The Run © **2014 Sydney Wray**

ISBN: 9781087903309 (Paperback)
ISBN: 9781087903316 (E-book)

Any reference to historical events, real people, or real places are used fictitiously. Names, characters, and places are products of the author's imagination.

Front cover image by Mirjana Krasojevic Knezevic.
Book design by Mirjana Krasojevic Knezevic.

Printed by IngramSpark, Inc., in the United States of America.

First printing edition 2021.

The Run Productions, Sydney Wray

The Run

Vol. 1

Sydney Wray

The Run Productions

To Craig, because this book wouldn't have
been possible without you

One

"You can't kick me out!" I stood, gaping as my foster mother catapulted the only bag I owned from the steps of our foster house.

She winced guiltily as my bag landed with a thunk. The situation was not registering, and I looked up from the bottom of the steps.

"It was either this or his explanation to the police," she said, crossing her arms and glancing down the street to avoid my gaze. "Juvenile jail is not fun."

I decided to reply with the most obvious question. "Where am I supposed to stay?"

"What about Lavender?"

I stopped, my heart beating fast. "This is the only place I've known."

"I want you to stay. I do, but-"

"-but what?" I interjected. "You cannot just kick me out! I'm sure that's illegal, dammit!"

Hellen shook her head adamantly; her short, curly, blond hair barely moved out of its orderly position. I watched her step forward and speak lightly, "Lindsey, I love you like a daughter, and I've had you under my roof since you were a little girl. I know you'll be fine." She reached into her pocket, checking behind her and pulling out five twenty-dollar bills. I looked at her, hoping she'd understand the dilemma. A hundred dollars wouldn't get me very far.

Hellen shoved it into my hand and placed a finger to her lips. "You take care now. You know my number if you need help." I wanted to tell her I would need help; I wanted her to know she was making a huge mistake. Hellen pinched my straight brown hair, softly touching the side of my bruised face.

I nodded, a tear dripping from the corner of my brown eyes. I bit my tongue to keep from either crying or screaming; I wasn't sure

4

which one. With tear stains and fading memories, I picked up my bag and walked away without a second glance.

~ 2 Days Earlier~

"Lindsey!" My name was yelled from the living room, where the television drowned any lingering noise. "Make yourself useful and get me another beer," he said without taking his eyes off the screen. No one was in the house but us. The kids were either at sleepovers, with Hellen to run errands, or playing in the backyard.

With a huff, I dropped my mechanical pencil against the kitchen table. Algebra obviously had to take a break. Reaching into the fridge, I grasped a cold bottle of beer and strolled into the living room.

My arm extended, but his eyes stayed glued to the screen. The reflection of blue and white danced on his dark eyes, and it seemed as if he noticed only the bottle's presence. Beer stains imprinted his dirty yellow T-shirt that stretched over the protruding beer belly. Walter's pathetic hand reached for the bottle, his intensive gaze not breaking attention. Right before his fingertips reached the sweaty bottle, I dropped it—with a smile.

The crashing sound startled him, anger flashing in his dark eyes by the time they settled on mine. "What the hell was that for?"

I shrugged, barely able to contain my smile. "Oops."

Walter stood abruptly, or as abruptly as his body allowed.

I fake gasped and placed a hand on my heart. "So you can stand!" I looked to the ceiling, shutting my eyes for effect. "Thank you, Lord, for this miracle."

He glared and raised a challenging finger. "You better watch yourself."

I raised my eyebrows, enjoying the moment of toying. I loved to watch fear in his eyes for once. "You better watch yourself." I waved a hand over my body. "If you even raise a finger to me, you'll probably be arrested." I was bluffing, but only to scare him.

"You're bluffing."

I shrugged. "I don't think you wanna test my knowledge."

He smiled and stepped forward. "I don't think you wanna try me." I shuddered as his toxic breath of cigarettes and alcohol fanned my face. He waved a hand to the ground, stepping around me and tossing over his shoulder, "Clean this up."

~~~~~~~~~

"Lindsey? Beer."

I groaned to myself, fed up with the recent beer runs. "No," I yelled out, returning to my book and squinting because of lack of light. Huffing, I looked up. My eyes hurt. I had only one lamp, and age was making it dim. Or the electric bill.

"Lindsey!"

I threw down my book and stormed down the white-carpeted stairs into the living room.

I looked square at him, giving a slight shake to my head. "Are you really that handicapped that you can't even take one step into the kitchen and get yourself your own damn beer?"

He looked up, shocked by my outburst. "You watch your tone."

"You're not my father," I said.

He stood with a vindictive smile. "Look, little lady, how would you even know what it's like to have a father? Isn't yours, oh I don't know, dead?"

The anger that was brewing began to rise up my throat. I'd seen enough movies to know the position a father holds; even as I thought it, I knew it was stupid. "Shut. Up."

He chuckled. "Oh, and where's your mother?"

I shoved him. "Don't you dare talk about my parents!"

6

He stopped laughing, his sick humor evaporating as he stumbled backwards. "You little-" I pushed him a second time, and he tripped backwards over the chair's arm onto the floor. It was my turn to laugh while I stepped forward, towering above him.

"You don't know a thing about my parents," I started, watching him rise to his feet slowly and look me in the eyes, "so next time you want to open your mouth about them-" I was interrupted by a hard slap across my left cheek. My skin prickled from it, but I regained my composure enough to hold eye contact. A sick smile captured his face, the twinkle in his eyes reminding me he was in control. I weighed my options; he was a stronger man, and I was a 5'5" girl with a small frame. The only thing I knew I still had were my words, "You're the most pathetic piece of shit I've ever seen."

A small chuckle jumped in his throat, and his meaty hands quickly grasped my shoulders to shove me backwards. I felt my body sail to the ground, the impact scaring me more than it hurt. For that time, it was he who stood above me with all the power in the world. "I would suggest you don't cross me again, and do as I say."

He straightened his back, his lower spine letting out a crack as he made his way back to the sagging chair. I watched him fall back into it, fixing his gaze on the television. The door cracked open slowly then, three of the kids peeking in. They were old enough to gather information and come to the result that I wasn't just choosing to sit on the ground. I pulled myself up, legs shaking, and walked down the hallway to the downstairs bathroom. I reached the mirror and turned my face, noticing the bright red mark that slightly outlined a handprint. I clenched my teeth, a tear dripping out of my eye and running down the same cheek. I quickly wiped at it, heavy adrenaline starting to pump through my veins.

Marching my way into the kitchen, I quietly pulled a beer from the fridge. My audience of eight year olds now sat quietly on the staircase, watching my every move. I was never one to be a role model. I glided back into the room with the bottle in hand, stepping up to him.

Walter looked up, glancing at the beer. "That's more like-"

I didn't let him finish. I swung my arm to the top of his head and slammed the bottle of beer down. Glass exploded around him, beer dripping from the tips of his hair.

I shook my hand, ridding the beer from my hands. "There's your beer."

~~~~~~~~

"I want her out!" Walter screamed from downstairs, his voice traveling through the house. I was standing in my doorway from upstairs.

"I can't just kick her out, Walter! This is her house!" Hellen's exasperated tone rang from the living room, and I could almost imagine her makeup-less eyes growing wide.

"Hellen," he started, voice dropping, "it's me or her." The once-loud voice turned into low murmuring, and I could no longer hear. I thought Hellen, the only mother I'd ever known, would've picked me over Walter.

I was wrong.

Two

Growing up without a mom or dad was super hard. Through kindergarten to second grade, it was strange watching my friends squeal and run to their parents after a long four-hour day of work. I would naively watch them with my big, brown eyes, observing the exchange of tight hugs and questions on how their day went. By the time I reached second grade, my request for a mom and dad at Christmas time stopped. I stopped thinking when they would come in and rescue me from horrid foster homes, which always seemed foreign and uncomfortable. I met my best friend Lavender at this time, though it wasn't love at first sight. At all. In fact, I'd say we were enemies since the day she stole my sand shovel. I was alone—big shocker, I know—and she had the audacity to interrupt my peaceful play time. Teachers always tried to get me to make friends, thought I was a lonesome cause, or something, but the truth was, I was just a kid who would like to stick to her own things. I looked up at her from my squat, the sun outlining her raven-haired head. She continued to stand there, staring at my progress. I continued my collection of sand castles in silence until the teachers called for us to go inside. For the following week, she'd continue standing above me and watching my art at work. I came to the conclusion that she had to be jealous. By the third or fourth day, the silence had obviously gone on too long. As I marveled at the castle I was creating and promptly began on my fourth and final castle, Lavender skipped over. Her sickly perfect curly hair swung back and forth.

She stood to my left, peering down at me like she had been doing for the past week. It made me angry. "What do you want?"

"You're not doing that right," she said, her arms swinging at her sides.

I frowned, patting sand into the mold. How could one do that wrong? "Yes, I am."

"Here, let me help." Lavender crouched down and started to pat the sand on top of my hands.

I shoved her away. "Stop!"

Lavender looked at me sternly. "Let me help!" To this day, we couldn't come to who actually threw the mold and how it ended up in the air. We both watched, our mouths open, as it flew through the air and into another boy. The mold ricocheted off him, falling to the ground of woodchips. He erupted in tears, though I didn't understand why, because it was a plastic mold thrown by the strength of six year olds. Lavender started to giggle and I joined in. From that day on, we became inseparable. Lavender helped me in so many ways, and I helped her too. I thought about those precious memories I had stored and tucked away in my conscience, as my feet slapped along the pavement to Lavender's house. I had no idea what to do; I was alone, and had no one but her.

Lavender had her own apartment in Brooklyn, and though I loved the constant noise that New York had to offer, I was busy dealing with my own noise. I climbed up the cement flights of stairs and easily found room 144. I knocked hard and heard quick footsteps. The door opened and Lavender stood there, her olive skin covered by a green face mask. She grinned at the first sight of me, the mask crinkling.

Our eyes met, and her grin slipped.

Her eyes widened. "What happened?"

"I need help."

~~~~~~~~

She ushered me in, shutting the door and guiding me to the black couch. I sat, and she crossed her legs. Then she crossed her arms. "What's wrong?"

I said it how it was. "Walter convinced Hellen to kick me out."

She blew out a breath, thoughts literally swarming in her mind. "You'll stay here, then."

I looked up at her from under my lashes. "I'm scared."

She raised her eyebrows, knowing me too well. "What did you do?"

"I threw a glass bottle on his head."

She shook her head, a smile tugging at her lips. "Leave it to you to mend things."

I let out a short laugh.

She stood, her skinny jeans pulling up with her long legs. She motioned to a room across her living room. "Put your stuff in the guest bedroom."

"I can't stay here forever, Lav."

"You'll stay here as long as you need."

~~~~~~~~

Plopping down my bag, I slowly sat down on the white bed, earning a squeak. Looking around, I blinked rapidly to stop the flow of tears soon to come. The brown lamp on the night stand was perfectly lit, reminding me of how dim my light was at home. None of this made sense; why did this have to happen? Why me?

I flopped back onto the bed, my head falling on one of the many pillows. My eyelids fluttered shut, the exhaustion from the day taking its toll and forcing my brain to erase the internal noise. I wasn't sure how long I had slept, but I woke up in a disorientated state and noticed a dark figure slipping through the door. I glanced to the small alarm clock on the nightstand next to the lamp, and I wasn't sure how

11

the lights had turned off. I read 4:07 a.m., and I glanced back to the figure now crossing the room and edging closer to me. My stomach jumped, and I slowly reached to my left and into my back pack. I made my hand crawl like a spider and immediately found what I was looking for. Out of the corner of my eye, the figure was edging closer. I jumped and pressed the trigger of my mace bottle.

"Aghhhh!"

"Aghhhh!" My terrified scream and his painful one combined. Words of wisdom: always carry a bottle of mace when you're a foster kid, but always check whom the person you're ambushing is.

The lights turned on shortly after, and by reflex, my arms reached up to cover my eyes. The intruder had clumsily found his way over to the light switch on the wall.

"Who the hell are you?" The boy demanded. His chestnut hair was messy. His green eyes were wide with confusion and red from irritation. My eyes darted to his shirtless chest and red-and-blue striped boxers. My eyes lingered over the deep indent of abs, and my state of delirium didn't help my wandering eyes.

"If you take a picture, it will last longer." He spit, reaching to the ground and throwing on a gray T-shirt he had taken off moments before.

"Who are you?" I sputtered, ignoring his rude comment.

He squinted. "I'd like to think you have the common decency to answer me first. You just sprayed me with mace."

I frowned, not enjoying his attitude, and crossed my arms across my chest.

"Lindsey. Lavender's best friend," I explained as if he should've known.

"Oh, I'm sorry, that wasn't included in the handbook."

I smirked. "Well, I'm sleeping here."

"So am I."

I bit my lip, not understanding. "And your name-" I stopped, the running footsteps sounding down the hall. Lavender appeared looking as if she had woken up in a nightmare. Her hair was in two braids, and she wore her shorts and tank top. I waited for her to explain the obvious misunderstanding, turn to the guy and tell him to get lost.

She held up her hands in surrender and bit her lip. "Sorry Linds. I forgot."

What? "Forgot what?"

She stepped forward, and I noticed a faint smudge of mascara. "This is a friend of mine."

I let out a sarcastic laugh and looked him over. "Looks like it." There was no way they were friends. The shirtless freak was about to climb into bed, obviously not realizing it wasn't Lavender he was joining.

She closed her eyes. "Really, he's a friend. He just needed a place to stay."

I made a face and looked at him, digging for some information. "And who's this friend?"

"This is Nathaniel."

I snorted, moving toward the bed and crawling under the covers.

Nathaniel watched as I took over my territory, motioning to the door. "So, if you don't mind..."

I laughed, giving a small beauty-queen wave and reaching to shut off the lamp light. The room was dark for only a millisecond before it was bright again.

I sat up, becoming irritated. "I'm sorry, last time I checked, this was my room."

"Last time I checked, this was my room." His voice had a soft, silky texture to it.

"Well, go find the couch, *Nathaniel*."

He glared, dramatically shutting off the light and leaving the room. I was left to my thoughts in darkness.

14

Three

He placed dramatically, grabbing the light and leaving the room. I was left to my thoughts. I stared...

I woke the next morning, carefully thinking of what I would do next. There was a boy less than ten feet from me, meaning I could no longer walk out looking like I had just woken up. I slid out of bed, crossing the short distance to the wall mirror. I peered closer; faint dark circles outlined my eyes, a pillow crease indented my left cheek, and my hair stuck out in messy angles. I smoothed out my hair to the best of my ability, then stopped. I leaned back, blinking. What was wrong with me? I huffed, turning and exiting my lair. I was craving a yogurt.

My bare feet slapped against the tile floor as I made my way through the white-carpeted living room and into the small kitchen. Standing next to the toaster, shirtless, if I might add, was Nathaniel. I ignored him and edged past the roadblock to the fridge. While searching for something to curb my craving, I heard him clear his throat.

I rolled my eyes, looking on the fridge door.

"Good morning."

found a strawberry one and whipped around. "Good morning."

He nodded in return.

I grabbed a silver spoon from the drawer, moving past him and toward the high chairs. I sat, feeling uncomfortable under his hard gaze. I ripped the yogurt top off, waving my spoon over his body. "Would you please put some clothes on? This isn't your man-cave."

He leaned backwards on the counter, raising an incredibly attractive eyebrow. His abs tensed. "Why, does it bother you?"

"No," I said a bit too quickly, and he responded with a sly smile.

I ate my yogurt in silence for the first three minutes, until it had obviously been too much for him. The toaster ejected his toast.

He plucked it quickly and tossed it on a plate. "What's wrong with your face?

I scowled, meeting his eyes. "Subtle."

"No, seriously," he defended himself, glimpsing my bruise.

I put down my spoon. "Are you referring to my overwhelming beauty, or my lovely complexion?" I put a mocking hand to my face.

He rolled his eyes, "Never mind," and left the kitchen with buttered toast in hand.

"Mornin'!" Lavenders' chirpy voice suddenly came around the corner.

"Finally!" I placed the last spoonful of yogurt in my mouth, jumping up. "Who is that?"

She cocked her head. "Haven't we been over this?"

"Briefly. But I want more information."

She sighed. "Of course you do."

I didn't say anything, only waited.

"He's kind of a friend of a friend. He needs a place to stay for a while. It's fine."

"So, you two... aren't... involved?"

"No. He's not my type anyway."

I nodded, dropping my voice to a rushed whisper. "Even though I have a strong dislike for him, he is exceptionally gorgeous-"

"I know." The devil himself stood there, smirking. "I am exceptionally gorgeous."

My cheeks burned in embarrassment. He placed a hand to his jaw bone. "Is it my overwhelming beauty, or my lovely complexion?"

I scowled, storming from the room and away from his laughter.

~~~~~~~~~

It had been radio silence from Hellen. I had to say, I was hurt she didn't care to check in and find out I wasn't dead in a ditch somewhere. But I ignored the feeling until it disappeared; there was

16

no time to be hurt. I had to go to school anyway, and I wouldn't risk being stuck with him.

The day consisted of, once again, the boring classes I was familiar with. Math, science, Language Arts, lunch, AP French, gym, home. Same schedule. When I got home that day without Lavender, who stayed after school to take a test she had missed, it was quiet. From the corner of my eye, I saw my bag being thrown from the guest bedroom.

I gasped. "Hey!"

I dropped my school bag and rushed to the bedroom door, stopping in the doorway. Nathaniel was lounged on my bed with his own bags sprawled throughout the room.

He saw me and got up. "Nice, huh?"

I gaped. "Where am I supposed to go?" I felt an overwhelming sense of Deja-vu.

His face came into a certain realization. "Oh, right! One sec."

I stood there, my arms crossed, as I watched him. He slipped past me, and in the midst, a waft of cologne covered me. He smelled good. Stop it, Lindsey!

Nathaniel picked up my bag he had thrown, returned to the room, and placed it in the corner. He grinned. "You can sleep here."

I stared at him. "Were you dropped on your head when you were a child?"

He didn't seem to notice the problem. "Oh. You're right." He gave me the 'one second' signal and ripped off a sheet from the bed and placed it cleanly on the ground, along with a pillow. He grinned his boyish grin. "See? I've got it all planned out."

I continued to stare at him. "How old are you anyway?"

"Eighteen."

"I can't sleep in the corner on the ground for the next few months, or however long I'm here!"

He cocked his head. "Why are you here?"

17

"That's not the point."

He smirked, then crossed his arms, mirroring me. "Oh, I see, is Daddy not getting you the Porsche you wanted?"

My stomach tightened and through clenched teeth, I muttered, "Shut up."

He started to pace. "Or are you angry with your mom for not allowing you to get a new pair of shoes you want?"

I didn't say anything.

He stepped forward. "It's not my fault you're a spoiled brat, who got everything she wanted when she was younger."

"Oh, really?" I stepped closer, inches from his face. He slightly gulped, probably taken aback by my forward respond. "It's pretty hard to get everything you want when your parents are dead."

~~~~~~~~~

I kept walking for a long time; blank thoughts clouded my mind and I must've been walking for a while. When I got back, it was dark. I had to return at some point, so there I was, walking back up the familiar steps to room 144. I opened the door without hesitation and saw Lavender.

"Hey." She popped her head out of the kitchen. "Where were you?"

I grimly smiled. "Just a walk to clear my head."

" 'Kay." She nodded tentatively, shooting me a message through her eyes. I read, *he's an asshole and I yelled at him.* "We're ordering pizza for dinner, if you're hungry."

"Okay, sounds great." I walked out the kitchen and past the bedroom where it had all gone down, expecting to see his bags still around the room. But it looked different, most definitely. All of Nathaniel's stuff had vanished, and my bag was perched carefully on the pillow. I stopped and entered. It was clean and seemed like it had even been vacuumed.

18

"I'm sorry."

I spun around and was faced by Nathaniel, who had a wounded expression. Lavender must've really given it to him. "I didn't know. It was terrible of me to say that stuff."

"Where's all your stuff?" I said, ignoring his apology.

He shrugged. "I should be the gentleman and give it to you."

Becoming angry, I shook my head. "Just because you found out about my parents doesn't mean you can pity me!"

He looked stunned. "I'm not pitying you! I gave you the room!"

I didn't have to explain myself. I didn't even know him. "Whatever." I edged the door closed. "Thanks for the room."

He looked at me, his green eyes shining with a certain type of concern. It made me angry. "Okay."

~~~~~~~~

I hated Nathaniel. Hated him. He thought of no one but himself. I could tell he was a serious player, and this certain opinion was really growing on me. Every time I returned from school and entered the apartment, Nathaniel had a different girl. The amount of hormones flying around were enough to choke me, and I didn't enjoy seeing Nathaniel in action. The newest girl was a tall blond, and she looked like a hooker. I wondered where he found them. You'd think the two would stop once the door opened with a noticeable amount of noise, but no. Not only did they continue, but it seemed to escalate. For several, several minutes. I heard her leave through my closed door, and I walked into the living room. I stared at him, falling back into the black couch.

"What?" he asked.

"You know, you didn't strike me as a hooker-type guy. But today," I paused, nodding, "today really confirmed my suspicions."

He glared. "She wasn't a hooker."

19

I raised an eyebrow. "Oh yeah? What was her name?"

He seemed to contemplate this question, then sputtered, "Jessica."

"You totally just made that up."

"Did not."

I crossed my arms.

Nathaniel got up. "I don't need this abuse from you."

I silently laughed at his word choice. "Abuse? That's a pretty big word for you."

He glared, reaching down into the fridge and grabbing a water bottle. "I am smart, for your information."

"You couldn't figure out how to work the gas station nozzle yesterday." Nate and I were put on grocery shopping duty yesterday, and him being him, insisted to drive because I was a "safety hazard." By the time we pulled into the gas station to refill the tank, he couldn't figure out how to a) open the gas tank and b) insert the nozzle properly.

He threw up his hands, cheeks reddening. "It was hard."

I snorted.

He stepped in closer, a sudden smile tugging at his lips. "You know what I think your problem is? I think you like me."

I laughed sarcastically. "You could be the last person on the earth, and I would never even consider you."

He shrugged and started to walk away. "We'll see about that." I stared after his broad shoulders, swearing to myself I would never become one of those daily girls.

Four

Walter was running after me. Sweat prickled my face as I sprinted as hard as I could. He couldn't get me, he just couldn't. The same thing repeated in my head, faster, faster, faster! I turned the corner of the pavement road and urged my long legs to go faster. For an overweight person, he was still quick. It was midnight and the whole neighborhood seemed like it was asleep. It felt like I was trapped.

Because I was.

"I'm gonna get you, Lindsey!" His voice was rough and I heard the effort that was made to make the statement.

I started to pant. Fear pushed me harder. My lungs gasped for air while my legs burned.

"Help!" I gasped. No one rescued me and the darkness seemed to swallow our figures up. He was getting closer, closer. I was falling back for some reason.

Walter finally reached me and- "Ahhhhh!" I woke up with complete panic in my eyes. A dream. It was a dream. Or a nightmare.

The door opened and Nathaniel's figure interrupted my thoughts. His hair was messy, again, and nothing but boxers clung to his hips. Gross. "Are you okay? I heard screaming."

I tried desperately to calm my breathing without him noticing. Perspiration made my white T- shirt cling to my body. He paused, beginning to take a few steps toward me.

 I put up a hand. "Don't."

He shrunk back and hurt flashed in his eyes for a brief second. Lavender suddenly appeared. "I heard screaming."

"I'm fine." I motioned for everyone to leave.

She hesitated. "Are you sure?"

I faked a smile. "Yeah, it was just a nightmare. No big deal." She slowly nodded and returned to her room.

I didn't need to look at him. I felt his presence. "I'm fine."

"Yeah but-"

"Can you just leave?"

He didn't say anything. He just left.

I was suddenly alone and secretly yearning for a person to comfort me. Because my best friend knew me so well, she came back ten minutes later to fall asleep with me.

~~~~~~~~~

"What happened last night?" Lavender finally asked, peering at me across the kitchen table. Nathaniel was sent out to food shop. Who knew what the idiot would come back with? Probably carbs, carbs, and some more carbs.

I shrugged. "Nothing. It was just a bad dream."

She let her shoulders drop in defeat. "Stop it."

"Stop what?"

"Stop acting like nothing's wrong!" she exclaimed before settling down and lowering her voice. "I know you get like this sometimes, but it's been especially bad lately." Her brown eyes, so similar to mine, searched my own. "Let me in."

I sighed after moments of contemplation. "Walter. It was about him." I gulped, remembering the terrifying feeling I felt the night before. "He found me."

She bit her lip. "What would happen if he did?"

"I don't know. I don't think it'd be good."

"We should do something." She turned, reaching into the fridge and swiping two bottles of water. She handed one to me, which I took graciously.

I let out a short, unamused laugh, unscrewing the cap. "Like what?"

22

"We can tell the police." Her earrings bounced against her neck.

"No, we can't," I began, shaking my head. Her arched eyebrows furrowed together in confusion, asking where the hell my logic was. "Questions would come up, and they'd find I wasn't living in my foster home."

She was still lost. "Tell me what I'm missing."

"They'd either send me back, or to a different home in a different state."

She finally nodded slowly. "Okay, we won't tell the police. But if one more bad thing happens, I'm doing something. Got it?" I didn't say anything and nodded in semi-agreement.

"How're your parents?" I asked slowly, watching her carefully. Her grip tightened slightly on the plastic water bottle, resulting with a crinkling sound.

"I think they're fine," she said lowly, reaching under the deep kitchen sink and finding a bottle of cleaning fluid, "I haven't been over much, but when I do they seem to hold it together for me." I could remember their fights like it was yesterday; their high-school sweetheart status and regard for their only daughter sparked their refusal for divorce. I watched her spray the blue liquid on the white countertops. She ripped a piece of paper towel off the role, wiping the counter down in circular motions. Cleaning was her telltale sign of self-distraction. She cleaned the entire island until every counter was sparkly white and clear of any debris. She crossed the short distance of the tile kitchen, past the framed hung pictures of her and I on the walls, and to the trash.

She took a deep breath, breaking the comfortable silence between us. "I'm just glad I have this place." I smiled for her, my gaze sweeping the very clean and cute kitchen. The opening and closing of the front door occupied the quiet agreement between us. Nathaniel appeared around the corner, carrying five or six bags in

23

one hand like it was nothing. I watched the muscles ripple in his arm and then intensify once he lifted his load up onto the counter.

He caught me watching and smirked. "Like what you see?"

"No."

He shook his head, smiling.

"You're cocky, you know that?"

He laughed. "I'd like to think of it as a charming characteristic of mine."

I grimaced. "Exactly - right there."

"What?" he demanded. "I'm just being normal."

"Your definition of normal is my definition of complete stupidity."

He sucked in a breath. "Harsh, Garland."

"Don't call me that." I shot back. He had slyly found out my last name the other day while taking a peek at my homework. I glanced at Lavender, who was busy measuring herbs for her new detox plan.

"What, exactly, is that?" I asked, curious.

She didn't sneak a glance at me and continued her steady concentration. "It's a mixture of mint and bark shavings from a rare African tree."

I raised an eyebrow, highly skeptical. "And where did you find this?"

"Amazon." She dumped the herbs into her cup of prepared hot water.

Nathaniel snorted. "Sounds like bull to me."

"You sound like bull." I rolled my eyes.

"That doesn't even make sense, sweetheart."

Lavender cleared her throat, holding her cup of tea with great admiration. "You guys sound like an old married couple."

I flashed a smile. "The only difference is, he's dead."

~~~~~~~

24

The same dream. Every night. Walter chasing me in a deserted park. By the fifth night, I searched my symptoms and expected to be told I was dying from a rare disease. What I read was interesting, though. Dreams that put the body in a stressful situation are the brain's way of preparing the individual for their flight-or-fight response. So, was I going to be stalked and attacked by the old man? I dug deeper in my research, and found a separate website titled *HealthyBrain*. I clicked on an article named, "The Inside Psychology of Dreams." Apparently, if a dream is repeated more than twice and the course of events in said dream are almost identical, then it was the body's way of transporting a message. I bookmarked both websites, knowing I was going to revisit them at some point.

Lavender's detox ended up giving her a side effect of drowsiness, which was a slight concern to me but beside the fact that she didn't hear my screams during the night. I swear, I was waiting for my dear heart to give out during the episodes and take its revenge on me in the form of heart failure. On a dreaded Monday morning, Lavender had jumped into the shower and left me alone with the curious beast. The guy had been glancing at me for all of twenty minutes, before I finally snapped, "What?"

"You're having nightmares every damn night."

"No I'm not."

He cocked his head. "Oh really? Then is that Lavender screaming, '*help, someone help me! He's chasing me!*'?"

I pressed my lips together in response, leaning back into the couch and letting my eyes fall into a concentrative stare. The TV was a great distraction that tended to be underrated.

He shook his head, annoyed. Lavender came prancing down the hallway, her hair wrapped in a towel, dressed in an outfit for the day.

I smiled in relief, trying to shove aside the way he was staring at me. "Ready to go?"

Lavender nodded, checking the messages on her charging phone. "Give me a second to do my hair." She paused, her nails clicking against the screen of her phone as she replied to a message. She finished, walking back in the direction of her room.

He turned back to me once she was safely out of earshot. "If they continue, I'm telling her."

I glared. "You wouldn't."

"I would."

"What's your problem?"

He leaned closer and I noticed a sprinkle of freckles across his nose. His eyes were a deep green and speckled with emerald. "This is not good. You need help."

I snorted. "Oh, you mean from a therapist?"

"I wouldn't object for you to get some professional help," He started with a slight undertone of sarcasm, and my look cut him off. "Who's the person in your dreams?"

"Why do you care?"

His lips parted in response, but was cut off by Lavender's call for me. Looking back at Nathaniel, I whispered, "Just leave me alone." I got in the car, ducking my head. I'd always liked Lavenders' car because she didn't have to share with anyone. Lavender is also a bit OCD, or at least I thought so. Even though she doesn't have a proper diagnosis, she doesn't like me rearranging her things, and her areas are freakishly clean.

"What's your guys' deal?" She asked me as she searched for the right key.

"Nothing," I said curtly.

"Oh yeah, that's believable."

I rolled my eyes. "Just start the car."

She did and we rolled out of the parking lot. She edged the car onto the highway, and we were officially en route to school. The car smelt of coconut shampoo and body wash. I inhaled deeply.

"Have you had dreams lately?" she asked causally.

"Yeah, have you?"

Lavender grinned. "You know what I mean."

"Lavy," I said in a singsong voice, unrolling my window and inhaling the New York air. She turned onto a busy street, the busy sounds of the city flowing through the car. "I'm fine."

"Are you sure?"

I rolled my eyes and looked at her. She concentrated on the road. "Yes, Lavender. I'm sure."

But I wasn't, but it didn't mean I was going to tell her.

27

Five

"Linds! Can you go to the store and get me my bread?" Lavender, as 'special' as she was, was allergic to almost everything. Gluten, soy, eggs. The list went on forever, really.

"Okay!" I called back. I finished the last sentence to the chapter of my book and went into the kitchen to get the keys.

I turned to walk out the door but was stopped by the 'O shirtless one.' "Hold up. I need something too."

I chuckled. "What, all out of necessary safety equipment?"

"You're disgusting." He pulled a shirt over his head, and jogged over to the fridge. I groaned, growing impatient as he searched for his next victim. An orange juice carton emerged in his hands, tipping into his mouth.

"No, you're disgusting. "I yelled to Lavender. "I'll get some orange juice too. I don't want to put us in danger of getting diabetes." I heard her laugh in response.

He made a face. "Diabetes isn't contagious."

I walked to him and pointed to his throat. "You've got a little-" at the last second, I flicked upward. "Now who's smart."

~~~~~~~~~

"You're a terrible driver!" he screamed as the car lurched forward once more.

"Shut up! You're making me nervous!"

His eyes were filled with pure terror as he gripped the safety handle above the door. His knuckles were white. The store was on the right, which meant I had to cut in front of three lanes, plus ongoing traffic. That was a problem.

I took a deep breath and he looked at me. "Wait, you're not going to-"

"Ahhh!"

"Ahhhhh!"

Our screams were combined as I cut the steering wheel quickly across the lanes. The car made a loud screeching sound and Nathaniel belted out, "HAIL MARY, FULL OF GRACE, THE LORD IS WITH THEE!"

I finally pulled into the parking lot of the store and forcefully hit the brakes. Our boisterous breathing filled the silence.

He stared daggers at me. "Do you even have your license?"

"Yes." It was quiet when I finally looked at him. "You're Catholic?"

He took a deep breath and stared straight ahead. "Nope." When the shock finally vanished, we tentatively opened our doors.

I tucked a piece of hair behind my ear, shaking. "Okay, so I'll get the bread. You get whatever you're getting."

He nodded, swiftly walking in the other direction.

I searched for the bread once I made it into the store and finally found it.

I paid for the bread at the register and finally found Nathaniel. He had a prescription bag in his hand, along with a box in a plastic bag.

I grinned. "Wonder what those are."

He scowled. "It's medication. For me."

"Whatever you say."

We continued to bicker until we exited the store.

I fell silent once my gaze settled on a terribly familiar person off to the side. My stomach lurched. Walter stood with a burning cigarette in his hands, his friend's arm encircling him.

Terror built up in my chest and I dropped my head. Nathaniel stopped talking and looked at me. "Hey, are you okay?"

"Can we just get to the car. Quickly," I mumbled.

He was confused. "Sure."

I watched the ground, but our path was suddenly interrupted by a beer glass that had flown through the air and hit the ground.

Nathaniel looked up. "Hey, watch it, man!"

"Nathaniel, shut up," I said quickly.

"Well, look who it is!" His voice entered my mind like a scary memory. Or a nightmare. The deep, gruff voice hitched my breath.

I held my head up and met his eyes.

"You know him?" Nathaniel questioned.

I didn't answer and only looked at Walter. "I'm surprised you had the energy to actually get up and come here."

He smirked. "Still the same, aren't you?"

"As always," I said curtly.

He pulled his mouth into a snarl and curled his finger as if saying come here. I contemplated this situation. He wasn't going to try anything in a public place. I stepped forward, a hard expression on my face. Nathaniel grabbed my elbow, his finger pressing into the soft parts. It felt like a fire sensation.

"Are you insane?"

"Maybe."

~~~~~~~~

He pulled me. "Let's go." I closed my eyes and let him guide me to the car. I turned my head and locked eyes with Walter.

"That's right, you better run."

I can't really explain what followed this statement. One second I was in the grasp of Nathaniel, and the next I was sprinting toward him. Anger was pulsing through my veins. It was no joke that the fact I wasn't taught certain morals as a kid resulted in my behavior. Think about it: Would a private school goodie-two-shoes sprint toward an older man to finished what she started? No, but I would. His eyes

30

widened as I drew closer and Nathaniel was running after me, his voice hanging in the air as he yelled at me to stop. But I was faster because of my advantage of time. I ignored his angry pleas, Walter's beady eyes following me. I finally reached Walter and shoved him as hard as I could. He lost his balance, stumbling backwards.

He spit to the side. "You little-" I didn't let him finish. I kicked his stomach, but he took his cigarette butt and pressed it cleanly on my arm. I cried in pain and went to hit him again when I felt arms enclose around my stomach. I was lifted off the ground and being carried by Nathaniel to the car. Anger was stuck in Walter's eyes and he went to follow but his friends stopped him.

He screamed. "Yeah, that's right. Bitch."

Six

"Are you trying to get yourself killed?" he yelled, shutting his door and resting his arms on the black steering wheel.

"No. I knew what I was doing."

He scowled and pointed toward my burned arm. "Yeah, looked like it. What are you, a member of the Fight Club?"

Okay, it was stupid. I accepted it once my blood was done pumping. I didn't' even know what I was trying to accomplish. It was silent the whole ride home, making an angry, awkward time. Nathaniel didn't understand my side of the story, and Lavender certainly did not.

"I'm fine."

We were soon in the living room, discussing the scene. Great.

"You know, I'm not nine," I reasoned, hugging a throw pillow to my chest, "We don't need a family meeting."

He threw up his arms and turned around. "Do you not understand the consequences of your actions? That guy, whoever he was, looked at you like you were a meal."

A thin funnel of angry tears made its way to my eyes. "Why do you even care?" I felt myself asking that question way too often. Why did he care? No one usually did.

He snorted.

Lavender cleared her throat. "Okay, everyone just needs to..." she finished with a motion.

I managed to smile.

"You're sixteen-"

"Seventeen soon!" I interjected.

She frowned. "As I was saying, you're sixteen. Normal teenagers don't go through this."

"I have you."

32

She shook her head. "We need to go to the police. Walter is dangerous."

"So, he has a name," Nathaniel murmured during his walk from the living room.

I stood up abruptly. "No! I'll have to go back into foster care! Once I turn eighteen, I'm free of it. Just two more years and I'm out."

"Whoa, whoa, whoa," He interrupted us both from his position in the kitchen, pointing a water bottle at us. "Take it back, for a sec."

I groaned, falling back into the couch.

"I don't think you two understand the severity of the situation."

"Sherlock, ladies and gentlemen," I said under my breath.

He ignored me, continuing. "If your removal from the foster home were to get out in any way, and people find out you are letting her stay with you," he was speaking to Lavender now, "you can get in a lot of trouble."

I closed my eyes. Sometimes, my stupidity astonished me. Of course, she'd get in trouble.

"Now, I'm not saying to go back there," he said, looking to me. "But I'm saying that there has to be an actual plan now that ensures the safety of you both."

It was quiet in the apartment, and then it clicked. "I could destroy my paperwork."

"Are you nuts? That'd be like dropping off the face of the earth. You could never get a family."

The last sentence sent a feeling of despair to my chest. "Lavender. It's been eleven years. I don't think anyone's looking for a sixteen year old."

She pressed her lips together, only because she knew it was true. Parents wanted only little kids. They didn't want teenagers.

"Then it's settled." I announced, looking at both of them. "I'll take my file."

~~~~~~~~

33

"We can't make big decisions like this so quickly. Where do we even get your paperwork?" I never did like the fact that a kid's life is recorded on a piece of paper. Our mistakes are basically based on the person we're perceived as.

I didn't have to think about it. "My house."

Lavender's eyes flicked back and forth, her tell-tale sign of heavy-thinking. Then she grinned and looked to Nathaniel .

"What?" he questioned.

"You're going with her." What? No.

"No!" We both said simultaneously.

He shook his head, his overgrown hair flying ever-so slightly. "I am not going with the crazy chic. Nuh uh. No."

I agreed. I decided to not touch on the crazy part; we were finally agreeing on something together. But Lavender didn't. And when Lavender made up her mind, she'd get it done. We later found ourselves sitting in her car outside my house. Nathaniel was pouting.

"I can't believe this is happening."

I rolled my eyes. "The feeling is mutual, buddy."

"Can you just go in already?"

"I'm waiting for a good time."

He gestured angrily toward the door. "There's no one home!"

"That doesn't stop neighbors from seeing." I explained, looking at him. The look he gave me changed my mind. "Okay, okay. Calm down, I'm going."

"You better," he muttered. I opened the passenger side door. (He made me sit shotgun because he claimed he wanted to live to the age of twenty). I made my way up the walkway. Reaching down and placing my hand under the carpet, I found the key. The bitter cold prickled my skin. I unlocked the door, glancing over my shoulder. I let myself in, heat hitting me full blast. They couldn't have gotten heat while I was there? I remember vividly the moments when my teeth were anxiously chattering due to the cold, and I always slept with two, thick blankets.

I crept forward, though I wasn't sure why because no one was there, and found Hellen's office. Where would files be? I searched the familiar room and spotted a metal file cabinet. I opened the cabinet with a click and sifted through the files of past, and present, kids. I looked through the present, and found many younger kids around ten through fourteen years of age. They were all familiar, except for one. She was about five and had light chestnut hair with dark, sincere eyes. Her bangs ended just above her eyes and her smile was priceless. Apparently, her name was Blaire Richman, and she was five. *It didn't take her long to replace me*, I retorted nastily in my head. I heard the door open. I froze and quietly closed the cabinet. Heavy footsteps sounded against the hallway and I heard heavy breathing. The footsteps were too heavy to be Hellen's, but the breathing matched Walter's cigarette-invaded lungs. My stomach churned and I pinched my mouth to keep from making a sound. My brain screamed at me to move to a safe place and I quickly responded. Moving to the opposite side of the door, I crouched behind it. I balled my fists, ready to swing. The footsteps continued to come closer and my eyes were wide. I listened carefully.

Step, step, step. Pause. I stopped and the adrenaline in my body seemed to kick in. The door opened slowly and I swear it seemed like a scene out of a horror movie. It continued to open as I prepared to launch upward. More, and more, and- I jumped up and slammed him right in the jaw. Let's just say, it wasn't Walter.

Nathaniel growled, rubbing his jaw in annoyance. "Do you have a knack for ambushing guys?"

"I thought you were someone else," I murmured. "Let's just get what we came here for." I returned to the filing cabinet and sifted through old files. If I wasn't in the old ones, I'd have to be in the new ones.

35

Nathaniel wandered nearby, his fingers tracing the dark desk. "I kind of understand why you don't want to come back here. This place is depressing."

"Ah hah!" I exclaimed as I found my familiar file, which held my life. Nathaniel came over and peered over my shoulder.

He smirked. "Nice picture."

I looked at it. It was pretty cute. My childish cheeks were plump and my eyes shined with a certain happiness that every five-year-old has. If only I knew what was coming.

I scanned the page, my eyes squinting every so often to read the blurred type-writing. A gasp hitched in my throat and I couldn't believe what I was reading.

In clear print, it read:

Adults/guardians of child: Lisa Garland, Peter Garland

Cause/reasoning of foster/orphan associations: Unable to care for Lindsey Garland

(If so) Guardians current address: 18 haddle peak drive, Richmond VA 23218

My lips parted in shock, and many sensations gripped my body. I couldn't decide if I should be happy or angry.

"Wait, so your parents are still alive?"

I didn't say anything. I nodded.

"Shit." He murmured.

36

Seven

I stormed inside the house, my file tucked firmly under my arm, and slammed the guest bedroom door. I didn't say anything on the car ride home. I sat on the bed, a familiar squeak sounding from the springs. I looked down at the file and clenched my teeth. My finger hovered above the sickening sentence,

Cause/reasoning of foster/orphan associations: Unable to care for Lindsey Garland.

Unable to care for Lindsey Garland. They had given me up. I was told they were killed. Did they request this explanation? Or was I taken away? A million thoughts swarmed through my head. I was five, but I didn't remember my parents. I heard low murmuring outside the door and suddenly Nathaniel appeared with Lavender. He crossed his arms and stared at the ground. Lavender looked headstrong.

"We've come to a resolution."

I looked up from under my lashes.

"You're going to Virginia."

I snorted.

"With Nathaniel."

I almost choked on my saliva. "What?"

She nodded. "With my car. Tomorrow."

I shook my head so forcefully I earned a whiplash. "This is ridiculous." I looked over at Nathaniel. "I'm not going with him."

"Well, you can't go by yourself."

I stood up and crossed my arms. "I don't even have to go."

"Don't you want to see your parents?"

I thought about this. "No, not really."

"Well, you're going."

I moaned. "That takes eight, nine hours to get there! Imagine me, in the car with him!"

"You're not all sunshine and rainbows either, sweetheart."

I glared at Lavender. "I. Am. Not. Going."

~~~~~~~~

I was only bringing one bag, but Nathaniel was bringing three. I smirked, eyeing his bags. "What are you, a teenage girl?"

He scowled, eyeing my bag. "What are you, a teenage boy?"

I shrugged. "I don't see the point in carrying so many bags."

"And I don't see the point in carrying so little bags." He retorted.

I bit my tongue, knowing I wasn't getting anywhere, and slammed the car door shut. Lavender waved from the balcony like a beauty queen, grinning. Driving on the highway with Nathaniel was awful.

"Read me the stupid directions!" he yelled at me.

"Stop yelling at me and ask me like a normal person!"

"The problem here is that you're not a normal person."

"I'm not the one who can't read!"

He scowled. "News flash, sweetheart! I'm driving!" Growling, I snatched the map and turned it sideways. Along with my head, I squinted to read the tiny lettering.

He snorted. "It looks like you're trying to read cryptic."

"Turn left onto Washington street.

He frowned. "That's not right."

"Jesus, Nathaniel! Just listen to me! I'm right and you're wrong."

"You're so pushy." He grumbled as he turned left onto the street. Several minutes later, we reached a dead end.

I didn't say anything and picked up the map again.

He looked at me. "Nice directions, Captain Genius."

"Well, you were yelling at me!"

38

"Oh yeah? Who said--" he cleared his throat, and tried an impression of my voice-- "just listen to me! I'm right, and you're wrong!"

I glared. "That doesn't sound like me.

He groaned. "I need to murder someone."

"Okay, turn around and come back the way we came."

He did and we later found ourselves on the familiar highway.

I studied the map. "Okay, we're gonna take a shortcut."

"Oh, this'll be good.

"Take exit 16, east."

He eyed me. "Why do I feel like this is wrong?"

"Just do it. You need to learn to trust people."

He made a strange sound in his throat. "Look what happened when I did."

I took a deep breath. "Just do it."

~~~~~~~~~~

"See! We're on the right way!"

He ignored me and clutched his stomach. "I'm starving." As if on cue, his stomach growled.

"Deal with it."

He gasped. "You are not a caring person."

"Thank you for noticing."

He pulled off the highway and found a drive thru into a McDonalds. "Hi, I'd like two boxes of chicken nuggets, one large fry, and a hamburger. Oh, and a chocolate milkshake."

I cringed at the amount of food he was ordering. No one replied and it was quiet. I turned, peering over Nate and laughed. He frowned. "Hello?"

I couldn't hold it in any longer, and I was grinning stupidly. "Um, Nathaniel?"

He turned around. "Yeah?"

39

I pointed. "You just ordered to a trash can."

Confusion was written on his face as his cheeks turned pink. "Whatever," he mumbled. He pulled up to the right station, and ordered the same thing. He finally noticed my presence. "Oh, do you want something?"

I was starving, but I didn't want to let him know that because I had recently pushed away the fact that he was hungry.

"Just a water."

He frowned, then turned toward the lady. "Hamburger, fries, and a water please?"

I raised my eyebrows. He pulled up to the pick-up counter. "You need food."

I pulled out my wallet, but he had already beat me to it. I sighed. "I could've paid for mine."

"You're a girl," he pointed out. And the moment was ruined. He handed me my food, and once I opened the greasy bag, I took back all that was said.

Eight

"We have to find a place to sleep tonight," Nathaniel noted as he glanced out the window. It was almost eleven o' clock, which meant we'd been driving for four hours.

My eyelids noticeably fluttered shut as I struggled to find a hotel. "Hotel, or motel?" I asked.

He cringed. "Hotel. You couldn't pay me to sleep in a motel."

I should've known. "Pretty boy."

"Are you naturally mean, or do you try really hard?"

I ignored him and pointed. "There's a hotel."

He pulled into the parking lot and parked the car. We went inside. The lady behind the desk had perfect hair; it was slicked back tightly in a bun.

She smiled as we approached the desk. "Hi, how can I help you?"

I smiled and politely said, "We'd like two rooms, please."

Nathaniel tugged at my arm and whispered in my ear. "We should probably get one room-"

"Not a chance, bucko." I turned back to the lady, but he grabbed me again.

"Lindsey." It was the first time he'd actually said my name. "We won't have enough money for the whole trip."

"Then we'll sleep in the car."

She typed rapidly on her keyboard, oblivious to our banter. She paused, biting her lip. "I'm sorry, but we have only one available room."

I stared at her. Nathaniel stared as well. We exchanged a glance. The room was nice and it had two big beds appropriately spaced from each other. A flat-screen TV was placed on the wall in front, a mirror on the side, and a nightstand separating the two beds.

41

I wandered into the bathroom and flicked the light switch. With marble sinks and shower, I nodded in enjoyment. Fresh white towels were folded neatly on the sink. I walked back into the room and crossed my arms at his lounged figure. "I want that bed."

He smirked. "Not a chance, sweetheart."

I grumbled, plopped down my bag on the right bed. "Fine, but you should know that the only reason why I'm not putting up a fight, is one," I held up a finger," you're too heavy."

He raised an eyebrow. "Was that a fat joke?"

"And two," I held up another finger, "because you're so close to the door, you'd be kidnapped or killed *first*." I shrugged. "At least I'd have time to escape."

He let his mouth drop open.

Within in minutes, the lights were off and it was silent.

~~~~~~~~~

"Nathaniel," I angrily whispered. "Nathaniel!" He was snoring so loud, I'm surprised half of Mexico hadn't crumbled away due to a faraway earthquake.

I checked the bedside clock: 3:12 a.m. I groaned and grabbed a pillow to my left, throwing it in his direction. I watched it fly through the darkness and hit him square in the face. I congratulated myself for my perfection in aim. The snoring stopped for a short moment, then continued shortly after like nothing had interrupted his stream of oxygen. This was not happening. I quietly slid out of bed and went to the bathroom. On my way, I reached under the coffee table and grabbed an empty garbage pail. Without turning on the light in fear of waking him up, I twisted the faucet of the shower and waited for the bucket to fill. The substitute for a bucket filled quickly. By the time the water nearly reached the brim, I deviously picked it up with trembling arms and slowly made my way to his bed. In one swift motion and all the muscle power my trembling arms could produce, I dumped it on his body. The water immediately grabbed its host, clinging to his shirt and soaking everything in contact.

I wish I would've thought to put it on video; it was that funny.

He sat up, gasping and sputtering. "What the...?"

I laughed hard, leaning back onto my own bed and clutching my stomach. His shirt clung to his chest, showing the indent of abs. His bed head dripped in water, while his face was a mixture of drowsiness and confusion. He hadn't processed the situation quite yet, making an even funnier moment for me.

"Why," he took a breath, "would you do that?"

"You were snoring."

He looked like I'd just told him his head was on fire. "And you couldn't wake me, oh I don't know, without water?"

Shrugging, I got back into bed. "Night."

~~~~~~~~

My dream had been peaceful and without the interruption of Nathaniel's snoring, but I dreamed-Lindsey suddenly felt like she was drowning. My eyes flipped open, revealing Nathaniel and my weapon of choice. The bucket dangled in his grasp. Cold water, not warm like I had oh-so-considerately chosen, clung to my skin and pulled escaped strands of hair out of my face.

"What is wrong with you?"

He shrugged, the shirt he had slept in hugging his body. I could still spot stains of water. "You were snoring."

I rolled my eyes. He was mimicking me. "I don't snore."

"How do you know?"

"Because I know," I sputtered.

He nodded sarcastically in an understanding way. "Right."

"I see that you're still damp," I observed, stepping around him to the bathroom.

43

"I see that you're still *wet*," he spit back. I bit my tongue, slamming the bathroom door. After we were both ready, I told him I'd meet him at the car and began to proceed downstairs by myself.

"What about breakfast?"

I paused in the doorway. "We can get something on the road."

"What do you think we are, made of money?"

I rolled my eyes. "You should take a Xanax."

"You know," he started with a bright smile, "you'd think a foster kid would gobble up any sighting of free food."

I stared, unamused. "Has anyone ever told you how funny you are?"

I shut the door, ignoring whatever reply he would come up with, and took the elevator to the first floor. Minutes later, (ones I'm sure that didn't include a concern of my whereabouts), Nathaniel appeared downstairs. I watched him ignore my presence and walk straight towards the cereal section, snagging one of every type of cereal. He then floated to a different table, plucking two yogurts from an ice bucket. I watched, a small smile tugging at my lips as he then found himself at the hot bar. He grabbed a few napkins with his unoccupied hand, putting three sausages on them. He dropped the serving utensil, rose and met my eyes. With his arms filled with four cereal boxes, two yogurts, a napkin filled with sausages, and two apples, he raised a challenging brow at me. I managed a laugh. He then ripped his gaze, snagging two more apples from a basket and a few plastic utensils, and without an intentional look in my direction, brushed past me and through the sliding glass doors.

Nine

I didn't really remember my parents or anything from my childhood before the system. It felt like my memory was wiped and my brain remembered only events that weren't necessarily positive. But, like I said before, anything before Hellen – zip.

I remembered telling Lavender when I was fourteen, "Do you remember your childhood?"

Her eyebrow twitched briefly, but it was so fast I had to make sure it was what I thought. "Yeah, totally."

I didn't respond, leaving myself to my own thoughts.

Lav had placed a hand on my arm as if reading my thoughts. "Don't worry about it. Sometimes, the brain has a way of erasing painful memories."

"You look like you're planning a murder," Nathaniel interjected, drawing me back to the present. "Should I be worried?"

"Shut up, Nathaniel." I shifted my body, leaning against the passenger side door. "Is it wrong to give a girl some peace?" Why couldn't he just give me a break?

I felt his eyes on me. "I feel like you have an invisible wall in front of you."

I sighed, watching the outside world whiz by. "What are you talking about, Nathaniel?"

"When someone cares, or tries to care about you, you shut them out. Why is that?"

I didn't answer, just rolled down my window and enjoyed the wind through my hair.

He rolled it back up. "Just give me the directions, so I can get out of this car with you."

That stung, though I wasn't sure why, but I acted as if it didn't. I grabbed the map. "Turn left there."

45

"Where?"

"There!" I pointed.

"Where is there?!"

Anger boiled inside me, and I grabbed the steering wheel. "There!"

He tried to yank it back, but we rolled off over a divider and into a lone parking lot. The car jolted forward.

"Are you insane?!"

I scowled. "I think we've established this."

"Oh, come on, Lindsey. That's the first freaking rule of driving! Didn't your dad-" he stopped short.

"Oh no, keep it coming."

"I didn't mean it like that."

"What did you mean it like?"

"Nothing!"

I had enough. I grabbed the door and yanked it open. Stepping out, I leaned against the car. I heard a similar sound, and he was suddenly standing next to me. "Oh, what-- you're gonna pout now?" He smirked, looking up to the sky. "Classic."

I ignored him, the sounds of cars flying by filling the space around us.

He laughed with no trace of humor. "I can't believe you! If one person makes one mistake, you freak out like it's the end of the world! Well, news flash, sweetheart. It's. Not!"

I turned suddenly and slapped him hard across the face. He was stunned. I was stunned, but not nearly as stunned when he grabbed the sides of my face, leaning in and pressing his lips firmly to mine.

~~~~~~~~~

46

I pushed him off me, my cheeks burning. I had to forget about the fact that Nathaniel had stolen my first kiss. "What is wrong with you?"

He blinked blankly. "Sorry."

"Sorry?" I yelled, incredulous. "*Sorry*?"

"I didn't mean that. I got carried away."

"So, you. . . kissed me?"

He shrugged, his cheeks a slight pink. "I don't like you in any way, so you don't have to worry." His tone was harsh and serious, and I believed him.

"Then why would you do that?"

"Can we just put it behind us?" he asked, staring straight at me.

A weird feeling churned in my stomach. "Fine." I opened the door and prepared to duck my head. "If you ever kiss me again, I'll do worse than slap you."

He shook his head, and mumbled as he crossed over to the other side. "And if you ever touch my steering wheel again..." he mimicked, the second part trailing off. Boys.

I turned my head to the side as he pulled the car into drive and maneuvered his way out of the parking lot. My fingers lightly grazed my lips. Had that really just happened? The next twenty minutes was filled with sheer silence and the obvious existence of both our silent thoughts. Nathaniel broke the ice first, clearing his throat and announcing that his twenty-four-hour hunger mark was taking its toll again.

"Of course, you are," I mumbled, pulling my hair into a messy ponytail.

"Can you try to be nice for at least five seconds?"

"Just find a place to eat." I waved off his question dismissively, shifting for at least the one hundredth time. "My butt is killing me from sitting in this car."

He put up a sarcastic, sassy finger. "TMI, sweetheart."

"Stop calling me sweetheart," I snapped.

"Okay, sweetheart." He grinned.

My stomach growled, and he chuckled. "Want some water?" I vaguely remembered the McDonalds scene.

"You're such an asshole." I hated swearing, but for some reason I wanted to hurt him.

Nathaniel rolled his eyes. "Have I ever told you that you have great comebacks? Really, award-winning comebacks."

"There's a diner," I said, ignoring him. He pulled off, parking the car. We went in and were seated by our Barista."

She nodded and grabbed two menus. We followed her and she placed them down. "You're waiter will be one moment."

"I'm getting a hamburger, and a milkshake."

"You really looked at the menu." I searched through mine.

He glared. "It's a diner. Who looks at menus in diners?"

"I do."

"Well that explains it."

"Explains what-"

"Would you like some drinks?" The waiter came over, her red lipstick so thick it was smeared onto her teeth.

I tried not to stare. "Water, please."

"I'll have the same."

"I thought you were having a milkshake," I said through clenched teeth.

"I changed my mind."

I glanced at the waiter, and she nodded as if she understood our hateful relationship. Moments later, she returned with our waters.

"Are you ready to order?" I couldn't stop staring at the red lipstick that managed to snag her tooth.

"A hamburger, please," Nathaniel piped up. She scribbled it down and looked to me.

I looked down, and I could almost feel Nathaniel's impatience and his growing hunger. My neck started to prickle with sweat. I was nervous.

"U-um-"

"Just pick something," he hissed.

"I can come back-" she started.

"-no stay!" I said a little too forcefully. Her eyes widened slightly. The other costumers began to look over, eyeing our dysfunctional table.

"Just order!" Nathaniel stared at me.

"I'm looking. Calm down!"

"She'll have a hotdog," he suddenly declared, looking at the waiter.

"I can't eat hotdogs."

"Why, are you a vegetarian too?"

I leaned forward. "What's that supposed to mean?"

"That you're incredibly inadequate."

I chuckled without humor. "Do you even know what that word means?"

He struggled. "Of course, I do."

I nodded sarcastically. "Sure."

Looking up at our waiter, I found her looking incredibly nervous. "Sorry."

"I'll come back..."

"No!" we both said in unison.

She shrunk back down.

I looked at our waitress, glancing at her name tag, then back to her. "Wanda, is it?"

She nodded.

"Do you have a son, Wanda?" I asked.

Another nod.

"Well, let's hope he doesn't turn out like this one," I said, pointing to my dining friend.

Nathaniel glared at me. "You see, Wanda? Do you see the verbal abuse I have to receive from her every day?"

Wanda looked back between us nervously, her lips parted and the mishap with the lipstick revealed itself again. She swallowed. "So, will it be a hotdog?"

I stared at her. "Fine."

~~~~~~

"I can't believe you made friends with our waitress."

"I can't believe you actually used the word, 'inadequate.' "

We had driven all day, and it was almost nine at night. Our destination was ten minutes away. My heart thudded, and I was a nervous wreck. I had no idea what to say to my parents.

"What are you gonna say to them?"

I shrugged. We eventually ended up at a red house, complete with a white picket fence. Flowers overflowed pots, and I smiled at the beauty of it all.

"Do you want me to come with you?"

I thought. "No, I'm good."

I got out of the car and walked up the front steps. My legs shook, and the cool night air chilled me. I forced my thoughts to not linger, because if they did, I would never make it to the door. My footsteps seemed to float over the pentagon-shaped tiles, and I swallowed. The doorbell rang a pretty tune and I waited. Footsteps came to the door. The blue wall opened, and standing there was a pretty brunette.

She smiled a polite smile. "Hi there, how can I help you?"

I cleared my throat. "This may seem crazy...," I hesitated, not sure if she wanted to have her daughter back in her life, "But I'm your daughter."

50

Ten

She laughed. *Laughed.* I stopped myself from making a face. "I'm sorry, but I don't have a daughter."

"Um, yes. You do." I shoved my file toward her. She studied it, then pressed her lips together.

"Oh, sweetie." The woman shook her head. "Could you come in for a moment? I'd like to explain it all." I didn't understand. Was this woman my mother or not?

I was suddenly angry. "Are you my mother?"

Worry reflected in her brown eyes. "Is your name Lindsey?"

"You still haven't answered my question," I said through clenched teeth.

She motioned to the door. "Please, just come in."

I stood silent, not wanting to follow her in. But all too soon, I found myself in a decorative living room, sipping fruit punch. The woman was rummaging in the kitchen, and shortly stepped back into the room I occupied. She held out a small white plate filled with cookies. I simply shook my head. I just wanted her to get to the point.

The nameless woman sat down on the perfect couch, her perfect khakis crinkling. She clasped her hands and placed them on her lap. "I'm sure you want me to explain." Um, yeah. I nodded.

She mimicked me. "I am not your mother."

My stomach sank. This whole trip was a waste of time. Being kissed by Nathaniel was a waste of time. Being with Nathaniel was an even bigger waste of time.

"But I do know who she is." She stopped. "I was a close friend of hers. We were practically sisters."

I waited for more. She started with, "Look, honey-"

"Don't call me honey," I snapped. Okay, maybe I was being rude. But who could blame me?

51

She pressed her lips together, and took a tentative bite of her cookie and corrected herself. "Lindsey."

I waited.

"Your father is no longer with us."

I was confused. "Where is he?"

"That's the thing." She paused. "He's passed."

He's passed. Her voice seemed to bounce in my head. I didn't have a dad. I wasn't so sure why it upset me so much in the moment, having already known for so long that I didn't have a father. Maybe it was someone finally looking me square in the eye and telling me he was gone. Really gone.

"Where's my mom?" I pulled myself to the corner of the chair, leaning forward.

She smiled, sending wrinkles to the corners of her eyes. "She's in Los Angeles."

"Los Angeles?" I questioned. "Los, freaking, Angeles?! That's, like, three thousand miles away!"

She shrugged. "Only six hours by plane."

My body heated up, and I rubbed my face. Then why the hell hadn't she come to get me? "I've never been on a plane."

"You will one day. Here." She got up, and made her way into the kitchen. I heard a drawer opening, and moments later she returned with a slip of paper.

"This is her address."

I peered down at her neat handwriting. "Why wasn't this on my files?"

"I'm not allowed to say any more. I'm sorry."

She was starting to get on my nerves. "What, the Swat Team is going to jump in through the windows and arrest you?" I joked.

The woman half-smiled. "I promised her."

I studied her, and she did have similar features that matched mine. Brown hair, brown eyes, and mocha skin tone.

52

"What is your name?"

"Call me Aunt Jess."

I most definitely would not. But I tossed her a smile anyway. "Thanks for your help."

She smiled and stepped forward with her arms wide. My eyes widened slightly, but I gently hugged her anyway. I followed her to the door, added an additional wave once I stepped out, and descended outside into the chilly air. The fresh oxygen was refreshing, and I breathed in deeply. Closing my eyes, I listened carefully to the trees swaying in the wind. It was so- *Beeeeep!* I jolted from my half-relaxed state, and stared wide eyed at the idiot in the car. He was beeping and waving his arms as if saying, let's go already!

I scowled, rolled my eyes, and strode to the passenger side, manipulatively taking my sweet time. Smiling shortly to myself, I could vaguely see his irritated expression.

"So what happened?" he inquired as soon as I entered the car.

I shrugged. I didn't have to explain anything to him.

"Oh what, you've gone mute?"

"Maybe."

He sighed, and started to press the key into the ignition. "Seriously, was that lady your mom or not?"

I sat quietly, deciding whether to go into detail. The car took a sharp, looped turn and I gently gripped my seat in order to stay in my upright position. "She's my aunt."

His head immediately swiveled to me, and I felt his shocked eyes bore into the side of my head. I continued. "My dad is dead and my mother is in Los Angeles."

I waited for a snarky answer, but received only a long period of silence. Glancing at Nathaniel, I saw that his brow was creased as if he was thinking of a puzzling riddle.

I looked out the window, enjoying the well-deserved silence. Trees blurred by and the scene occupied my thoughts. For as

53

long as I could remember, a window seat always soothed me. My childhood consisted of me being in a social worker's car when I was a child, waiting to be dropped off.

I leaned back in the seat, the silence causing unwanted thoughts to fester. The familiar scene of Nathaniel kissing me in the parking lot swirled in front of my eyes; his lips, pink and slightly parted, drew closer to me and - *no. What was going on?* This wasn't me. I sneaked a look at the boy sitting on my left, taking a steady breath. Yes, his hair did seem to perfectly stand inches high. His natural highlights did not get lost, as would be expected. A lone freckle hid at the corner of his eye, and his green eyes shone with concentration as they stared at the road ahead. A strange feeling began in the pit of my belly. I swallowed hard, returning my gaze to the window in an attempt to force it down.

I heard a long sigh interrupt the silence. "Okay, the answer is obvious, right?"

I cocked an eyebrow, looking at him. I was suddenly worried he'd caught me looking. *Answer to what?*

He kept his eyes on the road. "We're going to Los Angeles."

~~~~~~~~

I didn't say anything. I was too shocked. "I'm sorry. . . *we?*" I accentuated, clearly perplexed. He looked at me for a split second, his beautiful eyes boring into mine. *Did I just say beautiful?*

"*That's right.*"

"Why do you want to come?"

He smirked, a thin veil of ignorance suddenly plastered onto his face. *How could I ever say his eyes were beautiful?* I asked myself in a non-question tone.

"I don't. I'm only coming because Lavender will most likely make me."

54

I scowled. "Well, I don't want you there." A small voice nagged at me, though. *Did I?*

I glanced at him, that humorous smirk of his playing on his lips. *That stupid smirk.*

It was quiet for a few minutes. "Why are you even staying with Lavender?"

I rolled my eyes and looked to him, expecting his eyes to be on the road. But they were dead on me, his arms straight to the wheel.

As I quickly looked back, a weird feeling stirred once more in my belly. I took a breath to steady myself, and I felt normal again. Almost. "Like I have to explain to you."

"You do if you want me to pay for your plane ticket."

"I can pay for my own." *I really couldn't.*

"Whatever you say, sweetheart."

Eleven

For the next four hours, we sat in silence while listening to the latest songs on the radio. That is, until Shawn Mendes flowed through the stereo system. When the chorus came, I was ready. "We don't have to be ordinary! Make your best mistakes." I sang.

Nathaniel quickly switched it off. I crossed my arms. "Is there a problem?"

He looked over at me, that stupid boyish smirk glistening for a second, before he returned his eyes to the road. "I could deal with him," he glanced at me, "but a duet between the two of you is hard to handle."

"You're just jealous."

"Of what? Him?" Nathaniel shook his head. "Never."

"Mm-hm."

"I'm an amazing singer, for your information."

I nodded, not convinced. "Sure."

He reached over and hit the button. Immediately, a slow song blasted through the stereo. When the chorus came on, he started to sing. His voice was smooth and sounded like it had been coached.

Once he was done, I was dumbfounded. He was good. *Really* good.

"Why are you so good?" I asked, clearly perplexed.

He shrugged. "I went on *American Idol* and got to the top twenty."

I gasped. "Really?"

Nathaniel nodded. "Yeah, and the same day, I invented microwavable popcorn."

I punched his arm, and he laughed. "Hey! Don't assault the designated driver!"

"I'm an amazing driver," I pointed out.

He snorted, and put on his blinker to turn left across a three-lane expressway. "Remember this?"

Before I had time to think, he cut the wheel at a forty mph pace. The car responded with loud screeching and tire squeals. My heart jumped to my throat, and I fumbled around for something to grab. By the time he was finished, I was laughing so hard, tears formed at the tips of my eyes.

He just grinned. "My thoughts exactly."

~~~~~~~~~

After the little fiasco in the car that earned many negative looks from surrounding cars, conversation, (surprisingly) flowed easily. After five hours and forty-five minutes, we were pulling into the familiar apartments. He swiftly arrowed into the parking lot and the car came to a full stop. I sat there, engulfed by the sudden silence.

"Well," he started, "It's been fun."

I couldn't help but stifle a laugh. Pulling the door open, I lifted myself out of the cramped space. I stretched and yawned. "I'm. So. Tired."

"So am I." Nathaniel walked to the other side and pulled open the trunk. It didn't open.

He cursed under his breath and placed his palms on the bottom. With another tug, it still didn't release its pressure. I could tell he was really pulling hard.

I put my wallet on top of the car and walked over to him. "Here, let me help."

He nodded and I placed my palms in the same position his were in.

"Okay, on the count of three, we pull."

I nodded. "One."

"Two."

"Three."

57

Maybe we should've been smarter about where we placed our hands and where sensitive body parts were in contact. Or maybe Nathaniel could've grown a brain. Either one, we were faced with a success and a conflict. The good thing was that the trunk opened. The bad thing? Let's just say in the next moments of pulling it together, the lid slammed me square in the jaw. A severe pain hit me immediately and the next thing I saw was blackness.

Twelve

"You think she's in a coma?" I heard faintly. It was Lavender's voice.

"I don't know. But she's so much better this way," Nathaniel said. I heard a thwacking noise and I mentally smiled. Good old Lavender.

I was slowly resurfacing and managed to mumble, "I'm not deaf, you know."

"Dammit." Nathaniel cursed under his breath.

All I knew was that my jaw was numb. I opened my eyelids, spots swarming in front of them. Slowly, they adjusted to the sudden light and activity.

I sat up. Lavender's eyes were wide and she slowly let out a breath. I was lying on the couch.

"Oh my god, you're okay!" She smothered me with hugs, but she bumped my jaw.

I felt immediate shooting pain. Tears sprang to my eyes, but I quickly wiped them away. I hated to cry. Nathaniel noticed, but looked away when he caught my eye. His brow furrowed in confusion.

Lavender piped up. "You've been out for about an hour. I was so worried."

I blinked.

"And we think you might have bruised your jaw. Ice has been sitting on it for the whole time you were out."

I flinched and felt below my ear. It hurt.

Lavender shrugged. "The doctor said it would be painful for the next week or so and if it doesn't get any better then you should go and see him. You have to keep taking ibuprofen—two. And keep icing it."

I blinked at the amount of information. "Okay."

She had a permanent smile plastered to her face. Something was up.

"What's wrong?" I asked slowly, tentatively.

She paused, her smile faltering slightly.

"Lavender?"

I watched her slowly leave the room and return shortly with a small, rectangular makeup mirror. Lavender handed it to me so I could raise it to my face. A light crimson shade plus blue and purple was creeping out under my lower jaw.

My eyes widened. "What's wrong with my face?!"

She cocked her head, still slightly cringing. "It'll go down within a week-"

"A week?!"

"Or two," she finished.

My eyes were so wide I thought they'd pop out. I took a deep breath, my chest heaving. I did not want to show a lot of emotion. It took all of my strength to either not break into tears or smash everything in the apartment. I composed myself and out of the corner of my eye, I saw that Nathaniel was watching me with concentration.

"This is your fault." I stared daggers at him, and Lavender stopped me from leaving the couch to give him a piece of my mind.

"We *both* had our hands on the trunk, sweetheart," he started, defending himself.

I glared.

"Let's think about the positives."

I raised an eyebrow.

"You're alive. And awake. Everything's good." He grimly smiled, his tone resembling one of his many sarcastic remarks. "For a little bit, we thought you wouldn't make it."

"Your jokes fail to get any funnier."

He rolled his eyes, leaving the room. After he left, Lavender sat next to me and stared me in the eyes. "So? How was meeting your mom?"

I sighed, remembering the recent events. "She wasn't my mom."

Her mouth popped open.

"She's my aunt. My mom is in Los Angeles. My dad is dead."

She let go of a long breath. "Wow. I wasn't expecting that."

It was quiet for a few moments when a sudden question finally dawned on me. "How'd I get inside?"

She shrugged. "I was waiting for you guys to come back when someone knocked on the door really urgently. I ran to it and found Nathaniel standing there with an insane look in his eye. Scared, maybe. You were in his arms."

I was in his arms.

~~~~~~~~

"Go fish!" I happily said.

She groaned. "That's, like, the tenth time." I shrugged and watched her dig in the pile of cards.

She looked at me. "Do you have any two's?"

I scanned the cards in my hands and spotted a two. Sighing, I plucked it out and gave it to her.

Lavender chuckled. "I'm so good at this game."

I snort. "I have five pairs and you have one." We laughed and then our game was interrupted by the slam of a door. Nathaniel stood there, his eyes finding mine first. His gaze softened once he saw me, then he nodded at Lavender. "We should eat something easy for dinner. It'll probably be painful for her to eat."

By the time she nodded, he was already gone.

Thirteen

Pain. Every day. I could only eat soup, because every time I'd chew, my jaw would protest and send pain signals to my brain.

"Lavenderrr!" I groaned. Okay, I admit it. I was being a pain in the ass.

She appeared at the door, looking frazzled. "Yeah?" I gave serious brownie points to her, though; she'd been taking really good care of me. Nathaniel had been distant all week, barely looking me in the eye.

I stretched my jaw, regretting it as soon as I felt another pain. "My teeth have been hurting." The strange thing was, not only did my jaw ache, but my teeth had some serious issues as well.

"Your teeth?"

"Yes," I said, "I feel like my molars are going to explode."

She seemed to think about something. "Come with me."

"Why would I need to-?" She didn't let me finish. Lavender threw me a wave of her hand, leaving the room in expectation I'd listen. I sighed, slipping out of bed and throwing on an easy sweatshirt and yoga pants.

I let myself out of the apartment and met Lavender in the car. I closed the door. "Where are we going?"

"It's been two weeks, Linds. Plus, your teeth.."

"No!" Complete fear pulsing through me.

"Not the doctors. The dentist."

"The dentist?"

She looked at me. "Yeah. Your teeth shouldn't be hurting."

I shut my mouth. I hated the dentist, but if you knew Lavender, you would know that arguing did nothing. About ten minutes later, we arrived at the parking lot. I sat still, my eyes glued to my hands. I was terrified. "You know, now that you mention it, my mouth really isn't hurting anymore." As if on cue, my body decided to remind me of the pain I had been experiencing. My molars ached. I flinched.

"Come on. " She got out of the car and with hesitation, I followed.

When we got inside, Lavender marched me to the receptionist. She smiled, flashing teeth. "Hi girls, how can I help you?"

Lavender smiled politely. "Hi. My friend, Lindsey, hurt her jaw about two weeks ago. Her jaw should be healed, but now her teeth are hurting her."

She nodded, then looked to me. "What does it feel like, dear?"

I paused. "Aching. It feels like it's getting worse."

She tsked. "One moment, please."

Lavender nodded, and walked me over to a chair. She laughed when she saw my anxious expression. "You'll go over to a crazy, drinking, and smoking guy with all his dangerous friends around and throw a bottle on his head without any fear, but you're scared of the dentist?"

I dropped my voice to a whisper. "They are literally performing construction in your throat. And you're telling me you like that?" She managed a smile.

"Lindsey? The dentist is available for an evaluation." A receptionist came in, and announced it. I clenched my teeth. Ugh, bad idea. Pain.

Getting up, I took one last sweep of the reception room, (who knew if I'd be back), and followed the women through the door. She led me down a marble hallway, the sound of drills and dentistry filling the air. Once I entered the room, I was faced with another woman with almond-shaped eyes and dark hair slicked back into a ponytail. I smiled at her and slowly sat on the chair she'd indicated. She returned the gesture. "Hi, Lindsey. I realize you've been experiencing some discomfort."

63

I nodded, but eyed the table of sharp tools. *Maybe this is where I'd die*, I miserably thought.

"Let me just take a look in your mouth. Just lie back and get comfortable." I did as instructed in slow motion, but she just waited with a patient smile.

I opened my mouth wide, and she moved the overhead light so it was shining completely on me. She squinted her eyes as she looked, and quicker than it started, she moved back and moved the overhead light. Turning it off, she took off her gloves.

I was surprised. "That's it?"

She nodded. "Yep. The source of your discomfort is coming from your wisdom teeth. I'll have to remove them."

"What?" I half-yelled.

"It's normal for a girl your age. Many people get them removed."

"I thought they weren't removing them these days as much as they used to," I stuttered.

She shrugged, and placed her hands on her thighs. "I could tell with one glance that you need it badly."

She placed a hand on my shoulder to comfort me. "We put you under, so you won't feel a thing. And then when you wake up, all you can eat is ice cream."

"I'm lactose intolerant," I lied.

She smiled. "Gelato, then. Sherbet?" Oh, well, it was worth a shot.

"You can go back to the reception office now. I'll go make your appointment, immediately. How is tomorrow for you?"

"Tomorrow?" I asked in bewilderment.

"That's my next available appointment, and I don't want you to be in pain."

She guided me back, because I didn't think I could actually walk. "Same healthcare, right? CHIP?"

64

I nodded. I've been here before, and CHIP was the state administered healthcare to children through eighteen.

Lavender got up, and talked to the doctor. All I saw was Lavender's head bobbing in agreement.

~~~~~~~~~

"Okay, so the thing is..." Lavender started, leaning on her kitchen counter and looking at me.

"Yes?" I asked in a monotone.

"I can't go with you tomorrow."

I just stared. At that moment, my level of terror was climbing past one hundred. I was sitting on the couch, my body twisted so I could stare daggers at Lavender.

"I'll ask Nathaniel."

I should've almost expected it. My life was bad as it was, so why not appoint Nathaniel to be my medical supporter?

Nathaniel walked in the door, munching on a hamburger. He stopped when he realized we were staring at him. "What?"

Lavender talked first. "Lindsey is getting her wisdom teeth out tomorrow. I need you to take her."

"Where will you be?" is all he asked.

"Yeah, where will you be?" I piped up.

"I'm spending the day with my mom." She looked back at him and stuck out her lower lip. "Please?"

He shrugged. "Sure. But won't she be all loopy, or something?"

She nodded.

Nathaniel sighed into his hamburger, taking a bite and saying through his mouthful, "Great."

Fourteen

"Lavender," I moaned. "Don't leave me!"

She tossed away her apple core. "Lindsey. You're going to be fine. It's just your wisdom teeth. Nathaniel will be with you," she added, as if all the problems were suddenly fixed. As if.

I moaned again, terror gripping me. I eyed Lavender, and she looked at him as he walked into the room. "I have nothing to worry about, right?"

Nathaniel rolled his eyes. "Don't worry. I'll make sure she doesn't walk straight into ongoing traffic." He looked at me and sarcastically added. "We wouldn't want that, now, would we?"

Lavender warned, "Nathaniel. Stop it. You need to leave soon— your appointment is in--" she paused and checked the clock, "An hour. The dentist asked us to be early, to give you time to prep for surgery." My eyes widened at the word.

She shook her head, chuckling. Lavender reached me on the couch and gave me a hug. I closed my eyes, inhaling her vanilla scent. It made me feel just a little better.

She pulled away and clasped her hands. "Good luck."

And with that, she added one more nod toward Nathaniel. "Take care of her, please. I'll be back later tonight." He just nodded as we both watched her swoop out the door. The silence that ached on after she left felt intoxicating and awkward.

"I guess I'll go get dressed. We should leave in ten," he said, his eyes cast down.

"Okay." I was already dressed in white sweatpants and a tank top. The dentist had insisted I dress to be comfortable.

~~~~~~~~

66

"Nathaniel, I can't!" I screamed. I was having a panic attack. He was trying to pull my arm out of the door, but I was heavily refusing.

He looked slightly amused. It wasn't amusing. "Lindsey, get out of the car."

"I can't!"

He pulled harder, then realized it was the seatbelt that was keeping me in so tightly. Both our eyes locked on it. But he was faster. He lunged quickly and unbuckled it. The strap immediately undid itself and I had no protection. Crap.

I begged him with my eyes. "Nate, please!" He gave me a look, because it may have been the first time I'd ever called him that. C'mon. I had to do all the sweet-talking I could.

Nathaniel gave another tug, sending me flying out of the car into his chest. I thought to myself, *drastic times called for drastic measures*. I dropped to the ground and held onto the edge of the car.

"Lindsey!"

The next thing I knew, I was hoisted onto Nathaniel's back and dangling upside down. I felt him grinning.

"Oh, shut up," I grumbled. We entered the building and he put me down. He still didn't release his hold on me; good thing, because I probably would've run. I looked up at his handsome face and surprisingly swooned. He was—okay—stupid hot.

Nathaniel walked us over to the desk and smiled at the lady. Her eyes noticeably widened, and she fixed her hair. I rolled my eyes, but Nathaniel didn't seem to notice. Of course, he didn't—boys never did.

"Hi. Lindsey Garland is scheduled for surgery this morning." I noticeably cringed. He loosened his grip on my arm just a tad.

She fluttered her eyes and nodded, her gaze falling on me. "Right. We've been prepping for you. If you'll just follow me into the surgery room." I couldn't even nod my understanding. Tears started to form—I was so scared. Right before a tear would slip out and

67

roll down my cheek, I blinked rapidly in realization that he was still standing next to me.

He frowned, wiping the corner of my eye. His touch was like fire, but the shock on my face made him recover his original state. He looked embarrassed and quickly removed his finger. Clearing his throat, he nodded toward the receptionist. "You'll be fine. I'll be here when you get out."

~~~~~~~~

"Lindsey?" someone asked. "Lindsey, can you hear me?"

I slowly opened my eyes, spots swarming in front of them. My vision felt funny. I tried to speak, but something was blocking my voice. My brow furrowed in confusion.

"What-?" My word came out thick. I didn't understand why.

"Lindsey. Lindsey, listen." A short, Asian woman was talking to me. I looked at her, my eyes widening. "Oh, no," I cried, dropping my head," I've been deported to Japan."

Her brow furrowed, and my comment earned some smiles from her co-helpers. "No, no honey. You've just had your wisdom teeth removed. Your mouth is going to be a bit uncomfortable like this for a couple of hours, okay? But I want you to keep this ice on it." Someone handed her an ice pack. I grabbed the ice pack, and placed it against my cheek. I sighed loudly in contempt.

She smiled and held out her arm. "Let's get you home."

I accepted the request and let her lead me back into the reception area. I saw Nathaniel and squealed. "Nathaniel!" I gasped. He looked up in confusion. I ran clumsily, still dizzy and unsure of my movements, and threw my arms around his neck. "I missed you!"

"Um. Okay?" He patted my back.

The same Asian woman turned toward him. "She's going to be a little loopy like this for the next couple hours."

I turned toward her, and pressed the ice pack harder against my cheek. "I'm not loopy!" I sobbed, then studied her eyes. They looked like almonds.

"Okay, I think it's time to go," Nathaniel quickly said, eyeing my curious expression. He put an arm around my back to lead me away from the lady and out toward the parking lot.

He helped me into the car and went over to the other side. He started the ignition and we pulled out onto the main road.

I pouted. "Why can't I drive?"

"Because I want to live till I'm at least twenty."

My tongue seemed interesting at the moment, and I let it flop out of my mouth. I rolled it around and let it hiss like a snake.

"What are you doing?" came Nathaniel's amused voice.

"Don't laugh at me!" I exclaimed sternly. That just made him laugh harder. "Don't laugh at me! Why are you laughing?!"

He shook his head, and halted the car because of a red light. I looked out the window and spotted a homeless man. Rolling down the window, I yelled, "Hey, hot-stuff!"

He looked around, and smiled at me with a wink of his eye. The man blew a kiss to me. I gasped, holding out my hand and catching the imaginary kiss. The window suddenly rolled up, and I looked at the culprit. "Hey, I was making friends."

Nathaniel rolled his eyes, but I got distracted. Nathaniel was barely able to contain a smile as I looked at my reflection in the rearview mirror.

I frowned, cocking my head to the left. "My cheeks are fat," I decided.

He laughed. "No, they're not."

"Yes, yes they are! I have fat cheeks!" I wailed and started to pinch one. It felt like elasticity. "I'm like an inflated chipmunk."

He laughed again. "You're not an inflated chipmunk."

I continued to study my face, and then stick my fingers in my mouth. "What's this?" I grab something soft and spongy.

He looked at me. "Oh, put that back in. That's soaking up your blood."

My eyes widened. "That's blood?!" I rolled down the window, and tossed it out.

"Lindsey! Why'd you do that?"

"It was in the way."

I watched him shake his head, pulling into a parking space. "Let's just get you inside." The cute boy parked the car, climbing out and walking to my side. He opened the door and held out a helping hand. "I'm too fat!"

He rolled his eyes. "You're like, ten pounds."

"I can't tell if that's an insult or not."

He shook his head and grabbed my hand. I feebly got out of the car and let him lead me up the cement staircase and into an apartment. Once I got inside, I sat on a brown couch. "Where am I?"

He came over with a cup of water. "This is where you live."

I met his eyes, calmly asking, "Are you kidnapping me?"

He ignored me and handed over a cup of water. "Take this."

I obediently took a sip, then watched him sit next to me. I poked his cheek, and he laughed. "What are you doing, Lindsey?"

I poked it again, then gasped as if I've realized a certain phenomenon. "Are you Batman?"

"Sure."

"Oh, my god. Where's Superman?" I questioned, looking around. I got angry, then upset. "Where's Superman?!"

I started to sob. "Superrrrrmmannnnn!!" Jumping up, I ran around the table. He jumped up after me and tried to get me. It was like we were playing tag! I lunged, and he lunged.

"I'm faster than you," I proudly said.

"You sure about that?"

70

I nodded solemnly. "I'm going to the Olympics."

"Oh, really? Because the only cardio I remember you doing is dialing a restaurant to ask for delivery."

"Nate," I started, putting my hands on my hips and staring him down from my side of the table, "Didn't Lavender ever tell you I was an athlete?"

He raised an eyebrow, "Never mentioned it," and he suddenly jumped at me, taking me by surprise and slinking an arm around my stomach. Nathaniel gently carried me to the couch and placed me back down in my previously imprisoned position. I felt deep in thought as he took out his phone and scrolled through something called News Feed.

"Nathaniel?" I asked, my voice thick with cotton.

"Mm?"

"Why don't you like me?"

"What are you talking about?" His tone sounded bored.

I shrugged. "You never talk to me. And you're mean."

"I think you're the mean one."

I shook my head adamantly. "But I like you." My eyes widened. "Shh!" I said, putting a lazy finger to his lips to usher his silence, "I don't want Lindsey to know I told you." I looked around, making sure she wasn't there. Phew.

He cocked his head, eyes wide. "You—I mean—Lindsey likes me?"

I nodded. "Oh yeah. A lot. A lot, a lot, a lot, a lot, a lot, a lot."

He pressed his lips together, unresponsive.

"You know what's a weird word?" I asked. "Snorkel. Nothing rhymes with it. Snorkel." I laughed.

He looked at me and murmured. "Yeah, weird word."

71

Fifteen

I woke with sunlight pouring through the cracked shades. I winced, my eye catching a prescription bag and a glass of water. Good old Lavender. I got up, exercising my usual morning routine, and made my way out of the room. I spotted Lavender sitting with her back towards me.

"I survived," I said, very giddy.

She turned and smiled. Getting up, she made her way toward me. We embraced, holding onto each other lazily and not breaking contact

"I knew you'd be fine," she mumbled over my shoulder. "Did he take care of you?"

I repositioned my head on her shoulder. "I don't remember anything after the surgery, so I'm probably not the ideal person to ask."

Lavender laughed. "I'll ask him when he gets back."

I nodded. "Thanks for the water and my prescription."

"What water and prescription?"

I pulled away. "The one you left on the table."

She frowned. "I didn't leave anything on your table."

Nathaniel. I sighed and my head snapped up to the sound of the door opening.

"There you are," Lavender started. "How did it go yesterday?"

He took out his white earbuds, "What?"

"How did it go yesterday?"

He looked at me, then to her. "Why don't you ask the patient herself?" Lavender put her hands to her hips, her eyes zeroing in on him. Uh oh.

He held her gaze for only a few moments before finally breaking and shrugging. "It was fine. She was fine."

72

"Did you get any videos of her afterwards?" she asked. "I wish I could've seen that." I looked to him, curious. What, exactly, did I do?

Nate looked at me, blinking inquisitively. "No. No, sorry I didn't."

"Well, what did I do?"

"You mentioned Batman and snorkels. Nothing big." With that, we both watched Nate retreat from the kitchen and into the living room.

The kid acted more hormonal than a pregnant woman. I turned to Lavender, sharing a confused look. "How was your mom?"

She nodded, turning away and reaching into the fridge. "She was good. It was nice to spend time with her."

"Does she know I'm staying with you?"

She blinked to the floor, shutting the fridge slowly. "No."

"Oh," I started, "would she be mad?" Lavender's mother was the nicest woman alive, but tough as hell. Just like Lavender—only more. I shuddered at the thought of seeing her angry.

"I didn't want to find out," she admitted. Great, so I was even more of a burden than I thought. I was unintentionally forcing my best friend to lie to her own mother. "But I'm sure it'd be fine. You know she loves you." I knew she was only trying to make me feel better.

"What about Nathaniel?"

Lavender paused for a moment, reaching into the overhead cabinet and grabbing two glasses. "Yes. She knows about him." I tried to not feel offended; Nathaniel was a clearly more presentable person to tell your mother about than me. But even as I thought it, I knew it wasn't true. She was helping with Nathaniel for something I still did not know: my stay was illegal.

73

Sixteen

"Nathaniel. Nate. Natheo. Nathaniel!" I chanted, hovering over his bed. His eyelids fluttered open, and he grumbled.

"What do you want?"

I made an 'o' with my mouth. "Someone's grumpy." He rolled over and buried his face in the pillow on the couch.

I continued to push him. "Nathaniel!"

He groaned into the pillow, the sound muffled. "What?"

"We're going to be late!"

The plane would leave in three hours, and we needed to be there two hours in advance. Lavender had already left for school, while I told the school I'd be out sick for the next few days. Priorities, right? School could wait.

"Right. Five hours on a plane, with you."

I frowned. "Don't think I'm excited to spend time with you, either."

He rolled over, his eyes finally finding mine. They flicked over my face as if looking for something. "I don't believe you."

I raised a questioning brow. He rolled his eyes, sliding off the couch without another word. He reached the bathroom, shutting the door with a click.

We pulled off onto the JFK exit, and I was nearly jumping out of my seat. Okay, I had to admit it: I was more than excited.

"Have you ever even been on an airplane?"

I looked at him. "Yeah, the opportunities just fell in my lap during my foster years." We pulled up to the designated terminal, and he

74

opened his door. I did the same. The familiar traffic and noise of New York accompanied the loud sounds of airplanes taking off or landing.

Nathaniel grunted as he hauled the suitcases out of the trunk. "A little help here?"

I rushed over and reached under the bag to help lift. I touched his hand by accident, and felt a chilling warmth. He flinched as I touched him, and my face scrunched slightly. Why was he being so... cold? And weird. Most definitely weird.

We heaved it to the ground, and started on the next one. "Jesus, Nathaniel. How much stuff did you pack?"

"Nothing you need to be worried about." He shot back with edge.

Yes, we've bickered before. But our snits always lacked the seriousness his tone now possessed, and I wasn't sure how to feel about it. We retreated through the parking lot and over the crosswalk, entered the revolving doors and moved over to our airline. We reached a woman who was dressed in a very sophisticated uniform dress. Her hair was slicked back into a bun. She was very pretty, and as soon as she caught a glimpse of Nathaniel, she reached up and ran a hand through her hair. Oh, but of course.

She cleared her throat, batting her eyelashes. Jealousy ran through me. Nathaniel, as usual, didn't seem to notice. "Hello, and where are you flying today?"

"Los Angeles."

She nodded and began to type on her keyboard. "Names?

"Nathaniel Sky and Lindsey Garland."

Her gaze flickered to Nathanial, then back to me. "Very well, then." She looked down and continued to type. "How many bags will you be checking?"

I eyed his pile of bags, snorting unconsciously. They both looked at me.

Nate broke the staring contest first, refocusing on her once more. "Two for me and one for her."

She glanced at me ever-so-subtly, her eyes flickering quickly over me. I stared back, noticing what was happening. I almost wanted to smack Nathaniel and yell, "Do you not see what she's doing?"

I opened my mouth to give her a piece of my mind, but he grabbed my hand. Flashing teeth at the lady, he said, "My girlfriend and I are in a hurry."

My chest fluttered at the word, and I questioningly looked down at our hands. She pressed her lips together, her gaze dropping immediately to the keyboard. She typed harder than before. A few moments later, two tickets printed out and she handed them to us. After checking our bags, we turned the corner. He forcefully dropped my hand.

"I'm surprised you saw what she was doing."

"I'm not stupid. Or blind." I looked down as we rolled up to security. I took off my shoes and placed them and other things into plastic trays. The security man motioned for me to step forward and a warning immediately rang. Three security men raced toward me and pressed their hands to my sides. A strong, heating sensation crept up my neck—I probably looked just as guilty as they thought I was.

The lady closest to me huffed, and pointed to my hair tie. A piece of metal hid on the exterior. "False alarm, everyone."

I sighed in relief and continued through the security barrier. I watched Nathaniel's amused smile disappear and harden as soon as he reached me. "What are you, dumb?"

I shoved on my shoes, raising my eyes to his. "What is your problem?" I shook my head, grabbed my bag and stormed off toward the gate. Minutes later, Nathaniel found me in the waiting area. I didn't say anything and neither did he. Then a woman came on the

P.A. and announced, "Excuse me, all passengers who are boarding the 11:30 flight to Los Angeles. It appears that we have open seats, and if anyone would like to switch once they board the plane, please let a flight attendant know."

I glanced at Nathaniel, who had his head bent down concentrating on a flappy bird game. I weighed my options: sit next to Nasty-Nate for the next five hours, or relax in peace. My mind was made before the options appeared. Once we boarded, again without a word to Nathaniel, I quietly inquired with a flight attendant about changing my seat. He nodded promptly, telling me which rows were available.

"Where are you going?" Nathaniel asked me once we reached our seats, confused as to why I was walking further down.

I shrugged, smiling. "I took that open seat."

"Why?"

"Because I don't want to sit with you."

~~~~~~~~

Okay, it'd already been an hour and I was going out of my mind. It was a bad idea to switch seats, however awful it would've been to sit with Nate. I was caught in the middle of two men who seemed to be either brothers or friends.

"Harry, you cheated on my sister for my other sister. Do you now realize how messed up that is?"

I looked at Harry, waiting for his comeback.

"Technically, I didn't cheat," he defended, taking a huge bite of a Twix bar. Some bits crumbled and fell onto his white collared shirt, but he didn't seem to notice. Or if he did, he didn't care. "They were both okay with it."

My other plane buddy made an exasperated face. "And that makes it okay?"

I raised my hand. "Can I make a suggestion?"

77

They both looked at me and simultaneously said, "No."

I crossed my arms, spotting Nathaniel coming towards me in the aisle. He stopped and grinned, acknowledging my plane buddies. "Having fun?"

I tightly smiled. "Yep." No.

He nodded with his stupid knowing smile. "Okay, then," and he turned, going back down the aisle. My gaze followed him until he disappeared behind a navy-blue curtain. Where was he sitting?

"How about we reach a level ground?" Harry suggested, taking another bite of the Twix. More crumbs tumbled out, adding to the growing pile on the crease in his shirt.

I eyed the guy on my left, waiting. He blinked suspiciously, waiting as well.

"I'll forget about both of them," he started, but then made it worse, "but only if I can have your cousin." Ohhh, Harry.

I unstrapped my seatbelt and stood amongst the sudden yelling, knowing I was going to regret this at some point in my life. I sidestepped over Harry's feet and reached into the overhead bin, finding my bag, then shutting the bin. Nate had to be better than this! I wasn't even sure where he was, so I decided to follow the path he came from. I walked straight down the slim aisle, hitting some people with my bag in the process. I whispered my apologies in the process, my heart beginning to beat wildly in my chest. Where was he?!

"Ma'am," a flight attendant suddenly stopped me in the aisle, eyeing my bag, "Can I ask you where you're going?"

"Um," I stammered, "I'm trying to find my friend. I have a seat next to him."

"What is his name?" She eyed my bag once more, confused on why I wasn't sitting in my seat in the first place.

"Nathaniel Sky."

To my surprise, she nodded immediately. "That would be in first class. I'll take you there." I nodded. Whatever first class was, something told me it'd be better than Harry and his crumbs.

I followed her, and eventually ended up in front of another navy-blue curtain. "Right through here. Enjoy." I let myself in, stopping in my tracks. There were only nine seats, but instead of the original airplane seats, the ones in front of me were white recliners.

"Thought you'd never come," came a deep, velvet voice. I slightly jumped, looking to my left. He sat in the luxurious seat next to the window, smirking. There was an empty seat next to him.

I passed three passengers, sitting next to him. He looked at me. It was quiet.

I kicked my bag under my own seat because I couldn't reach the distance of the seat in front of me. "Just curious, but, how did you manage to..." I trailed off, waving a hand over the sectioned-off area of "first class."

"I have my connections." He said, eyes darkening for just a moment. Weird. "Why didn't you want to sit next to me?"

I looked at him and saw his eyes had softened. I shrugged. "You were being a jerk. Why?"

He took a deep breath, looking like he was contemplating the option of telling me or not. "I heard what you said a couple days ago. To Lavender. About me being arrogant."

I bit my tongue, realizing something very important in that moment. Nathaniel was... a human. With feelings. "I didn't mean that."

"Then why did you say it?"

I didn't know. "I don't know."

He snorted, looking away and out the window.

"Nathaniel?" I whispered.

He looked away from the window, his eyes boring into mine. "I'm sorry."

Seventeen

I wasn't sure how much time had passed, but my eyes were fluttering open. And my head was on his shoulder. But something about sitting there, with my head cocked onto his shoulder, felt right. I had this strange urge of wanting to be closer to Nathaniel Sky, when a certain realization hit me hard. Or a question. Or a fear? Did I have feelings for him? Butterflies flew around my tummy at the thought of being closer to him, and I sat up quickly. No. I was not going to be one of those girls. I was especially not going to be part of the oh-so-many girls Nate had in his life. I looked at his relaxed state, his lips that were slightly parted, his eyelids that fluttered open-

He caught me and smiled. "Is there something you'd like?"

I shook my head quickly, quite embarrassed. "There was..." I racked my brain to come up with something, "There was a bug on your face."

His forehead creased in a, what? expression. "We're on an airplane."

I bit my lip, shaking my head slightly. *Why was I so stupid?*

"Okay..." He said, dragging the y. He leaned forward and reached for his glass of water when the plane violently jumped. Water trickled down his chest, staining his shirt. He cursed and I couldn't contain my laughter.

He pretend-narrowed his eyes at me. "It's not funny."

I covered my mouth. "It really is."

"Oh, really?"

I nodded, and he slyly grinned while throwing the remaining bits of water on me. I gasped and stuck out my tongue. "Very mature."

"That's me."

"Excuse me, passengers. We will be landing shortly. The seatbelt sign is now activated, so please take your seats and fasten your seat belts." The seat belt sign blinked on automatically and I followed instructions.

"You're acting different today," Nathaniel mused, studying me.

My heart sped up, but I made myself slow my movement while buckling. "What do you mean?"

He shrugged. "Nice."

I laughed, my shoulders shaking. "Are you implying that I'm not nice?"

"Maybe."

I punched him in the shoulder and he grabbed the spot. "Ouch. That almost hurt." I rolled my eyes and prepared for landing.

~~~~~~

When we got off in the airport, I looked around once we got outside. Nathaniel came and stood next to me. "Where're we going?"

I ignored the question. "This is so cool."

He shooed it away. "I've been here a million times."

I let my eyes freely sweep the surroundings. "With who?"

Nathaniel was quiet for a moment, before he answered, "My parents."

I glanced at him, extremely curious. He'd never mentioned his family. "What are your parents like?"

He ignored me and checked his phone. "We have two days here, so we should probably get going and find your mom." I nodded, but he was already calling a car. Why hadn't he answered me? I wondered if he even had contact with them.

I watched him speak with an official-looking guy at a desk, who nodded. Nate waved me over, then motioned toward a black car that had miraculously arrived. The driver got out and smiled at Nathaniel, followed by a motion to the car. He disappeared and I frowned. "Isn't he driving us?"

"Nope." He placed our bags in the trunk. "I'm driving."

81

I opened the passenger side and ducked my head. "Why can't I drive?"

"I think we both know the answer to that question."

I scowled as he shut his own door, putting the car into drive.

"Why did you bring so many bags, anyway?"

He shrugged, pulling his seatbelt across him. "I like to have all my stuff with me."

"What?"

"I like to have all my stuff with me."

I shook my head. The statement was too weird. "I heard you. Why do you want to have all your stuff with you?"

"Can we just get to where we're going?" he snapped, and hurt flashed across my face. I quickly replaced it with a blank expression and he eyed me.

"Take a left up there," I pointed and he pulled out of the parallel parking space. Around two hours later, and still not being sure of where I was because I was too busy goggling at everything, Nate broke the silence in the car.

"Lindsey, it's getting dark. We should probably get to our hotel," Nathaniel said as we pulled down yet another alley.

I huffed. I had hoped we would find her house by now. "Fine."

He turned around and onto the nearest highway. In no time, we were pulling into a large, fancy-looking building. The building itself was dark lacquered and seemed to be smoothed over in some sort of shiny polish, and the windows showed large white curtains that flowed from the ceiling to the floor.

"Nice," I muttered.

"My parents are members of the hotel," he mentioned like it was nothing, "I already made reservations." Who was he, anyway? I pulled open my door and stood out to stretch. Almost immediately, two men emerged from behind a sliding glass door.

"Mr. Sky, pleased to see you. We'll take care of the bags."
Nathaniel nodded, handing the keys to the outstretched palm of the
man who spoke. I noticed that he avoided my eye contact, veering it
quite professionally and moving briskly past me. I followed him into
the hotel.

"Hi, ma'am. I'm Nathaniel Sky," he addressed the woman as if
just explaining his name cleared up everything.

I started to smirk, but the women behind the counter nodded
obediently. "Of course, Mr. Sky." Why did I think otherwise?

"You have a reservation for one room, is this correct?" she
asked, glancing to me, then him.

"Must've been a mistake. Can we have two?" he said
immediately, and, I have to admit;,my stomach did shrink.

She nodded again, typed furiously into her keyboard and
handed us both cards. "No problem. Enjoy your stay, Mr. Sky."

I smiled at her and walked down the hallway to the elevator.
Nathaniel was quiet, seeming to be completely engrossed in his own
thoughts.

"Here's your room." After we exited the elevator, he motioned to
a door.

Something was wrong. "Are you okay?"

He softly smiled. "Yeah, I'm fine. Goodnight."

And with that, Mr. Sky left me by my door.

~~~~~~~~

Knocking. That's all I heard. My eyes angrily opened and
I looked around. It was pitch black and I glanced at my bedside
clock. 2:23 am. Who would be knocking at 2:23 am? That called
for standard protocol. I jumped up and turned on the light, my eyes
squinting as they struggled to adjust. I searched for a weapon and
spotted the lamp. I ripped its cord out of the wall and crept to the

door. The knocking had lessened a bit but it wasn't gone, which made my anxiety rocket sky high. I took a deep breath, quick and steady, and yanked open the door in one swift motion.

"Ahhhh!" I yelled, prepared to attack, but the door revealed only Nathaniel. I dropped my lamp, biting my lip. Oops.

He looked startled as his arms stuck tightly in front of his face. "Whoa."

I wasn't in the mood. "What are you doing? It's 2:23 in the morning."

"Sorry," he shifted uncomfortably, shoving his hands into the pockets of gray sweatpants, "I didn't think you were sleeping."

"Was the darkness in my room not a big enough hint?"

His eyes were bloodshot, now that I looked at him closely, but he still looked unbelievably good-looking. "Sorry, I'll just go..." He turned to walk away, but I grabbed his arm. I mean, I couldn't just let the boy go back to his room and bask in loneliness. "Come on in." He hesitated as if deciding whether this was a good idea, but eventually followed me in. He sat on one of the many couches.

We didn't say anything, and the silence became strange and awkward. I couldn't take it anymore. "What's up?" What's up? Who would ask that at 2:23? Probably 2:25 by that point.

Nathaniel shifted, gazing deep into my eyes. "Do you remember anything about your parents?"

I was taken by surprise. "No." But then, the real question dawned. "Why?"

He sighed and placed two hands to his face. "Just wondering."

I checked my clock. 2:27. What a thing to wonder at 2:27, and he noticed my expression.

"It's just..." he noticeably paused, "I don't know. I don't know."

I'd never seen him that way, and it also made me want to comfort him. His shoulders were scrunched up toward his ears, and he blinked sleepily. I almost moved to his shoulder, but stopped myself. Wouldn't that be awkward?

"Can I ask you something?"

I checked the time. 2:32. I sighed, stretching out my legs. At that point, I didn't even care. Lay it on me. "What is it?"

"Why don't you cry?"

I stared, almost wanting to laugh. At, now 2:33, Nathaniel Sky had broken into my room and asked why I didn't cry.

I asked exactly what was on my mind. "You woke me up to ask why I don't cry?"

"Yes."

I struggled to hold a straight face. "Well, you see, I have this condition where my eyes don't secrete moisture and-"

"Shut up," he said, and my laughter immediately filled the room. But he didn't join in, so I let it fade. "Why do you care?"

His tired eyes finally met mine. "Because. Because maybe I care, Lindsey."

Crying and showing how I felt was a sore spot for me, and even Lavender knew better than to bother me about it. I mustered the lamest excuse I could come up with. "I don't need you to care."

"Yeah, well." He rubbed his face. "I can't tell you why."

"What?"

He stood abruptly. "I don't know why I care."

I took a soft breath. "Why are you here?" Here, as in my hotel room. Didn't he have better things to do? Like sleep? I knew I had better things to do—like sleep.

He answered me with a shake of his head, refusing to meet my eyes. I waved toward the door, flopping back onto my bed. "You know where the door is."

He muttered something under his breath before hoisting himself up. I glared. "What did you just say?"

He reared, facing me. "That here you go again, ignoring what's in front of you."

"And what's in front of me?" I asked.

He took a breath, his shoulders rising and falling slowly. "Me." Something about the look in his eye made me think twice about his one-word answer, and I remembered the way he kissed me on the side of the road.

"I think," I started, breathless and unsure of myself, "you should go."

Eighteen

I didn't know how to act the next morning when I saw him, so I started with a casual and hesitant, "Hey."

He walked up to me, his steps faltering only for a moment before shooting me a quick smile. "Hey. Ready?" His mood swings almost gave me a whiplash. Nate didn't wait for my reply as he turned and began the check-out process. Once we were back in the rental car with AC blasting and music loud enough to drown our thoughts, it wasn't until thirty minutes passed before I reached over and scrolled the dial down, the music slowly softening. His eyes were trained on the road, one hand on the wheel.

I studied his flawless features and asked, "Are we almost there yet?" Okay, I admit it, I chickened out. I was going to ask, "What happened last night?" But his face and eyes and lips distracted me from the main objective at hand, and I picked an easier go-to conversation starter.

He smirked and glanced at me for a moment. "What are you, eight?"

I felt as if I had almost imagined his red-stained eyes and exhausted mindset the night before. I frowned. "Jerk."

He briefly checked his phone. "We're actually... five minutes away."

I sat back in the seat, giving my confused brain a break from Nathaniel-induced stress. My stomach churned with nerves. I was finally going to meet my mom. He pulled off the highway and took a left on red. "We're supposed to continue this road for about a mile or two." The car entered a thick, beautiful bracket of overhang trees. I rolled down my window and stuck out my head, looking up into the sky. The green leaves, speckled with revealed patches of sunlight, hung close to the car. But I knew it was only an illusion. I smiled,

87

and returned my head. As soon as I got my head back in, I caught Nathaniel's eye. He immediately whipped back around to stare at the road ahead. I hid a smile, and we suddenly pulled into a road. Large houses sat acres from each other, and my eyes widened.

Nathaniel nonchalantly gathered in our surroundings. "Wow."

I nodded. "Wow is right." He gazed, seeming almost bored with the scenery. Or unfazed. The car rolled to a stop in front of a gray-bricked house, with flowers that burst from every corner of the steps. The doors, window frames, and garage doors were painted a slick, clean white. My eyes swept the perimeter, and I noticed that the lawn was cut evenly, possibly perfect.

"Maybe we have the wrong address," I said, my voice quivering slightly as I felt myself shrink back into the black cushion of the seat.

He shook his head. "Nope. This is it." And as if he didn't believe himself, he checked his phone and nodded to himself once he realized the GPS had brought us to the correct address. He gripped the steering wheel and with one hand put the car into park.

I took a deep breath. "I don't think I can do this." I looked down, noticing my hands were clenched. I suddenly felt his hand wrap around my tensed fists, and something made me instantly relax.

"Do you want me to come with you?"

I thought about this. Did I? He would definitely make it easier, but how could I answer questions about us? What was he… a friend-on-occasion-that-serves-as-my-travel-companion? "No thanks. Just, come back in like an hour or so."

I got out of the car, hearing the car roll back slowly as he departed. I bounded up the steps and inhaled the scent of flowers and freshly cut grass. I rang the doorbell, running a hand through my hair and trying to untangle the knots that had somehow gotten there from sitting still in a car. Moments later, no one answered the door, and I was starting to believe she was not home. I checked over my back, wondering if Nathaniel had left. His car was gone, and my stomach tightened. Did we have the wrong address? But suddenly, heavy footsteps sounded against the foyer inside and the door swung open. I began to smile, but it immediately slipped.

Walter stood in the doorway.

~~~~~~~~

I took a small step back, confusion running through me. I was starting to think confusion was my middle name. "What are you doing here?"

He grinned, revealing ugly, cigarette-stained teeth. "I've been waiting for you."

I made a face, immediately thinking of escape routes. Nathaniel was probably only halfway down the road by then. If I cut and run, maybe I'd catch up. I tried to keep my cool, trying to forget the devil in my nightmares was standing less than three feet from me.

"What do you mean?" I asked, trying to stall. Taking a tiny step back, I felt the edge of the step.

He laughed. "What are you, stupid? I've been waiting for you!" And quicker than I could process, he lunged forward and grabbed me. His grip tightened on my upper arm, pulling me inside. "Come on, Lindsey. Try to follow rules for once."

He spun himself around so I was in front of him, a position in which I could not escape. Tears started to prickle, but I breathed evenly as he shoved me inside. He shut the door behind us, and I heard the deafening sounds of multiple locks. Was it just me and him? Or were his other friends here too? He guided, more like forcefully pushing, me across the beautiful room and through a door leading to what I thought was the basement. I stared at the ground, concentrating on not collapsing onto my face. Seconds later, after climbing down the winding, carpet staircase, we reached a cement cellar which looked like it was half-finished. Stray pipes and tubes hung from the ceiling, and I studied my surrounding area. In the corner, one man stood, arms crossed. I had no way out. Was this another nightmare? I pinched myself in hopes of waking myself up, but I stayed in the scene.

"So, this is the girl?" The nameless person asked, his deep and gruff voice ricocheting off the cement floors.

Walter laughed behind me, a force pushing me into the middle of a room, where I was met with a fold-up chair and roll of duct tape. I couldn't help myself from snorting, the defense mechanism of humor rolling in. "Classic." I glanced to the man across the room. "Which one of you will be the lucky one to tie me up?"

Walter rolled his eyes. "Still haven't lost that sarcasm, have you?"

I kept going. "Did you guys watch all the action and horror movies?"

He shoved me down, my smile fading. Walter stood in front of me and began duct taping my waist to the chair. The man crossed the floor, beginning to help Walter in the crime.

I eyed Walter, who seemed to be having some trouble with the tape. I almost wanted to laugh, my fear evaporating for a few moments. The kidnapping was a fail, in my opinion. He hadn't even tied back my arms, which were crossed across my chest. I snorted once more, but soon pulled a straight face when he eyed me.

"Aren't you gonna tie back her arms?" the man asked. I glared at him, feeling a mix of being annoyed and impressed. I had to give him some more credit; he clearly had more than half a brain.

Walter sighed and came closer to me. Once my arms were tied back tightly, he stood back, surveying his masterpiece.

I looked up at him. "You must've been a stellar art student. Really, this is a prime tape-job."

"Paul, come here." Walter motioned to his partner-in-crime, ignoring my sass.

90

The man, Paul, stepped forward and nodded. "Well you could-" he stopped once he caught a glimpse of Walter's face, regretting the decision in offering feedback, "It's perfect." Hah.

"So now that you've tied down my weight of one-hundred-and-twenty-four pounds, are you going to tell me why you're in my birth mother's house?"

He laughed sadistically. I didn't find anything funny. "Your mother is dead."

I stared, confused. "Then why was I given her address?"

"Oh, by Aunty-Jess? If that's even her real name." He took my silence to continue his explanation. My eyes followed him as he paced. "Shortly after Hellen kicked me out of my house- "

"Since when was it ever your house?" I interrupted, irritated that he thought it was ever his home, but hiding my surprise that Hellen had finally kicked the toxins out of her life. But a small voice was nagging at me: why hadn't she come for me?

He ignored me and kept going. "So when I was packing my stuff up, I saw you break into the house with some guy—handsome fella, by the way—and watched you look for a file."

I tried to ignore the cold shiver running down my spine. He had been watching me—us—the whole time? I swallowed, officially freaked out.

"I then got the idea of messing with you."

"Wow," I nodded, "your life sure is filled with excitement."

He glared at me, his stubbly hairline inching forward in centimeters. "You thought your mother would be here." He grimaced. "God knows, considering your behavior, how awful she must've been."

I gritted my teeth, my hand clenching behind me. "Don't you dare talk about my mother. You never even knew her."

He mockingly laughed. "Neither have you." A shocking conclusion hit me. He was right.

"Now. Let's get to the real question. Why, on earth, did I do this?" he asked, still pacing while he clasped and unclasped his hands. "Because, sweetheart...." He paused for effect, and I faltered, the nickname reminding me of Nathaniel. How long had I been here? Would he even find me? "I want my revenge."

"How old are you, ten?" I interrupted, trying to stall.

He continued as if he didn't hear me, "And to do this, I am going to do everything you did to me."

I mock-laughed. "What? Get you kicked out of your only shelter? I'm sorry you have to live on the streets."

"Could you just shut up!" he shouted, his voice raising. Walter readjusted his collar, his face red. "First up," he stopped, and held out a hand to Paul, "a beer bottle."

Paul grabbed a bottle that was hidden in the dark and handed it to Walter. In one swift motion, he slammed the bottle on top of my head, the glass shattering around me. A sudden tiredness fell over me, and I was pulled into blackness. I couldn't see anything or even move, but I could still hear voices. Paul, maybe?

"This isn't part of the plan!"

Walter replied with a gruff tone, "How am I supposed to know she'd black out?" I heard footsteps coming toward me, then stop. Fingers were placed on my neck, remained for only a few seconds, then pulled away. "She's still breathing."

"Well, Jesus!" Paul said. Why was he yelling? Too loud. I wanted the voices to stop. I just wanted to rest in peace. Just for a few moments, but of course Walter had to ruin it.

"Calm down," his gross voice responded, "we just have to wait it out." I grumbled, annoyed with their constant yelling, and felt myself stir to life again. I lifted my pounding head, feeling like it was weighing more than it should have. I blinked repeatedly, my vision blurry. Everything become clearer with every blink. I took in my surroundings; the un-stained gray floor, pipes and yellow-packing

92

foam protruded from the ceiling and walls, and Walter. Walter stood less than three feet from me, smirking in content – though I wasn't sure why.

He glanced at Paul, "What did I tell you?"

I noticed then the beer dripping from my hair, and I gagged at the scent. A warm, trickling trail of something dripped from my forehead. I realized it was blood. Coming from where? My forehead? My already bruised jaw? With the thought of it, it ached subtly.

Walter was close to my face, and I spit on him with all the force I could muster. He closed his eyes and wiped my saliva from his cheeks. "Shouldn't have done that, sweetheart." Sweetheart. The name made me think of a certain someone. Where was Nathaniel? Before I could get lost in my thoughts, I felt him slap my cheek. Hard. His fingers just grazed my recovering jaw, but it was just enough force to cause pain. I bit my lip, trying not to cry.

Beer dripped from my hair, and I gagged from the scent. A warm, trickling trail of something dripped from my forehead. I realized it was blood.

Walter was close to my face, and I spit on him with all the force I could muster. He closed his eyes and wiped my saliva from his cheeks. "Shouldn't have done that, sweetheart." Where was Nathaniel? Before I could fall deeper into my thoughts, Walter slapped my cheek hard. His fingers just grazed my recovering jaw, which sent sparks of pain around my jaw and face. I bit my lip, trying not to cry.

"Next, on our list…" He continued pacing again. I just stared straight ahead, not meeting anyone's eyes.

"Who was the woman in Virginia, then?" I managed.

He stopped and shrugged. "Money is the key ingredient in bribing people." I shook my head. This wasn't happening. Blood trickled around the frame of my face. Or maybe it was beer.

"Next. You ruined my relationship with Hellen. Now, I'm going to ruin your relationship."

"I'm not in a relationship."

"Oh really? What about your friend Lavender? I know you're close."

"Touch her, and I'll make sure you pay."

He threw up his hands. "Who's in the chair, again?"

I ignored him.

"Anyway, say hello to your new home."

"Excuse me?"

He smiled and leaned close to my face. "I'm gonna keep you here. You don't have real family, and your files are gone." I thought back, remembering I had destroyed them. "You're a nobody." I realized he was right. My phone then rang, piercing the air. I froze, hoping it was Nathaniel.

Walter cursed, "You have a phone?"

I snorted. "What teenager doesn't?"

"Give it to me."

"No."

The ringing continued.

"Give it to me, dammit!" he yelled.

"No!" I yelled back.

He slapped me across the face. "Give it to me. Now!"

I wriggled my arms enough to be able to scramble for the phone with my fingertips in my back pocket, and heard it drop to the ground behind me. I pressed a button before letting it fall, though, hoping it was the answer key.

He grabbed it and stuck it in his pocket. "You should learn to listen to what you're told, Lindsey."

"What are you talking about, old man?" I sneered.

"That is how you became a foster kid, isn't it?" He inquired, a grin pulling across his face. He looked like he was keeping a secret. I didn't answer.

He raised an eyebrow, "Let's get something straight. No one cares about you and no one ever will, and that's the reason why I can keep you here. Lavender can be bribed, like your 'Aunt' (he made air quotations), in Virginia was paid to tell you you'd find your mother here."

A tear slipped out of my eye, but I bit my tongue to stop the flow. "You're wrong."

"No. I'm not." Laughter erupted from Paul and Walter. I stared at the ground.

"Lindsey. Don't move." A voice came from the bottom of the stairwell, and I looked up.

Nathaniel stood there, anger written over his attractive face.

Nineteen

"Nate," I said, my voice low and full of relief.

He didn't look my way, only stared straight ahead at Walter and Paul. "Take the tape off. Now." I've never seen or heard him so angry. "Or I'll call the police."

Walter stared at Nathaniel and slowly inched to my side. I tensed.

"Look, kid. You don't know what you're getting into."

Nate laughed, but there was no humor in his voice. "Oh, please. I think I'm smart enough to realize that this," he paused, and motioned to my trap, "is a failed kidnapping."

I noticed his phone clutched tightly in his hand, but he still stared straight ahead at Walter. "I'm not gonna tell you one more time. Un-tape her, now."

Walter swallowed, moving toward me. "So your big plan is calling the cops?"

"After I make your face uglier than it is now," he said as he clenched his fist, his knuckles white.

Walter smirked, arrogance dripping from a chuckle. "What are you, seventeen. Eighteen? Don't waste your time with this one," he motioned to me. I looked down, hoping Nathaniel would just walk away.

Nathaniel shrugged. "I think I'll take my chances."

Walter's face dropped, not expecting this heroic answer.

Nathaniel's eyes finally shifted to mine and his brow furrowed, then hardened. "What's on your face, Lindsey?" He asked softly, as if he already knew the answer.

My breathing shook as I inhaled. "Bl-" suddenly, something hard slammed against the side of my cheek, throwing my head to the side. I let a sob break through, but only one. The next few moments happened in a blur. Nathaniel cursed loudly as he jumped forward and threw Walter against the wall. I felt dizzy and had an overwhelming urge to fall into a deep sleep, letting the relaxing moment of darkness wash over me.

I was just about to happily give in when Nathaniel's voice yelled, "Stay awake, Lindsey."

I pushed a strong urge of energy into my eyes to force them to stay alert. But my head hurt; it hurt so much. Paul backed away from the fighting, looking scared. He turned and jogged back up the stairs. If I hadn't been so tired, I would've happily laughed. Nathaniel didn't seem to notice as he kicked Walter. And then it was quiet. The only sounds in the room were Nathaniel's heavy breathing. I wasn't sure how long the scene lasted.

I was exhausted. "Nathaniel. Is he-?"

"No. Just knocked out."

I nodded, then was silenced by Nathaniel's hands. He placed them both on my cheeks and wiped away a fresh tear. Or blood. Or beer. I wasn't so sure. "Everything's okay now."

I took a shuddering breath, my head pounding while I tried to nod.

His shoulders dropped a fraction. "I'm sorry I left you."

I shook my head, hard sobs suddenly passing through. "I-it-wasn't y-your f-fault."

He looked down at me, clearly surprised I was crying but trying to not act surprised. Like it would scare my tears away or something. "Let's get you out of here."

He bent down, pinching the edge of the tape and ripping it off my legs in one swift motion. By the time he reached my bare arms, he grimaced up at me.

I closed my eyes, preparing myself. "Like a Band-Aid." He ripped quickly, as per my instructions, and threw the discarded tape to the side. Walter still lay in a heap on the ground. Nathaniel moved

97

to my side, placing a hand on my lower back and the other in my hands. He helped me up slowly.

I swayed, spots running in front of my vision. "Whoa," he whispered close to my ear. I turned my head a fraction to the left, blinking in surprise when I realized he was closer than I thought. I stopped, suddenly aware of his warm hand pressed into my lower back and the other grasping my hands. He looked into my eyes, his gaze darting to my lips then back to my eyes. He didn't need to say anything; all I wanted to do was get closer to Nathaniel. I placed the hand he wasn't holding onto the back of his neck, pulling him in. He resisted for a moment, his eyes nervously darting across my face and finally landing on my eyes. He shortened the distance between our faces and pressed his lips lightly to mine, hesitant. It felt as if all the exhaustion and tension and behavior between the two of us fell away, and the only thing that was on my mind was his mouth moving in sync with mine.

He pulled back, looked into my eyes, and grinned. "You have no idea how long I have waited to do that."

~~~~~~~~~~

When we got back to the hotel, Nathaniel had insisted on staying with me in my room until I fell asleep. He appeared from the bathroom with a wet cloth in hand. He made his way over to my side of the bed, the TV softly humming in the background. I shifted a tiny fraction to make room for him as he sat on the edge of the bed, the mattress slightly dipping. He placed the cold cloth against my forehead, soothing my burning head. The shower I had taken had washed away the beer and blood, but my head was still hurting. [Sydney, I think the time since the jaw injury and the wisdom teeth extraction has been so brief that she would still be bruised (remember the blue and purple under her jaw?) and taking pain meds prescribed for the dental surgery. You have mentioned NONE

98

of this. Each time Walter hits her with a beer bottle, you need to have her wondering about the possibility of permanent damage to her face. Also, when he hits with great force, she will definitely pass out. Write that into the scene, with Walter waiting impatiently for her to wake up so he can hurt her some more.]

"How did you find me?"

He sat on the desk chair, not taking his eyes off me. I relaxed into the back of the bed, pillows supporting my back.

Nathaniel shrugged. "I didn't have anywhere to go, so I decided to just come back and wait for you. After forty-five minutes, I called you and it picked up."

"And that's when you heard Walter's voice."

He nodded, face hardening when he remembered the conversation he had overheard. "You shouldn't believe what he said."

I lowered my gaze to the white sheets.

"He's so wrong, Lindsey."

My gaze lifted to his slowly, and I whispered, "Thank you. For everything, I never thanked you for driving me...for taking me here."

"I did it because I have feelings for you."

My eyebrows raised. "What? Even the first drive?"

His mouth made a straight line. "Well, no. You're kind of annoying- "

I threw a pillow at him with a grin, cutting off his sentence. "Go to sleep."

"You can't tell me what to do," I said with a smile.

"When you get cat-fished by some guy who throws beer bottles on you, then I have the right to tell you to get some rest."

I sighed a tiny sigh. I wasn't tired anymore. "I'm not tired." I stubbornly pushed out my lip, and he laughed. Nathaniel got up and made his way to me.

He bent down and slowly kissed my forehead. "Please?"

I tried not to let him take advantage of this moment. "Nope."

99

He lowered his kiss, now pecking the top of my nose and murmuring, "Please?"

I started to fall into a trance and mumbled, "Mm, almost."

He grinned, and dropped his jaw to slowly kiss my lips. Fire exploded, and I happily agreed to keep my eyes closed for the next nine hours.

~~~~~~~~~

"Linds! The plane leaves soon. We should be there now."

I groaned and rolled over on my bed. "Why does it matter if we miss it?" My voice was muffled against the soft pillow blocking my mouth.

Nathaniel's voice was close to me, so I guessed he was picking up stray clothes of mine. Nathaniel had fallen asleep on the desk chair late last night. I only knew because his snoring had woken me up in the middle of it all.

"Because you can't miss school tomorrow." His voice trailed as he entered the bathroom.

I groaned again and curled up tighter into a ball under the blanket. I sighed and it was oddly quiet for too long. I didn't dare to peak, but spoke from under the covers. "Wha-"

Arms were suddenly wrapped around my waist, and I was easily hoisted into the air. "Nathaniel!" I yelled.

"I needed to get you up some way." He said into my bed head, dropping me on my own two feet.

"You're annoying," I muttered up at him, but my small smile gave me away.

He clutched his chest as if in pain. "That was harsh."

I shoved his chest and disappeared into the bathroom. After taking a long shower, (regardless of Nate's yells for me to hurry up), brushing my teeth and applying minimal makeup, we descended downstairs into the lobby. He checked us out, and by the time we made it through the security checkpoints and to our gate, I smiled smugly at him and dangled my damp hair. "Told you we wouldn't be late." I sat, exhaling for the amounts of time we probably had.

"All passengers for flight 261 from Hawthorn, Los Angeles to JFK, New York City: boarding for first class is now available. Any family with small children or people who need a little extra time are also able to board at this time."

I avoided his I told you so gaze.

~~~~~~~~~

"I have to say, first class is pretty great." I sighed as I stretched out my legs and snuggled into the comfortable chair. "I'm never going back."

"It's alright."

"First class is alright?" I questioned, raising my eyebrows at him.

He shrugged. "I'm used to it."

I held up a hand. "Settle down, Mr. Big Shot." I watched him smile, looking away. It faded quickly.

"What's wrong?"

"Nothing," he shrugged. I waited for a better explanation.

"Tell me,"

Nathaniel looked at me, searching my face. After what seemed like minutes, he finally sighed. "Fine."

I waited.

"I was raised with all this...stuff," he said, finally settling for a word. "It was cool for a little bit until I didn't really care."

I remained silent, urging him to continue.

"So, I left."

My eyes widened. Nate had *chosen* to leave his family?

He noticed my expression. "Never mind. It's not important."

I replaced my look with a blank expression. "No, tell me."

101

"It's fine." He took a sip of his water. I stared at him, thinking, if I do it long enough then maybe he would feel uncomfortable and finally fess up.

He eyed me. "Please stop."

"Stop what?"

I raised an eyebrow. "Staring at me like I'm your prey." I forced myself to not break my expression and continued to stare.

He released a breath. "Fine. They just put too much pressure on me, I think. Expected me to do this big stuff when I wasn't ready."

I was turned toward him now, listening.

"I felt suffocated."

"So, what happened?"

"I lived in my car when I left. Then Lavender took me in."

My eyebrow twitched, blown away with the amount of information he was sharing. "You haven't spoken to them since?"

He shook his head, the spiked overgrown hair flying a tad. "Nope."

"Why did you tell me they kicked you out when we first met?"

"I know, I'm an asshole, but I didn't want to be the asshole who shoved his perfect family in your face."

I slowly nodded. I guess that made sense. The rest of the flight lasted eight hours; I passed the time by watching movies and resting, so by the time we finally arrived in the heart of New York, I was weary. After picking up our baggage, we walked outside to find our car. The loud sirens, commotion and chilly air comforted me. By the time we were settled into the car, I glanced at Nathaniel and realized how much I had learned about him on our two-day trip. But I had learned nothing about where my mom was. Or if I even had a mother still living.

~~~~~~~

102

"You're back!" Lavender squealed, as we came barging through the door quickly. It was so cold.

I laughed as she engulfed us both with hugs. "We were only gone for two days." I plopped down my bag. Leaning against the sink, I wrapped my arms around myself and enjoyed the warmth of the apartment.

She dramatically sighed. "And it was the longest two days of my life."

I laughed and Nathaniel dropped his bags, adding to the pile on the kitchen floor.

"So? What's your mom like?"

I glanced at Nate. "That's a long story."

Twenty

"He what?" Lavender exclaimed, her face lit in exasperation. She gripped the table.

Nathaniel plopped onto the couch. "He kidnapped her."

"But that doesn't make sense." She shook her head. "The lady in Virginia-"

"Lied," I finished.

She frowned. "Are you sure?"

"That's what Walter said," I said, catching Nate's gaze on me.

His face hardened. "The guy's a phony."

"Except the fact that my parents really are dead." My sentence sent the two of them into silence.

Loud, anxious knocking interrupted the silence. Through the door came a muffled voice, "Police. Open up."

I froze, my eyes wide. Nathaniel jumped up quickly, barely making a noise as he held a finger to his lips and motioned to the next room. Lavender grabbed my arm, pulling me into the guest bedroom and shutting the door behind me. I was left alone. My hands shook; I knew what this was. It had to come eventually. I placed my ear to the door, straining to hear what was going on. All I heard at first was murmuring too low for me to make out, but it quickly escalated into yelling.

"Where is Lindsey Garland?"

Nathaniel's voice didn't seem fazed as he calmly answered, "I don't know."

"Son, you have three seconds to tell me the truth. Lindsey is a ward of the state, and cannot live on her own until she is of the age of eighteen."

"I'm telling you the truth. I don't know where she is," Nathaniel insisted. I sighed, closing my eyes and glancing around the safe and cozy room. I opened the door, stepping into the living room and in eye-range of the cops. Lavender stood to the side with arms crossed, her face slack and apologetic. I almost hit myself; here I was, putting others in harm's way for my own cause.

Twenty - One

"Lindsey? Dinner!" Hellen called from downstairs, her voice ricocheting off the walls I had once called home.

Small sets of feet ran from the hallway outside my door. I yelled back, "I'm not hungry!"

Hellen didn't answer, but I knew she heard me. Recently, I wasn't up to doing anything out of the ordinary. I shivered and wrapped my sweater tighter around me. My room, filled with darkness, seemed even lonelier than usual. I've been going to school, but haven't really communicated properly with Lavender. I've been too upset. I kept telling myself that it was only for one year.

Low knocking sounded outside my door, followed by the new girl, Mariella, who poked her head in. She was six and absolutely adorable.

"What's wrong, Lindsey?" she asked, voice squeaky.

She climbed into my bed and snuggled into me. I squeezed her. "I'm fine."

Mariella was quiet. "Does it ever get better?"

I frowned. "What?"

"You know."

I was dumbfounded. And speechless. What was I supposed to say to that? I settled with lying. "It does. I promise. You'll be adopted soon." I meant the last part; she was young, sweet, and the cutest thing. Why wouldn't she be adopted?

"You weren't," she replied meekly while playing with the strings of her pink shoes.

"I was different," I managed, placing a hand on her head and taking a piece of her soft blond hair between my fingers, "I promise that you'll be out of here soon."

Mariella nodded against my shoulder, then crawled out of the comfortable position. "I'm going to dinner."

I smiled, though I knew it was too dark for her to see, and whispered, "Okay."

And she was gone like that. I wasn't even sure if she heard me.

~~~~~~~~

I was reading my book when my window started to make noise. Looking up, startled, I squinted at the window. Something small suddenly shot up and hit against the glass, a tiny ping resulting. I jumped up and ran the short distance to the window. Unlatching the lock and lifting, I rested my elbows on the sill and peered down. Nathaniel stood there, a handful of pebbles in his hand, and was about to toss another one. Oh, Romeo. I swear, the scene looked like something out of a book.

"Nathaniel?" Nathaniel Sky was currently launching rocks at my window.

He stopped, his face lighting up as he looked up at me. "Hey, stranger."

I shook my head. "You're the biggest idiot alive."

"I am who I am."

"What are you doing here?"

Nathaniel grinned, flashing teeth. "We," he paused, dropping the pebbles and rubbing his hands together, "are going on a date."

I smiled. "Nate, I can't."

"Why not?"

I frowned. Did he not understand? "Because I may be in a situation where I can't leave the house after ten."

It was his turn to frown. "That sucks."

"Tell me about it," I muttered. "How did you know which room I was in?"

He sheepishly smiled. "I was hoping I'd get lucky."

I stifled a laugh, my hand flying up to cover it. I could only imagine the expression on Hellen's face if he had chosen the wrong window.

"Come on," he called up.

"I can't!" I hissed, a smile forming.

Nathaniel crossed his arms and tapped his foot.

I sighed. I wasn't going to win this. Pulling my head back inside the window, I tip-toed to my door, opening it slightly, and leaving it ajar. Slipping out carefully, I eased past the blue night light that illuminated the hallway. I sneaked a glance at myself in the hallway mirror and ran a hand through my messy hair. All the kids were asleep, but I spotted the kitchen light on. Hellen was still awake, which gave me no access to the door. I turned and slipped back into my room, suddenly slamming into a hard figure. I gasped, looking up. Nathaniel stood there, smirking. I pushed him back into my room and shut the door behind me.

"You're insane!" I whispered, staring wide-eyed up at him. He grinned and slipped his arms around my waist to pull me closer, clearly not caring. As he leaned down, my eyelids fluttered shut the moment he placed a deep kiss on my lips. The kiss lasted seconds, but it felt like an eternity. As he pulled back, he looked into my eyes. The moonlight streamed into my window, allowing me to see his eyes. The green tint seemed to shine brighter than usual. If that were even possible.

"Let's go," he whispered.

Once he turned, I nodded, letting out a breath I didn't even realize I was holding in. I followed him to the window.

Nathaniel slipped a leg out the window, then the second, and as quickly as ever, dropped himself. I gasped, rushing to the windowsill. Peering down frantically, I saw Nathaniel stood there grinning, perfectly fine.

I bit my lip, taking in the situation and thinking realistically, "I don't think I can do that." I eyed the ground from the second story.

He chuckled, "Probably not," and bent down to search through a bag I hadn't noticed. Moments later, he pulled out a long, red rope.

He unwound the tie and tossed the end up to me. "Now just loop the rope to a sturdy object. Like your bed or something."

I rushed to my bed and tied the rope around the strong post. Beds in foster houses were nailed to the ground for some reason; don't ask me why. It wasn't like some kid was going to steal a seven-foot bed. At least I hadn't come across one who had the desire to do so.

Walking back to the window, I nodded down at him. "It's tied."

He nodded and stepped closer to the wall. "Now just place your legs out the window like I did, and hold onto the rope. All you're going to do is hold the rope and walk backwards down the wall, so you're facing it."

I gulped, fingering the rope in my hands. I could do that. I peered over the edge, blinking. No, I couldn't.

"Don't worry, I'll catch you if you fall."

I scoffed.

"Don't worry, Linds, I'm right here." Something about his voice made me step out of the window. Before I could even register what I was doing, my second leg was out as well. I was sitting on the sill. I tugged at the rope from the bed, testing for durability.

Without thinking about it, I changed my position and was now completely outside the window with my feet planted against the wall. As quickly as I could, I walked down the wall. My weight added an amount of pressure to the rope. One step, two steps, three steps. I grunted. My hands were stinging and started to slip. Four steps, five steps, six steps. Almost there. But as quickly as descending down, the rope betrayed me and snapped. I was sent flying down toward the grass. I swear, at that moment, I felt as if I weighed seven hundred pounds.

I braced myself, waiting for the impact of the hard ground. But I never did. I dropped into Nathaniel's arms, a small grunt escaping his lips and a short breath from mine.

I looked up at him and he grinned. "Told you I'd catch you."

~~~~~~~~

"So where are we going?" I asked, blindly. Literally. Nathaniel had insisted on blindfolding me. As irritating as he was, I couldn't complain about his guiding hands on my waist.

"It's a secret."

"It's been, like, an hour!"

I heard him chuckle behind me. "It's been ten minutes."

"I can't believe you broke me out of prison," I said, my foot catching a tree root. Or a piece of trash. "Ow!"

"Watch your feet," he said in my ear, his warm breath tickling my neck.

"It's a shame I can't use my eyes," I complained.

"We're almost there." He guided me to the right. I heard soft, crunching sounds beneath our feet. It was suddenly quiet, and I didn't feel the presence of Nathaniel anymore. His hands were gone.

"Is this when you kill me?" I asked, only half-serious.

Familiar laughter erupted from the left of me. "Can you be quiet for at least a minute of your life?"

I bit my tongue.

He laughed, sounding closer again. "Okay. I'm ready."

I sighed dramatically, but I couldn't help the curious excitement bubbling up inside me. The blindfold suddenly slipped off, and I blinked. Lanterns. Everywhere. Ten, twenty, maybe even thirty small, powered lanterns were placed in random areas of Central Park. It was deserted, as expected, and illuminated only by the lanterns.

110

My jaw dropped, but not before my gaze shifted over to the ground. A clean towel was placed, along with a bouquet of flowers and a basket of something.

I whipped around and placed my hands on his chest. "Okay. How many Nicholas Spark's novels did you read?"

"Who?"

I rolled my eyes, grinning and looking back over the masterpiece. "Nate."

He gazed at me, as if anticipating what I was about to say. "Yes?"

"I love it. This," I gestured, "is probably the most amazing thing anyone has ever done for me."

Nathaniel grinned and exhaled as if scared of my reaction. "I'm so happy you like it."

"I love it," I corrected him. "How long did it take you?"

He bit his lip, thinking. "Well, Lavender helped." I smiled. "So probably about an hour or two to set it up."

"I'm so special," I cooed.

He stepped closer to me, closing the space between us. "You are." At that moment, in the middle of Central Park, I believed him one hundred and ten percent.

~~~~~~~~~

"This. Is. So. Good." I exhaled, closing my eyes. The warm brownies melted on my tongue.

"I have something for you," he said, reaching into his pocket and pulling out a slim, white box, tied with a skinny blue ribbon. Nathaniel handed it to me, and I grabbed it with trembling fingers. I pulled the ribbon, and it slipped off. Opening the lid, I gasped at what lay on a satin pillow. An infinity charm, connected with a chain.

"Do you like it?"

I nodded furiously.

111

Nathaniel got up and took the box from me. He disappeared behind me and swept my brown hair to the side. He put it around my neck, his finger brushing me as he connected it together. After he reappeared in front of me, my fingers held the pendant.

An idea popped into my head.

"Uh oh. Someone's thinking."

I grinned and pointed. "Wouldn't it be fun to climb that rock?"

He followed my finger. "Sure?" Then, "You might not be strong enough."

I slapped him as I got to my feet. Looking down, I mischievously smiled. "But I'm fast."

"I don't doubt it." Taking off at a sprint, I heard distinct laughter behind me. I pumped my arms and willed my legs to go faster. I knew I was ahead of him. I would've heard-

"Ahh!" I yelled, as someone grabbed my waist and hoisted me into the air. "Nathaniel! That's cheating!" I laughed.

He dropped me. "Sorry! I can't let you win, now can I?"

"You can't cheat in games with your girlfriend," I spilled, but as soon as it left my mouth, my face flushed.

He stopped, turning. His shoulders rose and fell with even breaths. "What?"

Oh, no. I went too far. I ruined it. "Nothing."

"Do you want to be my girlfriend?"

"That depends if you want to be my boyfriend," I retorted, falling into our usual banter.

"Yes, I do." I didn't have time for my brain to freak out before Nathaniel sprinted off. I took off after him. By the time I had reached the rock, I was breathing like I had run a marathon. I bent over and leaned into my legs, trying to control my breathing.

He wasn't even fazed as he watched me. "Come on, Gramma. Time to climb the rock."

"Whose idea was that again?" I asked.

"Yours."

"I take it back," I said, as I finally was able to sustain a standing position.

He gestured in front of him. "After you."

I walked forward and placed my foot into a crevice on the rock, pulling myself up. Moments later, we were both sitting about eleven feet from the ground.

I lay back and stared at the stars. Nathaniel followed my actions. "So are we just going to ignore what just happened?"

The elephant in the room revealed itself, but I willed it to disappear. "What do you mean?"

"God, you're annoying."

I sat up, leaning on my hand. "That's not very nice."

"Isn't that how our relationship started? From not being nice?"

"Well," I crossed my arms, "I guess we have to make some adjustments now that we're…"

He grinned. "Right."

I rolled my eyes, lying back down.

It was only a few minutes until he spoke. "What is it like?"

"What like?"

He sighed. "I shouldn't be asking, but-"

"Not having parents?" I interrupted. I knew the tone of the question. It was too familiar.

My gaze softened. "It's okay."

My stare returned back to the stars. "It's weird." I paused, squinting my eyes. "I remember, when I was little, I didn't really understand where my parents were. Like, say I was at school? And the kids, they would greet their moms and everything. And I would just stand there, seeing some woman I didn't know picking me up. And every time I would change homes, it'd be a different person."

He watched me intently.

113

"I think it was when I was…eight, when I began to understand. And about that same time, I met Lavender. That's why she is really close to me. She helped me understand."

He smiled warmly, looking to the side. My eye caught a black, ink-scrawled bird on the corner of his neck. "I've never noticed that before."

He looked at me. "What?"

"Your tattoo."

His face lit up in a crimson pink. "It's nothing."

"When did you get it?" I asked, curiosity striking.

He chose his words carefully. "I was eighteen. I'd always wanted one."

"What does it symbolize?" I asked.

"Why does it have to mean something?"

"I feel like it's a rule or something."

He blew out a breath and flicked his eyes to me. "It's an eagle."

"Are you big on America, or something?" I smiled.

Nate rolled his eyes. "It means freedom."

I nodded, knowing well enough that he didn't need a response.

"You know what I like about you?" he asked.

"That I'm annoying?" I joked. He suddenly appeared on top of me, his arms taut on either side of my body. My breath hitched as he hung inches from my face. The moon shone brilliantly behind him.

"No." He smiled, his eyes flickering back and forth across my face. "You're beautiful."

"You don't think I'm smart or anything like that? We live in a progressive era, you know."

He chuckled. "That's what I noticed about you when we first met. How clever you are."

"Mace bottles have that sort of effect on people, I agree."

He laughed.

"You didn't—I don't know—think I was crazy?"

114

"Oh, never. Not you." Letting his sarcasm show, he closed the limited space between us and pressed his lips firmly to mine. All I tasted was chocolate.

Twenty - Two

Lavender stood up ahead, placing books into her locker. Her dark hair was swept into a clean, tight ponytail.

I skipped to her. "Lavender!"

She looked surprised, as she warily said, "Lindsey."

I smiled. "Doesn't the sun look particularly exquisite today?"

"Sure."

"Hmm." Life was good. Wasn't it good?

"Are you okay?" she asked, as she shut her locker and tightened her grip on her books.

"Better than okay."

She thought, then came to a certain realization. "Ohh. It's about Nathaniel, isn't it?"

"Maybe."

Her eyes shot to my neck, then widened. "Did he give that to you?" Lavender squealed, earning a disapproving look from a nearby teacher. I pulled my hair to my side, covering the mark.

She stuck out her lower lip. "That's so cute."

"Speaking of cute, how is Andre?" Andre was a boy that managed to catch Lavender's eye, and she had been crushing hard for a few weeks now. They'd been on a few dates, but that was it.

Lavender grinned. "Amazing. I'm seeing him tonight." She paused. "You should come over."

"Won't you be gone?" I asked.

"Exactly. Your boyfriend will be there."

"When did I say he was my boyfriend?" I linked my arm with hers.

"Oh please," She waved it off, "Nate and I have become sleepover buddies. I got a rundown of the whole night last night once he got back. Complete with details."

I laughed.

Later that day, I visited Lavender's apartment. I'd managed to get permission from Hellen. Lavender had texted me after school to tell me she had gone to meet Andre early and that I was welcome to come over.

Nathaniel suddenly opened the door, munching on a bag of Doritos. His face widened in a smile. "What are you doing here?"

I smiled, stepping inside. Nathaniel closed the door and I looked around. "I missed this."

I sat cross-legged on the couch, and watched Nathaniel put away his snack and wash his hands. He joined me on the couch, facing me. "You know Lavender is out, right?"

"I know." I didn't know why I felt so nervous.

"Well, I'm glad you came. I wanted to talk to you about something."

I nodded, waiting.

"My parents called the other day."

My lips parted. "What'd they say?" The apartment seemed quieter today. The hum of the fridge filled the silence.

"They wanted me to come over. 'Make amends.'" He rolled his eyes, making air quotes with his fingers.

"Well," I shifted on the couch, "are you going?"

"I don't know."

"You should go," I said firmly.

He sighed, shoulders deflating a bit until his eyes met mine. "Will you come with me?"

My eyes widened. Was he serious? Me, the broken foster-girl, meeting the classy and wealthy family from the other side of the city? "Nathaniel. No. No way."

"Why not?" he whined.

"Because there's about a million and one ways for things to go wrong if I did."

117

"What does that even mean?"

"Because," I searched for the right words, "because I'm not someone you bring home to your Connecticut parents." Nate had briefly mentioned where he was from before he moved out; I was sure he thought I had forgotten the tiny detail.

Something flashed in his eyes before I could even be sure I saw it. Was it deja-vu I caught a glimpse of? He puckered out his lower lip and blinked rapidly. Oh no, there it was. I was about to say yes. Because as I stared at the beautiful boy sitting in front of me, his green eyes a brilliant emerald paired with his perfect face, I surrendered, "Okay, fine."

He lunged forward and smothered my cheek with kisses. I laughed, gently pushing him off me. "Okay, okay, lover boy. Settle down." He sat back. I changed positions again and lay back so my head was then resting on his chest. It rose and fell steadily, his heart beating in my ears. The slow rhythm began to increase slightly. "Your heartbeat is fast," I murmured.

He chuckled, chest jumping. "You make me nervous."

I snorted, unconvinced. "No, I don't."

He was quiet. "You don't give yourself enough credit."

I ignored his comment. "I make you nervous?"

"Yes."

I shut my mouth, careful not to ruin the moment. I had a habit of doing so.

"Do you play the guitar?" Nathaniel randomly asked.

"No-" He got up and I leaned forward to let him. He was gone for a few moments, then came back holding a slick acoustic guitar.

"I found it in your closet—well, my closet now." He answered my unasked questions. He sat down on the ground. I joined him and wrapped my arms around my legs. I took it from his outstretched hand and stared blankly down at it.

"Why does Lavender have a guitar in the closet?" I asked.

It took him a little bit to respond, but when he did, said, "Maybe she has a secret talent."

I laughed. "I wouldn't be surprised. Can you play?"

He nodded, and I gracefully gave it back to him. "Where'd you learn?"

"My mom made me take lessons when I was little," Nathaniel answered, sounding deep in thought; he was staring intently at the strings. He pinched the pick in his hand and strummed a chord. "She was hoping for something more traditional, like piano." He paused, rolling his eyes slightly, "Just another reason to disappoint."

He started to sing, "Every time I see your face, it puts my heart in a race. It grows ten times larger, then I start to think you're a charmer. Your laugh lights up your face, it makes me believe I've picked an ace. Ever since I've met you, I've been put in a daze. I'll be drawn to you forever, even on Sundays."

Nathaniel strummed the last chord, and it was suddenly quiet. I ignored the cliché-ness of the moment, too distracted by the thought of him having just sung a song I'd never heard. Judging by the shy look on his face, I guessed it was specifically for me.

"I had some spare time..." He trailed off, looking nervous. I had never seen Nathaniel Sky nervous.

I grinned, watching him place the instrument gently on the floor. For a moment, we just stared intently at each other. He didn't smile, but his eyes shone with a certain type of charm I knew only Nathaniel possessed.

And quicker than that, we moved to each other in unison and our lips met.

~~~~~~~~~

"Lindsey? Can you come in here, please?" Hellen's voice called to me as soon as I walked through the door.

119

I shivered. "Yeah." Making my way into the kitchen, I found Hellen by the stove, stirring something in the frying pan. Judging by the smell, my best guess was tomato sauce.

"Where have you been?" she asked me, a tone in her voice I've never heard before.

I shrugged. "Out."

Hellen turned around, her eyebrow cocked. "Okay." She slowly started to walk towards me. "Where were you the other night?"

"Here," I lied.

She nodded, and sat down on the chair nearby. "Does, 'here,' mean hanging on a rope outside?"

I froze. "Wha-"

A small amused smile formed. "Did you forget that your window is right above the kitchen window?"

I swallowed. I'm such an idiot.

Hellen sighed. "You know the rules, Lindsey. No one leaves this house after ten. Whether you like it or not, you are my responsibility until you turn eighteen-"

I cut her off with laughter that lacked humor. "Responsibility? Is that what you call kicking me out of my house?"

Hellen looked guiltily down. "Walter-"

"Oh yeah, who could forget Walter?" I leaned against the counter, trying to appear more relaxed than I was. I could feel the anger burning in my throat. "The fact that you chose him over me felt like absolute betrayal." I seethed, tears prickling my eyes. For some unknown reason, I didn't wipe them away.

"I ended it, you know," she lamely retorted.

"And that helps?" I half-yelled and stormed out of the room, my hair flicking. On my way to the door, I spotted Mariella on the staircase. Her hands gripped the bars.

Even over Hellen's angry pleas to stay, I ripped open the door and ran into the cold night air.

120

"I don't even know what to do," I admitted once I settled in at Lavender's apartment. "I can't go back."

"Then stay here," Nathaniel said.

I eyed the couch. "I guess I'll stay on the couch." And I moved to the linen closet to pick out a pillow and sheets.

"Or," he interjected, "you could sleep with me."

My eyes widened, and I turned around. He had an amused smirk on his face, "I didn't mean..."

I held up a hand with a smile. "I know what you meant."

The door jiggled, and Lavender walked in. "Hey!" she called, then spotted me. "I thought you couldn't be out at this time."

"She got in a fight with her foster mom," Nathaniel explained.

"Ahh." Lavender set her purse on the counter. "So you're sleeping here?"

"If that's okay."

"Linds, you could sleep in my bed for all I care." She grinned, grabbing ice cream pints from the freezer. "Sleepover!"

It was my turn to grin. "Thanks." I watched her search for spoons. "How'd your date go?"

"Amazing."

"Tell me about it," I squealed, watching her eyes connect with Nate's over my head for just one moment before grinning at me.

"Okay, that's my cue," he said, standing and moving towards his room. "Have fun, girls." Our night of ice cream and boy talk was just what I needed and missed. After Lavender retreated to her room and I was left by myself, I felt the loneliness creep in. The city that never slept played in my ears. I slipped out from under the covers, silently creeping to his door. I opened it and heard his snoring almost right away.

I shut the door with a click and walked to his bed. "Nathaniel. Nathaniel!" I shook him.

121

He slowly resurfaced and mumbled. "Five more minutes."

"You're an idiot."

He grunted, "I knew you'd come," and pulled me into his arms quickly, not saying anything else, and resting his chin in the nape of my neck. I turned, resting my head on his chest and tucking my head under his chin. He kissed my head and we fell asleep.

Twenty - Three

"It's like, one of my talents," I said, a grin forming.

Nathaniel shook his head. "No way. I once won an award."

I made a face. "For cherry knotting?"

He let go of a deep laugh. "You are literally the most gullible person I know."

I smacked his arm. "I am good at it, though."

"Oh, yeah?" he challenged, running a hand through his freshly cut hair that now stood only inches from his head.

I nodded and plucked a cherry from the bowl sitting between us.

He shrugged and followed my action. "I'll guess we find out, then."

I nodded, going to place it in my mouth, when I yelled, "Wait!"

He jumped, the cherry falling from his fingertips. Nathaniel's eyes were wide. "What?"

I giggled. "We need to make a bet."

He sighed, picking up the fallen cherry. "Fine. Loser goes streaking in Central Park. At night." Nathaniel finished, a smirk playing on his gorgeous face.

"I'm pretty sure that's a felony."

"Fine. Loser..." He seemed to be lost in thought.

"Kisses someone else?" I asked.

Nathaniel's eyes widened. "No way. Loser has to. . . steal something."

I frowned. "How about this? We both have different things."

"Fine, you steal something. I kiss someone." He shrugged.

"Well, why can't I kiss someone?" I asked.

"Because, you're my girl. And I don't want to see another guy touch you." He finished his statement with a whisper.

I smiled, thinking I could actually have a bit of fun with this one. "Then I get to pick the girl."

"Then I get to pick the place." He said in the same tone.

I nodded and shook his hand. "Deal."

And with that, we both plop our cherries into our mouths. I bite down on the pit-less cherry, and sour flavor bursts onto my tongue. I chew quickly, swallowing the cherry and getting to work on the stem. At first, I chew on it, trying to make it softer. When I thought it was soft enough, I used my tongue to cross the stem then loop it under. I sneaked a glance at Nathaniel, and his face was pulled into concentration, staring at the floor as he worked on his stem. As soon as it was looped loosely in my mouth, I stuck one end between my clenched teeth, and pulled the other end through with my jaw and tongue.

I grinned, a competitive spirit kicking through. The knotting scene was played within seconds, and I placed my fingertips to my mouth to pull it out. In unison, Nathaniel did the same. He grinned. "I won."

I gasped. "No way! We did it at the same time."

"Does that mean we have equal kissing abilities [activities]?" He smirked.

My face burned.

"I mean, I guess that makes sense," he said, grabbing another cherry and popping it into his mouth. He chewed. "Considering I taught you how to kiss."

My mouth parted a bit. "You're wrong."

"Wasn't I your first kiss?" he asked.

I raised an eyebrow. I loved teasing him. "I don't know, were you?"

He held my gaze, clearly unsure. "Alright, alright. I understand if you don't want to admit you lost to me..." He trailed off, and I hit him again. Nathaniel laughed. "I guess we'll both do the dares."

124

I nodded. That seemed fair enough. "Okay."

~~~~~~~~~

I tapped my chin, my eyes scanning the crowd of girls in Central Park.

Nathaniel didn't seem nervous. He'd probably kissed hundreds of girls, right? I spotted a girl around thirteen, and pointed, "Her."

He reared toward me. "Do you want me to be arrested?"

I chuckled. "I'm joking." And I looked around.

Nathaniel was grinning at a girl running nearby, her breasts bouncing as she took each stride. Her blond hair swayed back and forth. To be honest, she was hot. "Her." I shook my head quickly, an unfamiliar feeling of jealousy ebbing its way through my chest. "No way. I get to choose."

He seemed to pout, but then I spotted a girl around our age sitting alone at a park bench. She was reading a large book, stylish nerd-glasses perched on her nose. She had a mole on her left cheek, and she picked her nose, examined it, then placed her finger in her mouth.

"Her. Go." I pointed, and Nathaniel followed my finger.

He groaned. "The girl on the bench?"

I nodded with a sneaky smile on my face. "Go on."

He bit his lip. "Lindsey-"

"Go. Oh, and it has to be four seconds long," I added.

"When was that a rule?"

I grinned. "Just now." His shoulders deflated as he grudgingly took bounding steps toward the bench. I watched Nathaniel walk toward her and stop directly in front. The girl looked up, looking startled. She stood and pushed her glasses further up her nose. Nathaniel's body language was taut, making it look like his next move may ruin his life. But sooner than I expected, the romantic, smooth Nathaniel looped his arm around the girl's waist and pressed

125

his lips to hers. She jumped back slightly, then seemed to lean in to his kiss. But after all, it looked awkward. His body was so rigid, and anyone could've seen that he was not interested. I counted four seconds in my head, and he pulled away as soon as I hit four. His face was pulled into a cringe, but it disappeared as soon as the girl's eyes fluttered open.

I laughed. Nathaniel removed his arms and stepped back, when the girl lunged forward, throwing her arms around his neck and kissing him passionately. His shoulders were hitched up high, with his tense arms and hands held at his sides like he was unsure of what to do with them. I doubled over while my entire body shook with laughter.

~~~~~~~~

"That was the worst experience I have ever had." Nathaniel spit into the water we were passing and plopped a piece of neon-yellow gum into his mouth. He offered me a piece, and I did the same.

I laughed. "It wasn't that bad."

He cringed, the previous moment literally playing before his eyes. "She tasted like asparagus." I had no words. Minutes later, Nathaniel had taken me to the local pet store.

I turned toward him. "A pet store?"

"Yep. It's your turn."

I felt nervous, "What do I have to steal?"

Nathaniel continued to grin mischievously. "A rabbit."

My eyes widened as he grabbed my hand to pull me inside. The pet store manager looked at us, and said in a monotone, "Welcome to Pet Galaxy, where all your wishes come true."

I frowned as Nathaniel whispered in my ear. "The rabbits are in the back. I like white ones."

I chuckled and eyed the cashier. "Watch him."

He tipped his head. "Will do."

I sharply turned the corner to the back, where Nathaniel had instructed. Lining the walls, cages of a mixture of spotted, white, brown, and black rabbits sat. The colors swirled together. I unzipped my coat, preparing to take a rabbit. Nerves pulsed through me. What if I got caught? Could I get arrested for stealing a rabbit? I'd never heard of anyone getting arrested for stealing a rabbit. But quickly, I reminded myself that I had to do this fast. As per Nate's request, I spotted a black and white rabbit with ears that drooped down the sides of his face. Crouching down, I carefully opened the top of the cage to pick up the rabbit. Looking to both sides of the deserted aisle, I shoved him inside my coat, zipping it up. I quickly walked to the front of the store, and stopped beside Nathaniel, who was in a deep discussion with the cashier. The bunny moved inside my coat, and I tried to somehow cover it up by coughing.

The cashier looked at me. "Find everything you need?"

Shoot. I needed to get out of there. I tightly smiled. "Yes, thank you."

I turned to leave, but he asked, "Would you like me to check you out?"

I grumbled silently, and Nathaniel raised an eyebrow in my direction. At that moment, the rabbit decided to move as it crawled toward my neck. I frantically bounced, (the guy staring strangely at me), and I felt the rabbit inching downwards again.

"No, no. I was just looking," I assured him.

He nodded, seeming slightly suspicious. Was I just being paranoid? He returned to his comic book. I rushed out the door, Nathaniel laughing behind me.

"Did you get it?"

I glared at him but didn't respond. Moments later, once we were safely far from the pet store, I stopped and unzipped my jacket.

Nathaniel laughed even harder as I carefully pulled the frightened bunny out of the dark area.

His eyes bulged, and I tried to hold him in a comforting way.

~~~~~~~~

"I'm home!" Lavender called from the door.

I ran to her, grinning. "Hey, Lavii. How was your day?"

"Fine," she said slowly. "What's up?"

I shrugged. "Nothing much. Nathaniel and I cleaned and vacuumed."

"What do you want?" she asked, suspicious.

I sighed and grabbed her hand. Pulling her into the living room, Nathaniel stood among us. Her eye caught something, and she opened her mouth. The rabbit lay comfortably in the cardboard box Nathaniel had supplied, the bottom covered with newspaper.

She shook her head. "No way. Nu uh." Lavender turned around, throwing up her arms.

I pouted. "Aw, come on, Lavender! Please? He has nowhere to go!"

She sighed. "Where'd you even get it?"

"Him," I corrected.

Lavender rolled her eyes. "Him."

"We found him," I lied, glancing at Nathaniel.

She stared at me. "You mean to tell me that you found a pet rabbit in the streets of New York?"

It did sound crazy. Nathaniel laughed behind me, and I whipped around. "You don't help in these situations."

He shook his head, continuing to laugh. "She stole him."

My eyes widened, and I hit him. "Nate!"

"Ow! Would you stop hitting me?" he whined.

"Both of you, shut up." Lavender shouted. We stopped, looking at her.

128

She dropped her bag and crossed her arms. "I don't really want to know why you stole a rabbit. Yes, fine. He can stay, but if he goes anywhere near my room—I swear, Lindsey, I'll hurt you."

I grinned. Lavender disappeared, and Nathaniel bent down to the box. He stroked the rabbit's head, and he seemed to lower himself so he was flat against the bottom. "We need to give him a name."

I snorted. "How 'bout Nathaniel?"

"Is there a reason why you're so mean?"

I bent down as well, stroking his soft fur. "I'm mean only to people I like."

A small smile tugged at his lips. "I have a name."

"And that is?"

He turned his head, looking at me. "Nindsey."

I laughed. "Did you hear Lavender and I that night?" Lavender and I were laughing over celebrity ship names, where she decided to give Nathaniel and I one.

He shrugged. "Girls are loud."

I kissed his cheek and glanced down at the rabbit. "Nindsey it is."

Twenty - Four

I squinted my eyes, scribbling down my best guess for problem 29.

"Can you come down here please, Lindsey?" Hellen yelled from the kitchen.

I sighed, putting down my mechanical pencil and climbing out of bed. Making my way downstairs, I stopped at the kitchen doorway. "Yes?"

Hellen seemed to struggle with a plastic shopping bag as she hoisted it onto the counter. "Where have you been lately?"

"Out," I said, knowing I did not want to get into details. Stealing rabbits did not seem like something that Hellen would be very happy about.

She nodded, turning toward me. "Well, I just wanted to remind you of the annual Adoption Day coming up this weekend." Adoption Day was pretty self-explanatory. Every three months there would be an allotted day where possible adoptive parents come to the foster house to "pick" out their adorable child. I had missed the last one, because I wasn't exactly living at the house. Now, hence my age, Hellen found it sufficient that I just help set up and direct happy adults to the designated room.

"That's this weekend?" I asked, bewildered.

Hellen looked at me. "Yes, and you promised you'd be there."

I sighed. There was no getting out of this one, but a brilliant plan distracted me.

~~~~~~~

"No!" Nathaniel yelled, adding extra emphasis with his hands. "No, no and no. A thousand times no."

130

I stuck out my lower lip and followed him into Lavender's living room. "Please? Hellen won't really let me be eligible for adopting-"

He wheeled around, a frown on his face. "What are you talking about?"

I parted my lips. Wasn't it obvious? "I'm seventeen. A lot of parents don't want a seventeen-year-old-"

"That's ridiculous," Nathaniel spit out, stepping closer to me. "You are going to be eligible to be adopted tomorrow."

I frowned. "Yeah, but I just lead the parents into the room and introduce them."

He waved a finger, dropping his bag of Doritos with more force than intended. "Oh yeah? Well, I'm gonna be there."

I grinned. "Really?"

He softly smiled. "If it means that you get the opportunity to become adopted, then of course."

~~~~~~~~~

I adjusted my conservative white dress and breathed in the small mirror. Running a hand through my hair, I half-smiled.

Low knocking sounded against my door, and I looked up. "Lindsey, it's time. Parents are arriving."

Hellen.

I swallowed and shook my hair out once more. "Okay, I'm ready." My stomach swirled as I stepped out into the hallway. I hadn't done it for two years.

Hellen smiled at my complexion. "Wow. You look very pretty. The parents will love the enthusiasm from you when you introduce them to the kids."

I looked at her, expressionless. "I'm not introducing them."

She shot me a confused look.

"I'm going to be in that room where I can be adopted."

She simply blinked and I stepped down the stairs.

131

Once I had reached the end, Mariella tugged at my dress. She smiled up at me and motioned for me to pick her up. She was wearing a pink tutu. I did and when she was sitting comfortably on my hip, she leaned into my ear and whispered, "Am I gonna get adopted today?"

I looked at her, "Of course, you will," but frowned, suddenly realizing she had dressed herself. I eyed her messy hair. Hellen must've forgotten about the usual touch up.

I put her down and held out a hand. "Come here."

She grabbed my hand, and I led her to the bathroom in the hallway. "I'll be right back. Stay here."

She nodded, and I ran upstairs. Kneeling down under my bed, I grabbed a box. I quickly darted back down stairs and met her exactly where I had left her. I guided her inside and shut the door behind us. Grabbing a stool in the corner, I motioned for her to step on it. She did and I opened the box with trembling fingers. Inside lay a mixture of bows, clips, and ribbons.

Mariella's eyes couldn't have been bigger, and I chuckled to myself. "Pick out a bow. Your favorite color." She smiled widely and reached into the box, grabbing a soft pink one. She handed it to me, and I also picked out a comb. I brushed her hair and after I was done, the once knotty hair was clean-swept, knot-free, and shiny. I took the bow from her and clipped it in. Grabbing a piece of her hair from the front, I moved it back and made a slight bump. I then clipped in the bow. She looked adorable.

Mariella giggled at her reflection in the mirror. "Thank you!"

I hugged her. "You're welcome, sweetie."

She hopped down from the stool and ran out into the hallway. I picked up the box, and placed it under the sink. Noise was escalating in the house, and I smoothed out my dress.

I walked out of the bathroom and into the crowded room. Parents laughed all around, smiling and playing with a child.

132

Where was Nathaniel? I glanced to the door. He had promised me.

"Lindsey? Can you please get the cookies in the kitchen?" Hellen rushed past me and gave me a hopeful look. I half-nodded, and made my way into the kitchen, the noise level quieting a bit. I found the plate of cookies and reached for them. Arms suddenly wrapped around my waist, and I jumped slightly.

Nathaniel placed his head into the crook of my neck and mumbled, "Sorry I'm late. I couldn't find Nindsey."

I laughed and spun around, planting a quick kiss on his lips. "It's fine."

He stepped back, but his arms remained in the same position. "Shouldn't you be in there...?" He trailed off. "I mean, I'm not an expert. But seeing that everyone is in the living room, you should be to."

"Hellen asked me to get these." I explained.

He rolled his eyes. "I'll get 'em. Just go."

I nodded and started toward the living room.

"You look amazing, by the way," he added.

~~~~~~~~~

I'm starting to realize why I had stopped those things. There I was, sitting by myself. No one had talked to me the whole time, and it was starting to get embarrassing. Especially in front of Nathaniel.

"Hello." A pretty woman stood in front of me.

I looked up, startled, and wondering if I'd thought too soon. "Hi."

She smiled. "Do you live here too?"

I nodded. "I've been here since I was five."

She nodded, her mouth set in a straight line. "I understand. I was in a foster home myself." The woman sat down, and I couldn't have become more excited that she still remained. "It's hard."

I nodded.

133

"And I don't understand why a pretty, young lady like yourself is still here," she added.

I smiled. "Thank you."

"Polite too." She laughed. "What's your name?"

"Lindsey Garland-"

"Oh, Lindsey. There you are." Hellen suddenly came over. She looked at the nameless woman. "Excuse me."

The woman nodded.

Hellen looked at her again, as if remembering something. "Mariella is almost ready to go." So, Mariella was finally getting adopted! I couldn't have been more excited for her. She deserved a home. As if on cue, Mariella bounded down the steps with a suitcase in tow. Many adults cooed at her as she passed them, but she didn't seem to notice.

She reached the woman, and shyly smiled. "I'm ready."

The woman grinned widely, revealing white teeth. "Alright, honey."

Mariella saw me, and ran to my side. She cupped her hands and leaned into my ear. "Thanks for everything. You're my most favorite person in the world."

I grinned, thinking that that day had been worth something. I hugged her, a tear stinging my eye. I was going to miss her.

The woman looked at me and apologetically smiled. "It was nice meeting you, Lindsey."

I grimly nodded back. "You too," and I glanced at Mariella's gleeful face, "she's a great kid."

~~~~~~~~~~

The adoption day was over, and I was mad. I stomped over to Hellen, "Why would you do that?"

She looked startled. "Sorry, honey?"

I glared. "Why would you interrupt our conversation? It was going great, and she could've adopted me!"

Hellen parted her lips. "I'm sorry. Really, I am." Yeah, looked like it.

I scoffed as she left me alone in the room. Someone touched my shoulder, and I turned around to find him.

"Are you okay?" Nathaniel asked, his eyes searching my face.

I plopped down on the couch and covered my face in my hands. "No."

He rubbed my back, as I felt him sit down. "It's going to be fine, Linds. You will be adopted."

I didn't know what I was thinking. Who would want me? I removed my hands and whispered, "You can't promise that."

He seemed to understand my reply. "I know. But I am anyway."

I nodded as Nathaniel placed his index finger and thumb over my chin, gently moving it towards him. He leaned in and placed a kiss on my lips. Giggling came from the corner, and I pulled back. Many of the foster kids stood behind the door, their heads poking out. I couldn't help but smile.

Twenty - Five

"I'm kinda freaking out," I admitted, biting my nails.

Lavender gestured. "Don't worry about it. I thought his parents were excited to meet you!"

I shrugged, repositioning myself on Lavender's bed. "Yeah, but still. I know he'd feel so much more comfortable with me, but I'm nervous. What if they don't like me?"

Something flashed in her eyes before she rolled them. "Everyone likes you. And Nathaniel will take care of you."

I smiled at the mention of his name. "You're right."

~~~~~~~~~~

I shut the door to the house and started up the stairs. Half of the kids were playing in the living room, and their screams filed the space inside the walls. Hellen bustled down as well, then jumped when she saw me.

She placed a hand to her heart. "You nearly gave me a heart attack."

I didn't say anything. I was still angry with her for ruining my conversation.

"Where have you been lately? Remember our deal..." She cocked her head, moving the basket of laundry to her right hip.

I rolled my eyes. "I've been with Nathaniel, and Lavender. And yes, I won't forget the police hauling me out of Lavender's apartment. I'm home every night before twelve."

Hellen nodded. "So, is Nathaniel your boyfriend?"

"Yep."

She smiled. "That's good. He seems like a nice boy. I'd love to meet him officially one day."

136

I half-nodded and started up the steps again. "Oh wait, I forgot." I turned around. And faced her. "I have this dinner thing tonight, so I won't be here for dinner."

"Who is this with?"

I silently sighed. "Nathaniel. With his family."

Hellen nodded. "Okay. Just be careful, okay?" She spun around and disappeared behind the wall. Be careful? I rolled my eyes and turned to jog up the stairs and into my room. Closing the door behind me, I leaned against it and shut my eyes. This was going to be one interesting night.

My phone buzzed and my eyes fluttered open. Grabbing it out of my pocket, I read an incoming text from Nathaniel. Don't worry about tonight. I'll pick you up at six :)

I sighed, shutting my eyes once more. I was mentally envisioning an outfit perfect for the chilly weather of November. Knocking sounded against my door. I groaned, expecting it to be Hellen as I swung around to grab the handle. It was the new girl, Tanya. Because Mariella had been adopted, we had unoccupied space. I hadn't exactly talked thoroughly to Tanya. We only exchanged hellos and welcomes. As I looked closer, I realized she was actually really pretty. Her dark skin let off a glow, and her long eyelashes curled ever-so slightly. Tanya was chewing vigorously on neon green gum.

I smiled, recomposing myself. "Oh, hey Tanya. What's up?"

"Just wanted to ask if I could borrow your toothbrush."

I couldn't help but make a face. "Excuse me?" That was unsanitary on so many levels.

She laughed, instant dimples appearing. I liked her laugh. It was full of life. "I'm just kidding, girl." And she laughed again. "I just wanted to talk. You know, you're the only one that's close to my age in this place so..." She trailed off.

"Come on in."

She nodded, slowly following me back inside my room. I shut the door and made my way to the bed. Leaning against the wall, I was somewhat comfortable. I watched Tanya instantly take my desk chair as her seat.

It was silent for the first few moments until I had to break the ice. "How old are you, again?"

"Sixteen."

I brightened. "Wow. I've never had anyone close to my age before." I thought, then held up a finger. "Wait, that's a lie. There was this boy once, and I had a crush on him. Little did I know, it couldn't go any farther than that."

"How old were you?"

"Six," I answered curtly, but completely honestly.

She laughed. "I get that. A lot, actually."

"Really?"

Tanya nodded, then stared at the ground. "That's actually how I got kicked out of my previous foster home." I made an 'o' with my mouth.

She sighed and finally met my eyes. "Wanna know what happened?"

"Only if you want to tell me." I didn't want to barge into her personal life.

Tanya shrugged. "Nah, it's fine." She repositioned herself. "My foster parents were really good ones. And they were one step away from adopting me."

My eyes widened, but she held up a hand. "Yep. Anyway," she paused, "Their foster kid and I liked each other. And this went on for about a year or two. It was just a stupid crush, nothing more. So, I didn't think anything of it, ya know? But one day, he thought his foster parents were out. He kissed me, and they saw." I couldn't hide my shock.

"And, as you know, it's against all rules to have any relationship with a foster brother or sister. His parents were worried their son would get in trouble, so they stopped my adoption and sent me off."

It was quiet, signaling she was done. "That's ridiculous."

She shrugged. "I don't know. It doesn't matter. I'll be eighteen soon and out of the system."

I half-smiled. I had thought that one sentence at least one hundred times.

"So? Have any cool stories for me?" She mused, her eyes lighting up in amusement.

I shook my head. "You have no idea." So, I told her. How Hellen kicked me out, to having to stay at Lavender's, about Walter, meeting Nathaniel of course, our trips, the kidnapping, and my escapes with Nathaniel. And by the end, we were laughing like best friends.

"That's crazy!" she squealed, and rolled over to high-five me. "So much better than my story." I crossed the room to my closet, beginning to choose an outfit for that night.

"Wait, wait. So you stole a rabbit?"

I whipped around with a grin. "That's what you wonder about that whole story?"

She shrugged.

I sighed, thinking of the rabbit. "Nindsey, that's his name, and he's at Lavender's house. I'll bring him by to meet you one day."

"Deal." She grinned. "You're seeing him tonight?"

My stomach churned at the mention of my plans. "I'm meeting his parents."

"Oo. Harsh."

I nodded. "I know. I'm freaking out."

"What time is he picking you up?"

"Six."

Tanya checked her phone, then gasped. "Um, hello? That's in an hour."

139

I jumped up. "We sat here for two hours?"

"I guess so," she said. "Do you want some help?"

I crossed the room and checked a drawer. "Do you have any makeup?" I was a lost cause.

"I should. I want to go to cosmetology school."

I spun around. "So you'll do my makeup?"

"I'd be offended if you didn't ask." She rolled her eyes. "Get dressed, then meet me in my room. Oh, and bring a sweatshirt. I don't want to get makeup on your outfit."

I nodded and watched her leave my room when I suddenly shouted, "Tanya?"

"Yeah?" She shouted back.

"Hair?" I laughed.

"Obviously."

~~~~~~~~

"Sit still!" she ordered, and I giggled.

"Sorry, sorry! I've never had anyone do my-" and I broke down giggling again. The brush she was using against my eyelids was ticklish.

"And.." She paused, and the brush continued to wisp away, "done!"

My eyelids opened, and I gasped at my reflection. My eyes, with a subtle smokiness, seemed wider than usual. She hadn't used much, and it was just enough to make it look natural.

"You're amazing."

Tanya beamed. "Thanks." She placed a brush in a bag nearby and picked up the heating curling iron. "Hair."

I sat back and let Tanya get to work. She made random curls in my hair and finally after about ten minutes, set down the iron. Tanya returned to my head, and started to separate the curls. The once-before tight ringlets fell around the frame of my face, now soft waves.

She grabbed a comb and ran it through my scalp lining, separating it and making a parting.

"Done." She sighed. "Pretty, yet simple. You're not going over the top, but you still look like you care."

I hugged her, surprising myself but ignoring it. Since when did I give hugs to people I barely knew? "Thank you. Really, I owe you."

The doorbell rang, and I heard the kids yelling to Hellen. I stood up, and looked at Tanya. "I look okay?"

She surveyed my outfit. "You might even look better than me."

I laughed, lightly shoving her. I had paired black skinny jeans with an oversized crème sweater. Tanya had also let me borrow some ringlet bracelets and a few rings.

"Gotta go. Thanks again." I waved, and disappeared from her room and into the hallway.

I jogged down the steps, and my eyes met Nathaniel. He was in deep conversation with Hellen, who laughed every so often. Most of the kids stood around, peering curiously at the cute boy in the foyer. He was wearing jeans and a long sleeve colored shirt.

His eyes suddenly shifted to mine, and he broke into a smile. "Lindsey."

I had never loved my name more than I did at that moment, but I teasingly responded with, "Nathaniel."

He shook his head with a small smile. "Ready?"

I nodded, hearing footsteps behind. "Whoa." Tanya's voice muttered in close to my ear. I carefully elbowed her behind me. She snorted, leaning against the railing. I walked down the remaining steps and grabbed his outstretched hand.

~~~~~~~~

I placed my palm on the cold window and watched my handprint disappear as I removed it.

141

"Having fun?" Nathaniel teased. I looked over and found him smirking at me. I had to distract myself in some way.

"Ha. Ha."

He laughed.

"Where are we going?" I asked, staring out the dark windows.

"Ridgefield. It's about an hour or so away."

I nodded. "Will we get back in time?"

"Oh yeah."

I nodded again and stared out the window.

A few moments passed, then my peripheral vision revealed Nathaniel's head turning toward me. "What's on your mind?"

I frowned, peeking at him. "Nothing."

He smirked. "Lindsey, come on. If I know one thing about you, is that you never shut up." I hit his arm.

"Ouch, please don't assault the driver."

"You deserve it."

"No but really, are you okay?"

I sighed. "I'm just nervous about meeting your parents."

He was quiet. "It's going to be fine." I couldn't tell if he was trying to convince me or himself.

~~~~~~~~~

"I might throw up." I gripped my door handle, my gaze fixated on the mansion in front of me. A mansion, I kid you not.

Nathaniel chuckled, his arms crossed as he stared in amusement. "This reminds me of when I took you to get your wisdom teeth extracted."

"I had a good reason for that." I looked into his eyes and might've even detected fear. Of course. I almost slapped myself. Here I was, acting like a selfish brat, when he was probably more freaked out than me. I composed myself, pulling myself together.

He held out his hand. "Please?"

142

I took it immediately, reminding myself of how he must've been feeling, and stepped out of the car into the homey neighborhood. He shut my door and looped his arm around my back. We walked up the stone steps and walkway, past the night lights that shone over the perfectly trimmed grass. We were soon at the door. The large house was made completely of gray stone, with white double doors adorned with gold handles. It had a looped driveway, leading into two white garage doors that guarded the sides.

We stopped, and I glanced at Nathaniel. "Are we planning on standing here the whole night, or...?" I teased. It was my attempt to make him feel better.

He took a shaky breath, a small smile stretching his gorgeous face. "I'm nervous too."

I reached up, and squeezed his forearm. "It's gonna be fine. I'll be with you the whole time."

He looked at me. "Thank you for coming. You look beautiful, by the way." My stomach fluttered, and I smiled at the ground. His outstretched arm pressed the doorbell. Barking sounded immediately and pounding claws against the door.

I looked at Nathaniel in question, and he was grinning. "The only thing I missed."

I've always wanted a dog when I was a kid and asked for a puppy every Christmas. Hellen insisted we weren't allowed, so I eventually gave up. I think she had lied about not being allowed; I was more than certain other foster houses had animals.

Amongst the dogs, the door clicked and swung open to reveal a very attractive brunett, with a fragile frame for a body. Her smile was evident as she stared at Nathaniel. Her emerald green eyes shown, complimenting her sophisticated black dress and heels. Then, she looked at me. Her smile faltered for just a moment before she regained her previous state. "Hello, dear." The woman, whom I

143

assumed was Nathaniel's mother, reached forward and grabbed her son into a delicate hug. Nathaniel hugged back.

She reached back and motioned. "Come in, come in."

Nathaniel held out a hand, signaling for me to proceed first. I obeyed and soon found myself in a large foyer. The walls, a crisp white, accented a beautiful chandelier that cascaded from the high ceiling. A large German shepherd suddenly ran into the room, jumping onto two hind legs to embrace Nathaniel. His tongue flopped effortlessly as he licked him. I grinned when the dog jumped down then jumped on me. Nathaniel sprung forward, laughing slightly as he grabbed the dog's collar and pulled him off. I didn't mind, but I still admired the way he was so protective.

"This is Snoopy," he answered a dawning question that I was soon to ask.

I laughed at the irony in that, looking at the daunting figure of the black and tan dog.

"He seems big and ferocious, but really he's the biggest baby," he informed me, scratching behind Snoopy's ear. The dog's back leg began to pound against the ground in enjoyment.

I turned toward Nathaniel's mother and held out a hand. "It's so nice to meet you."

She grimly smiled, as she shook my hand. I watched her eyes, as they quickly scanned my body. "You too, um..." She trailed off as if searching for my name.

"Lindsey." I filled in the awkward silence. That was strange.

"Lindsey. I'm Laura, Nathaniel's mother of course." She stepped backwards. "Why won't you kids come on into the living room? Dinner is almost ready and Nathaniel," I glanced at him, who was currently rubbing circles into Snoopy's tummy, who was rolled over, "you might want to wash your hands."

Nathaniel looked up and swallowed. "Sure, Mom." He got up from his kneeling position and placed his hand on my lower back.

Laura eyed this, but turned before I could catch her eye. Laura led us into another room that was quite similar to the last. Here, four long, leather couches sat in a cube-like space. A big, flat screen TV perched above a stone fireplace. I sat down and Nathaniel sat next to me.

Laura seated herself in front of us and blinked, a silence falling over the three of us. Maybe I had made a mistake by coming. "How have you been, Nathaniel?"

"Fine."

I definitely made a mistake by coming.

"How old are you, Lindsey?" Laura asked.

I swallowed. Shouldn't Nathaniel have told her? "Seventeen."

"Nathaniel turns nineteen tomorrow," she quickly retorted.

My head swiveled toward Nathaniel. "You didn't tell me that." As soon as it left my mouth, I bit my tongue and willed myself to stop sabotaging myself. How bad must it have looked to Laura that I didn't know her son's birthday?

He looked guiltily at me. "I didn't think it was a big deal."

I bumped him playfully with my shoulder. "Of course, it is."

"I assume you're still in school?" she asked, still looking at me but obviously throwing it in Nathaniel's face.

I nodded, a smile still on my face.

"Do you plan to go to college?"

"I'd like to. I just hope the foster care won't hold me back-"

"Foster care?" she interrupted, concern lacing through her voice. I looked at Nathaniel again, growing irritated. My age was one thing, but the foster system? Had he told her nothing about me? "Yes. I've been in foster care since I was five."

Nathaniel had his head bowed, staring at the ground.

"I'm sorry, dear." Her voice softened. "That must be tough." The door slammed shut in the foyer, making me jump slightly. A tall,

145

attractive man waltzed into the room, a large grin plastered on his face. He was almost identical to Nate.

"Nathaniel." He held out his arms for an embrace. Nathaniel awkwardly patted him.

The man looked at me. "Hello." His voice was tentative, unsure of what I was doing sitting on his couch.

I smiled, standing up to shake his hand. "I'm Lindsey. I'm sure you've heard much about me." The last sentence I meant to throw in Nathaniel's face.

He shook his head, his eyebrows drawn together as his gaze darted to his son. "I'm afraid we haven't." His father seemed nicer than Laura.

I nodded, trying to hide my hurt.

He grinned wider, trying to make up for the latest depressing sentence. "Come on into the kitchen! Dinner is almost ready. I'm Scott, by the way." We all stood, Nathaniel's hand finding my lower back. I avoided it, stepping around the table and trying to pretend I hadn't noticed his affection.

"Lindsey, do you like salmon?" his father asked, looking back at me as he guided us all through to another room.

"I've never had it."

His eyes widened in a surprised way. "Your parents have never made salmon for you?" I blinked, swallowing hard. I became angrier with Nathaniel every passing second. "I'm in the foster care system. I don't know my parents."

He looked shocked. "Oh, wow. I'm sorry." Like I hadn't gotten that one before. I half-smiled.

Scott looked at his son, his gaze hardened just a tad. "Show Lindsey to the dining room. Dinner is ready." Nathaniel nodded and guided me into yet another room. It was in the shape of a rectangle, with a long dining table. Places for three were set out, and I frowned knowingly. Nate shifted beside me, clearly uncomfortable. He

146

looked down, as his mother scurried by with a placemat, plate, and silverware in her hands. She smiled at me as she left, and I stared at Nathaniel.

"Did you not tell your parents I was coming?" I asked in a low tone.

Nathaniel shamelessly looked at me. "I'm sorry."

"Why didn't you tell them?" I hissed.

He sighed and finally met my eyes. "I didn't get around to it."

"That's the most ridiculous thing I've ever heard-"

"Here we are!" Laura came in, holding a tray of filleted pink fish. Her voice was more enthusiastic, and I felt uneasy with the fact that she had to fill the awkwardness. Scott came in behind, holding a few other trays, placing them down and taking the seat at the head. I sat and Nathaniel sat next to me. Laura left the room again and came back in holding trays of delicious smelling food.

"It looks amazing," I said, staring hungrily at the plates in front of me. Nathaniel grabbed the large spoon and served various foods onto my plate. I didn't thank him. After everyone was served, I grabbed my fork and placed it in my left hand. My knife, on my right, dug into the soft fish.

I took a bite and swallowed. It was amazing, and Scott chuckled at the look on my face. "Good, huh?"

"Really good!" I exclaimed, and took another bite.

"It's Nathaniel's favorite," Laura smiled, "but I'm sure you know that." I nodded tightly, a weird feeling developing in my tummy. The passing seconds in this house made me feel like I hardly knew my boyfriend.

"So, Nathaniel," his dad cleared his throat, "where have you been living?"

Nathaniel stared at his plate, moving a lonesome potato back and forth. "Can we discuss this later?"

147

Scott looked confused. "Sure." He looked at me. "Where is your foster home?"

I took a sip of water and placed it down. "Downtown Manhattan."

Laura and her husband nodded. "Well, I wish all the luck to you."

"Thank you, sir," I replied, and stabbed a potato. Stabbed. After dinner was finished, Laura disappeared into the kitchen with our dishes. I stood as well, excusing myself.

"Laura?" I asked as I stepped into the big kitchen.

She swiveled around and smiled. "Hi, honey. Everything okay?"

"Yes. I was just wondering if you needed any help?"

She shook her head. "You're our guest, no need."

"No worries, really," I insisted. I had wanted to give Nathaniel time to talk to his father.

"My husband doesn't understand why I like to wash the crystal myself." She offered without any questioning on my behalf.

I eyed the dishwasher layered with the dirty china dishes. I was curious. "Why do you?"

She shrugged. "I've always liked washing the dishes since I was a little girl," she paused her washing of a glass and threw me a smile, "There's also something satisfying about cleaning a crystal glass."

I nodded, stepping up the sink and peering into the soapy bubbles. "Do you mind if I help?"

Laura passed me a glass without another world. She was smiling to herself, her long, dark eyelashes pointed toward her soapy hands. I submerged it into the water, the comfort of warm water tickling my skin. We washed in silence; the sound of sloshing water and foamy soap filled the beautiful space around us. I gently scrubbed the glass, dunking it into the water and back out. The motion threw me into my thoughts; Why was Nathaniel being so

148

secretive and strange? Was he not telling me something, or was I imagining it?

"Mrs. Sky," I started, "I hope you don't mind me asking, but, why did Nathaniel leave a couple months ago?"

She looked at me. "He didn't tell you?" I shook my head.

"It's a big story, but," she paused, looking confused, "did he tell you he left a couple months ago?"

I nodded.

Laura shook her head. "Nathaniel left three years ago. When he turned sixteen."

~~~~~~~~

"It was nice meeting you, Lindsey." Laura hugged me and I stepped up to Scott.

He smiled. "I enjoyed meeting you too, Lindsey. Come by any time! You're always welcome." Scott half-hugged me, planting a kiss on my cheek. I let Nathaniel say his goodbyes, and together, we walked out into the cold. It was silent as we walked to the car, my shoes making the only sound. I was confused and angry as hell. What hadn't he told me? Nathaniel crossed over to my side and opened my door. I got in without a thank you, and I'm pretty sure he noticed. He shut the door and crossed to the driver's side. When he got in, his breath was visible in the cold temperature. Nathaniel started the ignition and clicked on the heat.

"I'm sorry I didn't tell them you were coming," he finally said.

I shrugged, turning toward the window. It was almost silent the whole way back to New York until he rolled to a stop in front of my foster house. I checked my phone, and it read 10:50. Just in time. I unstrapped my seatbelt, letting it fly back and barely looking at Nathaniel.

"Thanks, it was nice meeting your parents." I went to grab the door, when he softly grabbed my elbow.

149

I stopped, not looking at him.

"Lindsey, I said I was sorry."

I nodded, even though I wasn't exactly angry with him for that. I was confused, for the most part. "It's fine." But even in my tone, I could still sense that it was off.

He could too, but nodded anyway. "Alright. I'll see you tomorrow?" I looked at him and awkwardly nodded. He leaned in for a kiss, but I turned my head at the last second, changing it to a kiss on the cheek.

He leaned back, his head down. "Please, Lindsey. What's wrong?"

I sighed, not able to take it anymore. "Your mom told me that you left three years ago." Nate didn't say anything, so I continued. His face was blank.

"You told me you only left a couple months ago. So why didn't you tell me you left years ago?"

"I didn't think it was a big deal," he said, still not meeting my eye.

I sighed, and reached out to softly grab his chin, turning it to face me. "It is a big deal."

But something still ached in my stomach, and I knew it was coming up soon. "Your mom also said something about why you left."

He sighed, closing his eyes and turning away. "I knew this was going to come up some time."

He was scaring me, because for some reason, something didn't feel right about what he was about to admit.

Nathaniel turned toward me, so his entire body was facing me. "When I turned sixteen, I met this girl. I really liked her, but my parents didn't approve. They thought her lifestyle wasn't a good influence on me." I didn't interrupt him. My breathing slowed.

"We'd be in fights all the time, and even though they insisted I couldn't see her, I snuck out to meet her anyway. They eventually found out what I was doing."

"What happened?"

"I moved out, and lived in my car."

I swallowed, still watching his facial expressions. "What was this girl's name?" Nathaniel looked at me, bowed his head, and whispered in the saddest tone I've ever heard,

"Lavender."

Twenty - Six

I turned into a sprint, my feet pounding hard against the pavement. I turned the corner of the houses, jumping over a curb and regaining my speed. My heart beat fast, probably confused as to why I was running. My house was looming in the distance as I ran. I was doing everything I could to forget the recent weeks' memories. I had broken up with Nathaniel. Or, I wasn't exactly sure what had happened. I hadn't explicitly said, "I'm breaking up with you," but I also didn't exactly say, "Okay. I'll see you tomorrow." I had simply broken his gaze and got out of the car without a second look. I had gone full-on radio-silence. My phone had suffered 27 missed calls from Nathaniel, and 22 missed calls from Lavender. It had almost become an art of mine to avoid Lavender in school. I knew she'd been trying to find me, but I'd been dodging her at every corner. I hadn't spoken a word to her since the day of the meeting with his parents, and I didn't intend to anytime soon. My best friend failed to mention to me that she had basically been his first love, or like, or whatever. The thought made me even more angry. I felt like an idiot while the two of them shared glances and walked around me when I knew nothing. Like I was a pawn in their secrecy. I slowed to a jog, my heart beating fast. I doubled over, resting my hands on my knees. The truth was simple, and I was then seeing it: Nathaniel and I were something that never should've happened. I wanted to move on.

~~~~~~~~~

Low knocking sounded against my door, and I sat up with a jolt. It was quiet for the first few moments when the door finally opened a crack. "Lindsey?" It was Tanya, and I looked up.

"What's up?" I asked, forcing a grin.

She eyed me, and shut the door. Tanya sat down on my bed, still studying me. "Are you okay?"

I smiled wider. "Yeah, why?"

"Because about a year ago, my friend broke up with her boyfriend. She cried for a week, and didn't talk to anyone," she answered in a monotone. "You're carrying on like Santa has picked you to be the Chosen Elf."

I laughed at her analogy and shook my head.

Her gaze softened. "Lindsey, I don't understand-"

"I'm fine." I reassured her.

"Has he called you?" She asked meekly, as if unsure of the answer.

I shrugged. "Yeah."

Tanya cocked an eyebrow.

"Twenty-seven times." I paused, and held up a finger. "Wait, make that 28. He called this morning."

Tanya's eyes widened. "Twenty-eight times? That's insane. That's, like, borderline stalking." She reached into a bag and pulled out a chocolate chip muffin and Starbucks cup. "Here." I licked my lips, and took the goodies from her. Taking a triumphant bite, I immediately rejoiced as chocolate melted into my tongue.

Tanya got up, and I parted my lips. "Where are you going?"

"Out," she answered, then spun around. "Just so you know, if I had a boy who called me 28 times?" Tanya shrugged, flashing me a lopsided smile, "I wouldn't give him up."

~~~~~~~~~~

I pushed open the double doors to school and stepped inside. I turned toward the south building where my locker was. It took me five minutes to speed-walk, and I was soon standing at my full-length red locker. Speed walking had become an art of mine as well. I spun the code, and the familiar click soon came.

"Hey, Lindsey," a voice said. I spun around and was face-to-face with Todd. I'd known Todd since I was in kindergarten, so we were good friends.

I smiled. "Hey, Todd."

He nervously smiled, dimples appearing. Huh, I thought. Kinda cute. "I was just wondering if you wanted to go out sometime." I opened my mouth to inform him of my boyfriend, when I stopped myself. I no longer had a boyfriend, so I was single. Why not?

"Sure, Todd. Sounds like fun.

"Cool. Do you want to go see that movie that just came out? It's at, like, eight." He shifted, seeming nervous.

I cocked my head, switching my heavy books from my right to left arm. "The horror one?"

He nodded, then stopped himself. "Only if you like-"

"I love them." I forced a grin. "See you then."

He nodded, and took off the opposite way. When I got home later that day, I automatically checked my phone for missed phone calls. But nothing was there; no blink alerts, voicemails, texts.

~~~~~~~~

Two weeks. Two weeks since I'd last spoken to my best friend. And Nathaniel. I'd forced myself to think of Todd, though. My date with him was tonight. Tanya was teaching me how to properly apply makeup.

"Hey, when you're a famous makeup artist one day doing celebrities' makeup, I want to be able to brag about Tanya Williams doing my makeup." I bit my lip to make my giggling subside.

I heard her laugh and put down something. I opened my eyes, and this time, the only thing that she had added was mascara. I frowned. "Why not shadoweye?"

Tanya raised her eyebrow. "It's eye shadow, by the way, and this is just a date. It doesn't look like you're trying too hard. Plus,

154

you don't really need much." I nodded, trying to make it seem like I understood.

"Are you meeting him there?" she asked, checking the time.

I nodded and stood up. This time, I was wearing a simple pair of skinny jeans, and a white winter cardigan. I had pulled my hair into a pretty ponytail with a skinny braid on the side.

"Thanks, Tanya," I said, giving her a one-armed hug.

She grew quiet. "Are you sure you want to do this?"

"Do what?"

She tossed me a knowing look. "You know what I mean."

I shrugged. "It's not going to hurt anyone."

Tanya nodded. "Get out of here, already."

I laughed and walked out of her room. "Hellen?"

I heard her answer from the kitchen, so I jogged quickly down the steps to meet her there. "Is it okay if I take the car?"

She mixed the hot pot of pasta, cocking her head. "Sure. Where are you going?"

"I have a date," I said.

Hellen smiled. "Nathaniel?"

My stomach twisted. "I broke up with Nathaniel."

Her smile dropped, along with her hold on the wooden spoon. "Why?"

I shrugged. "I don't know. Can I take the car?"

She confusingly nodded. "Sure." I was gone before she finished.

~~~~~~~~~

"No, way!" I laughed, tears forming at the tips of my eyes.

Todd laughed. "Yep. He poured the whole thing in. My mom was horrified."

"I'm sure she was! Bleach is an issue!" I laughed again as we walked toward my car. We'd finished the latest horror movie about a Ouija board. I thought it was good.

"Do you wanna go somewhere else?" he asked, his eyes flickering from my face to his car.

I grinned. "That depends. Where's the destination?

He grimaced. "Well, if you don't mind, my mom's apartment first."

I slowly nodded, and he pressed his lips together, eyes glued to his phone. "She asked me to stop in and grab something from her. But after, I was hoping maybe we could go to that new bakery. Okay? I have a strange craving for their chocolate cake." He grinned a boyish grin.

I laughed. "That sounds amazing right now, actually."

"So you can follow me if you want," he said, back stepping towards his car. I found myself nodding. It was official: my life was a fiasco. It turned out, his mother's apartment was in Lavender's complex. I got out of my car tentatively, looking around for a certain someone.

He locked his car and came over to me. "She's on the second floor."

Lavender's floor, I frowned. He caught me. "Are you okay?" I nodded.

I felt him come closer to me, touching my arm. "How about you just stay here." He smiled warmly, and I felt bad that I made him feel like I didn't want to meet his mom. It had nothing to do with that. His troubled gaze softened and I lightly pinched my forearm. I made an effort to not flinch. I didn't know why I was being so strange. "I'll only be a few minutes."

He exhaled and held out a hand. I grabbed it, but it felt wrong. It's just nerves, I told myself. But as much as I told myself this, a small voice kept nagging at me. It's because of Nathaniel, it retorted back. He squeezed it, smiling. "Be right back." I leaned against the car, watching him walk away from me and up the stairs. I searched for Lavender's room. The night was cold and bitterly nipped at any exposed skin. I'm sure my cheeks were a flushed red, and I pulled my scarf tighter around my neck. My eyes landed on it, and I prayed that the usually open curtains at the small window were shut. Of course, they were wide open, light pouring from the window. I glanced away. As promised, Todd was back in just a few minutes. We drove out of the complex, but I couldn't help but feel that Nate's green eyes were on us.

~~~~~~~~

"The cake was amazing," I said, as I licked my lips.

He grinned. "I'd thought you'd like it. Their bakery is the best in the area

We continued to stroll down the strangely deserted pathway. "Why did you ask me out? All of sudden, I mean?"

Todd's faced reddened. "Well, I've always kind of liked you." My mouth fell open.

He continued, scuffing his shoes slightly as he walked. "I was going to ask you a couple months ago, but this girl told me you had a boyfriend." Lavender.

"But then I heard that you were single."

I looked at him. I had stopped seeing Nathaniel only about two weeks ago, and he asked me before then. "Who told you that?"

"I just heard it around," he answered, then finally looked at me from a period of silence. "So... this guy. Was he special, or something?"

I made an inquisitive face. "Why?"

"I can tell by the way your face changed when I mentioned him," he answered briefly, yet unmoved as he stared warmly at me.

157

I shrugged, desperate to change the subject. "He was. But, that's just it. The key term, was." I let out a short laugh, looking down. My stomach churned as I said it, though I tried to push it down. He smiled and stepped forward, leaning in. My breath hitched in my throat, and I had the sudden feeling of- abort! Abort!

"Then I hope it'd be okay if I could do this." His hand, foreign, found my cheek. He stopped. "Can I kiss you?"

Twenty - Seven

He watched me uneasily as I wracked my brain for an appropriate answer. What was I supposed to say? I had never been asked before, and I've only ever been kissed by-ahem- him, and he didn't exactly ask me. A swirl of a memory swooped in and I blinked furiously.

I stopped, suddenly aware of his warm hand pressed into my lower back and the other grasping my hands. He looked into my eyes, his gaze darting to my lips then back to my eyes. He didn't need to say anything; all I wanted to do was get closer to Nathaniel. I placed the hand he wasn't holding onto the back of his neck, pulling him in. He resisted for a moment, his eyes nervously darting across my face and finally landing on my eyes. He shortened the short distance between our faces and firmly pressed his lips to mine-

"Lindsey?" Todd asked, unexpectedly inches from my face and waiting for an answer.

I felt a slight hitch of breath in my throat, and I suddenly seemed claustrophobic. I numbly stepped backwards, hurt flashing across his face. I mean, I had just started to know Todd again. I needed time to... what exactly? Move on? Get to know this very handsome boy in front of me? I didn't know.

I shook my head and my lips parted to say something. He pressed his lips together in a firm line and looked down.

"Sorry. I shouldn't have-"

"It's me," I quickly substituted. "Another time?"

He looked at me, dumbfounded. "Sure." And we continued on our walk back to the cars.

~~~~~~~~~

Thanksgiving, I wrote, *commemorates a feast held in 1621 by the pilgrims and the Wampanoag. It's the precious time in which families gather, and give thanks for everything they cherish.* I ended with a triumphant period and shoved my pen back in my bag. Holding the remainder of my essay up to the dull light, I grinned in relief. I was done.

"You're done with that already?" Tanya stood by my door, peering at my paper. Tanya was in my English class, even though she was younger. Apparently, her English skills were advanced, and my school rewarded her with 12th-grade English.

"Yep." I looked at her. "And no, you cannot copy my paper."

She puckered out her lower lip. "Aw, come on. Mrs. Dempsey won't know the difference. She can barely read her own handwriting."

I laughed. It was true; most of the students created a rumor that she was 96, but obviously that wasn't true. Eighty at most. "She's not stupid. Go write your own."

She sighed, flicking her ponytail. "Fine. Oh, by the way. How does Thanksgiving work around here?"

I swiveled toward her on my chair and nodded. "We basically just have a regular sit-down Thanksgiving dinner. Nothing special."

Tanya nodded. "What about Christmas?"

"Tree, decorations, presents from people who feel bad for us. The usual." I filled in the information, watching her reactions.

She traced her finger against my wooden desk. "Has Nathaniel contacted you recently?"

I thought, taken aback by the randomness. "No. Why?"

"Because I saw him the other day..." She trailed off, biting her lip.

I put down my pen and crossed my arms. "Tanya."

"Yes?"

"Spill."

160

She scrunched up her lips and finally met my eyes. "I saw him with a girl. They were holding hands."

My heart shuddered half a beat and an odd feeling filled me. Though I couldn't place my finger on it, it definitely resembled jealousy. I imagined how he acted around her, and if he did the same things with her that he did with me. The thought made me so sad. "What did she look like?"

Tanya squinted her eyes. "Blond. Tall. I didn't see them for that long." I let go of a breath I hadn't realized I was holding in. Had I expected it to be Lavender?

"Where did you see them?" I softly asked, staring at the ground. I looked up when it suddenly grew quiet. Tanya had her face pulled into a confusing frown. "It was weird. I saw them in the parking lot at school. How old is Nathaniel again?"

"He doesn't go to our school," I answered numbly. "Why would he be in front of our school?"

"Would he be picking up Lavender?" she offered.

I shook my head. "Lavender has her own car." A dead silence hung in the air. "Weird."

~~~~~~~~~

"Come down here, please!" Hellen yelled from downstairs and I jumped out of bed.

I talked while I hopped down the stairs, "Hellen, I have a lot of homework to do and-" I stopped short when I caught a glimpse of a pretty girl standing in the foyer. Lavender. I tried not to glare, mostly because I was shocked she was standing in front of me.

Hellen cleared her throat. "I'll give you girls some time to talk." She whisked away in my peripheral vision, but I barely noticed as I stared at the person I had neglected to speak to in the last three weeks. That's, like, a century in girl years.

161

"Lindsey." It was said more like a statement as my best friend stared at me. She numbly reached behind her and started to wrap a piece of her hair around a finger—her tell-tale sign of nerves.

I didn't answer.

"Can we go somewhere and talk?" she asked, glancing at the rising noise in the living room. I nodded and without asking Hellen, I slipped out the door without grabbing my coat.

~~~~~~~~

I gripped my hands around the mug in front of me, staring down at the chocolatey-substance brewing. Whip cream was artistically spun in a swirl. I took a sip. Lavender sat across from me, sipping on an iced-mocha. I didn't meet her eyes. Why did I agree to this again?

"I'm sorry," she bluntly stated. I met her eyes, which were blinking rapidly. Light brown mascara caked onto her eyelashes, her emerald green eyes shining with a look I wasn't sure of. Her green eyes reminded me of Nathaniel, and I looked away.

Lavender smirked at herself. "I mean, that's where I should really start. I should've told you about Nathaniel and I-"

"Why didn't you?" I interrupted, setting a hard gaze.

Lavender parted her lips. "Well, when you guys first met, I saw something. And I knew you'd never had a boyfriend before, so when you asked me that morning if I were involved with him, I quickly said no."

"I wouldn't have cared even if you did! And what does it have to do with me being single? Is that such an embarrassment?" I raised my voice, earning a look from a nearby customer.

Lavender's eyes widened. "Of course not. It's just," she sighed, "I'm sorry."

I looked at her and after moments of brief sanity, nodded. "Okay."

Lavender exhaled and smiled. "I missed you."

162

"Me too," I admitted. "How is he?"

She looked down, then at me. "He took it pretty bad in the beginning."

"Really?"

She looked at me like I was crazy. "You're a catch. And he lost you."

"And now?"

Lavender made a face. "He has a girlfriend."

I blinked and decided to lie. "So do I."

"You have a girlfriend?" She smiled.

I blinked. "Boyfriend."

Lavender didn't smile. She remained expressionless. "Who?"

"Todd. You know, that boy from-"

"I know who he is." She curtly nodded and gripped her cup. "Do you forgive him?"

"I think so. Did you know he didn't even tell his parents I was coming? And that he lied about the fact that he left his parents three years ago?"

Lavender nodded. "He gave me the whole story once he got back that night. He was wrong, Linds, I know, but he was really torn up for about a week or two. He didn't expect you to break up with him."

It was like my brain was doing cartwheels, hopping from one insured idea to the next. "We should all do something together." What?

"Together?" Lavender repeated.

I bit my lip. "You know, you and Andre, Nathaniel and his girlfriend, and Todd and I."

"Why?" he asked, confused.

"I think it will help things," I said, "Nate and I...we just have to accept the fact that we've moved on."

She didn't look like she believed me. "What do you propose we do?"

Think of something! "Your apartment. Just a normal hangout?"

Lavender warily smiled. "Sure. I'll talk to Nathaniel and Andre." We clinked cups and smiled at each other. It was good to have my friend back, but I knew it would take a while for me to regain some trust. And she knew that. But the question was, what had I gotten myself into? Was I ready to see Nathaniel? With another girl?

~~~~~~~~~

We got out of school on a Tuesday, but I still had one thing to do. I slammed my locker door and readjusted my backpack strap. I scoured the halls, looking for Todd. After all, he was my (read: boyfriend), and I had to invite him to the party at Lavender's that I had so brilliantly thought up. My plan: march straight up to him and kiss him. My palms grew sweaty as I spotted Todd leaning against his locker, reading something on his phone. I paused and took a hesitant step toward him. I found myself standing there within seconds and he looked up.

"Hey," Todd said with a friendly smile.

"Hey." I smiled and thought back. Did I forget to put that mint in my mouth ten minutes ago? Oh gosh. But I tasted a faint peppermint and relaxed. "I wanted to talk to you about something." He pocketed his phone and raised an eyebrow.

I licked my lips. "So, the other night, when you were going to kiss me... I didn't return the gesture because I was caught off guard." I tried hard not to laugh at my stupidity. Caught off guard? He even asked me.

He squinted, a humorous smile forming on his lips. "I asked you." Crap. Don't ask me what was running through my mind when I placed my hand on his arm and kissed him. It lasted a couple seconds, but his kissing skills almost rivaled those of Nathaniel's.

164

Almost. I leaned back and waited for a response. Todd only grinned, leaning in to kiss me once more.

~~~~~~~~

"Can you please grab the mashed potatoes in the kitchen?" Hellen asked me, looking frazzled. Thanksgiving and Christmas were the most nerve-wracking times for her. Though I didn't know why; it's not like she had to buy presents. They're supplied to us from churches and shopping stores.

"Hey, chop chop. I want me some mashed potatoes." Tanya suddenly stood in front of me, clapping her hands.

I laughed and turned around. Taking the bowl, I walked into the dining room and placed it on the table. A turkey, mashed potatoes, stuffing, sweet potatoes, and pie sat on the table. I was impressed. The first year I was in Hellen's care, the Thanksgiving was pretty bad. My eyes shifted to the dining room and I laughed at the irony of having a nice Thanksgiving in a foster home. The plates and cups were made of Styrofoam and the silverware of plastic.

I eyed Hellen in amusement.

"What?" she asked, placing her hands on her hips.

"Oh, nothing."

Tanya came up behind me and murmured in my ear. "Better than most homes."

That was true. Many of the foster homes didn't even celebrate Thanksgiving.

"Kids! Everyone, we're ready!" Hellen yelled from the kitchen, bustling in with a bowl of sauce. I sat, and Tanya did the same next to me. It was a little hectic, but after everyone had sat down in a mannerly way, we dug in. We weren't allowed to pray, because the government sees it as an, "unlawful treaty of whether or not the child him/herself wants to oblige to Christ."

165

After a few moments of clattering forks and kids screaming, Hellen clapped her hands as if wanting our attention. It quieted almost immediately and ten heads swiveled toward her. It was then when she began her speech, "Happy Thanksgiving, children. Some of you, " she shot Tanya and me a look, "may be wondering why this meal is so extravagant." Many of the smaller kids made a face at her word choice. "I am pleased to announce that five of our children have been chosen and applications have been approved for adoption." Something jumped in my stomach as I watched her prepare to announce the names.

"Bailey Michaelson," a four-year-old scamp who was rather rambunctious, "Luke Tanner," a six year old who kept to himself, "Danielle Nimp," a six year old who was best friends with Mariella, "Mathew Reese," a nine year old that talks to me frequently, "and Tanya Wilson."

I reared toward her, a big smile on my face. "Congratulations!"

She blinked, very still. "Is this a joke?"

I shook her shoulders. "No!"

She blinked again, her shock wearing off as a tear hung in her eye. After the first tear trickled down her cheek, they all started to run down, "I've," she sobbed, "been-been waiting so-so long for this-s."

I hugged her and murmured, "You deserve it." And she did.

Twenty - Eight

Tanya was officially adopted and gone. Lavender and I were getting back to becoming what we were, and the "hangout date" was tonight. I didn't have the right to complain about it because I was the culprit who arranged it in the first place. Tanya's new adoptive parents lived in Michigan, so she pulled out of my school and took a plane to her new life. I was happy for her. I was just wanting my foster-years to be over. One year left. I grabbed my phone, jacket, and checked myself in the mirror once more. Before Tanya left, she kept her promise of teaching me how to properly apply makeup. It was shaky at first, but with each day's passing, I was improving. I jogged down the stairs, swinging open the door and meeting the cold. Todd was meeting me there so I could just drive directly to Lavender's. Taking a deep, wavering breath, I climbed into Hellen's car. I hadn't spoken or talked to Nathaniel in a month, (let alone seen the boy,) and I was worried. Starting the ignition, I pulled out of the icy driveway and started toward Lavender's apartment complex.

~~~~~~~~

"Hey, beautiful." I heard someone say as I got out of the car.

I looked up with a smile and spotted Todd slinging an arm over my car. He had on jeans and a brown snugly coat.

I shut the door and walked over to his side. "Hello."

"Ready for this?" he asked, moving a strand of hair away from my face.

I nodded. Todd laughed, leaning in and kissing me. His breath tasted of clean mint, and it took all of me to break away from the moment.

"We should go inside," I whispered, something stinging my eye.

Todd nodded, gently grazing his thumb over my cheek. Slinging an arm over my shoulder, we walked up the stairs to her floor. "Why didn't you tell me Lavender lived here when we came that night?"

I shrugged, staring ahead. "I guess it slipped my mind."

"Mmhm." He cocked an eyebrow, doubt seeping through his reply.

I leaned into him as we approached the door. Loud pop music sounded through the door.

I took a breath, staring at the white paint.

"You okay?" he asked, glancing at me.

I barely looked at him. "Yeah." There was no way I was telling him of my recent relationship with the boy we were about to encounter. Can you spell awkward? Todd knocked on the door, his arm still over me. I suddenly felt claustrophobic again and edged away slightly.

The door swung open, Lavender standing there. She smiled, "Hey, guys. Todd, it's so great to see you again."

"You too, Lavender."

Lavender motioned us inside. "Come on in." I pushed away my nerves, not pondering, and stepped inside. I immediately smelt pizza, the cheese and sauce wafting around me.

"Smells good." I bumped Lavender as she walked past me.

"It's amazing what a takeout menu will do," she whispered, grinning and moving ahead. I laughed and took off my coat. Todd took mine and set it down with his. We walked in together and I was soon in front of a very cute boy whom I assumed was Andre, who was a little taller than Lavender. His chin stubble contrasted beautifully with his olive-skin tone, and his black hair hung perfectly. He was laughing at something Lavender said. She touched his chest, giggling.

Andre looked at me and smiled. "Hey, I'm Andre." He held out his hand. "Lavender has told me a bunch about you."

I smiled. So, she did. At least someone did. "Same. It's great to meet you."

Andre bro-slapped Todd. "Hey, man. Todd, right?"

He nodded. "Yeah. Lindsey's boyfriend." I flinched slightly and looked down, my entire face heating. Had I really just done that? I saw Lavender watching me, but I ignored it. Loud laughter erupted from behind us and I spun around. Nathaniel came out of his room, hand in hand with a blond girl. Her blond mass nearly shouted "hair extensions," and the makeup was a little bit much. Was I being too harsh?

"Oh!" she squealed, almost shattering a glass sitting next to me. "They're here, Nathaniel!" She rushed forward, enveloping me in a hug. She smelled of some lilac perfume, and... it immediately came. Nathaniel. She smelled of Nathaniel. Todd got his hug next and I peeked at Nathaniel. He wasn't even watching me, just grinning dumbly at the blond.

"I'm Aubrie." The girl—Aubrie—said. The girlfriend, I assumed. I looked at her, something embedding itself in my stomach. I knew what it was so I ignored it.

"Hi, I'm Lindsey. Nice to meet you." I mustered a warm tone.

Todd suddenly slung his arm around me, smiling at them. I tensed at his sudden touch, but he rubbed my arm. I sensed Nathaniel's eyes finally fall on me, but I didn't look at him enough to decide what his expression read. I didn't care, anyway. An awkward silence continued until Lavender cleared her throat.

"The pizza is ready." That did it. We all grabbed a plate, piling our plates with the baked dough.

Aubrie made a face, peering at the pizza. "Oh, um, sorry. I'm gluten-free." I snorted softly to myself, veering away from the kitchen and into the living room. We all sat in different areas, chatting and eating pizza. Todd was making jokes every so often and I laughed. He was funny.

169

"This was a great idea, Lindsey," Andre said, taking a bite of crust and giving a piece to Lavender. Shoot. I didn't want anyone to know it was my idea! Or, if I'm being honest, I didn't want Nathaniel to know.

"I have an idea," Aubrie said as we all continued to eat.

Lavender looked at her. "Yeah?"

"We should play Spin It." She grinned. I glanced at Lavender, questioning her with my eyes, hoping she'd know. She looked at me blankly, then at Aubrie.

"How do you play that?"

Aubrie put down her water, water as in a single meal, and leaned into Nathaniel. "Well, basically you get a ketchup bottle, or a bottle of some sorts, and spin it-"

"Like spin the bottle?" Todd interrupted.

Aubrie shook her head. "Kinda. So, let's say Lavender were to spin it, and it landed on Andre. Lavender would ask, Truth-Dare-or-Snog-"

"Snog?" I questioned.

"Would you stop interrupting her, Lindsey?" Nathaniel shot at me. I tried not to stare. It was the first thing he had said to me. In fact, it was the first time I heard him say my name in weeks. Aubrie ignored him. "Snog means kissing. It's like an English way of saying kiss. But the rule is, you can't kiss the same person twice."

"Seems easy enough," Todd said, glancing at the group. Everyone nodded, but I had a distinct feeling that this was going to get very bad, very quickly. Lavender stood, collected some of the plates and walked into the kitchen. We all assembled ourselves in a circle. Todd next to me, Aubrie across from us, seated next to Nathaniel, and Andre next to me. The music lessened a bit and Lavender came back with a mustard bottle.

"Is this okay?" she asked Aubrie.

Aubrie nodded and chirped, "Perfect."

Lavender handed it to her and took a seat between Andre and me.

"Who wants to go first?" Aubrie asked the group, her yes flickering over each of us. No one replied, so she shrugged, placed it in the middle, and spun it. We all watched as it slowly decreased its speed and landed on Nathaniel. "Truth, Dare, or Snog?"

Nathaniel's eyes flickered quickly to me, then Todd. He smirked. Smirked. "Snog." And with that, he leaned in and deeply kissed Aubrie. I stared at the floor, hating feeling this way. Why had I wanted to do this again? After a few seconds, they pulled away and it was Nathaniel's turn. He spun and it landed on Todd. Phew! Not me.

"Truth, dare, or Snog?" Nate asked.

Todd blinked. "Snog." And he leaned over to me, catching me by surprise, and enveloped my lips with his own. When he pulled away, I was out of breath. Nathaniel blankly stared at Todd, almost looking...bored. He motioned for him to spin. He did, and this time it landed on me.

"Truth, dare, or Snog?" Todd asked, wiggling his eyebrows.

I thought. "Truth." I wanted to play safely.

Todd looked slightly disappointed with my answer, but nodded anyway. "How many boyfriends have you had?"

Crap. That was why I didn't play this game in eighth grade. But I came up with an answer quickly. "One." Todd, looking surprised, leaned in and pecked me on the cheek.

I couldn't look at Nathaniel; I know what I had done was horrible, but I didn't want questions to arise about my past with him. Even though I scolded myself to not peek, of course I did. He was staring blankly again. Right at me. A sniff came from Lavender, but I ignored her.

I lowered my gaze to the mustard bottle and spun. This time, it landed on Aubrie again. "Truth, dare, or Snog?"

"Snog." Aubrie leaned over and kissed Nathaniel. His jawline was taut as she did so. My belly ached. Afterwards, she spun. It landed on Nathaniel.

"I feel like these things are always rigged," Lavender murmured next to me, huffing. I nodded, agreeing with her, and turned my attention back to the game.

Aubrie asked Nathaniel, "Truth, dare, or Snog?"

"Dare," he answered almost immediately.

Aubrie grinned. "Show me one hidden talent I don't know about you." A memory suddenly swooped in without warning.

And with that, we both plopped our cherries into our mouth. I bit down on the pit-less cherry and *sour flavor burst onto my tongue. I chewed quickly, swallowing the fruit and getting to work on the stem. I chewed on it first, trying to soften it. When I thought it was soft enough, I used my tongue to cross the stem and loop it under. I sneaked a glance at Nathaniel and his face was pulled into concentration, staring at the floor as he worked on his stem. As soon as it was looped loosely in my mouth, I stuck one end between my clenched jaw and pulled-*

"As a matter of fact, I do," he said, yet in a tone I knew too well. Cocky. He got up and disappeared into a room. Moments later, he came back with a guitar and sat on the couch.

"I was waiting to sing this for you, but I think this is the appropriate time." Nathaniel said to Aubrie, my stomach pulling into knots, knowing he was shooting that comment at me. He wasn't going to do what I thought he'd do...He looked down at the guitar and he strung a familiar chord. Nathaniel began to sing,

"Every time I see your face, it puts my heart in a race. It grows ten times larger, then I start to think you're a charmer. Your laugh lights up your face, it makes me believe I've picked an ace. Ever since I've met you, I've been put in a daze. I'll be drawn to you

172

forever, even on Sundays.." And he strummed the last chord. I stared at him, shocked.

I felt Lavender's piercing vision against my head, but I couldn't shake the feeling of betrayal. How many girls had he sung this song to? Or was he just trying to get me back for kissing Todd? Shouldn't I be the one who was angry with him, not the other way around?

Aubrie cooed. "Aw, Nate!" And she kissed him. I got up, stepping over the bottle and through the circle of "fun." I made my way to the door, opening it, and closing it with more force than intended. I had forgotten to grab my jacket and I crossed my arms, leaning over the railing. It smelt of snow as I stared up at the dark sky. Suddenly the door opened and I turned around, my gaze settling on Lavender.

"Hey," I mumbled, returning my gaze to the sky.

She ambled over to me, holding out my jacket. I took it with shaking fingers, "Thanks."

Lavender nodded. "Want to tell me what that was all about?"

I shrugged.

"Because it looked like you two were about to start a wrestling match."

I managed a smile. "I would've won."

Lavender laughed. "I wouldn't doubt it." She looked down, then to me. "But really. What was with the song and the kissing and the stares..."

I looked at her. "He wrote that song and sang it to me when you were out with Andre one day."

She clenched her jaw. "I'll kill him."

I shook my head. "It's fine."

"No, it's not fine. What he did in there was really low." She half-smiled, squeezing my shoulder. "You need to talk to him." I watched her walk back inside, the earlier music streaming through softly as she opened her door and it fading once the door closed.

I followed her and returned to my earlier position next to Todd.

He leaned into my ear, murmuring, "Are you okay?"

I nodded curtly and stared straight at Nathaniel, who was watching me. "Spin it."

He hesitated at first, but eventually spun the bottle. It landed on me. "Truth, dare, or Snog?"

"Snog," I answered immediately, leaning into Todd and performing my task.Todd's face revealed he felt taken aback when I pulled away, a dazed look playing with his eyes.

I spun the bottle. This time, it landed on Lavender. I winked at her and she returned a small nod. "Truth, dare, or snog?"

She huffed. "I guess I'll pick Snog."

Andre laughed. "You better."And the night ended with kisses.

Twenty - Nine

The dreams were back. Walter, chasing me in a park. I couldn't exactly understand why I was still terrified of the drunk man who had done horrible things to me. I woke up with a scream, my chest heaving and adrenaline pulsing through my veins. I slid out of bed, checking the time. It read 10:45. I brushed my teeth and washed my face. I made my way downstairs, the house being oddly quiet. It was a Saturday and usually the kids were hyper. Turning the corner, I stopped dead in my tracks. Walter stood at the stove, stirring something which smelled of bacon. I recognized his dense body, his piggish legs. Placing a hand to my mouth to mask my breathing, I slowly and cautiously took a step backward.

"Good morning, Lindsey." I paused, closing my eyes and hoping for the ground to swallow me up. Walter turned around, wiping his hands on a dish towel with a sly grin. "That's no way to treat an old friend."

~~~~~~

"What are you doing here?" I asked, mentally searching for a weapon. I didn't think a lamp could do any damage.

He shrugged, throwing the towel down and checking his bacon. "Hellen and I are meant for each other."

I snorted, crossing my arms and subconsciously tugging my pajama shorts down. "Are you sure about that?"

"She went to the park with the other kids," he said, ignoring my sarcastic question. "She didn't want to wake you."

I sighed. "Shame. I could've avoided you."

He pulled out a plate and slid the bacon onto it. "Oh, she didn't tell you?"

I raised an eyebrow.

"She's letting me live here for a while," he continued.

My heart faltered, skipping a beat.

He chuckled, catching onto my facial expression. "Didn't expect that, did you?"

"You kidnapped me," I said in a shaky voice.

Walter chomped on a piece of bacon, looking off into the distance. "That was fun." I didn't answer, just watched him.

He looked back at me, leaning onto the counter. "But what wasn't fun was that pretty boy who attacked me." I didn't say anything.

"Where is he?"

Nathaniel. I had to protect him. "He moved," I lied.

"Hm. Shame. I was really hoping I'd see him again. Show him how to really fight."

Walter started to pace, taking a bite of bacon. "You know, if it wasn't for him, I could've gotten away with it."

"I doubt that," I retorted quickly. "I still have the option of telling the police, you know." He stopped and took bounding strides toward me. I tensed and stared into his bloodshot eyes.

"I don't think that'd be a good idea," he said in a husky voice, anger seething through his eyes. My instincts screamed at me to run, but it was like I was frozen in place. "Because I could always deny, deny, deny."

I glared. "I have witnesses."

"Oh really? Well, no one witnessed you attack me that night. Remember the beer bottle?"

I did. "Self-defense," I offered.

He snorted and backed away. "Like anyone will believe you. I don't think you realize that I could get you kicked out of here faster than anything, so I'd watch your behavior if I were you."

"But you're not me."

176

His smile dropped. "Watch it."

"Oh, I will." And I backed up, slowly making my way upstairs. I reached my door, and quickly shut it behind me. I locked it and slid down onto the floor. I was in a bad situation, and I reached for my phone. My fingers hovered over the keyboard, wavering. My first instinct was to call him. But I knew I couldn't, and I didn't want to involve him anymore. I dropped my phone on the ground and leaned my head against the door.

~~~~~~~~~~

I laughed. "No way."

Lavender nodded. "Yep. And he won't tell me what he's getting me for Christmas." I leaned against Lavender's kitchen counter and watched her wipe it down. Such a clean freak. My phone buzzed, and I checked the text: *Hey beautiful, how about a date tonight? ;)*

I sighed, and put it away. Lavender watched me. "Todd?"

"How'd you know?"

She made a face. "Because I can tell from your reaction." I shrunk, feeling bad. Lavender crossed the kitchen and motioned to the living room. I followed her and sat on the couch. She sat as well, facing me.

I looked at her. "Am I a bad person?"

"Huh?"

"My reaction. I should be smiling from a text from my boyfriend. And instead, I sigh," I said, my phone buzzing again.

I opened it: *What do you say?*

I ignored it, putting my phone away and biting my lip. "Am I?" I watched her contemplate her answer precisely.

Lavender leaned forward. "You really want me to tell you what I think?"

I nodded, encouraging her.

"The truth?" she repeated.

177

I nodded again furiously.

Lavender sighed and tucked a piece of her hair behind her ear. "I think that you don't even like Todd. I can tell when you love something, and he's not on that list."

I was quiet, as I watched her continue to speak.

"I honestly think... that you still have feelings for Nathaniel. Deep feelings, that you still can't shake away, no matter what." I coughed, trying to cover up the silence that hung in the air.

"You know I'm right," she pointed out, smiling. "Look, Lindsey, it's your choice. If you like Todd, then stay with him. Just don't lead him on, because that boy is head over heels for you." She got up, disappearing into the kitchen. I numbly pulled out my phone and texted Todd.

~~~~~~~

Todd nervously drummed his fingers against the wooden table, licking his lips.

I took a sip of my hot chocolate and watched him. "You okay?"

"You tell me. Usually when your girlfriend says she needs to talk, it's either a break up call or a pregnancy issue. And I don't think it's choice B."

Definitely not choice B. "Todd-"

He groaned, slapping his palms against the table. "I knew it."

"Just...hear me out."

He nodded and stared into my eyes.

I looked at the wooden table and scratched at a dent. "You're an amazing guy. But...I really don't think we're meant to be together. I probably should've done this in the beginning, when we didn't end up kissing on our first date. I just don't want to commit to a guy as sweet as you, when I'm not feeling it. Do you know what I mean?" I looked up from the dent and saw him nodding.

"Can I ask you something?"

178

I nodded.

"Does this have anything to do with Nathaniel?"

I froze. "No." The dent was deeper.

~~~~~~~~~

We got out of school the following few days. I hadn't asked Hellen about Walter yet, but I was planning to. As soon as I returned home, I found Hellen and the kids decorating the tree.The new boy, Jason, ran up to me as soon as I came in through the door. "Wanna help hang the candy canes?"

I smiled and placed down the keys. "Sure." I let him lead me to the tree and grab the handful of red and white candy canes from the nearby table.

I noticed all of the decorations and looked over to Hellen. "Wow, people were generous this year."

She nodded, and hung a reindeer ornament. "It was weird. An anonymous person donated all of this stuff at the center."

I returned to hanging the candy canes. "Weird." That was my chance. "Hey, Hellen? Can I ask you something?"

"Sure, hon."

I cleared my throat. "In private?"

Hellen stopped midway and placed down the ornament. "I'll be right back, kids."

And I walked out of the room, leading into the kitchen. I turned toward her. "Why are you letting Walter stay here?"

She made a strange expression. "I don't know what you're talking about."

"C'mon, Hellen-"

"Lindsey. I'm not lying. Why would you think he's staying here?" Something inside me stopped. It was like all the fear in the world was hitting me in full blast. I was just about to inform her he was in our kitchen, cooking bacon, when I remembered his threats.

179

"Oh. Okay," I said, barely hearing myself. Maybe I had dreamt it. I started to walk out of the kitchen, but stopped when Hellen opened the fridge and asked, "Where'd all the bacon go?"

Thirty

"Just come over and I'll be there soon," Lavender said, her voice bouncing as she seemed to be running.

I repositioned the phone to my ear. "Since when do you run?"

"New hobby. See you in a bit."

I hung up, distracted for just a moment, and grinning. I started the ignition. As I drove to Lavender's, I tried to remember where she had hidden the keys. As soon as I got there I went straight to the door, searching around. I bent down, peeking under the mat. Bingo. I sighed, standing up again and unlocking the door. I smiled at the smell of cookies, and warmth. Christmas was Lavender's favorite holiday, and she was always festive. I put my keys on the counter and strode into the living room. Pulling out my phone, I scrolled through my junk mail.

"What are you doing here?" a voice asked.

I jumped slightly, looking behind me. Nathaniel stood there, shirtless.

Awkward. I stood up, taking a breath and forcing my eyes to stay on his face. "I'm meeting Lavender here."

He nodded, looking around the room and obviously avoiding my gaze.

I had to say what was on my mind. "Where's Aubrie?"

Nathaniel raised an eyebrow. "She's not in the picture anymore."

I snorted.

"What?"

I started to pace. "Oh nothing. Just, I feel bad for any girl that will eventually end up with a person like you."

Nathaniel looked taken aback, hurt flashing across his face. "You're not a walk in the park either, sweetheart."

Something exploded inside me. "Did she realize that you're not the person you say you are?"

"Excuse me?"

"Nothing." I returned to what I was doing. My phone was then taken from my grasp.

"What are you talking about?" he asked, phone in hand.

I stared at him. "Please. You act like this big-shot, when really, you're a lying loser who'll do anything to keep a secret. Not to mention a player," I added childishly.

He sarcastically laughed, stepping closer to me. "At least I don't bottle up all my emotions inside and constantly act like everything is okay."

I glared. "What, gonna pull the parent card again?" Nathaniel stopped edging closer, his fury dying. I backed off as well, immediately feeling regret. I know he hadn't meant it when he said it.

"I'm sorry," I murmured.

He looked up, shaking his head. "No. You shouldn't be the one apologizing. I've been a jerk." I didn't say anything and watched him hold up a finger. He disappeared from the room, and moments later came back in clothed in a maroon T-shirt. He walked to the couch, patting the seat next to him. I agreed after moments of contemplation and sat next to him.

"We need to talk," I reasoned, sighing.

Nathaniel nodded. "What do you want to start with?"

"That night," I said, almost in a full whisper.

"What do you want to know?"

I watched him. "Why didn't you tell me you left three years ago?"

"Because of why I left three years ago. Our relationship was so new, and I didn't want to jeopardize it." He paused and held out a hand. "Can I take your jacket? It's a long story." I slid out of my jacket and handed it to him. Once he came back from the front door, he started up again, "Lavender was my girlfriend. I was young and immature-""So nothing has changed?" I interrupted with a small smile.

He rolled his eyes, continuing, "I would always sneak out and see her. My parents didn't like her and didn't approve of her lifestyle or the way she dressed. Everything about her, they just didn't like. To this day, I still don't know why. So I was fighting with my dad one night, telling him I loved her and wanted to spend the rest of my life with her." He snorted. "He was angry, and told me I was a disgrace to the family for going against his word. So I left that night."

He swallowed, pausing. "I slipped out the window with all my stuff, stole the car and credit card, and lived in my car for about two months. Then I stayed with friends and hopped couches for awhile. Lavender and I slipped apart quickly. But after we came in contact again and she found out I didn't have anywhere to stay, she offered me a room." Nathaniel paused, his gaze flickering to the floor. "Did you know I was supposed to go to Harvard?"

I shook my head. I knew Nathaniel was bright, but I didn't know about his college plans.

But something still didn't make sense. "But that night, in the hotel room. I asked you about your parents and you told me they were wealthy and 'showered,' you with gifts..."

Nathaniel pressed his lips together. "I didn't think it was the right night to explain. It was a big day-"

I sarcastically laughed, irritated. "Are you serious? You know me, Nathaniel. I could've dealt with it, the truth. Besides," I paused, "if you had told me the truth in the first place, things would be different right now."

He nodded. "I know. And I'll regret it for a while."

I stared into the eyes I had originally fallen for and tore away from them. I couldn't.

183

He started up again. "We decided to just be friends. It was better that way, anyway. She offered me a room and gave me time to think about it."

I tucked a piece of my hair behind my ear. "So that night we met-"

"Was my," he stopped, thinking, "first night. That's why Lavender didn't tell you at first. She didn't even know I was coming."

I was quiet. "Thank you for telling me."

"Anything else you want to know?"

There was. "How many girls have you sung that song to?"

He closed his eyes. "I hated every second of that. I only sang it to her to get under your skin. I really did write it for you."

As if suddenly remembering something, he cleared his throat. "How are you and Todd doing?"

All I wanted to do was tell him I broke up with him. That Todd and I weren't meant to be, but Walter came into mind and I paused. I needed to protect him, and I wasn't so sure I felt the same before. "We're good."

~~~~~~~

I slammed the door shut and threw down the keys. I spotted Hellen in the kitchen, reading something online.

I walked into the kitchen and grabbed an apple. "Hi."

She turned. "Hey, hon. Oh, before I forget!" Hellen stood up from her computer, and pushed her glasses further up her nose. "Did you finish the list of caroling songs?" Every year on Christmas Eve, Hellen drags us all out to go caroling on people's doorsteps. I'd managed to skip out on the last one and spend the night with Lavender, but there was no way I was getting out of it this year. Hellen also asked for donations to The Foster Association and usually succeeded. We'd also had some pretty good singers, too. I remember I loved to do it when I was younger, but the embarrassment set in once I hit twelve.

I nodded. "Yes, but is there any way I could-"

"No. You're the oldest, Lindsey. The kids look up to you, and you're coming with us."

"Can I bring Lavender?"

She seemed distracted as she started to read something again on her computer. "Sure. What about Todd?"

"I broke up with him."

Hellen stopped what she was doing and took off her glasses to properly gaze at me. "Wow."

"What?"

She shrugged. "Well, you sure go through a lot of boys."

What? I stared at her. "Are you kidding me right now?"

"I'm just saying that you've gone through two boys in the last month."

Something inside me put up a wall, blocking any tears to leak. I stepped closer, narrowing my glare. "You have no right to tell me what I'm doing. You're not my mother, and I will never see you that way-"

"Lindsey, don't be disrespectful," Hellen interrupted, looking exasperated. I left the room.

~~~~~~~~~

"I'm sorry I got you into this," I grumbled, stuffing the Santa hat on my head.

Lavender laughed, wrapping a scarf around her neck. "I love this stuff! Remember when we were thirteen and doing this?"

I laughed at the memory as I slipped on gloves. "Don't remind me. What are you doing tomorrow?"

"Going to my mom's."

I nodded, swallowing. "What about Nathaniel?"

"What about Nathaniel?"

I blinked, watching the younger kids flip through their music. "I mean - where is he going for Christmas?"

"I think he's just staying at my apartment." I would've guessed so.

"Okay, everyone ready?" Hellen came bustling into the room, clothed in the traditional Santa-hat, and gloves. She passed out folders of music and wearily looked out the dark window. The streets were lit up with Christmas lights wound around the light poles, and the sky threatened to drop snow at any second. According to the weather report, New York would receive a record-breaking amount of snow this winter. I loved snow.

"It'll be better if it snows. You know…add to the scene?" Lavender piped up, noticing Hellen's expression.

Hellen nodded and smiled at everyone. We had practiced for two hours earlier that day and already had the solos and harmonies set. I was an alto, whatever that was, and Lavender was put into soprano so she could lead the hard parts for the little kids. I opened the door, my boots clicking against the wood floor. Cold hit me immediately, along with the delicious smell of approaching snow.

"Come on, everyone," I ordered, waving my black binder filled with the designated songs. Within moments, everyone was out and we were stepping up to our first house. Time to harass a family.

Hellen whispered loudly, "First song! All I want for Christmas is you! Ray, that's you." Ray, a twelve-year-old girl whose voice was absolutely amazing, nodded. Hellen knocked, and quickly ran back to our formation. I turned on the speaker as the door swung open, Mariah Carey's version of Karaoke filling the air. An old woman stood there, crossing her arms.

Ray started, "I don't want a lot of for Christmas! There is just one thing I need. Don't care about those presents, underneath the Christmas tree. I just want you for my own, more than you could

186

ever know. Make my wish come true-ue. All I want, for Christmas.. is.. you." She finished, the beat speeding up. The old woman was clearly impressed, clapping her hands. Our mixture of off pitch voices began. For the next house, Hellen knocked on the red door. The snow started to fall lightly, dusting the streets. I snuggled tighter into my scarf. The curtains on the front window flew open a crack, revealing an old man. He frowned and the curtains swung back. I tried to contain my amused smile.

"Patty, those orphan carolers are here again!" he yelled from inside.

She yelled back, "Don't open the door!" Moments later, the lights in the whole house went out. I tried to cover my laughter. Lavender was jabbing my side.

It was quiet. "Well, that went well."

~~~~~~~~

I happily sighed once I sat on the couch. My aching legs definitely protested. We did a total of ten houses, and standing in the cold singing songs with frozen lips was possibly the worst torture I wouldn't inflict upon my own enemies. We'd gotten a number of donations, even from a man who slammed the door in our faces before we had even started the word to "Jingle Bells." I massaged my freezing fingers and tried to restart circulation.

"Everyone take off your coats! Jason, you too, bed." Hellen ushered everyone.

The majority of the kids ran upstairs. Lavender found the spot next to me. She rested her legs on my lap. "Ahh." She exhaled, closing her eyes.

"Comfortable?"

"Mm."

It was silent until Lavender took a small breath. "What's going on with you and Nathaniel?"

187

I was surprised. "Huh?"

"You heard me."

I shook my head, even though her eyes remained shut. "Nothing. I just think that we were something that wasn't meant to really happen." I only heard her even breathing and she didn't respond.

Thirty - One

"Wake up, wake up, wake up, wake up, wake up!" Someone's voice rang through the air, followed by running feet. I groaned, rolling over and tucking my head under my pillow. I learned to hate Christmas by the time I was thirteen. All of the gifts were from, again, supermarkets or big-box stores. And even though there was a tag that noted whether it was for a certain gender or age, it was never something you even wished for. Don't get me wrong – I was thankful. But the gifts were never personal. I squeezed my eyes shut, willing my brain to slip into the blissful moments of sleep, when my door swung open and a body leapt onto me. I let out a gasp and stared up at Jason.

He grinned. "Get up! it's Christmas!"

"I'll get up soon," I mumbled, rolling back over.

"When's soon?"

I thought. "One hundred and twenty minutes." I hoped he didn't know how many minutes were in an hour.

A girl's voice suddenly appeared. "Which is two hours, Jason. Come on, Lindsey. Hellen is making hot chocolate."

I peeked from under my covers and spotted Ray leaning against the doorway. Her brown hair hung loosely around her shoulders. She glanced at me with a look of "nice try."

I looked back and forth between the both of them, and finally sighed. "Fine." I slid out of bed, watching Jason jumping up and down excitedly. I felt bad for him; it was his first year in Foster Care. I heard his parents had died suddenly in a car accident, and he of course, was used to the normal Christmas. Of course, I personally had no idea what took place on a "normal" Christmas morning. All my information came from movies. Jason had no idea what was coming. I brushed my teeth and slipped on a sweatshirt. I ambled down the steps and peered into the living room. About seven kids sat around, staring at the empty tree. I raised my eyebrows. That was strange. Usually there was at least one gift for everyone.

Hellen came in behind me and grinned at everyone. How could she be smiling at this moment? "I have a surprise for you all."

"Does this involve gifts?" Ray asked sarcastically.

The door swung open, and in came a man dressed as Santa. "Ho, ho, ho! I heard some very special children lived here, and my elves forgot their house!" All the kids jumped up, gasping at the visitor. Santa laughed, shutting the door and making his way into the living room. He sat on the couch, and everyone gathered around him. I stood from the staircase, smiling at the surprise and watching their excitement.

Santa chuckled and reached into a large brown bag. He dug around and pulled out a red package decorated with bows. "Where's Jason?"

My eyes darted to Jason and he grinned, holding out his hand. "Here!"

Santa smiled, handing Jason his package. The same process continued. Santa dug in his bag, calling out a name and handing them their gift. Every child got at least two or three gifts. I eventually sat on the stairs, watching the festivities.

"Where's Lindsey?"

I looked at Santa.

He saw my expression. "What, you thought Santa forgot about you?" I laughed and got up. Santa handed me a large box, winking as he did so. I crossed the room to the couch. The kids yelled in excitement to each other. Placing a finger to the edge, I ripped the wrapping paper off. When it was completely exposed, I opened the cardboard box. I opened the box within it and found it was filled with green and red tissue paper. I glanced to Santa, and he shrugged with a smile. Directing my attention back to the box, I pulled out the paper one by one. Soon, the paper littered the floor. I saw a simple piece of paper lying on the bottom. One sentence was written on it, where it told me to leave the house and turn left for thirty steps. And dress warm. I kid you not. I looked at Hellen and she shrugged also. Did she know what this was? I got up immediately and slipped into boots. I left without a goodbye and peered at my map.

I turned left at my sidewalk and continued for thirty steps. I laughed to myself at the specificity. I counted my steps, and slowed once I came up to a stop light. The streets were somewhat deserted except for a few lonesome cars. It was only around eight. Way too early. I squinted my eyes, covering my mouth as I spotted another package in a tree. I looked around, expecting to see the culprit behind it. Maybe Lavender? I made my way to it and started to hop. Oh, the life of a short person. After many attempts, I managed to get the package to fall to the ground. I opened it with trembling fingers. The mixture of adrenaline and cold was affecting me. Inside lay another piece of paper. It told me to continue straight for one hundred steps. I snorted, but did as told. One hundred steps later, I found myself outside a store located on 70th street.

A man stood there, holding a box. He looked at me, studying my face. "Are you Lindsey?" I nodded, and he handed it to me. I watched him walk off without another word, and I opened the box. Again, I found another piece of paper with a direction. It told me to walk four blocks. I did and slowed once I realized where I was. It was Central Park, and lying on the snow ahead was the largest box of all. A breath hitched in my throat, a certain horror dawning on me. Was this Walter? Playing a joke on me? Was he luring me into another trap? I took tentative steps toward the box. The snow crunched under my feet with every step. I reached it and kneeled. My name was printed in perfect script on the box. A big bow was wrapped around it, coming from the bottom up. I undid the soft ribbon first. I carefully let it fall to the ground. I then ripped the paper off. Inside the box was

191

more tissue paper. But this time, a large yellow folder was on the bottom. I took it out and spotted a bench up ahead. I made my way to it and sat down. I opened it cautiously, hoping it wasn't a bomb of some sorts. That would seriously dim the Christmas mood. A breeze blew across Central Park, blowing my wispy hair into my face. I shivered. I pulled out another single piece of paper. I was confused at first, but I dropped everything once I realized what the paper said.

Day release.

Lucy Eleanor Platt, and David Platt would like to take custody of Lindsey Jennifer Garland for three hours and forty-five minutes. (3h-45m) on December the 27th.

I looked up, parting my lips. Why would they want to meet me? Snow started to fall. It added to the already white ground.

"Lindsey." A voice came from behind. I jumped slightly and whipped around. Nathaniel stood there, surprisingly, dressed from neck down in a Santa suit.

My eyes widened. "You were Santa?"

Nathaniel smiled and nodded. "I was also the anonymous person who donated all those ornaments and Christmas decorations."

I smiled wider. "Really? And all those gifts today "

"I bought them. Also got each of their names and their wish list from Hellen."

I stepped closer, clutching the day release form. "That's amazing."

"Did you open your present?" He asked, looking at my hand.

I nodded. "You obviously knew what it was."

192

Nathaniel nodded and stepped closer to me. "Do you remember that adoption day, when that woman sat down and started talking to you?"

I nodded.

"Well, after Hellen interrupted, she stopped me and asked me about you. I gave her the information she needed, and she later asked for a Day-release form."

I made a face. "Then why is the date written for December?"

"I don't know. I guess they waited to fill it out." His eyes searched my face. "Are you excited?"

I took one more step, closing the space between us. "Too excited. It's amazing, actually. I might get adopted." My brain was doing flips. Was this a dream? Nathaniel softly smiled and gently moved a stray strand of hair away from my face. He kept his fingers on my cheek, his eyes slowly blinking. I closed my eyes, enjoying the feeling of his hands on me.

"Nathaniel," I whispered.

"Yes?"

I reopened my eyes. "Kiss me."

A quick flash of shock registered across his face, until he grinned one of his boyish grins and slowly leaned in to plant a soft, well-deserved kiss on my lips. Christmas may be one of my favorite holidays now.

Thirty - Two

"Spin! Spin, spin!" I giggled, watching Nindsey spin around as he followed my command, (and also the treat that was pinched between my index finger and thumb.) Arms suddenly looped from behind me, gently picking me up with strength I still didn't understand.

I laughed. "Nathaniel! Let me go!"

I heard him chuckle as he nuzzled my neck. "You're just so irresistible."

Chills ran up my spine. "Why, thank you."This was my moment. I reached behind me and jabbed his sides with my pointer finger. He dropped me immediately.

"Ow," I jokingly muttered, rubbing my lower back.

He had a strange look on his face. "What did you just do?"

"I tased you." I looked up at him.

"What does that mean?"

I triumphantly sighed. "Never mind. It's too challenging for your brain to understand." Nathaniel grinned and rushed toward me. I squealed and tried to stand, but it was too late. He grabbed my waist, and pinned me on the floor by my wrists. Straddling me by his legs, he started to tickle me. I laughed immediately, almost screaming, until tears leaked out of my eyes.

The front door opened, and in came Lavender. "What is going on in here?"

"Lavender!" I sputtered. "Help me."

"I swear, you two are going to get me arrested one day. People were staring at our door like someone was getting murdered." She dropped her purse on the table and crossed the kitchen. Nathaniel reluctantly got off me and leaned against the wall. Lavender disappeared from the room, and I exhaled, covering my eyes with my hands. My body was tingling.

"How are you doing?"

I peeked from my fingers. "I was just attacked. What do you think?"

He chuckled. "No, I mean how are you doing in general? Like with Hellen and the release day?"

I sat up, leaning against the couch. "Good. Hellen's the same old, same old. The release day..." I trailed off. He waited.

"I'm nervous," I admitted. "What if they don't like me?"

He scooted closer, caressing my face with his finger. "Who wouldn't like Lindsey Garland? It's impossible."

"I'm having the dreams again."

Nathaniel's romantic smile was replaced with a concerned look. "About-" I nodded.

He sighed. "Why do you think that's happening?"

That was it. I didn't want to; I really didn't want to, but I had to. "I came down one morning, and he was in my kitchen. Everyone else was out-"

"Did he hurt you?" he immediately asked, searching my cheeks and neck with his hands.

I smiled, taking his hands and pulling them off. "I'm fine. It's just—he's back." Nathaniel stood and held out a hand to me. I let him pull me up, and he guided me to the door with his clasped hand.

"Where are we going?" I asked.

"The police station," he replied nonchalantly.

~~~~~~~

I watched Nathaniel's gestures as I sat clasping and unclasping my hands. The nerves pulsed through me as I studied the nods from the policeman. Moments later, Nathaniel's head swiveled toward me.

He nodded, and I stood. Walking across the fancy marble floors, I reached the 6-foot man.

He presented me with a warm smile, wrinkles joining at the forehead. "Hello, Lindsey. My name is Officer Steve. Would you mind joining me in my office?" Wonderful. I had to talk about it now? But I nodded anyway, and glanced at Nathaniel.

"Alone." Steve cleared his throat. I should've known. I think Nathaniel knew too, because he offered me a knowing smile.

Steve gestured forward. "If you'd follow me, please." As I followed Steve, I glanced back at Nathaniel. He was making his way to the waiting chairs. I noticed his back muscles tensing as he took each step. Still following the policeman, I watched the buzz that took place. A woman was biting her nails and crying about something. A man, clearly agitated, tapped his foot and drummed his fingers against the wooden coffee table. The last one I caught a glimpse of was a little girl, sitting by herself. A policeman stood nearby, murmuring to another officer.

"Right in here, Ms. Garland." Officer Steve interrupted my thoughts. He was standing outside an office door. I walked in, taking a seat. Apart from the hastily stacked papers, the room was quite neat,

Steve closed the door and sat across from me, folding his hands over his desk. A document sat in front of him. "Now, can you tell me how you know Walter?" I hesitated. Was this going to do more harm than good?

He noticed my hesitance. "Lindsey, it's okay. We're going to keep you safe." We're going to keep you safe. I took a breath, and told him everything. From what I'd done, (including that my acts were purely defensive), to the kidnapping, and the recent bacon events. And the threats. Who could forget the threats? When I was finished, I watched his facial expressions carefully. They were hard to study. Just a blank face and a few nods.

He was quiet. "And you didn't tell anyone about the kidnapping?"

I hung my head. "No. I didn't think it was-"

"That is a serious crime. Not to mention trespassing in a government-owned facility." He shook his head. "And what happened after he hit you?" Something dropped in my stomach. I had wanted so badly to admit it, but could that lead to Hellen's arrest?

Officer Steve noticed my troubled expression, and his expression softened. "You need to tell me, so I can file a proper report and line up the exact offenses and facts."

Offenses. That word rang in my head. But quicker than I'd expected, it fell out. "I was kicked out of my foster house."

He looked taken back. "By Walter?"

"No." I shook my head, taking a steady breath for what I was about to admit. "It was Hellen, my foster mom." A quick intake of breath escaped from his lips, and he scribbled something on his paper.

~~~~~~~~~

Nathaniel jumped up as he spotted me. "So? What happened?"

"Walter is going to be arrested."

He smiled. "That's good, right?"

I rubbed my forehead. "I told him about Hellen." I spilled almost immediately, the guilt building up.

"What she did was illegal, Lindsey."

"That doesn't make it any better." I stared at the floor.

He was quiet, until he gently raised my chin. "Hey, I'm sorry. I know it must've been hard to do that."

"What if she gets arrested?" I asked, concern lacing through my voice.

"I'll guess we'll find out," Nathaniel murmured, motioning to the door. The ride back to my house was almost silent. I was scared of the fate that awaited Hellen. It'd be completely my fault, and I didn't know if I could live with that. But as Nathaniel rolled up to the house, it was the same boring project-house that stood there daily. Nathaniel parked and got out. I watched him cross to my side and open my door. Words. I couldn't make any. He put a hand to the small of my back and guided me into the house.

As soon as I entered, I called out, "Hellen?"

"Yes?" she called back.

I let out a sigh. She hadn't been arrested.

"See? She's fine." Nathaniel faced me, kissing my forehead softly. I nodded. The guilt would've been too much.

"Wait, aren't you meeting Lucy?" He suddenly pulled away.

I gasped. I had completely forgotten. "Can you drive me?"

"Of course."

~~~~~~~~

I walked into the coffee shop and looked around. The smell of coffee and pastries wafted around me.

"Lindsey?" I looked to a familiar, pretty brunett whom I assumed to be Lucy.

I smiled. "Hi."

"David is at the table. Come on over." Lucy put an arm around my shoulders. A man, also brunet, sat at a table while squinting at a menu. He looked up and smiled immediately. He wore a dark suit with a red tie.

"You must be Lindsey." He shook my hand. "I'm David. Lucy has told me much about you." David glanced at Lucy, "You weren't kidding. She is beautiful."

My cheeks warmed. "Thank you."

"Sit down." He pulled out the chair for me. Lucy sat down next to him and put her hand in his.

"So, you're eighteen?" David asked, folding the menu in front of him and getting right to it.

"Seventeen."

He nodded. "Great. Do you have any plans for college?"

"I was thinking about NYU, but it's super hard to get into it. Only a few slots are available," I explained, sitting up straighter.

"Well, I know you're a bright girl, and we'd love to help you get there." David said, which made me feel comforted. "We live in Chicago, however."

Something inside me paused. "Oh. You must've driven far."

"It was worth it," Lucy interrupted. "We have Mariella at home with my mother."

I had forgotten. Lucy had adopted Mariella. I smiled. "How is she?"

"We love her," Lucy cooed. "She's an amazing girl." The next hour and a half were pleasant, amusing conversations. David was very nice, and I liked them both. They asked about the foster house, school, and friends. It was the most comfortable I've ever felt with adults.

"And no one has ever wanted to adopt you before?" David asked.

I swallowed, taking a sip of my iced-coffee. "No. They haven't."

"I know Lucy was in the foster system until she was eighteen, so it sounds hard. I'm sorry you've had to go through that," David empathized.

"Speaking of foster systems, the time has flown by." Lucy grimaced, checking her wristwatch. Already? "We should get you back."

I shooed it away. "My boyfriend can bring me back." And I pulled my phone out, texting Nathaniel. He answered almost immediately, telling me he'd be there in five.

"We'd love to meet him." Lucy smiled, looking genuinely interested. Exactly five minutes later, Nathaniel walked in. I waved at him, standing. He paused, looking unsure whether he should intrude, but I waved once more to come. They'd said themselves they wanted to meet him.

Lucy stood, along with David, and shook Nathaniel's hand. "It's so nice to meet you, Nathaniel."

I'd remembered they'd met at the house on adoption day. "You too, ma'am." Nathaniel reached over to David, and introduced himself also.

"Well, we'll see you soon, honey," Lucy said, surprising me with a hug.

"Really?" I asked, against her neck.

She pulled away. "Of course! We're setting it up as soon as we get home."

I nodded, smiling. So they weren't done with me.

David hugged me, telling me it was a great time. They gathered their things, and Lucy grazed her thumb against my forearm. "See you soon, hon." And that was that. They both waved and put their arms around each other's waist.

"So, how'd it go?" Nathaniel asked, raising his eyebrows.

I grinned after them. "Amazing."

~~~~~~~~~

Nathaniel, again, walked me to the door and inside. We shut the door, and the usual chatter from the kids greeted us.

"I'm really happy for you, Linds," Nathaniel whispered, looking at me in a way that I loved.

"I am too-" a knock interrupted my reply, and I frowned at him. Holding up a finger, I crossed the room to the door and opened it.

A small gasp escaped my lips as I looked at the two policemen standing on the doorstep. "Hello. Is Hellen O'Brier here?" I barely nodded before they came in and shut the door themselves.

Hellen came down the stairs, holding a laundry basket. "Who's at the door-" she stopped short once she got a glance at our visitors. "Hello. Is there something I can help you with?"

The policemen shared a look, and the male cleared his throat. "Actually, there is."

He pulled out handcuffs, and her eyes widened. Nathaniel stood to the side in alarm, barely moving. "Hellen O'Brier, you are under arrest for inexcusable acts of the banning of a child owned by the government." *Under arrest. Owned by the government.* These two sentences rang in my head.

The entire room fell silent as Hellen simply dropped her basket. She walked to the policeman. He cuffed her while reciting, "You have the right to remain silent. Anything you say..." His words became fuzzy as my vision was enveloped in tears and shock.

Thirty - Three

I was quiet as I watched various women and men enter our house. Each social worker held official bundles of papers snug under their arms as they crouched down to a child that was assigned to them at the moment of their loss of family. I pulled my jacket tighter around my shoulders and my knees higher up on the steps. I painfully watched Jason's bottom lip quiver in fear and confusion. He didn't understand what was happening. I couldn't help but feel it was all my fault. I squeezed my eyes shut, rubbing my temples and trying to neglect the swooping memories from last night

"Where are you bringing Hellen?" I asked frantically, staring wide-eyed at the policewoman in front of me.

She sighed, bringing her hands to her hips. "Miss, I'm going to have to ask you to calm down."

I felt Nathaniel's hands reach my shoulders as he whispered into my ear. "Lindsey, back up a bit." Frustration screamed inside of me, but I did as suggested and stepped back slightly. The woman seemed to drop her hitched shoulders a fraction and I widened the condensed space between us.

"What is going to happen to Hellen?" I asked again, my tone softening. My gaze flickered to the living room where the children sat.

She sighed, blinking. "Ms. O'Brier will be transported to the police station, where our detectives will question her."

I nodded. *"Okay, then what will happen to our house?"*

She eyed the living room. "I'm not authorized to give you any information-"

"Please." I begged with my eyes.

After many seconds of contemplation, she nodded and motioned to the kitchen. Nathaniel and I did as told and we joined in a circle.

"Your foster home will have its authority revoked, and every child will be transported to another house. Separately," she explained, pressing her lips together.

"Ms. Garland?" A man dressed in a suit tapped my shoulder, awakening me from my trance.

"Yes?" I asked, standing up.

"Are you okay?" he asked, leaning closer.

My lips parted. No. "Yes. Where is Andrew?" Andrew, my assigned social worker, was nowhere present.

"I will be taking you to him. He is meeting us at Town Hall." He placed a hand on my back and guided me to the door.

I stopped. "The Town Hall? On 43rd street?"

He nodded.

"Why are we going there?"

He smiled and continued to the door. "You'll see."

~~~~~~~~~

"Lindsey," Andrew walked toward me, his arms outstretched.

I returned a small hug and gave him a questionable eyebrow. "Why am I here?"

"Follow me," Andrew said, walking across the marble-based floor. Our relationship was something between friendly and business. I did and entered a conference room. Something jumped in my stomach as I faced Lucy and David. They were in deep discussion with another man, papers laid out on the table. Andrew brought me to them and sat me down across from the adults.

"Hi, sweetie." Lucy reached for my hand and squeezed.

I swallowed. "If you don't mind me asking, what am I doing here?" Andrew sat next to me while Lucy and David smiled at each other.

203

"Well," David started, "because your house has been decertified, and the children are being moved to other homes, it would subtract months of preparation of being able to adopt you."

Adopt you.

Lucy grinned. "So, if you'd like, we're offering you a place in our family."

It was as if everyone around me was obliterated. That one sentence caused the most happiness I had ever felt. I had been waiting to hear that for twelve years. And it'd finally come. Tears erupted and rolled down my cheeks. I nodded, unable to speak.

Lucy laughed softly as she rubbed my arm. "I'm so excited to welcome you into our home, honey."

David smiled. "We are going to have a beautiful future." He cleared his throat. "There is one thing." My eyes met his.

"We live in Chicago." He said in a tone I could identify easily. A tone that stressed, *Do you really want to do this? Do you want to risk the things that you'd be leaving?*

I nodded, taking the pen and carefully signing my name on the dotted line.

~~~~~~~~~

I was walking on clouds as I noted the beautiful New York air around me. The cold nipped at exposed skin, so I snuggled in tighter to the new cashmere scarf Lucy had given me. Everything seemed clearer today; the naked trees, the frozen lakes, and the buildings seemed to have a glow. I turned left at the sidewalk, making my way to Lavender's. I was still in too much shock. By the time I arrived to Lavender's, I climbed up the steps in a happy daze.I reached the door, thinking of my new family. My new sister, who still doesn't know of my adoption. We were keeping it a surprise. The door swung open, interrupting my elated thoughts. Nathaniel stood there, a soft smile on his face. At that moment, everything dropped inside of me. Nathaniel. How did I manage to forget about him? He still didn't know about Lucy and David. Time stopped for a moment while I started to rethink my choices.

He grabbed me in a bear hug, mumbling in my ear, "Lindsey, I hope you're okay." His smell overwhelmed me. Mint and clean dryer sheets. I squeezed tighter, turning my head to the side against his chest. He released me, trailing me inside. Lavender spotted me and rushed over to pull me into a hug. Lavender. She didn't know. They thought they were comforting me about the house. About Hellen. The adoption was soon a thought existing in the back of my mind as I hugged my best friend.

"We have news," Lavender said when she released me.

I looked at them both.

Nathaniel leaned against the counter. "I was alerted about Walter."

My stomach tightened at the mention of his name.

"He's in prison."

I nodded. "For how long?"

"They called it a, 'B Violent Felony,' which means that he'll serve up to 5-25 years in prison. He is serving 15 years. You'll be long gone by then."

Long gone? I frantically asked myself. *Did he know?* "Long gone?" I asked, trying to sound nonchalant.

He chuckled. "Well, yeah, you'll be thirty-two years old."

I exhaled. "Oh." I was signed for leaving after the New Year's holiday. Lucy and David thought it'd be a good idea to finish off the year and semester in school so I'd have time to say my goodbye's. I had exactly two days. It was the 29th.

"And I have one more thing," Nathaniel added, averting his gaze to the countertop.

"What's that?" I asked, watching his actions.

"It's about Hellen. Because her case is similar to your report, we were also alerted of Hellen's whereabouts." Nathaniel paused. "Her license to foster has been suspended and she is serving one month in prison."

My mouth dropped open. "She's in prison?!"

Lavender reached me, slinging an arm over my shoulders. "It's okay."

I looked at Lavender, the one person in the world who had been there for me through everything, and the guilt settled. "Can I talk to you for a second?" Lavender half-nodded. I grabbed her forearm and led her outside. I shut the door.

She looked at me. "Why are we outside?"

"Because I don't want him to hear," I whispered.

Lavender cocked her head. "What's up?"

"I got adopted today," I softly said, unable to keep it in anymore.

Her eyes lit up and screeched, "Are you serious?!"

"Shh!" I placed a finger to my lips.

Lavender jumped at me, hugging me hard. "That's amazing!" she whispered.

I smiled, leaning into the hug.

She leaned back. "Wait, why don't you want Nathaniel to know?"

I lowered my eyes. "Because they live in Chicago."

I didn't see her reaction. I only saw her jumping fade.

After moments of silence, she finally said, "Lindsey, you have to tell him."

"I don't want to."

"You're going to have to eventually." Lavender chuckled, smiling. "I am so happy for you. I love you."

I hugged her hard, mumbling. "I love you too." I was going to miss her so much.

~~~~~~~~

I packed the last suitcase, looking around the bare room that I'd called mine for the last twelve years. I sat on the squeaky bed, memories flooding the scene.

"Hellen?" I ask, dragging the ll. "Is this my room?" I glance at the bare room, noticing that the walls most certainly were not pink, and my dressers were most certainly not white. Where are all my things? I wonder.

Hellen comes over to me, and places a hand on my face. "Yes, sweetie. You'll stay here until you've gotten adopted."

"What does that mean?"

"It means this is your house, until someone wants you to come to their house. For good." She explains, smiling like this makes sense.

"So this isn't my house forever?" I ask, still not comprehending what this nice lady is telling me.

"No, honey. Not forever. Think of it as a pit-stop."

I nod, thinking I understand. "Okay."

A new one swooped in before I knew it.

"You have to be quiet!" I whisper to the girl whose name symbolizes a strange plant. I grab her hand in mine and carefully tip-toe along the wall.

"What is this place?" she asks, her voice booming.

"Shh!" I say, and continue up the steps. "It's a pit-stop."

"What's a pit-stop?"

"Shh!"

I lead her into my room, and close the door.

Lavender looks around. "Is this your bedroom?"

"I guess." I shrug, plopping on the floor. I am sharing with another girl, but she rarely speaks to me.

"Do you want to play Barbies?" she asks, sitting down and giggling.

207

I glance around the room. I had no Barbies. "Let's play something else."

"Do you want to draw? I'm real good at drawing." She grins, smoothing down her pigtail.

I look at my hair, which is nowhere near the perfection of hers. There are just so many kids in the pit-stop that Hellen is sometimes overwhelmed. And even though I ask every morning, she never does braid it. "Nah."

And it's gone. I sighed, patting my suitcase next to me. This house may never regain its prior position, and it could be bulldozed down for all I know. But it's still hard to part. I had to see Hellen.

~~~~~~~~~

I entered the prison, shuddering. Teenagers and adults sat grumpily, glaring at nothing in general. Walking up to a woman in a booth, I cleared my throat, "Hi."

"Hi, miss. Is there something you need?" she asked, chomping on gum.

"I'd like to visit Hellen O'Brier."

The woman nodded as she typed on a computer. "I'll call her in. What's your name, Miss?"

"Lindsey Garland."

She typed again and signaled to the sheet in front of me. "Please write the time, your name, and the person you're visiting." I did and let a policeman lead me into a room. Men and women sat in a glass booth accompanied with a phone. He led me to the end, and I smiled as I saw Hellen. She did also, and signaled for me to pick up the phone.

I sat and picked it up. "Hi."

"Hi, hon." She grinned, stress wrinkles clearly visible on her face. "Happy New Years, by the way."

208

"I need to tell you something," I quickly said, watching her adjust her seating.

Hellen half-nodded.

"I got adopted."

Her face brightened. "That's wonderful news, Lindsey."

"And I want to apologize for-"

She shook her head. "You have nothing to apologize for. I pushed you out of the house illegally." Hellen paused, shaking. "I deserve this. And you deserve a new life."

A tear rolled down. "I want to thank you for everything you've done. I still remember the first time I came to the foster home, and you tried to explain everything to me."

Hellen smiled at the memory she was picturing. "I remember."

"When are you leaving?" she asked.

My lips parted. "Tomorrow."

"Wow." Hellen grinned. "Where are you going?"

"Chicago."

"You know I used to live there." Hellen laughed.

"Really?"

We laughed as she told stories of her mischievous self.

"I should probably go," I finally said, avoiding her eyes. I didn't want to stay for long.

"Yeah." She exhaled. "You're going to have an amazing future."

I nodded and hung up the phone.

I pushed myself up and offered her one last smile. Even through everything, I was going to miss her. Even through the bickering, she still meant something. I made my way out of the waiting room, pulling my hat on when I remembered something. I stopped, wondering whether this was a good idea. And finally, I turned myself around and headed back to the counter.

"Back again?" The clerk asked, still chomping on that piece of gum.

I nodded. "I was wondering if you had Walter Drake imprisoned here?"

She turned toward her computer and typed in the name. "Yes. We do. Would you like to see him too?"

I wrote in my name, next to his, and the date. "Yes, please." The woman made another call and pointed me into a different room on the right. I followed her finger, and opened the door. Walter sat in the first booth, a sick grin plastered onto his face. I sat down, letting the sick feelings pool in. I didn't care. I had to do this. Grabbing the phone, I listened for him to speak first.

"Lindsey," he purred, chuckling slightly. "Look where I am!" I didn't answer.

"This is because of you." Walter's face turned hard, and he leaned forward.

"No," I calmly said. "You've done this to yourself."

He smirked. "Don't worry, when I get out-"

"I'll be long gone," I finished. Courage was building up. The glass barrier between us was satisfying.

He mockingly smiled, leaning back. "So, to what do I owe the pleasure?"

"I just wanted to see your rotting face behind this glass, and me, free as a bird on the other side." I laughed at myself.

"What, you've got nothing else to do? You come here, alone if I might add, just to toy with me? Can I remind you about your lack of family?" He paused, smiling. "Oh, that's right, you have none."

I shrugged. I thought of Lavender. Of Nathaniel. Of Lucy and David. "That's what you think. Goodbye, Walter." I hung up, catching a glimpse of his confused expression while I walked away from the man who once gave me nightmares.

~~~~~~~~

210

"Where have you been all day?" Nathaniel asked me, leaning forward and kissing my cheek. "It's almost twelve." I almost didn't hear him over the commotion in Lavender's apartment. She was having, for the first time, a New Year's Party.

"Sorry, I had to finish some unfinished business." I grinned. After visiting my two prison mates, I took a short trip to Central Park. I needed some alone time, and though, yes, it was kind of creepy, it was just what I needed. The lights and music from Rockefeller Center reached the Park. Out of all my time in New York, I had gone only once to the ball drop. It was crazy and way too public for me, so Lavender and I usually stayed at her apartment. But this year, her apartment was filled with people. It was so crowded that the door was left open because we all could've suffocated from the lack of space.

"Uh oh." Nathaniel chuckled. "Do you want a drink?"

"No, thanks." I yelled over the noise, shaking my head. I checked the clock—five minutes to twelve. I should've told him by then. I needed to tell him. I was leaving in less than twenty-four hours.

"Nathaniel." I placed my hand on his arm. "I need to talk to you."

He nodded. "Talk."

"No, outside." I watched him. Nathaniel looked confused, but followed me outside anyway. The noise level was worse outside, so we descended to the back area on the banister. I blinked up at his friendly face, wanting more than anything for him to come with me. I was being selfish, I decided. He not only deserved to know, but I shouldn't be asking to have the best of both worlds.

It was quieter there and I started to speak, but was cut off by everyone's screams, "10!" *Already?!* I started to panic.

"9!"

"What's wrong?" Nathaniel asked me, searching me with his eyes

"8!"

The tears started to come. "I need to tell you something."

"7!"

"What? I can't hear you," Nathaniel yelled back, leaning closer.

"6, 5!" The numbers descended as I searched for the words.

"4!"

"I got adopted," I finally said.

"3!"

His face lit up. "That's terrific!"

"2!"

I shook my head. "I leave tomorrow."

"1!"

"What?" His face dropped.

"Happy New Year!"

Thirty - Four

I pinched the bed fabric, rubbing it between my fingers. Glancing around the hotel room, I rubbed my tear-stricken eyes. Lucy and David were meeting me at noon, which, I thought, checking my phone, was approximately four hours away. Nathaniel hadn't talked to me since the night before. Did I really want to go to Chicago? Maybe I hadn't thought it over enough. Did I really want this? Yes, I'd gain a family. But at the same time, I'd lose my New York life. The only thing I'd ever really known. Not to mention Lavender. And Nate.

If he still is yours, a voice nagged at me. *Right. If he still is mine to lose.*

My bags and overall belongings were packed in tight, already heading to Chicago in a U-Haul. All I currently had was a backpack Lavender had given me for a birthday once, filled with clothes, phone, and a book. It was time to leave, with or without a goodbye. And I knew just the place to spend my last few hours. I sighed, resting on the large boulder Nathaniel and I had found on our first date. It was a dark, gray day. It was one of those times when the weather wasn't even sure of itself. Would it be snow? Or snow mixed with rain? I let the cool breeze blow back my hair, pulling my coat tighter around myself. It was cold. I heard faint crunching behind me, but didn't turn around. Even though this part of the park was usually vacant, there were always some joggers lurking.

"I knew you'd be here." A familiar, deep voice came from behind.

I parted my lips, still not facing the visitor I'd been hoping for all morning. "It's calming."

The crunches came closer. "Tell me about it."

I closed my eyes, allowing my emotions to run free. I felt the cold atmosphere and listened to New York's sirens and horns. My five senses went into overdrive. "It feels like home."

I breathed in deeply, continuing. "It also smells good. In the park, I mean."

A low chuckle erupted from behind. It was closer.

"And I love it," I finished. Finally, I opened my eyes and found him standing next to the boulder. He was staring out onto the water in front of me. His hands were tucked into his front jeans pockets, and he wore a gray hooded sweatshirt. He was also wearing one of my favorite blue beanies. It was soft and smelled like him.

"Nate, I'm sorry." I whispered, staring out over the frozen water.

"I know." Nathaniel jumped with ease onto the tall rock and sat next to me. "But how I reacted was wrong. And I'm sorry."

"You shouldn't be sorry," I said, ashamed of myself. "I should've told you as soon as I found out. But I waited until the last possible second—literally." I managed a small laugh.

"But you were scared." Nathaniel seemed to finish for me, as if reading my mind. I watched him continue to stare at the water's edge.

"And I know what that feels like," he said, looking down.

Nathaniel finally met my eyes and caressed my cheek softly. "Lindsey, you have to listen to me." I waited. The more I looked at him, the more I wanted to stay.

"You've wanted this for so long, and I want you to be happy." Nathaniel looked deeper into my eyes. "But I'm happy with you." A tear formed like glass on my eye. He firmly shook his head. "You want a family...you need a family." He paused, a look of pain flashing across his face, but it disappeared in an instant. "Don't let me keep you here."

"Nathaniel-"

"Don't," he said more firmly.

214

"But I'll miss you," I whispered, gently taking his hand on my face.

"We'll text, call, anything. And we'll see each other again." Nathaniel half-smiled.

"Long-distance relationships never work out."

He laughed. "How do you know that?"

I shrugged, sniffling. "Movies."

He laughed harder, squeezing my hand. "I feel like all your knowledge comes from movies."

"It probably does." I laughed.

Nathaniel tucked a piece of fallen hair behind my ear. "We'll figure it out. And I'll come visit."

I nodded, another tear falling. Nathaniel wiped it away.

"Nathaniel, I'm scared," I revealed, sobbing into his shoulder. My breathing escaped in hitched breaths as I cried.

He rubbed my back and murmured to himself. "Me too."

~~~~~~~~~

"You better call me every day," Lavender said, bumping me with her shoulder.

I laughed, taking a sip of the warm tea. "You bet."

"What school are you going to?" Nathaniel asked from the living room, as he sifted through possible movies.

"I don't know yet. But apparently, it's like a real, traditional school where Lucy and David went too," I yelled back, wrapping my hands around the mug.

I heard him grunt and shook my head to Lavender. "So, tell me," I started, wiggling my eyebrows and leaning forward, "what did you say to him?"

She placed a sarcastic hand to her mouth. "What makes you think I said anything to him?"

"Because you're you," I said with a smug smile.

215

"You've got a point." Lavender returned my smile, turning around to the sink and placing her own mug in it.

I glanced at Nathaniel, who was still sorting through movies. I lowered my voice. "What did you say to him anyway?"

"That he was being a jerk and needed to think clearly." Lavender bit her lip. "Then I threw a cup of water in his face."

I laughed. "Are you serious?"

She nodded and slung an arm around my shoulders. "All for you."

"Okay, how about *Finding Nemo or Paranormal Activity 4*?" Nathaniel called from the living room, holding two movies in his hand.

"*Paranormal Activity.*"

He grinned. "That's my girl."

"Does my vote count?" Lavender asked.

"Does it have anything to do with *Finding Nemo*?" Nathaniel asked with a raised eyebrow.

"Maybe."

"Then no," he replied sweetly and threw *Finding Nemo* to the ground. "*Paranormal Activity* it is." I smiled and jumped onto the couch. Nathaniel turned on the movie and returned to the sofa. I leaned forward and he sat next to me. I rested back again, my head leaning on Nathaniel's chest and my legs spread out over Lavender's lap.

"Why am I the footrest?" She asked.

"Shh. The movie is starting." I put a finger to my lips.s

~~~~~~~~~

Although hearing the adoption speech was one of the happiest moments of my life, this could definitely register for being one of the worst. I couldn't stop crying, for one thing. Lavender hugged me while Nathaniel stood off to the side, his hands shoved into his pockets and his head bent. Lucy waited at the door, smiling sadly. I had called her asking if she could pick me up at Lavender's.

"You're going to be fine," she whispered into my ear, squeezing me. "I promise."

I nodded against her head, another tear leaking. "I love you, you know."

"I know. I love you too. Now go help your boyfriend," she added with a laugh, pushing me slightly.

I nodded, turning to Nathaniel. "You know, I'm glad you broke into my room that night."

Nathaniel laughed, shaking his head. "Now somehow, I don't think a lot of people have the experience to say that."

I grinned through my tears. "Probably not."

He stepped closer, reaching out and wiping away a tear. "I'm just happy you're actually crying."

I shoved him. "Shut up."

He grinned, letting me grab him and wrap my arms around his waist. He rested his head on my own, and rubbed my back. "We don't have much time."

"I know."

"And Lucy is watching, so I don't think I can really kiss you right now," he added with a laugh.

I looked up at him. My chin was against his chest and I whispered, winking, "Then I guess she'll have to deal with it."

Nathaniel smiled. "I was going to say that anyway."

He suddenly looked at Lucy, then at me, and shock filled his face. "Shoot. I forgot to give you something."

I raised an eyebrow, confused. "Okay?"

Nathaniel turned to Lucy. "Do you mind if I give it to her personally? It's in the house."

Lucy smiled, shaking her head slightly. "Sure, honey."

217

I was still confused. Nathaniel took my hand, leading me back to the apartment. Once inside, I looked at him, "What is it you have to give me?"

Nathaniel grinned and rushed to my lips. I jumped back slightly, unprepared for this. But all too soon, I leaned in. He pushed me against the wall as he grabbed my chin. Suddenly, Nathaniel gently picked me up by my thighs, carrying me to the kitchen. I continued to kiss him, then stopped. I laughed, "What are you doing?" Nathaniel just grinned and sat me on the counter. I wrapped my arms around his neck, leaning my forearms on his shoulders and was inches away from his face as I gazed adoringly into those emerald green eyes I loved so much.

Nathaniel smiled, leaning back. "I didn't just bring you up here for this."

"Oh, really?" I asked with a sarcastic bite. He rolled his eyes, turning and leaning behind the white kitchen counter. I watched him grab a large cardboard box, stepping back to me in two steps. I undid the cardboard folds, peering in. I wasn't sure if I wanted to nostalgically cry, or laugh in his face. I settled with a little bit of both

~~~~~~~~

I waved to Lavender and Nathaniel before getting into the car. They stood together, arms wrapped around their chests. They grinned, waving back. Believe it or not, it took a lot of my energy to convince myself to get into the car. I shut the door.

Lucy smiled at me. "Ready?"

I looked at her, smiling softly. "Ready." And I was. She put the car into drive and rolled out of the parking lot. I watched the most important people in my life until they became only a speck in the rearview mirror.

Thirty - Five

Once out of the four-door Jeep, I tentatively stepped onto the pavement driveway. Tall trees, along with cold-frosted grass stood around the semi-mansion. Four to five acres abutted the large gray house. I spotted a white barn in the distance. The sun was just starting to set

"Your house, is—um," I searched for the right word, but eventually spoke the obvious choice, "nice."

Lucy laughed, climbing out. "It's your house, too." I nodded, still trying to wrap my head around the fact that I had a house. The entire trip was filled with laughter. I felt like Lucy was a really cool girl I had met and befriended.

"We told Mariella last night and she's been dying to see you." She grinned. "She helped set up your room too."

"My room?" I asked. I'd expected to sleep in a guest bedroom or on a couch. Usually when I'd come to a new foster home, they sometimes wouldn't have rooms available in time.

"Of course, hon'!" Lucy exclaimed, coming over to me and slinging an arm around my shoulder. "What, you thought we'd stick you on the couch?" I nervously laughed and let her guide me to the brass door.

Lucy opened it, stepping in and I stepped in after her. A crystal chandelier hung from the high ceiling, and I looked around. A wooden staircase, adorned with white railings, continued underneath the chandelier. To the right, a long dining room table sat in the middle. To the left was the biggest library I've ever seen.

"Well, I'll give you a tour-"

"Lindsey!" A high-pitched voice screamed from the side and something clashed into me. A gasp escaped from me, and I looked down at a small, curly blond whose arms folded snugly around me.

"You're my sister now! Can you believe it?" Mariella yelled, bouncing back and prancing in place. No, I couldn't. I hugged her, not realizing how much I had missed her. She was always my favorite.

"Well, I'll get dinner started. We're having spaghetti and meatballs. I hope you like that, Lindsey." Lucy smiled toward me. "I know Mariella loves it."

My little sister nodded furiously.

Lucy laid a hand on her daughter's hand, playing with a piece of her blond hair. "Where's Daddy?"

Daddy? Mariella called him "Daddy"? I glanced at Mariella, expecting to see a look of confusion, but instead found a knowing nod. "He just ran out to do a night check at the barn."

Barn? Lucy saw my expression and chuckled. "We have horses. Mariella will show you tomorrow." Lucy wiggled her eyebrows at me. "So, Lindsey, do you have anything to show Mariella?"

I was still trying to grasp the fact that they had horses in their backyard, when I caught onto her expression. "Yes!"

Mariella looked up at me. "What is it?"

I shrugged, "I guess we should just check in the car." Lucy tossed me the keys. Mariella grinned, grabbing my hand and nearly flinging open the door. I jogged as she ran down the pathway and to the black Jeep. She released my hand, hopping in place and watching me struggle with the keys.

I unlocked it and reached into the back. I retrieved a cardboard box and nodded toward the house. "We should open it inside." Once inside again, I set the box carefully on the ground and watched Mariella crouch beside it. Lucy came back into the room and stopped by me. Mariella lifted the lid and gasped at what was inside. A black and white bunny popped out.

"What's his name?" she squealed, lifting her up.

I smiled to myself. "Nindsey."

After a delicious meal of spaghetti, my new family introduced me to my bedroom. The walls, painted a light blue, stretched across a forty-foot room. It came with a balcony, my own bathroom stocked with new makeup, brushes, and shampoo products. According to Lucy, it was the best makeup on the market. Like I'd know. But when they finally showed me my walk-in closet, adorned with new clothes, I nearly cried. Lucy had bought me the types of clothes that Lavender and I drooled over. David had selected a black plasma screen TV and had it perched in front of my bed. The bed, dressed in white and blue sheets and pillows, sat on a stepped-ledge.

"Alright. Here we are." David said the next morning, pulling into the school's parking lot. Wait, scratch that. *It was barely a school*, I thought as I stared wide eyed at the dark-brick exquisite building in front of me. I watched students amble around Windsley Prep. They talked and laughed with their friends.

"It's great here, you'll see." Lucy had squeezed my arm, before opening her door. Mariella was to be dropped off at school at 9:30, and it was currently 8:00. Another thing that was different from New York: the times were something I'd have to get used to. In New York, school began at ___ and finished at___.Here, we started at 8:10 and finished school at around 3:00. After entering the building, I gaped at the number of awards on the wall. Honor roll, various athletic awards, and even cooking awards hung neatly on the red bulletin board. Now, I wasn't sure if I was being dramatic or not, but it seemed like everywhere I looked someone's eyes were on me. Or maybe not me, but Lucy and David. Kids were looking at them like they were some sort of royalty. I'd have to ask someone about that. The whole staring-thing started to unnerve me. I was already nervous enough. I wore a casual dress I had found in the closet, and I started to rethink my options when I glanced at everyone else and their clothing option. The pairs of jeans blended together in one big swirl. Nerves started to rise in my throat. I clutched my backpack straps tight and followed Lucy and David around the corner. We ended up in a large office, a framed portrait of a man hanging above the door. A secretary glanced at the visitors and stood up immediately.

"Mr. and Mrs. Platt! Hi, how are you?" she asked, smoothing down her uncontainable head of red curls.

Lucy smiled politely. "I'm great, Fran. Is Steve here?"

"Right in his office—he's expecting you." David nodded and let Lucy lead the way. He placed a hand on my shoulder, guiding me.

The same man I had just seen in the picture sat at a desk, typing away. He looked up immediately. "Lucy, David! How nice to see you again!" Lucy and David seemed to be familiar faces in the halls of Windsley Prep.

The man, presumably Steve, stood up and walked around his desk to shake their hands. He turned to me. "And you must be Lindsey. It's so nice to meet you. I'm the principal of Windsley Prep."

I smiled, shaking his firm hand.

"I have her files all ready." He released my hand and retreated behind his desk, grabbing a manila folder. "Lindsey, you're ready to go," Steve started, "but first, I'm going to call up Mandi. She's the same age as you, and she'll be shadowing you for the day. We want you to be as comfortable as possible." I nodded and watched him cross the room and dial a number on the conference phone.

"Hi, Barbara. Can you please send Mandi Williams to the office?" A pause. "Alright, thanks." He said into the phone and hung up. "She'll be here any moment."

"Will Lindsey receive her schedule?" David asked, straightening his tie.

"Ah, yes." Steve picked up a slip from the desk and handed it to me.

222

I glanced at my classes. Spanish (R-3B), AP History(R-8C), Calculus (R-92D), AP English (R-46A), Lunch (Main Hall), Study Hall, (R-3B) , (R-1E) Psychology(R-32B)

The numbers and letters looked like some sort of jibberish. Steve chuckled at my expression. "Don't worry, Mandi will direct you to your classes. I have to say, for being in such a low-income school her grades were quite high." He looked at me. "I'm sure it must've been difficult to obtain your 4.0 average in such a school." I tried not to make a face. I couldn't help but feel a bit defensive. Yeah, sure the toilets were kind of scary and the text books weren't in good shape, but the teachers worked hard at what they did. It wasn't that bad. Lucy watched me and parted her lips to say something when a petite brunet entered the door.

"You wanted to see me?" she asked, her tone bored. Her dark outfit went with her hair.

"Yes. This is Lindsey Garland, a new student. I'd like you to help her throughout the day and introduce her to some people." Steve sat midway on his desk.

She looked at me, scanning my body quickly with her brown eyes. I suddenly felt self-conscious of my outfit. "Okay. Let's go."

I smiled at Lucy and David, following Mandi out the door. She led the way out of the office and turned right. I followed her and jogged to catch up.

"So, I have Spanish first period and-" She whipped around, her eyes settling on me and glaring slightly. "I don't want to be a babysitter." My mouth parted, but nothing came out. She didn't wait for a response, and she turned back around to enter a classroom. The brown lining of the doors gleamed, and I felt particularly out of place. I wondered if this type of school was like the one Nathaniel attended. I stood frozen and watched her through the door as she sat down at her desk again to return her stoical expression to the teacher.

"Thanks for the help," I muttered.

~~~~~~~~

I somehow made it to Spanish, but was completely lost for History. The bell had rung ten minutes ago. I was walking around the hallway looking like a lost explorer as I repeatedly glanced at my schedule and the golden plaque number on the brass doors. I hadn't seen Mandi since, and no one even gave me a glance. A panicky feeling settled in my stomach as I started to think of the consequences. I was once sent to the principal's office for dumping a bucket of sand on a kid's head, (I was seven), and even then I didn't get consequences.

"Lost?" A low chuckle came from a tall, blond boy in front of me. I looked up, startled, and was taken back by his piercing blue eyes. He had cropped blond hair that was more of a handsome look as opposed to a hot look. He clutched his black backpack, waiting for an answer. I grimaced, showing him my paper.

He scanned it for just a moment, then handed it back to me. "I can bring you to History right now. It's on my way. And I have two classes with you so you could just stick with me." The boy handed it back, smiling. "Aren't they supposed to give you a shadow-buddy or something?"

I smirked, taking the schedule. "Mine ditched me."

He sucked in a breath. "Oo, harsh. Well, come on. I'm Alex, by the way."

I fell in step next to him. "Lindsey. What are you doing in the hallways anyway?"

"I was training."

Alex caught my confused look and laughed, "If you're on one of the athletic teams here, you can get here early and skip at least one hour of your classes to do conditioning."

I noticed some water driblets on his hair and nodded.

224

"So where are you from?" he asked, pushing open a door and holding it for me.

"New York City."

"Oh, wow. Mostly everyone here is from here." Alex shook his head. "We never have new kids from out of state." I climbed the last step and opened the door. He motioned for me to go ahead first and I smiled. Such a gentleman—but I had mine back home. The thought of Nathaniel made my insides squirm.

"What's your elective again?" he asked me, peering at my crumbled schedule.

"Psychology...?" It came out like a question, unsure if psychology was an elective.

Alex nodded. "I have Design."

I noticed room 8C and pointed. "Is that it?"

"Yep." He strode to the door and reached for the brass doorknob.

I touched his arm. "Wait. I'm really late."

"I've got it." And he swung open the door, obviously interrupting a lecture.

Alex suddenly started to breath heavily, sputtering in between words. "Mr.-Minx-I'm-so sorry. This elderly...woman fell in the parking...lot. And Lindsey," he paused and took a deep breath, "was so kind here to stop...and...help her up."

The teacher, Mr. Minx, raised a brow. "Well, you're here now. Lindsey, right?" He held out an arm to the class. "Take a seat."

I nodded and glanced at gasping-Alex. He secretly winked and turned back to the teacher. "Thank you, sir, for understanding. I'll see you fourth period." Alex let himself out the door with more of a hope in his step. I caught him smiling. I took a free seat in the back of the class. It seemed as if I'd made a friend.

~~~~~~~~

225

"Who are your parents, again?" Alex asked me, cringing at his baloney sandwich and tossing it back in his bag.

I leaned against the tree, watching students rush by. Half the lunchroom was outside. "Lucy and David Platt."

He nearly choked on his water. "The Mr. and Mrs. Platt?" I raised an eyebrow, not catching on.

Alex started to chuckle. "What, you don't know what your parents have done for this school? They're legendary."

"How so?" I asked, taking a bite of my apple. Wait, shouldn't I have known how my own parents were legendary? I chewed hard. The whole blending-in-thing was already failing. I didn't want to be known as the foster girl.

He snorted and turned toward me. "Well, for one, your dad was football captain and scored a full scholarship. He was, like, really good."

I raised an eyebrow. David played football?

"Your parents have, like, donated a trillion dollars to this school," he continued.

I laughed at his exaggeration. "A trillion?"

"Mm." He reached into his bag and took out a bag of crackers. "How do you not know this?"

I almost stopped chewing, not wanting my story to be uncovered yet. A familiar face suddenly came into view. I pointed. "That's her. Mandi, my shadow buddy."

"More like your ditch buddy," he mumbled, but followed my finger. "Ah, that's Mandi Williams. Super weird chic."

"How so?" I asked, taking a bite and watching the brunett. She crossed the manicured lawn with her phone in hand.

"Rumor is she was an orphan and a widow took custody of her. I feel bad for her, though; she's had it pretty rough. The woman who took her in died soon after. So now she's in an aunt's custody." Alex explained.

226

"Is that why she's weird?" I asked tentatively, my hands going numb.

"No." He shook his head, throwing me a smile, "We're not all Satanists here, you know." I smiled.

"She just doesn't talk to anyone." Alex stopped then started again. "She had a boyfriend once. But I think he cheated on her."

I tsked. "That's awful. Have you tried to talk to her?"

"Oh, yeah. But she scares me," he whispered the last part, shaking his head.

I laughed.

~~~~~~~~~

I dropped my bag on the marble floor, still getting used to my surroundings.

"Do you want a snack, honey?" Lucy asked, opening the fridge.

I shook my head. "No, thanks."

Mariella came in through the door, carrying her own bag. "I'm hungry."

Lucy lightly laughed. "Of course, you are. I'll get something for you, but in the meantime, why don't you show Lindsey the horses? I'll go with you on a trail ride."

Mariella dropped her hot-pink backpack and grabbed my hand. She led me outside and across flat land.

"How many horses do you have?" I asked, searching the green field.

"Three. One for each of us. Mommy will probably buy you one," she said, taking large steps. I was no expert, but horses had to be expensive. We reached a barn that was painted white with black trimming. Mariella loosened her grip on my hand. She slid open the door. Once inside, I peered at the large horses in their stalls. The aisles were at least 12 feet wide, and was that a bathroom I spotted?

227

"My horse is at the end. Her name is Sunny," she explained, walking to the end and unhooking a rope.

"This is called the cross-ties. You put it on their halter when you groom them." Mariella opened the door, revealing a white pony just the right size for her.

"Be careful, honey." Lucy's voice boomed from behind us, lifting up into the tall barn. She carried a bag of apples and carrots. Another bag was filled with crackers, which she handed to Mariella.

"I know." Her small reply was filled with concentration. She held Sunny's halter and led him out to the aisle.

Lucy came beside me and handed me legging-like pants and a pair of boots. "Breeches and boots. For protection. That way if you were to fall off, the horse wouldn't drag you." I gulped. If I fall off? Drag me?

She laughed, catching my worried face. "Don't worry. I'm going to give you my horse, Red." She grabbed a lead line off the wall, and crossed the aisle to another stall holding a tall spotted horse. "She's a sweetie." Lucy handed me the rope and positioned my fingers correctly. She then pointed to the posts beside the stall and instructed me to clip him on. She handed me brushes. I carefully petted Red, giggling as he shut his eyes and blew out a breath.

My phone buzzed, interrupting the calming moment. *Hello, beautiful. How's Chicago without me? ;)*

"Lindsey there's a bathroom down there. You can go change and I'll get your tack out." Lucy pointed to a room down the aisle, and I made a face at the word, "tack."

"Saddle, bridle," she made a motion with her hands.

I set down my phone and retreated to the bathroom.

~~~~~~~~

Mariella giggled under her breath as she watched my continuous failed attempts. But to defend myself, I had tacked the horse up correctly. Well, except for the incident. Lucy had instructed me how to tighten the girth beneath the horse's belly, which I did, but Red obviously didn't like me. He had blown up his stomach with air, so when I stuck my foot in the stirrup and went to swing my leg over, the entire saddle slipped down and I was basically hugging a horse sideways. And as if it couldn't get any worse, Red decided he was tired of standing and took off on a walk mid-process. Have you ever side-hugged a horse, stuck in a stirrup, and taken a ride that way? I think not.

Lucy shook her head, a small hidden smile beginning to make its way. "We'll have to get you your own horse." Lucy motioned to the field outside, and I walked with Red beside me.

"Look—mirror Mariella. I'll stand next to you." Lucy led her own horse over to mine, and they nuzzled noses. It was a nice, chilly day. The sun was barely out; the entire sky was almost covered in a sheet of clouds.

Mariella grabbed a fistful of Sunny's mane, stuck her foot in the stirrup, and lifted herself into the saddle. Like a pro. I took a breath, and pointed a finger to Red. "You better not move." Lucy gripped his bridle. I grabbed his mane, stuck my foot in the stirrup and even tested for any weight issue. Feeling none, I swung my leg over the horse's back.

My eyes were squeezed shut. "Did I do it?" They cheered. I reopened my eyes. I was atop Red's back. Lucy mounted easily, and her horse moved over to mine. She leaned over and showed me how to correctly hold the reins. I watched Mariella canter her horse in quick circles.

"She's pretty goo," I said, still not able to take my eyes off her.

"She wants to become an equestrian," Lucy said to my side. "She wants to start jumping soon."

I nodded. "Were you...?"

Lucy looked at me and softly smiled. "Yes. But I got injured at nationals, so it ended my career. Now I just ride for fun."

I pursed my lips together. "I'm sorry."

"Everything happens for a reason." Lucy shook her head with a smile, pinching my leg. "Anyway, do you want to know how to move your horse?"

I nodded.

"Squeeze your legs against his sides. That's how you make him move. For direction, just pull on the reins in the direction where you want to go. To stop, pull gently back on the reins." She demonstrated each one to me while riding Black Jack, David's horse.

"Okay." Here we go.

Thirty - Six

I laughed hard, rubbing my fingers over my infinity necklace—the one Nathaniel had given me on our first date in Central Park. Alex continued his story, laughing here and there. He was so funny.

"You should come to my house sometime," I said, sitting back onto the tree.

"Sure. I'll just tell my dad I'm going to practice." Alex smiled, biting his apple.

I cocked my head. "Why can't you tell him where you're really going?"

He looked up from his apple, parted his lips, then a blank expression swept over his handsome face. "That's another story for another time."

~~~~~~~~

"Wow. This is your house?" Alex asked, his eyebrows raised so high that they aligned with his blond hairline.

"Yep." I squinted, a sarcastic smirk playing, and pointed to his mouth. "You've got a little drool..."

"Ha. Ha."

I rolled my eyes, smiling. "Come on inside."

He followed me through the back gate and up to the patio.

"Are those horses?" he asked, pointing to Red grazing in the distance.

I gasped, following his finger. "I thought those were just big dogs!"

Alex shoved me from behind. "I've known you for almost a month, and I swear you get more sarcastic by the day."

"Do you want to go ride them?"

"Um, yeah," he said in an, "um duh," way. "Lead the way."
I started up to the paddock.

~~~~~~~~~

I repositioned my fingers on the reins and dismounted. I watched Alex dismount with ease. The creek nearby trickled water noisily, and the horses' ears perked towards the sound of it. I led Red to it and watched him stretch his neck to lick the surface. Alex's horse, Black Jack, mirrored Red.

I tied his reins to a tree trunk and sat on a rock nearby. Alex did the same. We sat in comfortable silence until I cocked my head and asked, "Does your dad know you're here?"

"No. He thinks I'm at practice."

"Why can't you just tell him?"

"Because he wants me to play football, and I hate it." He shook his head.

"How long have you played?"

"Since I was ten. So that makes seven years."

"You must be good," I said. He shrugged in response. I watched Black Jack nuzzle Red's neck. "Maybe you'll learn to like it."

"Maybe. So, tell me about your old school," Alex asked without preamble, his head swiveling slightly in my direction.

I froze and rubbed my hands over my thighs. "What do you want to know about it?"

"I'm curious."

I parted my lips, not wanting to tell him yet. "Well-"

"I know."

I looked at him, confused. I looked at his small smile turning the corners of his lips. "Huh?"

Alex returned his gaze to the horses. "I know about your adoption. I know you were in the foster program."

232

My mouth dropped. He laughed. "I heard Mr. and Mrs. Platt adopted a seventeen-year-old girl from New York, and when I heard who your parents were-" he shook his head. "I knew the first day I met you."

"Why didn't you tell me?" I felt stupid.

He shrugged. "I didn't want to scare you away. I wanted it to be something you chose to tell me on your own time."

I laughed. "I didn't exactly tell you on my own time."

Alex laughed. "Sorry. Do you miss it?"

I looked at Alex, studying his handsome features. "New York?"

He nodded.

"I do. I miss my best friend. And my boyfriend." Out of nowhere, I swear, I broke down in a sob. The horses' heads rose in our direction, their eyes wide. Alex's head immediately snapped to me. He scooted over and placed an arm around my shoulders. I rested my head on his chest, feeling the tears pool out. He smelled like horses.

His other arm rubbed my back in circular movements. "Can't you go visit them?"

"I want to. But I'd have to ask Lucy and David, and I only got here a month ago."

"When's your birthday?"

"March." I sat back, wiping my eyes.

"That's spring break time. You can go then." He smiled.

~~~~~~~~

I leaned against the wooden kitchen table. I watched Lucy and David work together on dinner. They seemed so in love. "Can I ask you guys something?"

David looked at me, smiling as he wiped his hands on a cloth. "Sure, hon'. What's on your mind?"

233

I took a breath. I had told Lavender about my plans, and her excitement was insane. "I was wondering if I could visit New York for my birthday present. It's during spring break." I waited for their answer anxiously, watching their traded glances. They both faced me and crossed their arms.

David started. "Well, we'll have to talk it over. But if you that's what you're asking for—then yeah, maybe."

Lucy glanced at David. "The thing is, we were thinking about going away as a family for spring break. But if you want to go there, then maybe we could go with you."

No! I wanted to go by myself. "Oh, you don't have to come with me."

David chuckled and turned to Lucy. "That's code word for, 'no way.' " I nervously smiled.

They both looked at me before David cleared his throat. "We'll talk it over."

~~~~~~~~~~

I stepped up to my bed and flopped myself down. Holding my phone above my face, I tapped Nathaniel's name and held the phone to my ear. He picked up immediately. It would be our first actual call since I'd left. Both our lives had been so busy that we couldn't find the time to set up a phone call. How pathetic was that?

"Hello?"

I smiled, my insides crumbling. Even his voice helped me feel at home. "Hey, stranger."

"Lindsey!"

"Don't you have caller ID?"

He groaned. "I broke my phone. I had to get a new one."

"How'd you break it?" I asked, crossing my legs in a bent angle.

The line went quiet, and I could almost see him contemplating his answer. "Uh, well," he cleared his throat nervously, "I might've dropped it in my bowl of soup."

I broke out in laughter. "How did you manage to do that?"

Nathaniel laughed. "It just happened. Lavender helped me soak it in rice, but it still didn't work. So I got a new one."

"Since when do you eat soup?"

"Soup is good."

I shook my head. "I miss you."

"I miss you too. It's so boring here without you. Lavender is killer-"

"-I heard that!" A voice yelled in the background.

I heard him chuckle and yell back, "I intended you to hear it!"

Lavender's voice was clearer now, and I heard a slap along with Nathaniel's protest. I smiled.

Lavender was on the phone now. "Hey. How is this the first time we've talked since you left?"

"We texted," I reasoned, wincing.

I heard her snort, and I imagined her eye roll and knowing smile.

I sighed. "I know. I'm sorry. But I have something to tell you guys. Put it on speaker."

"Will do," Lavender confirmed, and there was a pause as she shifted the setting, "You're on."

"You know that my birthday is in March?"

"Mmhm," they said in unison.

"I might be able to come and visit for spring break during my birthday time-"

Cheers erupted before I could finish. I grinned against the receiver. "Lavender, is it okay if I stay with you?"

"No." Her voice dripped with sarcasm. "Um, yeah! I'd be offended if you didn't!"

I laughed and heard Nathaniel. "Can I talk to my girlfriend now?"

"I'm not stopping you," Lavender said to him.

"Alone."

Lavender groaned. "Fine. See you, Linds. Call me tomorrow. I still need to hear all about your school and everything."

"Oh, yeah that needs to be told in person."

"Uh oh." She laughed, and suddenly Nathaniel was on the phone.

"Hey."

I smiled. "Hi."

"So, spring break is about four weeks away. Now I actually have a reason to buy a calendar."

"That's good. I'm really excited."

"Yeah. Me too. Go to bed—it's late."

I sighed. "But I want to talk to you."

"Then stay." I did.

Thirty - Seven

I ventured downstairs after finishing my homework for the night.
The aroma of dinner was wafting past the kitchen and through the
house. My stomach grumbled. I checked the clock on the wall, it
reading ten past five.

"Hey, love," Lucy said from the stove. She stirred something
in the frying pan and placed a lid on it. "Done with homework?" I
nodded with a smile, taking a seat at the wooden table. Mariella
was scribbling in her coloring book with Nindsey asleep in her lap. I
glanced at my new family, more than content. Everything had finally
fallen into place. David looped his arms around his wife's waist,
planting a kiss on her forehead. I smiled. Nothing could have ruined
what I had. A hard knock on the door suddenly interrupted my happy
thoughts. David, Lucy and I exchanged an odd look; it was late for
someone to be visiting. Lucy wiped her hands on the dish towel and
retreated to the door with her clicking heels. David shrugged in my
direction, and I did as well. I grabbed a red crayon and bowed my
head to the coloring book Mariella was working on. A man's voice
erupted, but I didn't look up as I continued scribbling in the red rose.

"Sweets," Lucy said, her tone light and cautious.

I looked up into the eyes of a friendly looking man, and I smiled
and stood up.

"Hi," I greeted, shaking his hand.

He smiled. "Hello, Lindsey. It's nice to meet you." A flash of
confusion ran across my face when he spoke my name. How did he
know it?

"My name is Craig, and I am your assigned social worker."

My entire body ran numb, my heart beating rapidly. "My...what?"

Craig pressed his lips together. "I'm afraid we have a problem."

237

"What kind of problem?" I sat on the chair, Lucy next to me. She looked like she was trying to cover her concerned demeanor. David came from the kitchen and handed Craig a glass of water. He brought Mariella and Nindsey out of the room before joining us at the table.

Craig smiled his thanks and returned to the conversation. "We've had an anonymous complaint about your home here."

"What kind of complaint?" David asked, his tone slightly angry.

Craig opened a folder, slipping out a piece of paper and glancing at it. "Unfit guardians, slight abuse, and unfit home-environment."

"That's ridiculous," David spit out, standing up and crossing his arms.

"There's obviously some mistake," Lucy said, shaking her head at nothing in particular.

Craig grimaced. "I can assure you, there is no mistake."

"Well, obviously there is!" David yelled, slamming his hand on the table. I jumped.

Lucy stared at David. "David, calm down. We'll figure this out."

]"What's going to happen to me?" I suddenly interjected, my eyes squeezed shut. Another family? Orphanage? Foster home? The possibilities were endless.

Craig sighed, setting down his piece of paper and folding his hands. "Because there is even a complaint filed, Lindsey and Mariella will have to be removed from the premises until the court's verdict- "

"Whoa, whoa, whoa," Lucy said, slicing her hand in the air. "You're taking both of my daughters? And what is this court date you're speaking about?"

"Because they are both adopted, they will both have to be taken from the house. Although there is something I may be able to

238

do about Mariella. She has been here longer...about," he stopped, shuffling in his papers, "five months?"

"Around there," David confirmed.

Craig nodded, continuing, "Unfortunately, I don't think there is anything I can do about Lindsey's removal. She's only been here for about a month, I presume?"

"Yes."

"So there's nothing we can do?" David asked.

"I'm afraid there isn't."

~~~~~~~

"Lavender, it's happening all over again. I'm going back into the foster system."

"Shh-no. No, you're not, Linds. It's just temporary," she soothed. "I really wish I could get down there right away, but I have midterms all week. My mom will never let me go."

I nodded, pressing the phone harder against my cheek. "I know." There was a pause. "Lavender. What am I going to do?"

"You're going to do what you've always done. You're going to march right into that place like you own it, and conquer it like you've done with everything else you've had to deal with in your life." She said matter-of-factly.

"Okay," I whispered. "I'll talk to you later."

"Okay. Love you."

"Love you too." After the line went dead, I stuck my head in the pillow and screamed.

~~~~~~~

Because there was a "possible" threat concerning my home in the social worker's eyes, I had to leave the next day. School was not mandatory for me. I had to become settled into another house.

239

"Lindsey, we're going to get you out of this." Lucy rubbed my arm, her other hand clinging to David's. I nodded. I hoped so.

"As soon as possible, I promise you. Just hang in tight, and we're going to try to schedule the court date for sooner." David shook his head in anger.

"Lindsey Garland?" I turned around and faced a tough-looking woman with black hair.

She held out her hand. "I'm Jennifer Oat, but the girls call me Miss. I expect you to do the same." I struggled to keep my face as pleasant as possible. My eyes kept darting to her black hair, obviously dyed from blond to its color now. The roots were edging further down, and I mentally cringed. I managed a nod and followed her desperately-overdue-for-waxing eyebrows in the direction of the house. Lucy's wave was soft until it fell limp in the air once the door close. I pulled my suitcase along with me and up the steps. The house was red with white trimming and ugly cement poles. It reminded me of a prison.

Miss opened the door and motioned for me to enter. I did and immediately smelt a stale odor that seemed to linger in place as my nose became accustomed. An old wooden staircase rose upward in front of me and a living room sat to the left. There was no room to the right, but a hallway that ran along the staircase.

"The bedrooms are up the stairs, and you'll be sharing with Hanna. She's your age. I'll have the girls introduce themselves to you before dinner. Your room is to the right, and you take the free bed in the corner." Miss instructed like a sargeant drilling orders, and I found myself nodding robotically along. I climbed the steps, my suitcase hitting each step. Miss followed behind, glaring at my suitcase.

I stopped, meeting her gaze.

Miss looked at me. "Most girls here don't even have a backpack."

240

"My adoptive parents bought this for me," I explained. It's not like it was my fault the other girls didn't own something like mine.

"Exactly my point." She raised her eyebrows, and I pursed my lips, turning around and climbing the steps again.

I got to the top and looked around.

"In here," Miss said, bustling from behind me and into a room to the right. I followed her and glanced around. For the most part, it was bare. The walls were only decorated with one photo of a celebrity. Boring white sheets tightly wound around the bed. I walked to the far corner and hoisted my suitcase onto the bed.

"Dinner is in an hour. I expect you to help out. We do a lot of chores here," she finished with a motion of hands. I was half-tempted to ask if this house was a boot camp, but I decided it was best not to.

~~~~~~~~~~

I walked tentatively down the staircase, grazing my hand against the smooth wall beside me. Like everything else, it was also bare. I hadn't seen or met anyone other than Miss. For some reason, I wasn't nervous. Maybe I was just over it all. I walked down a hallway Miss had pointed out to me moments before, hoping I had gotten the directions correct. I entered a room, filled with mixed laughter and silence, I knew I had gotten them right. Around five or so girls stood around a kitchen, cooking what seemed like pasta. But one boy stood out. His brown hair was swept to the side and his eyes were something that really made him stand out. They were brown, which could be mistaken for being one of the boring colors, but I assure you, it was almost the opposite. There was a certain spirit in his eyes.

I watched the boy smile at something a girl said and continue to cut a tomato. He caught my eye and stopped smiling. His face hosted a look of curiosity. "So you're the new girl." He glanced over my outfit. The noise dropped immediately, and six pairs of eyes trained in on me.

I cleared my throat. "I'm Lindsey."

The boy nodded. "Interesting."

I cocked my head, crossing my arms with a sly smile. "And why is that interesting?"

"Just because. Ladies," he beckoned to everyone in the room with a tone of sarcasm, "let's introduce ourselves to our newest member."

A petite girl closest to him smirked, running a hand through her fiery-red hair. "At least you don't have to share a room with her."

The boy tsked at the girl, whom I assumed was Hanna. "Hanna, no need to be rude."

Hanna rolled her eyes, and resumed her task of cutting mixed vegetables. "Kiss my-"

"Language," the boy interrupted sternly, but with a small smile. He plucked a sliver of green pepper off her plate.

"Oh, please, Caleb," a brunet piped from the fridge. "You've received two yellow cards from Miss because of your language. One more, and you're on to another home."

The boy—Caleb—smiled and shrugged. "And I've learned my lesson twice, haven't I?"

"Yellow card?" I questioned, taking a step closer to them all.

Caleb glanced at me. "Something the Miss came up with. Kind of like...a warning. You get three warnings, you're out of the house."

"Kind of harsh, isn't it?" I asked.

"Probably." He chomped on a carrot. "But it definitely controls us all."

"Controls...?" It came out like a question. Why would we need to be controlled?

"Well," he started. "Some psycho girl ran away from this place a little bit ago. No one's found her since." Everyone seemed to stop a

242

beat and look at Caleb. The girls exchanged a glance, but it was over as fast as it had started.

I put my hand to my mouth. "That's awful."

"Eh. She's probably fine. Andy was strong." Caleb seemed to be talking to himself now.

Miss suddenly came into the room. "Oh, good. You've met everyone. But I still want everyone to gather in the living room."

Caleb groaned. "I hate the group talk."

"Well, we have a new member. So please, everyone, stop what you're doing for the time being and take your places in the living room." She waved her arms. Everyone dispersed from the room, and I followed. I ended up in a medium-sized room, similar to the one I had lived in in New York. I sat on a single chair, folding my hands in my lap.

Someone cleared their throat above me, and I looked up. Hanna stood there with a look of annoyance. "That's my seat."

I nearly laughed. What were we, in middle school? But I jumped up anyway, "Sorry." I wanted to get out of here as soon as possible, but that didn't mean making it miserable for myself while I was there.

"Don't apologize," a blond-haired girl said behind me. She gazed up at me with a bored look. "Hanna has some... issues."

"Shut up, Tara. At least my family didn't abandon me when I was five," Hanna clipped.

I parted my lips in shock. That was a terrible thing to say.

Tara laughed bitterly. "At least I don't-"

"Girls. That's enough," Miss boomed and sat down next to Hanna. "Now, you all know how this works. We're all going to go around the room, state your name and age and something about yourself." Everyone looked at a younger looking girl next to Miss.

She took a deep breath. "Hi, I'm Corrie, short for Cornelia."

"Hi, Corrie." Everyone else chorused sarcastically, like we were at some sort of mental-health therapy group. I bit my tongue to keep

243

myself from laughing. It looked like Caleb was the head of it. He chuckled silently and gave an amused gaze to the group. Miss gave them a look of disapproval, but nodded at Corrie.

"I'm fifteen and am being released in a month."

Caleb was next. "Hi, I'm Caleb."

"Hi, Caleb," everyone chorused.

"I'm seventeen, and cannot wait until I turn eighteen. I'll be out of the foster system."

"Neither can we," someone muttered, jokingly.

Everyone laughed, and next was an older-looking girl. She had large, dark eyes and looked Hispanic. "Hey, I'm Lina. I'm sixteen."

Two more girls, then it was Hanna's turn. She looked directly at me. "I'm Hanna, and I'm eighteen." A flash of confusion flickered across my face. Shouldn't she be out? But it was too late to ask any questions because it was my turn.

"Hi, I'm Lindsey," I started.

"Hi, Lindsey." The kids chorused.

I suffused a laughed. "I'm seventeen and..." I searched for a fact and settled on the only thing in my head, "...and I'm only here because someone filed a complaint on my adoptive parents."

"What foster home are you originally from?" Lina asked.

"I came from New York. I've only been adopted for about a month or so."

Caleb stretched back. "Ah, so you're a newbie."

I smiled. "You could say that."

"Who filed the complaint?" he asked, leaning forward to rest his elbows on his knees. A flash of curiosity flickered in his eyes.

I shrugged.

"Do you have any idea of who it is?" Another shrug. It didn't matter anyway. What's done was done.

"Okay." Miss stood up. "Back to cooking."

~~~~~~~~

244

I sat cross-legged on my bed, peering out the dark window. I'd already had my turn in the bathroom and was waiting for Hanna to come back in. Once she did, she rolled her eyes at me.

"I'm sorry, do you have a problem with me?" I asked, starting to get angry.

Hanna shrugged and sat on her own bed. Her red hair was pulled into a braid. "You're just one of those girls."

"And what kind of girl is that?"

Hanna raised an eyebrow. "You're the kind of girl that fools everyone. The kind that acts sweet, but really isn't. I can see right through it." She whispered the last part.

I was shocked. She didn't even know me. "You don't even know me!"

"Will you shut up?" she angrily whispered. "Miss will hear you, and we'll both get yellow cards."

"I don't like being blamed for something that's not true."

She snorted, and lay down. "Whatever. Just stay away from Caleb...he's been through enough."

"What's that supposed to mean?" Where did she get the idea that I was trying to pursue him?

"It means to stay away from him." And she clicked off the lights.

~~~~~~~

I was up half the night. Mostly because it was so quiet. I was also sleeping on a lumpy mattress that squeaked with every move. Seriously—every move. And while lying there in the darkness next to another girl who hated me for some reason, the shock of the whole episode was wearing off. My chest rose and fell steadily and shallow. How had I gotten myself into it again? *I missed home*, I thought. But at that moment, I wasn't sure which home I missed. By the time my melatonin finally took over my thoughts, I fell asleep. When I woke up in the morning, I checked Hanna's bed. She was gone, though.

245

Her bed was perfectly made, too. Feeling lethargic, I rolled over and went back to sleep. It was Sunday and the house seemed quiet enough. I knew Hellen let us all sleep in a bit on Sundays, so maybe Miss would too. Sleep fell over me quickly, but I wasn't sure how long I slept before Miss stormed into my room. I jumped, the door banging against the wall. She stood there with her hands on her hips. I was starting to think it was her signature pose.

"What are you doing?" she demanded.

"Sorry?" My voice was scratchy and I'm sure there were pillow marks on my cheek.

"Why aren't you up with the rest of the group?"

I probably looked even more confused.

"It's Sunday, which means chore day," Miss explained.

"I'm sorry, I didn't know I was supposed to be up."

Miss held a finger in my face. "I don't tolerate lying in this house. Hanna told me she told you last night and even woke you up this morning."

"She didn't wake me up." I was so confused.

Miss looked angrier, and her face grew red. "Yellow card!"

"No—I"

"Downstairs in five minutes." And she left just like that. Tears clouded my vision. I just didn't understand why she was so mad. I glanced at the bedside clock, and it read 8:43. I got up and dressed myself quickly in a long-sleeved white shirt and black jeans. I quickly brushed my teeth, washed my face, and ran a moisturizing cream though my hair. I decided I'd be makeup-shamed if I put anything remotely close to a beauty product on my face.

When I reached the bottom of the stairs, Miss handed me a vacuum. "Living room needs vacuuming."

I nodded, but glanced around. "Where is everyone?"

"Eating." She replied like it was the obvious answer.

"Can I eat first?"

246

"They've already done their fair share of cleaning. It wouldn't be fair if you just ate without cleaning first."

So, it was a prison.

She took my silence as a cue to continue, "Lindsey, something you need to understand here is that I like order. I like structure, and my methods really do make a better person. Vacuum first, and I'll give you your next job." Miss walked off. Trying to control myself, I bit my tongue and retreated to the living room. I turned on the switch. The vacuum roared to life, and the room was immediately filled with a loud sound. I pushed the vacuum back and forth. It left a path. I glanced behind the couch, and I cringed. The wooden floor was covered in dust. I moved the vacuum in front of the large window. I pushed it back and forth, but saw something in my peripheral vision. I stood ramrod straight and stared wide-eyed out the window. What I saw nearly made my heart skip a beat. Nathaniel stood there with his hands shoved in his pockets, rocking back and forth as he stared at the house. He looked as if he was contemplating something. I watched him, and he looked both ways before stepping onto the road and toward the house. He took bounding steps. He wore his favorite long-sleeved blue shirt and jeans. He hair had grown out a little, making it stand much taller, but it was pulled back under my favorite black hat.

I shut off the vacuum, biting my lip. Was this a dream, or was he really there? I pinched myself to make sure it was reality. I left the vacuum standing at the window and sprinted to the door. My footsteps pounded against the floor, and I didn't care about being quiet. I ran down the steps, and he stopped mid-step. His eyes found me, and a grin stretched across his face. I heard Miss calling my name, but I didn't care. I wanted to tell her and her chores to go to hell. I threw my arms around his neck when I reached him. He wrapped his arms around my waist, picking me up gently.

"Lindsey," he whispered huskily into my ear.

I squeezed tighter.

Thirty - Eight

"Do you understand what you've done wrong?" Miss asked me, peering up at me with a look of disapproval. All I could think about was Miss ripping me off Nate and telling him to leave. I just wanted to do was talk to him, not sit in a chair and be scolded by a woman I barely knew.

I rocked back and forth, avoiding her gaze. I was angry. The woman had literally ripped me away from him. "Yes." No.

"You've violated the rules. Running out of this house is completely unacceptable, especially for a cause as ridiculous as that one," she reprimanded, huffing. "Now, because you're new, I am not going to give you a yellow card-" Oh darn, I thought sarcastically.

"I will let you off with a warning." There was a pause. "Lindsey, look at me when I'm speaking to you." I met her gaze.

"Do you realize the consequences of becoming removed from this house by force?" Miss asked, blinking. I shook my head.

"Because you are temporarily, by government order, in my custody, your removal can result in... well..." She trailed off. "You can be put back into the program."

My eyes widened. "Oh."

"You already have a yellow card. Don't make me give you another. You're dismissed."

I bit my lip, spinning around and retreating to the kitchen. I still had more chores. I sighed, lifting up a bag of garbage and hobbling out the side door to the garbage bins outback. I dropped the bag on the ground with a grunt. Low chuckling erupted from behind me and I whipped around. Caleb leaned against the wall, covering his mouth.

"You know," he stood from his leaned position, "that was ballsy."

"Yeah, well let's just say I didn't get off easy."

"Oo." He winced. "Yellow card?"

"Nah, just a warning," I sighed, crossing my arms and glancing at my surroundings, "but an insane lecture."

"That is one of her strong points," Caleb said. "Don't worry. I get those at least once a week. She's usually all talk and no action. You've got nothing to worry about. Just stay out of trouble."

"Will do."

"So," he stepped closer, "who was that guy?"

"My boyfriend."

"Hm. He lives in Chicago?" Caleb asked, still not breaking his intensifying gaze.

"New York."

"Ah. Interesting." He tossed his head.

"Why is everything interesting?" I asked with a growing grin.

"The world is interesting," he simply stated, and went in through the side door.

~~~~~~~~

Now that I was resettled—temporarily—with Miss, I returned to school. Fortunately, Miss's home was in the same school district, and the bus stopped right outside her door.

I smiled when I saw Alex. "You're actually someone I'm excited to see."

"Trouble in paradise?"

"You can't imagine what this house is like."

He grimaced, throwing an arm around my shoulders as we walked. "That bad?"

I met his eyes. "Okay, I'm not trying to sound like some Windsley Prep princess, but...she took away my phone."

We rounded a corner, and he nodded. "Well, you do sound like one of us."

I laughed along with him. "At least you'll be out of there soon."

I closed my eyes for a second. "Let's hope so."

"Hey, watch where you're going," a voice snapped.

I reopened my eyes, only to set my gaze upon my shadow buddy.

Mandi's eyes darkened. "Oh. It's you." Did I have a sign on my head saying that it was okay to hate me for no reason? Mandi and Hanna seemed to think so.

I brightened my smile sarcastically. "Nice to see you too, Mandi."

She rolled her eyes at the two of us and shoved her way between us to her next class.

Alex threw his arms in the air at her departing back, and yelled, "What? You couldn't have gone around us?"

I smacked his stomach, laughing. "Come on. We're gonna be late for lunch."

Alex growled but walked outside with me. We took our usual seats against the large oak tree.

"What do you have for lunch?" I asked, peering into his paper bag.

He unwrapped something and made a face. "Baloney. Again."

"Why don't you just ask your parents to make you something different?" I asked, biting into my apple. "Or why don't you make your own?"

"My mom doesn't listen and I don't have time to make my own." He tossed his sandwich back in.

"That's what school lunches are for," I said, motioning to the lunch line inside.

Alex made a disgusted face. "I'd catch cancer from that food."

I laughed. "You can't, 'catch' cancer." I swallowed, thinking of when I told Lavender we needed a new carton of orange juice so we wouldn't catch diabetes from Nate.

"Believe me, you'd think otherwise if you've ever tried their pizza. It's like bread and dirt."

251

I shook my head, smiling.

He found a bag of celery sticks and started to chomp on them while squinting into the distance.

"So," I started, "how's football?"

"Um," he squinted harder, "fine."

I waved a hand in front of his face. "Alex? You okay?"

"Correct me if I'm wrong, but you've got an insanely attractive yet creepy guy staring at you from the parking lot." Alex bit his celery stick.

I started to turn, but he held up a cautious hand.

"Slowly."

I rolled my eyes, smiling. "Okay, fine. What does he look like?"

"Mm, he's got brown hair and a hat on."

My heartbeat increased. "What else?"

"Uh, wait. He's taking off the hat and running a hand through his hair…which is pretty long. Guy needs a cut-" I whipped my head around, and sure enough, it was Nathaniel. I jumped up, dropping my lunch box and jogged across the lawn and parking lot to him. I heard Alex's panicked yells, and hoped for him to shut up. I didn't want him to cause any attention. I was so close. Just a couple more steps. I reached him and wrapped my arms around him. He did the same.

He sighed into my ear, hugging me closer. "You have no idea how much I've missed you."

I breathed a deep breath and mumbled, "I know." I leaned back, smiling. Nathaniel's lips tugged upwards, and his hand that was held firmly on my waist pulled me closer. My lips met his. A small butterfly feeling happened once we kissed. It happened only when we hadn't kissed in a while.

I pulled back after a few moments, staring into his green eyes. "How did you get here?"

Nathaniel looked up toward the sky. "Well, if you must know, I walked."

"You walked?" I laughed.

"Still as gullible as ever." He grinned.

I slapped him.

"Ouch. And violent."

"Seriously, how'd you know where I was?"

"Lavender told me to drive my butt here as soon as she got off the phone with you. She explained the whole thing. Speaking of..." I waited.

His voice softened. "Why didn't you tell me yourself?"

I swallowed. "I just...didn't want to be a drama case anymore."

"Well, I hate to break it to you, Linds, but this qualifies for a phone call." He squeezed my sides playfully.

I nodded. "Okay." I stepped back, intertwining my hands in his. "I can't believe you're here. I didn't think you were real when you came to Miss's."

"Miss's?" he asked, confused.

I rolled my eyes. "The foster mom. She insists we call her Miss."

He held up a finger. "There's something very wrong with that." I nodded in agreement.

"Well, she was just charming when she pulled you off me." Nathaniel grinned, grazing my cheek with his finger.

I laughed. "That's her. Charming as ever."

"How is that place anyway?" We walked to his rental car and leaned on the hood.

"Interesting." I smiled at my use of Caleb's word, "Let's hope I'm not there for long. I just want this court date to come faster."

"Court date?" A flash of something flickered in his eyes, but it was gone before I could decipher it. Nathaniel pressed his lips together in a firm line.

"Yeah, so you know someone complained about Lucy and David?"

He nodded, tucking a stray piece of hair behind my ear.

253

"Well, the procedure is that I have to be removed, then wait for the court date. Then the judge decides what happens to me."

"That's not fair. Someone already adopted you. Why would you have to be removed?"

"My adoption is so recent and I'm officially out of the state's hands after two months. It's only been one month."

I heard him grind his teeth. "That's crap."

I let out a laugh. "Yeah, it is. Anyway, enough about me. How's life in New York?"

Nathaniel repositioned himself so he was facing me. "Boring. You're not there, so my lips aren't exercised."

"You're gross."

He grinned, taking my face in his large hands and kissing me. Someone cleared their throat, making Nathaniel pull away grudgingly.

Alex stood there awkwardly, his hands pushed deep into his pockets. "Uh, hey. I just wanted to let you guys know a teacher has been alerted of an, 'intruder,'" he made air quotations. "You better get out of here." My shoulders dropped in defeat as Nathaniel growled in annoyance.

"Who are you?" Nathaniel asked, glancing around before hopping off the hood.

"My name's Alex. Nice to meet you." Alex held his hand out, but it hung limp for a few moments before Nathaniel finally shook it. I shifted, sensing Nate's vibe.

"You too. I'm Nathaniel." He introduced himself, a stone hard gaze setting into Alex's eyes. Something about Nathaniel's body language made me blink. It wasn't jealousy, but something else I couldn't quite put my finger on.

"You better go," I said with a sigh, breaking the silence.

Nathaniel broke his gaze away from Alex, and smiled once it settled on me. "Probably. I have to go back to New York soon, so can we see each other again tonight?" I nodded, letting him kiss me sweetly on the cheek before watching him climb into the rental car.

~~~~~~~~~~

"Lindsey? Lindsey." Someone shook me and whispered my name urgently. I groggily opened my eyes. Morning already? But the room was dark. It cast a light glow on Caleb's face. "Caleb?"

"Get up and get dressed. We're going somewhere." He left the room.

I checked my phone, cringing as the bright light hit my face. I shined it on Hanna's bed, but it was empty. Shocker. My clock read 2:23 a.m. Why would he be waking me up at this time? I checked my messages and bit my lip as I read the constant messages from Nathaniel. I must've fallen sleep! A low, reminding knock sounded at the door, so I quickly shut off my phone and started to get dressed. Because of the darkness, I found a dirty pair of skinny jeans and a blue Windsley Prep sweatshirt. I ran a quick hand through my hair, untangling the knots that had made their way to my head during the minimal amount of sleep I had gotten. In less than five minutes, I was downstairs in front of the door. Caleb, Hanna, Corrie, Lina, Piper, and a girl whose name I forgot stood there silently. Caleb held a black duffel bag.

"What's going-"

"Shh!" everyone chorused.

I shut my mouth and followed Caleb's motions. Everyone followed him out the door and onto the front doorstep. We watched him shut the door tentatively. He still held a finger to his lips. Everyone followed him down the step and turned left at the sidewalk. We were around four blocks away, and right when I was becoming quite angry for walking aimlessly at night with no explanation, Caleb suddenly turned sharply into an alleyway.

255

I stopped, looking around. It was so dark that I couldn't make out anyone's faces. "What are we doing?"

"It's called Expression," Lina said, smiling as she passed me.

"Expression?" I questioned, watching Caleb unzip the mysterious bag.

Hanna groaned. "Why did we have to bring her anyway?"

"Because she's part of us now, so deal with it, Han'." Caleb handed me a cool bottle.

I squinted at it, trying to make out the tiny print. "Is this...?"

"Yep," Caleb said with a grin, "spray paint."

My eyes widened slightly. "Isn't graffiti illegal?"

"Only if you get caught," Lina called from the wall, already shaking her bottle and spraying.

"Just go with it. It's fun—trust me," Caleb said, grabbing my arm and guiding me to the wall on the end.

I bit my lip, eyeing the long alleyway. I know I shouldn't have done it, but they had included me. They obviously wanted me here... right? "How do I do it?"

Caleb stopped halfway and leaned over to me. "Shake the bottle first." I did and waited for the next instruction. "And just spray away. Usually in circular patterns or curved lines. Whatever you want."

I nodded, blinking, before carefully applying pressure to the bottle. It sprayed blue/gray, and with every stroke, I became relaxed. "This is fun!"

"So is working in peace," Hanna grumbled.

I frowned at her remark, but returned to my work. "So, why is it called Expression?" Everyone seemed to stop a beat and look at Caleb. Hanna shot me a look but I ignored it.

Caleb didn't seem to notice everyone's lingering eyes as he continued to spray. "A girl named Andy brought us all out here one night. She called it Expression."

Andy... I'd heard that name before. "Isn't she the one who ran away?"

His face noticeably tightened for a moment. "Yeah." And that was that. The only sound audible in the abandoned alleyway was spraying, until, sirens. Police sirens. I nearly dropped my can, staring wide-eyed at Caleb. Everyone stopped immediately, looking around to detect where the sirens were coming from. Then, we knew. The lights flashed nearby while policemen jumped out and pointed at us. It all happened in a blur as I stood frozen watching everyone drop their cans and run. Caleb grabbed my arm, pulling me away. We started to sprint in the opposite direction, then stopped when flashing lights appeared there as well.

"Caleb," I said in panic, my head swiveling in both directions as the policemen crowded in.

"Stop right there," one of them boomed. In a moment, we all became handcuffed.

Thirty - Nine

"You know," Caleb's voice echoed against the cement walls, "this is something we'll all be laughing about in the future."

"Hardly," Lina curtly objected.

I sat up from my head-holding position, sighing. "This is bad."

"Oh really, Sherlock? Figure all that out on your own?" Hanna glared from the corner, crossing her arms and leaning against the wall.

Anger seethed through me. "What's going to happen now?"

"We'll have one call each to whoever we want, and then wait until someone bails us out." Caieb explained the procedure like he had studied it, blinking nonchalantly at the floor.

"You explain that like it was a personal experience," I said cautiously and curiously. He winked at me. Movies.

Clanging of keys suddenly appeared in front of us. We all looked up eagerly. We'd been sitting in the holding cell for nearly an hour. A police officer stood there with fumbling keys, opening the gate. "You kids have one call each. Make it count. Follow me." I nearly laughed. We were foster kids; more than half of us didn't have anyone to call. Everyone but Caleb and I shook their head at the officer, signaling they did not need the phone. Just another reminder of our lovely lives. I stood from the uncomfortable bench, following the police officer out to the phone. It felt good to not be behind bars. I never thought I'd have to say that. I was first at the phone. Sighing, I dialed a number.

"Hello?" Nathaniel's sleepy, confused voice.

"Nathaniel?"

It was quiet. "Lindsey...?"

"Hey," I said cautiously, not knowing how he'd react toward my first crime.

"What's this number you're calling from? And it's like four in the morning."

"Yeah." I said slowly. "The thing is—I'm in a holding cell."

"What?!" he yelled. I heard a bed springing in the background, and I could imagine him jumping up in alarm. "Why, the hell, would you be in a holding cell?"

"I might've committed a crime of graffiti." I winced guiltily. The police officer snorted nearby.

Nathaniel exhaled after a moment of silence. "How could you be so stupid? You're waiting for a court date, Linds. This could really hurt your chances." I knew it could. I didn't say anything.

"Well…are you okay?" Nathaniel asked, his voice softening.

I rubbed my eyes, staring at my feet. "I think so. I'll be bailed out of here soon. I'm sorry I didn't text you back. I fell asleep."

He chuckled. "I don't care about that. I just care whether you're safe or not."

"I'm fine."

The officer pointed at his watch and I pursed my lips together. "I gotta go, Nate. Someone else needs to use the phone."

He groaned. "Okay. I'll call you in the morning." I nodded more to myself and hung up. Caleb stepped up to the phone, dialing a number. I stood behind him, watching him pause over a number, then sigh and place the phone on the hook.

Caleb looked at the officer. "I don't need it. I changed my mind."

He nodded, motioning us back into our holding cell down the hallway. Once we were inside, Hanna glanced at Caleb from the ground.

"Who'd you call?" she asked skeptically, pulling her legs up tighter. She was leaning against the wall, on the ground.

Caleb shrugged. "Someone who's not important." Lina and Hanna eyed each other but went back to their boredom-based daydreams.

259

Clanging against the rims of the bars sounded for a few moments, paused, then started up again. I finally looked up, my eyes setting on Caleb's hunched shoulders facing away from me. He held his key chain from his pocket, moving back and forth against the bars. "Caleb?"

"Hm?"

"Shut up."

Caleb stopped, turning around as he rolled his eyes. He pointed his key chain of a dolphin at all of us. "You people," a dramatic pause, "are mean." I half-smiled, shaking my head as he turned around again and leaned against the bars.

"Officer?" he lazily called.

Moments later, the same officer who had arrested us appeared, his raised eyebrows indicating his lack of interest. "Yes?"

"Nature's calling," Caleb's monotone voice stated. Lina chuckled to herself against the wall.

The officer motioned to the toilet in the vacant corner. "I'm not stopping you."

"Have you noticed this cell is filled with girls?"

The officer shrugged. "Ask them to close their eyes." And he walked off.

Caleb faced us, sighing. "Well, isn't he charming?" I laughed. Caleb eyed the toilet, then made his way to the corner as he started to unzip his pants.

"Whoa, whoa, whoa." Hanna stared wide-eyed at Caleb.

"What?"

"Don't even think about it."

"I have to pee," he whined.

"Suck it up," Piper grumbled from her sleep-like position.

Caleb stuck his tongue out at her, but thankfully re-zipped his pants. The next hour was filled with dazed sleep and minimal

260

conversation until the officer came back once more and started to unlock the door. "Okay, everyone out."

I jumped up, my legs wobbly. We all filed out, following the officer.

"Uh oh," Caleb mumbled near my ear.

I looked at him, raising a questionable eyebrow. "What?"

"Look who's here." I did. Standing there with a flat look was Miss.

~~~~~~~

"Everyone sit in the living room. Immediately." Her tone was scary as she tossed her purse onto the steps. No one objected as we clumped into the living room. I took a seat next to Caleb. It was silent as we waited with our heads down for Miss to join us.

"What made you leave at two in the morning?"

"The world is different at two in the morning." Caleb smiled, looking up at Miss with a cheeky expression.

"This is not the time for jokes. I was awoken by a call in the middle of the night from the police station. They told me my foster children were currently in a holding cell."

"Wait," Hanna started, "you knew we were there?"

"Of course, I did. I went right back to sleep and picked you up in the morning. It serves you right to have to sit in a holding cell."

"What happens now?" Piper asked.

"All of you receive yellow cards."

Caleb suddenly looked up, his face suddenly serious. "But that means-"

"Yes, Mr. Jacobson. Three yellow cards within one month, and I'm sure you know what that means." Hanna looked up, shock and concern plastered onto her face. I could understand; Caleb was like a brother to her.

261

"All of you will receive extra chores and house arrest with the exception of school. Caleb, I have contacted your social worker and you will be on your way to another home by tomorrow." The room fell silent as we stared at Caleb.

~~~~~~~~

"This sucks," I muttered, wiping the glass window.

Hanna smirked from behind me as she cleaned down the counters. "Tell me about it."

I rubbed harder on a spot. "Has she always been like this?"

"Not really. But you know," she paused, checking for Miss, then whispered, "it probably has something to do with age, if you know what I mean." We both collapsed into laughter, back to our cleaning. It was quiet for a few moments.

"How long have you known Caleb?" I asked Hanna.

She glanced at me, biting her lip as if deciding whether or not to tell me, then shrugged. "Ever since I've been here. So that makes it...five years."

I nodded, curiosity striking me. "Who's Andy?"

"Why?" she asked curtly.

I was taken aback. She had been so nice then turned so mean within seconds. "I was just wondering."

Hanna sighed, turning on the faucet. "Sorry. It's not something I should be telling you. Andy is..." she shook her head, "...a story you need to ask Caleb for."

~~~~~~~~

Hanna was finishing up her last chore when Caleb knocked on my door. I looked up from my school book, half smiling.

"Hey."

I closed my book. "Hey."

262

Caleb stood there, shifting from heel to toe awkwardly. "So, you wanted to know who Andy was?"

I parted my lips, managing a lame response. "Um-"

"It's okay, Hanna told me." He strode over to my bed and sitting on the edge. I remained silent, watching his thinking face.

"I was seven when I came here. I was just starting to understand what my life meant." He blinked. "Changing from house to house was very confusing. I'm sure you know what that feels like." He threw a lopsided frown in my direction. I nodded, expressionless.

"I was scared and upset. I was taken from my mom when I was seven. No one knows where my dad is." He shook his head as if he were getting off track. "Anyway, we were told a new girl was coming to stay with us. I didn't care really. At that time, I thought girls were covered in cooties." I smiled.

"Her name was Andrea, but she insisted everyone call her Andy. Long story short, we bonded. By the time we were fifteen, I believed I loved her."

Caleb paused, sadness flashing in his eyes. "She was amazing, but there was always something to learn about her. People just... stuck to her. It was easy to be her friend because she wasn't complicated. Everyone liked Andy." He stopped, wincing, His tone was becoming haunting, raspy, as he was reminiscing about his deep memories.

He clenched his hands, blinking sadly. "I don't know. She was incredible."

"Where is she?" My tone had dropped to a whisper without me even knowing it.

"She ran away. I woke up one morning and Hanna broke the news to me. There were police cars parked in the driveway. I didn't believe what anyone was saying because I didn't think she'd leave without a goodbye. But her clothes and everything was gone."

263

"And she didn't say goodbye?" I asked, shocked. It seemed as if their relationship was important. Why wouldn't she say goodbye?

He paused. "She left a letter."

"Did you read it?" I asked, pinching the bed fabric.

"No. I never did." His face was blank at this point.

I didn't understand. "Why didn't you?"

"Because I was too hurt. She had broken my heart and left without a proper goodbye." Caleb finally met my eyes.

It was quiet until he finally leaned forward to stand. "Just one question." I raised my eyebrows.

"Why did you call your boyfriend when you have a family?"

"I didn't want them to be disappointed."

Caleb nodded, looking like he understood.

"Caleb, wait," I said.

He glanced at me.

"You should read it. The letter. Trust me, you might lose it and you'll regret that you never got to read it." I reasoned, my tone soft yet pleading.

Caleb half-smiled. "I'll never lose it." Something about his tone made me later realized that the letter was the last thing he had of her. Opened or not, I became to realize that it was important no matter what.

Forty

I smiled, watching Mariella, Lucy, and David climb out of the car. Mariella bounded up the steps, barely checking for her parents, who followed. I went to open the door and embrace my family, but I froze over the doorknob, remembering Miss's rule. I already had two yellow cards, and I did not want to earn myself a third one before my court date. So I waited for Miss to bustle into the room and open the door for me. I tried to not roll my eyes. I watched Miss lean down, smiling at Mariella.

"Well, hi there. And what's your name?' Miss asked, her tone soft and so kid-friendly I almost did a double take.

"Mariella," she replied, and I stepped from behind the door.

Mariella's face lit up when she saw me. She ran through the door and bombarded me in a bear hug. She was only to the height of my belly button, so I bent to pick her up and rest her on my hip. I planted a kiss on her cheek, and she snuggled closer into my neck.

"I've missed you," she cooed. I squeezed her tighter and smiled at Lucy and David as they shook Miss's hand. I let down Mariella and hugged them in turn. Lucy smelt of a faint Channel No.1 perfume, while David smelt of a husky cologne mixed with paperwork and ink.

"Well, come on into the living room." Miss motioned, her hospitality shining. I've never seen her so nice before. Lucy and David stepped inside, looking around. Mariella grabbed my hand, and Miss led the way to the living room. Lucy and David sat together, while Miss took her main chair. Mariella sat on my lap across from everyone. A water pitcher sat on the coffee table with elegant glasses I'd never seen before.

"We really appreciate you opening your home like this until we get this resolved," David started, half-smiling. As I looked closer, I noticed faint dark circles under his eyes. He looked stressed. And tired.

"Oh course, Mr. and Mrs. Platt." Miss smiled, revealing her clunky teeth.

Lucy looked around, frowning. "If you don't mind me asking, where is everyone? There are other children here, correct?"

"Oh, yes. They're at the park, filling out their community service hours. Lindsey was excused for today because of the court date," Miss explained, taking a sip of water.

I mentally cursed, averting Lucy and David's befuddled stare.

"Community service?" David questioned, leaning closer to Miss and glancing quickly at me for some kind of reassurance.

"I'm sorry," Miss raised an eyebrow, "I thought you already knew."

"Knew what?" Lucy asked, her tone tentative. Mariella sat suddenly silent, sensing an intense discussion was impending. I stared at my nails, my lips pressed into a firm line.

"Last week, the kids slipped out of their rooms at two a.m. and went downtown to an abandoned alleyway. They were sketching graffiti on the walls-"

"What?!" Lucy nearly jumped out of her seat.

Miss winced, knowing it was only going to get worse. "When they got arrested, and were kept in a holding cell for the night."

"Arrested?!" It was David's turn to explode.

Lucy bit her lip, placing a hand on her husband's thigh. "How were we not informed of this?"

"I was told they each had one call, so I assumed..." she trailed off, looking guilty.

David and Lucy's gaze turned to me. His voice softened. "Why didn't you call us?" He almost sounded hurt.

"Wait." Lucy interrupted my response. "Who did you call?"

I swallowed hard. "Nathaniel."

266

"Who's Nathaniel?" David asked, though he looked at Lucy.

"Her boyfriend," Lucy told him. A look crossed her face that looked like she understood a bit more. Everyone's eyes settled on me.

Miss cleared her throat. "So, is Nick-"

"Nathaniel," I corrected.

"Nathaniel," she repeated, "Is Nathaniel the young man who visited you the other day?" I swear, at that moment, I wanted to dump the pitcher of water onto Miss's head.

"Visited you? What kind of home is this? Aren't we supposed to be informed about the discrepancies that take place here? Especially when they're having to do with our daughter?" David fired off questions, clearly quite agitated as he clenched his fists.

"I'm very sorry," Miss apologized, glancing at each of us and pursing her lips. "I'll give you some time." And with that, Miss left the room with my secrets remaining behind.

"What's...discrepancy mean?" Mariella suddenly asked, reaching to the cookie plate and choosing a pink-sprinkled one,

Lucy ignored the question and turned toward me. "Honey, why didn't you call us that night?"

I chose my words carefully. "I didn't want you to think I was some troubled kid. Like maybe, if you found out I got arrested...you wouldn't want me anymore."

"Lindsey, listen to me. We adopted you for a reason," Lucy said lightly.

"And you're our daughter, which means our responsibility," David jumped in.

"Okay." I nodded. "I'm sorry."

~~~~~~~~~

"Are you ready?" Lucy's reflection appeared behind me.

267

I looked at her in the mirror and smoothed down my reserved maroon dress, which clung appropriately and skimmed my knees. "I think so."

"I'm sure the judge will approve your application just by looking at you."

I made a face. "Something about that sounds illegal."

Lucy laughed. "I didn't mean it like that! You're a beautiful, responsible young woman, Lindsey."

We traded a smile before I checked once more over my dress, suddenly frowning. "Responsible enough to do something as stupid as decorate walls with graffiti?"

Lucy softly smiled and placed a hand on my shoulder. "We're not perfect and we all make mistakes. I'm sure you've learned your lesson about graffiti."

I lightly laughed. "I did."

"You know, when I was your age, I got arrested with my friends," Lucy admitted, raising her eyebrows.

I whipped around, looking at her instead of her reflection. "Really? For what?"

Lucy checked her watch. "You know, we really should get going."

I nodded sarcastically. "Uh huh."

By the time we left and got to the city, I stood in front of the Chicago Family Court, breathing nervously. On this day, I'd either be put back into the foster program, or back into the custody of Lucy and David. All because of a false complaint.

David came from behind me. "You okay, honey?" I managed a nod.

"Whatever happens in there, we will fight it if it's not the right decision. You're not going back into the system, I promise you." I clung to his promise, hoping he was right. I didn't know if I could handle another house. Lucy and Mariella finally met us and we entered the building. It was a nice day; blue skies with temperature in the low fifties. I'm not saying it's perfect, but it's definitely better than below zero. Once we pushed through the double doors, the smell of wood and paperwork attacked my senses. Mariella's eyes were as wide as saucers as her head moved slowly to gather the information around her. Lucy led the way to the decorative waiting area while David took care of the paperwork. I didn't say much as I stared into my lap.

"What's wrong, Lindsey?" Mariella asked as she attempted to crawl into my lap to comfort me.

"Honey," Lucy motioned to Mariella, adding a slight shake of her head. Mariella may not understand some things, but she definitely can tell the difference between a nod and shake of the head. She backed off and let me have a moment. David called to Lucy, and we all stood. A man clothed in a sharp, black suit was standing next to David. They exchanged light conversation.

The man smiled at us, his dark eyebrows rising. "Hello, my name is Andrew. If you'll just follow me, the Judge is ready and Craig Leeman is also ready to defend the complaint."

"I'm sorry?" I questioned.

"Craig, your assigned social worker for this case, will also defend you. But I've read your case, and I don't think anything will need to be fought. Today is mostly the judge's decision." I nodded, still not understanding. I thought the complaint was anonymous. We followed Andrew down long hallways and finally onto an elevator. The elevator rose upwards, and I pressed my hands against the wall as I gazed out the clear glass. We were currently rising above the city of Chicago. After, he led us to large double doors. He pushed them open and we entered a court room. Craig sat at a desk to the left, and a tired looking man sat at the judge's desk. The desk to the right was vacant. I glanced behind me, watching Lucy, David, and Mariella sit in the wooden benches.

"Now," the judge suddenly boomed, "I don't want to drag this out. So, there will be no defending today. I am simply going to hear both sides of the story briskly once more, and that will confirm my decision of Lindsey Garland's placement. Are we clear?" I nodded as the courtroom fell silent.

"First, we will hear from the defendant." The judge motioned to someone. My stomach went cold, as it was quiet for a few moments. Slowly, I heard creaking and footsteps. I turned slightly in my chair, shocked on many levels. Alex walked slowly and tentatively to the stand. How had I not seen him when I came in? He avoided my gaze, but when his eyes finally flickered to mine for just a moment, I glared. I wanted to show him the shock and utter betrayal I felt. I remember Nate the day he met him; was it his intuition that noticed something off with Alex? He looked extremely guilty. He winced from my glare, his eyes falling onto the wood in front of him. A policeman came to him and held an opened bible. Alex placed his hand on it and repeated the sentence after the guard.

"I swear to tell the truth, the whole truth, and nothing but the truth, so help me God," Alex quietly said.

"Mr. Freeman, what was your complaint?" the judge asked.

Alex took a deep shuddering breath. "I complained about abuse and unfit guardians." There was some shuffling behind. I heard David's low grumble.

"And what is your reason for this?"

Alex seemed to contemplate his answer. Maybe he was trying to remember what he clearly rehearsed. "I witnessed it."

"That's a lie," I blurted, venom in my tone. Alex shrunk into a slightly hunched position.

The judge shot me a look. "Please." I shut my mouth.

270

"And what exactly did you witness, Mr. Freeman?" The judge resumed his questioning.

"Lindsey's father hit her multiple times."

A memory clouded my vision of Walter.

He stood up abruptly, and before I knew it, slapped me hard across the face. Before I had time to be shocked, I felt another hard blow to the side of my face-

"And her mother did nothing," he finished. The judge nodded, motioning for him to return to his seat. Alex slowly walked past me without a word, though I felt his strong gaze burn into the side of my face. I refused to meet his eyes.

"Lindsey?" The judge looked at me.

I stood and walked to the stand where Alex had been. My lawyer stood from his spot, folding his hands and smiling at me.

"Lindsey, how long have you been in the foster system?" the lawyer asked.

"Thirteen years," I answered immediately.

"And you were finally adopted when you were seventeen years of age?"

I nodded. "Yes."

He nodded, seeming to have proven an invisible point. "Lindsey, will you please pull your hair back for one moment?" I did.

"Judge, do you see any marks of hitting, as the witness said, on her face?" The judge studied my face and shook his head. The lawyer went on to say how Mariella was taken care of perfectly, and there were zero signs of abuse with her or even me.

I left the stand once it was time, and the courtroom fell to silence as we awaited the judge's decision. "Okay. I've come to a decision."

"I've decided to release Lindsey Garland back into the custody of Lucy and David Platt with further occasional inspections." A

271

relieved sigh released from behind me, but I didn't care. I jumped up and hugged my family.

~~~~~~~~~

"We have an early birthday surprise," Lucy finally said, setting down her glass of white wine. Everyone excitedly looked at me, and it was surprisingly quiet for a restaurant.

I grinned. "Really?"

Lucy smiled, looking at David who cleared his throat, "We've talked to your friend—Lavender, is her name?" I laughed.

David chuckled. "Anyway, she's invited you to stay in her apartment for the time during your spring break. And wait for the biggest part..." He cocked his head to Lucy.

She grinned. "Your flight leaves tomorrow night at eight."

My mouth fell open. "And school?"

Lucy, the coolest mom, said, "There are only three more days of school until spring break officially starts, so you can take those off."

I held up a hand to my mouth, trying not to cry. "Oh, my gosh. Thank you so much." I hugged them each and tried to calm the excitement. I was going to see Nathaniel and Lavender in less than twenty-four hours.

Forty - One

I tapped my fingers against my thigh excitedly, grinning as I glanced out the window to my city. New York was still as beautiful as ever.

"Turn here," I reminded the taxi driver.

He nodded, spinning the wheel and turning into the designated street. A gate blocked our entrance. "Do you know the code?"

"Pound 441," I replied, trying to contain my excitement. I watched him lean out the window and type in the number. The gates swung open on command. As he drove through with reckless speed that could be seen only in the city, he hit the brakes.

"$56.29," he said, his accent thick.

I riffled through my wallet. My fingers skimmed past my new credit card, recently given to me by David, and handed him cash. "Thanks." He grunted in reply and I lifted my suitcase out of the car. I watched the taxi drive through the exit gate and breathed in the warming air around me. I noticed the bare trees around. The clouds were gray with impending rain. Arms suddenly wrapped around me from behind, and I jumped in fright. A head nuzzled into my neck, and I smiled as I caught a whiff of his scent.

"Nathaniel," I sighed happily. I turned around in his grasp and looked into the green eyes I recalled so well. They shone with a mixture of happiness and boyish excitement.

"Hello, beautiful." He grinned. It was one of those rare moments when I saw him without a winter hat. His brown hair still stuck up in a sexy angle, though, and he wore a long-sleeved white shirt with dark stone-washed jeans.

"Hi," I breathed a reply, not concentrating on words but trying to fathom how this beautiful creature in front of me belonged to none other than myself.

Nathaniel lightly chuckled as he caressed my cheek with his thumb. He threw an arm over my shoulder, using his other arm to rub my arm. "Let's get you inside." I nodded eagerly. We walked to her apartment, talking in easy conversation. We were steps away when suddenly the door flew open and slammed against the inside wall. Lavender stepped out, her arms crossed. Nathaniel obediently lifted his arm from my shoulders and let Lavender fling herself on me. I laughed, hugging her back. I sighed in her grasp. I missed it so much.

"I can't believe you left me for that long! I was stuck with this one," she mumbled into my shoulder, sticking out her tongue at Nathaniel.

I grinned, winked at Nathaniel and sarcastically said, "Oh, how horrible."

"That's what I said." He disappeared into the house with my suitcase.

She stepped back, walking into the apartment. "Now, I need to hear all the details of your first prison experience."

"Oh, but of course." I grinned, throwing an arm around her shoulder. We walked through the door. Lavender shut the door and I glanced around. The same things were still there. The wide hallway was to the kitchen, and the living room that connected to another hallway and bedrooms. The only things different were the party decorations adorning the apartment. Streamers and a cookie cake decorated the kitchen.

"What's this?" I asked with a grin, peering at the cake's inscription. It read: Welcome Back!

"Nathaniel insisted." Lavender rolled her eyes.

"It was your idea." He came into the room, shoving her shoulder lightly as he passed to stand next to me.

"But you insisted."

He looked at me. "It was a group effort."

I laughed. "Well, thank you. I really missed you guys." I grinned at the two of them, happy to be home.

~~~~~~~~~

I walked out of Nathaniel's room into the hallway. Nathaniel was supposed to stay with me, but he slept on the couch instead. Lavender was at school since the New York and Chicago spring break sessions were not in sync. The kitchen was quiet and I spotted him rummaging in the fridge. I crept behind him and when I got close enough, wrapped my arms around his waist. He jumped as I laughed and stepped back.

"I wanted to get you back for scaring me yesterday." I leaned against the counter, crossing my arms and cocking an eyebrow.

Nathaniel half-smiled, as he seemed to be avoiding my gaze. Weird. "I don't get scared."

"Oh, really?" I asked. "Because I think I just did."

He was looking at me with a soft and intense look. I'd only ever seen him look at me once before like that. But as quick as I saw it, it was gone and was replaced with something else. "I'll—uh—see you later." He turned to leave.

"Where are you going? Can I come?" I asked, furrowing my eyebrows.

Oh, just the gym. I'll see you later." Nathaniel caught my eye once, but pecked me on the cheek. I frowned as I watched him walk out into the April air. Shouldn't he have wanted to be with me as much as he could?

~~~~~~~~~

"This is so much fun." I laughed uncontrollably as I twirled in a circle on the ice.

275

I heard sputtering behind me. "Glad," she heaved, "you're having fun." And then she lost her balance on one foot, and her entire stance collapsed onto the ice. I tried not to laugh as I planted fake-concern on my face and held down my hand. Her cheeks were rosy pink, and her hat slid forward, covering her eyes.

Lavender was many things, but athletic was not one of them. My poker face started to crumble as my giggling conquered and broke through.

Lavender's lips were taut, and she sarcastically smiled up at me, "Think that's funny?" I nodded, still laughing. Lavender sighed, and reached for my hand. I went to pull her up, but went the opposite direction when she pulled down. That was that. I burst through with a laugh I didn't even know I was capable of and covered my face. The ice was cold against my legs.

Lavender laughed next to me. "I told you I was a bad ice skater." I looked around at the indoor ice arena. I was hoping we could've skated at Rockefeller, but it was closed off. Kids from the age of fourteen, to sixteen skated around us. The skill averaged between beginner and trained figure skaters.

"People are looking at us like we're insane," I mumbled under my breath.

Lavender glanced around, her hat inching forward and her hair sticking out in wide angles. "I don't see anything." I laughed and helped her up. Before we started to skate, I told her to take off her hat and fix her hair. She looked at me dumbfounded, but did it anyway. After her hair was smoothed down properly, I stuck the hat on carefully. She then looked like the model she usually appeared to be. Teenaged boys glanced at her with awe and elbowed their friends noticeably. I shook my head as I watched Lavender's oblivious state.

"How's everything with Andre?" I asked, pushing off with my left skate.

"We're okay," she said, her eyes trained on the ice in front of her.

"Just okay?" I asked lightly.

Lavender shrugged. "Things have been off. But I'm sure we'll get through it." I gently nodded, tossing her a smile.

"So," she started with an entirely different tone, inching awkwardly forward with her skates, "how were the love birds last night?"

I shrugged. "It was great. We watched a movie and then-"

"Did some canoodling...?" She interrupted, wiggling her eyebrows at me.

I made a face. "Canoodling?"

"You know...a little smooch-time?"

I laughed hard. "I was going to say we ate ice cream, but yes. We did some canoodling."

"Knew it." She snapped her fingers, grabbing my arm for balance as we picked up the pace. I was quiet. But he was so weird this morning, and I couldn't shake the feeling. Maybe he was just in a mood, and I should've just put it behind me. It might not have had anything to do with me, after all.

"Okay, what's wrong?" Lavender suddenly asked.

I looked at her, startled. "Nothing."

"Lindsey. I will push you down if you don't tell me this instant." She waved a finger in my face, her tone firm.

"Are you sure you can?" I asked, eyeing her wobbly stance.

"Once I get off this ice, I can't promise you anything," she said sweetly.

I sighed, giving up. "I may be just overreacting, but he was acting strange this morning. Like, he was quick to leave and avoided my eyes."

"It may have nothing to do with you," Lavender said as she suddenly began to move more fluidly.

"That's what I thought." I crinkled my brow.

"And remember," she lost her balance for one moment before regaining herself, "it's Nate. He's always weird."

I shook my head with a smile. "I'll just wait it out and see how he acts tonight."

Lavender nodded. "Good idea. Which reminds me, does pizza sound good?"

~~~~~~~~~

I sighed in delight, enjoying the New York pizza melt in my mouth. "So. Good."

Lavender nodded, switching her weight from foot to foot. "I know."

"I mean," I started, swallowing, "Chicago has good pizza, but New York will always have my heart." The box was propped open on the counter, and we hadn't made it to the kitchen table. The door clicked open and in came Nathaniel.

I brightened as he strode into the room. "Hey!" I hadn't seen him all day.

He managed a smile. Key word: managed. "Hey. How was your day?"

I tried not to look disappointed with his lack of emotion, then reminded myself to stop being that kind of girl. "Fun. Lavender and I went ice skating."

Nathaniel nodded and ran a hand through his lengthy hair. "Cool." The room fell silent, and I glanced at Lavender. She gave me a slight nod, which signaled to me she understood my concern.

"So, where were you all day?" I asked, breaking the ice.

He shrugged. "Out." I nodded, irritated with his lack of detail.

"Let's watch a movie," Lavender suggested, raising her eyebrows and smiling at each of us.

"Sure." I nodded.

"But, it has to be Nemo." Lavender pouted.

I dramatically sighed, looking at Nathaniel. "What do you think?"

He played along. "I guess we could."

She clapped her hands. "Yay. I'll get it set up." When she disappeared from the room, I edged closer to Nathaniel and bumped my hip with his.

He smiled for real. "Yes, Miss Garland?"

"I missed you today, Mr. Sky." I smiled and stood on my tip toes to lightly kiss his lips. I pulled back a bit, and his hand found its way gently to my jaw and his other arm wrapped around my waist. We kissed again until he pulled away, a look of something flashing in his eye. "I... I missed you too."

I pressed my forehead to his, half-smiling as I gazed closely into his green eyes. There looked like there was a lot going on. I just couldn't figure it out.

"Nemo is ready!" Lavender called from the living room. He sighed and held out a hand.

~~~~~~~~~

The whole night consisted of normal-Nathaniel and awkward-Nathaniel. He slept on the couch, again, and woke up to the smell of pancakes. I quickly brushed my hair, teeth, and washed my face before I met Nathaniel and Lavender in the kitchen. They were laughing as Nathaniel seemed to be flipping pancakes. He told a joke, and she laughed hard.

"Morning." I felt like I was interrupting something.

Lavender grinned. "Hey."

Nathaniel looked behind him. "Morning, sleepy-head." Normal-Nathaniel was present. I smiled.

"When did you get up?" I asked, glancing at the clocked above the stove. It read: 10:26.

279

"Around an hour ago, and I know your favorite is chocolate chip pancakes. So," he paused, reaching for the bag of Nestle Chocolate Chips, and tossing it to me, "I went to work."

"And I just got up," Lavender said, sipping a cup of apple juice.

"Since when do you drink apple juice?" I pointed at her cup.

"It's my guilty pleasure." She hid her face behind the glass. Lavender didn't like sugary things.

"Lav, a guilty pleasure may happen once or twice a week," Nate said with a grin, "You have apple juice almost once or twice a *day*." I managed a laugh, but I couldn't help but feel left out. I knew it was only as simple as apple juice, but how much did I really miss while I was gone?

"Whatever." Lavender rolled her eyes and grabbed a plate behind her. She loaded it with pancakes, then handed it over to me.

"So, this has nothing to do with my birthday tomorrow?" I asked suspiciously. When I was thirteen, Hellen had forgotten my birthday for three years in a row. I was really upset, so Lavender picked a random date to be my, 'half-birthday,' even though she had no clue what a half-birthday stood for. Even though my half birthday is September twenty sixth, I had decided not to spoil the generosity that had gone into her planning at the time. I eventually told her later on, but she just laughed and named the day to be my, 'Almost half-birthday." It took a while to explain this story to David and Lucy, but they got the point.

Lavender had a faraway look in her eye. "That's tomorrow? I had no idea." After a breakfast of pancakes, Lavender announced she had to visit her mother. She also wanted to give Nathaniel and me some alone time. It was silent in the living room as I lounged on the bean bag chair in the corner. Nathaniel lay on the opposite one.

"Do you want to tell me about that graffiti?" he abruptly asked.

I groaned and put a hand to my face. "Not one of my best moments."

"Understood."

Nathaniel stood up, and held out a hand to me.

I raised an eyebrow. "Are we going somewhere?"

He nodded. "Follow me." And I did. I immediately guessed Central Park, but we actually drove past it. He brought me to a place I had never been to before. It was the artsy side of New York, where talented and aspiring artists painted anything around them that was without a color. When he parked his car, he crossed to my side and opened the door. When he caught a glimpse of my gleeful face, he didn't acknowledge it and shut the door. I ignored it. I glanced around in awe as Nathaniel retreated to the trunk. Men and women all around me painted murals on the buildings, pavement or even paper.

"Let's go." He enveloped my hand in his own. Clanging sounded as he guided me somewhere, and I looked over to his opposite shoulder. A black drawstring bag hung around his shoulder. I looked at him in question, but he just smiled. Around ten minutes later, we ended up behind the last building that faced the water. He let go of my hand and removed his bag.

"What are we doing here?" I asked, watching Nathaniel undo the bag.

I started to laugh when he pulled out four bottles of spray paint. He grinned, stood up and jiggled a can. "Don't worry. It's completely legal."

Nathaniel handed me two cans: blue and red. "Now, I'm sure you know how to do this?"

"I might've had a little experience."

"Just spray away."

"What should I do?"

"Anything you want." He started his spraying. I nodded, smiling and biting my lip. I pressed the trigger and a pretty red mist sprayed out. It was quiet for a while as we both worked. I already knew what I was doing.

"Have you been here before?" I asked curiously, looking to the left of me at Nathaniel. He was cute when he worked. The corner of his tongue was slipping out of his mouth.

Nathaniel shook his head. "Nope." I continued to look at him, unable to break my stare. He was so unbelievably beautiful. His jawline was taut, and it accented his tan face.

"I have peripheral vision, you know," he joked and looked at me. I smiled and we held a comfortable stare. Suddenly, his face was clouded and he looked down.

"What is your problem?" I asked.

"What are you taking about?" He asked, still spraying.

"You've been so..." I trailed off, searching for the right word, "weird!" Nathaniel continued to spray, a look of knowing plastered onto his face.

I was sorting through rambling ideas, not even sure of what I was saying. "Are you cheating on me, or something?" I raised my voice.

He dropped spraying immediately and actually looked at me. "No! God, no! Why would you even think that?"

"I don't know, Nathaniel. Maybe because you've been so weird in the past two days. Maybe because it doesn't seem like you want to be around me."

"I've been fine," he mumbled and returned to spraying.

I stomped to his side and grabbed the can from his hand. Throwing it aside, I took a good look at his face, when it hit me. I took half a step back. "Oh, my god." I whispered to myself.

Nathaniel continued to spray, refusing to meet my eyes.

"Say it," I said evenly.

He shook his head.

"Say it."

Nathaniel didn't even shake his head this time. He just stared motionless.

"Say it!" I whispered, swallowing.

"A family is more important," he said, his voice barely audible. I clenched my jaw.

"I can't." His voice trembled.

I shook my head. "Say it!"

"I love you," he finally admitted, shaking his head. "I love you."

I stepped back, fear striking me. I wanted to say the same phrase, but I couldn't bring myself to do it. The words were on the tip of my tongue, but I couldn't. "Don't."

"Don't?!" he repeated angrily.

"Just, don't!" I yelled, crying.

"I can't help how I feel." Nathaniel stepped close to me.

"I almost lost them—my family. I can't lose them again. And when you tell me you love me," I stop, and whisper, "you'll make me even more miserable when I'm in Chicago."

"That's why I didn't want to tell you," Nathaniel said firmly. "At all."

"So, you avoided me?" I questioned, angry. "How would that solve anything?"

"I hoped it would go away if I tried to ignore it." Nathaniel paused. "But when I look at you...I know I can't ignore it." I was lost for words.

"A family is more important at this point. Please, forget I said anything," he pleaded, searching me with his eyes.

I shook my head and whispered, "I can't." How could he expect me to do that?

"Try."

Anger rushed through me. "You shouldn't have told me."

"It's not like I had a choice," he said coldly, then regained his warmth quickly and lowered his gaze to the ground. "Forget I said anything."

Forty - Two

Three more days, I said to myself. Only three more days until I finish the dreadful years of high school and head off to college. I still hadn't decided what school I'd be attending.

"Ms. Garland? The answer please?" Mr. Buchanan called from the front of the room, raising his eyebrows.

"Um," I stuttered, returning from my daydream state and glancing at my notes, "The Industrial Revolution?"

"Ms. Garland, we are finishing up the chapter of World War II, not the Industrial Revolution." He sighed. "I know you've all finished your SAT's and finals, but we have to finish reading this chapter –" Binggg! The bell sounded. Rustling of papers and scratching chairs filled the room as students hurried out of the classroom. Currently, I had no friends at Windsley Prep. Mandy wasn't an option, and I was ignoring Alex to the best of my ability. I could survive three more days without a walking buddy in the hallways. When I reached lunch, I glanced around the crowded cafeteria for a place to sit. Feeling slightly like the new kid, I decided to eat outside. Sitting at one of the vacant picnic tables, I bit into an apple Lucy had packed me.

"Lindsey."

Recognizing the voice, I snatched my brown paper bag and started to stand when Alex put a hand on my arm.

"Please," he pleaded with his eyes, "let me explain."

"I'm not in the mood to deal with you right now," I answered, glaring.

"Five minutes. Just give me five minutes, and if you still don't want to talk to me, I won't talk to you ever again." Alex held me in his gaze, eyes wide.

I contemplated this, and slowly lowered myself to the bench. "Five minutes."

He nodded, sitting across from me and pressing his lips together. "I'll start from the beginning." I didn't reply and watched him continue.

"As you know, I'm not very close with my dad or his relatives. One of his step brothers was just arrested and put in prison-"

"Walter?" I interrupted, wincing. Even though this man was in prison, he still found a way to ruin my adoption.

Alex looked taken aback. "Yeah... How do you know him anyway?"

"Doesn't matter," I said dismissively.

He shook his head. "Well anyway, Uncle Walter knows I live in Chicago, and for some reason he knows you and your whereabouts." I clenched my jaw. Hellen must've told him. By accident?

"So," he paused, looking guilty, "he promised me that if I ruined your adoption, he'd help my relationship with my dad." I shook my head, "This still doesn't make sense. So, when you first met me that day in the hallway..."

"When you told me your name, I knew who you were," he finished.

"So you pretended to be friends with me, get me to invite you to my house, and then make false complaints about my family to the police?"

Alex averted his eyes. "Yes, in the beginning. But as I came to know you, I really started to care about you, Lindsey. For a long time, you're the one good friend I've had."

"Maybe because you do twisted stuff like this," I hissed, not feeling bad at all.

"I felt really bad about telling the police those things. I almost didn't, but that day my dad was yelling at me and insulting me. I remembered why I had agreed to Uncle Walter's deal in the first place, and it just happened." He scratched his head, trying to make me see his regret.

285

I stood up from the table with my bag in my hand. "Your five minutes are up."

~~~~~~~~

"Ready?" Lucy grinned, glancing at the hairstylist standing next to me. I nodded, smiling. Suddenly, the chair was spun and I found myself staring at a beautiful reflection. My hair, curled because of the graduation cap I would soon be wearing, was styled perfectly. My makeup was done by a true expert, and Mariella giggled beside me.

"You look so good!"

I smiled at her. "Not as good as you." She wore a sheer pink dress which was fluffy and stuck out. Her hair was done by Lucy herself, and the light pink bow I had given her in the foster house was clipped on the side.

"Now, we just have the dress left." Lucy clapped her hands together. "I'm so excited!"

I smiled. "Me too." Not exactly. I was graduating without friends and without a definite plan for my future. I was hoping Nathaniel was included, but I didn't know where our relationship stood. Every time I thought of him, his pained expression entered my mind before he confessed his love for me. I couldn't be hurt; I refused to be hurt. Lucy drove us home and pulled my sleek dress from the plastic. When I had picked it out, I hadn't expected it to look so good on. I didn't think a dress as simple as a white one would look so stunning.

Lucy gasped and stood from my bed as I exited my bathroom. "That dress is beautiful!"

"I love it."

Lucy's smile faded, and patted the bed. "Come sit, honey." I did, folding my hands in my lap.

"Are you okay?" she asked, raising a perfectly arched, waxed eyebrow.

"I'm fine," I lied.

286

"Lindsey," she sighed, cocking her head, "I can see right through you."

I dropped my forced smile, frowning. "I miss them."

Lucy nodded. "I thought so. But you can see them next year, right?"

I inwardly sighed. "Yeah, I guess so."

"Come on, hon'. We can't be late to your graduation. And your speech!"

~~~~~~~~~

"Harry Truman!" The headmaster announced, shaking Harry's hand and licking his fingers for the next diploma. I moved up in the line, readjusting my black cap and waving a hand in my face. Weeks before, we were given the caps and told to personalize them. I plainly wrote, "Just Keep Swimming," with the small, familiar blue fish. I couldn't think of anything in particular. What I was intensely nervous about was my speech. One morning, when the bell had rung and I was rustling papers frantically, my English teacher, Mrs. Ross, had gently stopped me.

"You're a wonderful writer, Lindsey," I remembered her saying, smiling. "And I'd like to offer you the honor of representing our senior class.

"Isn't that what the valedictorian is for?" I dumbly asked, tucking an escaped strand of hair behind my ear.

"Yes, but I've specially requested to have an assistant speaker."

I bit my lip. "What do I write about?"

She waved a nonchalant hand. "Life experiences. How certain events have prepared you for the moment of graduation and your future. I understand, however, if you'd like to decline this..."

"I'd love to," I finished for her, half-smiling. How hard could it be? I stepped up to the front of the line, smiling at the principal.

287

"Lindsey Garland." Loud cheering erupted form the left of the stands, along with light, polite clapping from surrounding families. I laughed at my family's excitement and stepped up to the outstretched hand. I shook it and grabbed my diploma. After pausing in front of the podium for snapping pictures, I ambled back to my chair. A few words were distributed from teachers, a humorous story from a student, then, finally, my name was called. I breathed, trying to calm my rapid heartbeat. Although I've always been quite good at public speaking, I didn't cure the impending nerves. Once I was behind the podium, my entire class sat in front of me, holding blank stares. When I first came to Windsley Prep, I didn't want anyone to find out about my foster care secret. Now, I felt it was time to let them know. I looked over the crowd, half-smiling and leaning into the microphone.

"When I was five, people called social workers entered my life. They were friendly enough, but it never made sense to me. That thought soon changed," I glanced at my scribbled paper, "Over a year later, I was put into the foster system. Scary, unfamiliar homes were among some of them. Only one became my temporary and main household during the years of adolescence, to where I am now." I spotted Alex in the second row, a surprised and attentive look on his face.

"I must assume most of you were raised within a loving environment, along with enjoying perfect schooling and acceptance." I paused, shrugging, "I didn't have that. I realized too late that the foster system had control over my life." I noticed some murmuring in the crowd. "Though my foster mom tried her hardest," I paused for a moment that was just long enough for those close to me would notice, "the little things still weren't the same. Vacations, birthdays, and holidays were some of the many things I missed out on. I didn't get to have shopping trips or nail days. I didn't have a mom to stay up late with to talk about boys." I felt the vibe in the crowd shifting from surprise, to pity, and finally settling on exactly what I wanted to avoid. I jumped to my next sentence.

"Now," I said, with a tone of humor, "before most of you interrupt this sad speech to give me a hug of reassurance, I have to stop you." Low laughing interrupted the pity.

"Because of my life experiences, I have to believe that those years of the foster environment have built me into the woman that is standing in front of you today. I was at long last adopted, only a little over five months ago, and living with a family that I never would have even dreamed of having. I am graduating with excellent grades, and a positive outlook on what my future holds. So, as my cap does say," I grinned, "Just keep swimming. And please, don't give up when things get hard. Because I assure you, they will. But one thing that's definite," I said, wrapping it up, "whether you're short," I paused, pointing a finger at myself, and earning laughter, "or tall, we are all capable of striving to the best of our ability." Loud clapping and cheering erupted from the stands and chairs of students. I smiled for real that night. Lucy and David stood, clapping their hands wildly and grinning.

~~~~~~~~~

David slid a piece of vanilla cake onto my plate, chuckling at something Lucy had said. "Well, I thought it was very well done! Really, Lindsey. You're a great writer."

I plopped a piece of cake into my mouth. "Thanks."

"You looked good up there, Lindsey," Mariella said, raising her eyebrows mischievously. "Boys were looking at you." I laughed immediately, watching the expressions of Lucy and David. They couldn't contain their laughter as well as they sat at the kitchen table.

"Oh, I almost forgot!" Lucy suddenly said.

"What?" I looked at her.

"I left something in your room." Lucy stood, but I stopped her.

"No, I'll get it. Where'd you leave it?" I asked, standing up and putting down my fork.

"On the stool, in your closet." I nodded and jogged to the staircase. Once upstairs, I opened my white doors and stepped inside. I glanced around and finally spotted a small bag on the stool. I reached for it, peeking inside.

"Don't snoop," a voice from behind me whispered. I jumped, dropping the bag and whipping around. Lavender stood there, grinning, "This closet is bigger than my house."

I squealed, rushing forward and grabbing her in an embrace. "I can't believe you're here!"

"I know!" she said, laughing. A tap came on my shoulder, and I turned around. Nathaniel stood there, grinning and trying not to spew laughter.

"Nate!" I yelled, wrapping my arms around his shoulders.

Nathaniel kissed my forehead, and I stepped back. "Have you guys just been hiding in my closet?"

"For two hours, yes." Nathaniel shook his head. "It was excruciating being trapped with this one." He pointed to Lavender.

"Mmhm," she looked at me, "You're lucky I was here. I had to stop him from looking in certain drawers."

I laughed, swatting Nathaniel and eyeing my bra drawer, which was open a crack. "Oh really?"

He faked a sputter. "Lies!"

"I'm assuming you've found them, judging by the squealing?" Lucy stepped into the room, smiling.

I crossed the room to hug her and mumbled into her shoulder, "Thank you. For everything."

She rubbed my back. "Of course, Lindsey. Of course."

Forty - Three

I couldn't control my laughter as I watched Nathaniel try to attempt mounting one of our new horses, Sugar. Lavender laughed with me, turning her head and shielding her humorous grin from Nathaniel's vision.

"It's harder than it looks," he yelled, frustrated, standing on the ground but holding his foot in place on the stirrup. He pointed to Mariella cantering in the practice sand ring. "I mean, that's not normal."

"Here," I finally said, taking pity while I handed Black Jack's reins to Lavender and crossed to Nathaniel's side. I instructed him to take his foot out of the tangled stirrup so I could untangle it.

"There," I patted, loosening it to make it drop lower. After readjusting the other side, I instructed him to place the left foot on the stirrup. He did, with his tongue pinched cleanly in the corner of his mouth out of concentration.

"Now, hop twice and lift yourself over the saddle." I stood in front of Sugar's body to keep him from possibly moving. Because of Nathaniel's awkward movement of mounting, he might accidentally urge Sugar forward, which would be bad for everyone.

Finally, Nathaniel sat in the saddle. Lavender clapped, and cheered, "Finally!"

He shook his head. "Now, uh, move...?" His command came out like a question, and I tried to control my growing smile. I stood on my tiptoes, rearranging Nathaniel's fingers correctly on the reins, and looked up at him from the brim of my helmet. "To make him move, urge him gently forward with a squeeze of your legs. To signal him left, pull the reins left and the same with the right."

But he only stared at me, a soft smile. "You're sexy when you teach."

291

I chuckled, my cheeks growing warm, and cautiously stepped away. "Ready?" He nodded, so I collected Black Jack's reins and mounted. I motioned for everyone to follow me single file—the necessary rule for trail riding. I loved taking one of the horses out into the woods. David was adding on a new section to this property, not that it needed it. Once we reached the other side of the white gate, I stayed behind so I could lock it once more. Some new horses were grazing inside the paddock, and I didn't want them to wander off. Lavender was in front, moving up and down in time with Red's gait. I clicked to Black Jack, and his ear twitched and swiveled obediently toward me. I tapped his sides, and he immediately responded with a clean trot, taking me to the head of the line.

"Show off," Lavender muttered as I passed.

I laughed, and glanced back. "Do you want me to teach you?"

"Do you want me to die?" she called out in the same tone.

"Aw, come on! It's fun."

Lavender sighed dramatically. "Fine."

I nodded. "Okay, I'll bring you guys to the wider field." It was quiet as I led them to the left, past the low trickle of water. A comfortable, peaceful silence fell over us. The only sounds that filled the air were the combined noises of the horses' hooves and occasional snorting. Ten minutes later, we reached the field.

"Wow," Lavender breathed from behind me.

I grinned proudly. "Pretty, huh?" The field, which was currently beginning to green again from the frigid temperatures of the long winter, stretched across a beautiful four acres with slight rolling hills. We ended up in a horizontal line, descending down the slight hill. I suggested everyone slightly lean back so we wouldn't add extra pressure to our horse's back. We reached the bottom, and Lavender grinned excitedly.

"Okay, now I'm excited."

I nodded. "It's really fun. See, all you basically do is tap their sides and click with your tongue. You can also grab a fistful of his mane, to hold balance and slightly raise yourself off the saddle and lean forward to stare in between his ears."

"Too many words," Lavender said. "English, please."

I laughed. "Just tap his sides and you'll move naturally with his gait."

Lavender nodded. "Okay, that doesn't sound too hard."

"You know that feeling you get in your stomach when you go on a ride at the fair?"

"Yeah?"

I laughed. "That's what it'll feel like in the beginning, but it's such a rush that you'll forget about it. Just don't fall off."

She snorted. "I'll keep that in mind."

Nathaniel looked at me. "Can you teach me—*Agh!*" He didn't get to finish before Sugar decided to make a run for it. I gasped, watching Nathaniel struggle to stay on the saddle while Sugar stayed in a ground-eating gallop. Her long white legs spread over the grass as Nathaniel hopped awkwardly and violently on the saddle.

"Pull back on the reins!" I screamed. Either he didn't hear me or didn't know what the reins were. Sugar kept up her pace. I kicked Jack's sides, and we took off at a gallop to catch up. But I wasn't close enough, because I watched Nathaniel tumble off the right side into the grass. He groaned, and rolled over onto his back. Sugar slowed to a canter in the distance, and I slowed with a quick dismount.

I kneeled next to Nathaniel, holding a hand to his face. "Are you okay?"

"I," he calmly said, "hate horses." Red snorted next to me.

Nathaniel pointed in Sugar's direction. "I'm bringing that horse to the glue factory." Sugar raised her head at him, snorting and flicking her tail, almost as if she understood.

293

I handed Nathaniel an ice pack, and he climbed up to sit on my cleanly made bed. Lavender was still riding with Mariella. He put it on his stomach, wincing.

"I'm sorry." I frowned, picking out a piece of grass from his hair. "You sure you don't want me to bring you to the hospital? You had a pretty bad fall."

"Nah. I'm fine, just a bit sore."

"Well," I wiped some dirt off his cheek, "at least he didn't buck."

His eyes widened. "That sounds dangerous."

Nathaniel put down the ice pack, staring warmly into my eyes. "I've missed you, Linds."

"I missed you too."

He leaned in, kissing me softly for a moment. The kiss deepened as he placed one arm around my waist, and I threw an arm around his neck to bring him closer. His body was pressed hard against mine as we moved fluidly. He suddenly picked me up and gently placed me on my back as we still kissed. He ended on top of me, kissing my neck. Suddenly, a barrier fell in front of me as he began to tug at my shirt.

"Nathaniel," I pleaded. He stopped immediately, looking at me and moving a strand of hair away from my face.

"I'm," I paused, not wanting to say this. "I'm not ready," I lied. Nathaniel nodded complete understanding as he leaned back. I propped myself up on my elbows, biting my lip to keep from crying. That step with Nathaniel meant more commitment. I reminded myself how it would feel if I were to take that step, then have him leave. If I couldn't admit my imminent love for him, how could I do that?

When Lucy found out Nathaniel had fallen, she went into parent mode.

"Honey, does this hurt? Tell me if this hurts," she soothed as she dabbed a warm cloth on this forehead.

He chuckled. "I'm fine, really. Thank you."

"Well, Sugar is a new horse. I'm sure he was nervous in those surroundings, and Lindsey should have never put you on her." She frowned in my direction, and I shrunk, knowing she was right.

Lavender parted her lips. "It was just a freak thing, Mrs. Platt."

"Horses are unpredictable," Lucy agreed, handing Nathaniel a glass of cold water. "That's why David and I were a little iffy on it in the beginning."

"How'd you two meet?" Lavender asked, smiling.

Lucy thoughtfully glanced at the ceiling. "My husband? At a resort."

"Exotic," Lavender commented.

Lucy smiled at Lavender. "Yes, it was quite magical. And at the time, I was actually engaged to someone else, and I even invited David to my wedding!" All three of us gasped.

Lucy took a seat, taking a sip of her white wine. "He and I became good friends, actually. Always joking and laughing. I started to lose affection for my fiancé."

"So what happened?" Nathaniel asked.

"Well," Lucy paused, "it was his birthday and I just had to get away from him. I left him a note with my engagement ring, and headed to the airport."

"On his birthday!" I exclaimed.

Lucy winced. "Yes, not one of my finest moments. Anyway, I haven't even gotten to the best part yet!" We waited.

"I was in the airport, headed to New York City, when my flight was cancelled and I ran into David. It turned out his flight was cancelled too because he was on the same flight as me."

Lavender clutched her heart. "It was fate."

"I believe so," Lucy agreed, smiling. "And then it just went from there."

~~~~~~~~~

"What movie?" I called out, sorting through our collection. Nathaniel was busy in the bathroom, while Lavender lounged in the couch. It was quiet.

"Okayy," I said, dragging the 'y.' "We have *21 Jump Street, The Other Woman*, and some other foreign comedy-"

Soft crying interrupted me and I turned around, alarmed. "Lav?"

I instantly got up, and sat beside her with a hand on her back. "Are you okay?"

She wiped her phone then heaved a crying sigh. "We broke up."

"What?" I asked.

"Yeah. He invited me over to his house one day, and I saw him kissing some girl in a car."

"I'm so sorry, Lavender," I soothed, rubbing her back. "You don't need him."

"I miss him." She sniffled. I had never seen her like that.

"Why didn't you tell me?" I asked, worried.

"I wanted to, but I never had a good moment to bring it up."

"Don't worry. He's an idiot for cheating on you." I shook my head, angry at myself for ever thinking Andre was a good guy.

Nathaniel came into the room and took one look at teary-eyed Lavender. "Is this strictly girl problems?"

"Sorta." I mouthed to him to drop it, and he did, bending down to read my movie selections.

"I vote Nemo," he declared.

I frowned. "But that's not one of them-"

"I want Nemo." Nathaniel smiled, knowing it was Lavender's favorite movie.

I made an "o" with my mouth, sitting up to look for it. I had the best guy in the world.

Forty - Four

"I can't believe you're leaving tomorrow," I pouted, laying my legs across Lavender's lap.

"I know," she sighed. "Two weeks wasn't enough."

Arms suddenly came from behind me, and a head nuzzled my shoulder. "And to think we'd leave you all alone with this closet."

I smiled, scanning my en-suite bathroom and large walk-in with various drawers and mirrors, adorned with multiple pairs of shoes, handbags, and clothes. "I'll just have to come visit you guys again."

Nathaniel kissed my forehead and lounged on the nearby couch. "When's our flight again?"

Lavender closed her eyes to remember the crucial detail. "Ten-thirty p.m. So that means we'll have to leave here around seven." Nathaniel groaned, running a hand through his gorgeous hair.

I gasped, a brilliant idea flashing in my mind. "What if I come too?"

Lavender clapped her hands. "Road trip!"

"But we're going on a plane," Nathaniel pointed out, raising an eyebrow.

"Same thing." She shooed it away. "Go ask Lucy!"

I removed my legs from her lap and stood. "I'll be right back." I left my bedroom and jogged down the long, wooden staircase. Every step left a loud noise which ricocheted off the walls. Lucy was reading some type of document in the library.

"Hey, can I ask you something?" I asked, poking my head in. She nodded without diverting her attention and motioned for me to enter.

I leaned against the bookcase. "So, I was thinking... would it be okay if I went back with Nathaniel and Lavender tomorrow morning?"

Then Lucy finally looked up with parted lips, plucking her reading glasses off her nose.

"Lindsey..." she trailed off, biting her lip with some sort of disapproval. I just raised an eyebrow, not reading her reaction with ease.

"I wanted to talk to you about that."

"About what?" I asked, my tone softening.

"I don't think that's such a great idea."

"Why not?"

"I'm not trying to sound harsh, but do you really plan to travel back and forth to see him? You need to think about your future, Lindsey." Lucy blinked, her tone holding no hint of remorse of any kind.

"He is my future," I argued. Is this what mother-daughter fights were?

"What about college? You've gotten many acceptance letters, but you haven't even looked at one."

"I'm taking my time," I numbly said.

"The deadline to your answer is soon. As your mother-"

"You are not my mom," I shot back, angry. Okay, maybe I was being a tad harsh. Or really harsh.

Lucy frowned, sadly looking at me. "As your guardian," I noticed a flicker of correction, "I want the best for you."

"Nate is in my life, Lucy." I leaned on the chair for support. "I've already lost him once, and I didn't like how that felt. I'm not prepared to go through that again."

"I'm not saying to end things with him," Lucy soothed. "I'm just stressing your options here. I know what it feels like to miss a man— and I see it in your face every day you're not with him." I didn't say anything.

"It's not fair to you," she said.

I theatrically rolled my eyes. "Oh, come on."

299

"Excuse me?"

I shook my head, preparing to exit the room.

"I don't want you to have unhappiness caused by a boy that probably won't be in your life-"

"I'm going to marry him," I interrupted, my brain doing flip flops.

Lucy pressed her lips together, "Lindsey..."

"Please butt out of my life." I turned and left the room.

~~~~~~~~~

"You okay?" Nathaniel's husky voice was near my ear as I stroked Red's blaze.

I dropped my hand, turning around and facing him. "Why wouldn't I be?"

He glanced to Red, then back to me. "No reason...just, you didn't come back to your room."

"Did you hear the argument?" I whispered, noticing his tone.

Nate paused, but nodded anyway. "Yes."

"Lavender, too?"

He shook his head. "I went down to talk with Lucy about you coming, but stopped when I heard."

"You shouldn't have heard that," I said, humiliated and turning around to pet Red again.

Nathaniel came around, pinching my chin between his index finger and thumb and giving me chills. "Did you mean it when you said you'd marry me?" I blushed. Here I was, unable to tell the poor boy I was in love with him, and I was saying that I'd marry him.

"Lucy will forgive you, you know," he said, a guilty look on my face.

"I'm not sure about that."

"She loves you, Linds. You know that." Despite everything, I nodded. I knew.

300

He suddenly looked down and stepped away, grunting. "I should check on Lavender."

"I'm sure she's fine," I said, frowning at his sudden wish to exit.

Nate actually met my gaze, his own softening. "I told her I'd be back soon..." His remark stung. Why didn't he want to stay with me? He was leaving in less than twenty-four hours, and he was going to go to Lavender? But I watched Nathaniel's broad back disappear out of the barn.

Away from me.

~~~~~~~~~~~

The next day, Nathaniel was still being strange around me. At breakfast, I barely spoke to Lucy. I was too ashamed of what I'd said to even look at her, and I was still upset with what she'd said. David noticed my behavior.

"What's wrong, hon?" David asked me, quickly sliding papers into a folder he needed for work.

"Nothing." I kissed his cheek. "Have a good day at work."

He frowned, but looked at Lavender and Nate. "I'm having a late night tonight, but it was nice meeting you two." They smiled their goodbye, and David left. I slid next to Nathaniel onto the bench.

I kissed his cheek, but he quickly half-smiled before standing. "I should see if Lucy needs any help." I didn't bother with him as he went into the kitchen.

"What's with him?" Lavender asked, taking a bite of her toast.

"I have no idea." I met her eyes, taking a sip of my water. I didn't want to be on a bad path with him. Was he weirded out by the fact that I said I'd marry him? Great.

"I was thinking we should go have a girl's day. Get our nails done?" Lavender said, changing the subject wisely.

I smiled for real. "Sounds like fun."

I laughed, stepping through the front door with Lavender trailing. "Your manicurist was totally talking about you!"

"Well, I did ask to change the color twice." She winced, but laughed anyway. "I should learn Mandarin. Next time I'll be able to figure out what they're saying." I dropped my wallet on the kitchen's island countertop, studying my nails. I'd chosen a clean white, and Lavender had finally settled on a black.

I looked down at my toes. "They did a good job."

"Definitely," she agreed, looking at her own.

"Lindsey?" Nathaniel stepped into the room. It was close to six, and they had to leave soon. "Can I please talk to you?"

My smile faded into a look of seriousness. "Sure."

"Mind if we go to your room? It's quiet there." I glanced at Lavender, who looked at Nathaniel with an odd expression, her head tilted. I eventually nodded to him and let him lead the way.

Once we made it, I closed the door. "Is everything okay?"

He stuck his hands in his pockets, a look of torture on his face. "Lucy is right."

"What?" My stomach went cold.

"She's right about me holding you back."

I stepped closer to him. "What are you talking about?"

"I'm holding you back...my being in New York. You can't keep traveling back and forth. I won't be that selfish." He stared into my eyes.

"Selfish?" I said. "How could you be selfish?"

"You have a family that loves you, a bunch of college options, and a perfect life laid out in front of you." I struggled for a response. He blinked slowly. "I don't belong in that mix."

"Stop." My breathing started to shake. "You know that's not true. Lucy...she's just worried for me. But I don't care." I stepped up to him, holding a hand to his warm cheek and looking into his green

302

eyes. Those gorgeous green eyes had been the first thing I noticed about him that night in Lavender's apartment. "You belong in that mix. I need you to be."

He was shaking his head. "No, I don't." His green eyes were covered with a thin line of tears. "Then say it."

I knew what he was referring to. I shook my head, knowing I couldn't. "Nate, I can't."

His voice dropped to a whisper. "Three words."

The phrase was on the edge of my tongue, threatening to break the divide that was blocking its way. I whispered, "Can't you just know it instead of hearing it?"

"I need to hear it."

I thought of the feelings I'd feel once he was gone, and how they would intensify once I told him the three words. I hoped they would somewhat diminish if I didn't admit what he was looking for in return. But I was being dumb. They wouldn't ebb. They were there, whether they came out of my mouth or not.

"Lindsey, I'm going to do what I asked you here for." His soft words broke my brimming thoughts.

I held in a sob. "Please don't."

Nathaniel wiped away an escaped tear. "I need to let you go."

"Nate," I sobbed, "Please, no. We can figure it out—you're making a bigger deal than it is." Amidst my pleading, I felt the hated desperation leaking in. I didn't want to be that girl, but I realized in that moment that it was the most natural response I could have had.

"I'm not." He said, reaching both his hands up and running them through his hair—his tell-tale sign of nerves. And of doing something he didn't want to do.

My mind was scrambling to keep him with me, physically and emotionally. "Can we please figure it out?" My world was falling apart before me, and I felt my voice in the argument crumbling. I felt him straying further from me, and my words of pleading were becoming

303

fuzzy. He wasn't listening anymore; his mind was made up. I think it was that that scared me more than ever. He stepped closer. He had said all he needed to say. I knew that, but I didn't want to admit it to myself. He leaned in, closing his eyes and kissed my forehead. I shook with tears, trying to expand the moment, which lasted seconds.

"Goodbye, Lindsey."

I didn't follow him as he walked out of the room. The door shut with a click.

304

Forty - Five

"Please leave your message for-" I groaned in frustration, forcefully hanging up my phone and cutting off the robotic voice. Why wasn't he answering? After nine times of continuously redialing Nathaniel, I had almost given up. But then I thought of Lavender. Quickly, I pressed a number on my speed dial and waited impatiently for Lavender's bubbly voice.

"Hello?"

I sat up immediately from my lying down position on my bed. "Lavender? Is Nathaniel there?" My voice was scratchy and tired.

"Well, hello to you too," she grumbled.

"Sorry." I couldn't stop now. "Can I please talk to Nate? Is he there?"

The line paused for a moment, then I heard Lavender's uncertain voice. "He's not here right now - he just went for a run." I paused, closing my eyes. My heart was racing while I tried to understand what was happening. I was in shock. None of it felt real.

"Lindsey? Are you okay?" Her voice cut into my thoughts.

I bit my lip. "I'm coming to your house."

"What?"

"I'll be there in a few hours." I hung up without waiting for her answer.

~~~~~~~~~

Stealing Lucy's credit card wasn't the difficult part, but as I pulled up to the airport in a taxi, the rising guilt was almost suffocating. Lucy and David thought I was currently trail riding, and I wondered how long it would take them to realize I was on a plane headed to New York. My thoughts were a confused jumble. I wasn't

305

about to give up Nathaniel for a ridiculous decision he'd made out of guilt for me.

Once I got through the security lines, I reached my gate within record time and boarded within 20 minutes. I sat down with my backpack at the window seat, and sighed as the seats filled in around me.

Within the same amount of boarding time, the flight attendant's voice filled the cabin, "Good afternoon, passengers. Thank you for flying with JetBlue, and we hope you enjoy your journey with us today. Flight time from Chicago to JFK New York City is two hours and fifteen minutes. Prepare for take-off by making sure your seat is in its full upright position and your tray table up and locked." About two hours later, I arrived. Watching the tall buildings whiz by was comforting as I sat in the back seat of the taxi. It'd been around three hours since Chicago, and I'd received no calls from Lucy or David. After punching in the code, the driver pulled into the parking lot in front of Lavender's apartment.

"What's a young girl like you doing alone in the city?" he asked, eyeing me as I got out of the back seat.

"I'm a foster kid," I explained, biting my lip. "I don't have anyone that's missing me."

He frowned, but accepted the cash from my outstretched hand. The driver shifted into drive, but leaned over to the window. "Look, kid, I don't know your story. But there's gotta be someone out there who misses you."

The thought of Nathaniel hit me. Maybe he didn't want me after all. "I don't know." I finally answered truthfully, and with a shrug, he swung into traffic. I walked up to Lavender's door on the third floor and knocked. I heard approaching footsteps from inside, and the door swung open, revealing Lavender.

"You have some explaining to do." She crossed her arms.

"Missed you too," I said with a grim look. I went to step in, but she blocked my path. "Oh, come on, Lavender."

"You're not stepping into my house until you tell me what's going on. I don't want to harbor a known fugitive."

I let out a laugh. "Trust me, I don't have a criminal record." I went to step in once more, but she again blocked my way. "Lavender!" I forced a broad smile.

But only a serious look replaced the smile I thought would exist. "What's going on." It didn't come out like a question.

I groaned and held up my hands in surrender as I looked to the right nonchalantly. "Nathaniel broke up with me, okay? And it was for a stupid reason and I'm not going to let him go like that." It was quiet, so I finally met eyes with Lavender. She stepped to the side of the door, meaning I could enter.

Once inside, I dropped my bag and looked around. "Is he here?" Lavender eased slowly into the room, a frown on her face.

"What?"

She didn't answer.

"What, Lavender?" I asked again.

Lavender sighed. "He left."

"Left?" I repeated, the words feeling like sandpaper in my mouth. "What do you mean, left? Did he go to the store or something?"

"I mean, he moved out and I don't know where he is." She nervously tucked a piece of hair behind her ear.

I shook my head, not understanding. "But you said this morning he went for a run."

"I lied."

"I don't-" I started, but she held up a hand.

"He didn't tell me where he was going or why. He just said he needed to figure some things out. He told me not to tell you, and that he would call you and explain immediately after."

I checked my phone and gazed over the notification: "no missed calls."

"He hasn't called me since you guys left Chicago. So, like, three days," I said.

Lavender just shrugged. "I didn't know he broke up with you. I'm sorry, Linds."

I leaned on the counter. "And he hasn't called you?" A look passed her face.

"He called you..." I said almost in a whisper.

"Only to assure me he was okay and somewhere where he'll be in a good state of mind. Whatever that means..." She saw my expression. "I'll call him now, if you want."

I nodded, numb. She grabbed her phone from the charging dock and scrolled through her contacts. When the phone started to ring on speaker phone, she handed it to me.

Nathaniel answered the phone after the fifth ring with a husky, tired voice, "Hey, Lavender."

"Nathaniel?" I asked, placing the phone on the counter and leaning over it. There was a long pause, then his line went dead.

Forty - Six

4 years later

I walked into Professor Darby's second period class where
he lectured on politics and persuasion. Three years ago, striving to
become a lawyer seemed intimidating to me. It was the summer of
graduation I rarely thought about—or more like—avoided to think
about. The monstrosity of the actions I had taken after the boy issue
was cringe-worthy. But as a mature woman, I occupied my mind with
more thought-consuming information. I sat down on the aisle, Mac at
my elbow, and focused my concentration on the professor standing
in front of the class. Within minutes, students filled all empty chairs
and the room grew silent.

"Okay, where did we leave off yesterday?" Professor Darby's
voice boomed across the rows of college students. A student raised
his hand nearby, and the professor motioned to him with a tip of his
coffee cup.

"We were discussing quotes near the end," the student said
confidently. I pulled up a fresh document on my computer and
readied myself to type.

"Ah, yes. I presume most of you remember the quotes we
discussed?" Professor Darby asked. The door suddenly swung open,
but I didn't direct my attention to the visitor. I did this many times in
my first year, and got myself into trouble for paying closer attention to
the visitor than to class discussion. It was lawyer training—train your
mind to concentrate on one thing. I listened to a girl quote something
Aristotle said, when suddenly, the ringtone of a phone split the air.

My stomach dropped as I hurriedly scrambled for my phone to shut it off.

"Miss Garland, you know how I feel about disruptions!" Professor Darby pierced me with a laser stare.

"Sorry," I sputtered, finally finding my phone and turning my ringer off. I noted Lavender was calling me—typical. I almost smiled at her bad timing, but the current situation restrained me. My cheeks burned as the professor's eyes zeroed in on me.

"Can we continue, Miss Garland?" he asked, tapping his foot. I started to reply, but stopped when my eyes shifted to a man standing next to Professor Darby.

Something rolled in my stomach, as I tried to fathom who he was. It was Nathaniel, but it didn't look quite like him. He still had that overgrown, shaggy hair, the overly attractive yet handsome face, and those green eyes I used to love about him. But the haircut complimented his many mature features. Black stubble grew at his chin, with a jaw line so accented it made me falter. If it weren't for the eyes and what they held, I possibly wouldn't have recognized him. The thought scared me. Nathaniel seemed to recognize my last name, or maybe he had caught a glimpse of me, but I was sure he remembered me. He stared at me, mouth open slightly as if he couldn't come to the reality of an older Lindsey sitting in front of him.

"Miss Garland?" my professor asked again, impatience coloring his voice.

"Yes, Professor. I'm sorry for the disruption," I replied, taking my eyes off Nathaniel and returning my attention to the professor, who nodded and suddenly seemed to realize Nathaniel's presence.

"Ah, class? This is my substitute for the week: Mr. Sky. I expect you to treat him with respect, as you do me. Mr. Sky is an intern from Washington, where he is practicing law there as well. This week, we will be doing something special with the second years. In this class, I will be holding mock court sessions. Mr. Sky here, will be the interrogator and I will be the judge." Professor Darby explained with motions of his hands, then checked his watch. "And I think it's time already."

Shuffling erupted immediately over the loud protests of Darby. "But remember, your case starts tomorrow. These sessions will tell me if you're ready for my internship in the spring!" Everyone filed out along with myself. I didn't want to speak to someone from my past.

"Miss Garland?" the professor called. I stopped in my tracks. Turning slowly around, I made my way to him. Nathaniel stood to the side, reading something without batting an eye in my direction.

"Who was that, ever so, important call from today?" He raised an eyebrow.

"A friend of mine, which leads me to wonder about her timing, because she should also be in class." I let out a small laugh, which turned Nathaniel to glance up.

"Well, tell your friend she should be in class. And for you, turn off your phone. If it happens again, I will excuse you from my class," he said with total sincerity. I swallowed, but nodded and turned on my heel to leave the large room.

~~~~~~~~

"He's in my class," I blurted. Lavender glanced up from her half-eaten Chinese box.

"Who..." She trailed off, raising an eyebrow.

I hadn't said his name verbally in over a year, but finally swallowed and said, "Nathaniel."

Confusion clouded her vision for just a moment before her eyes widened. "Nathaniel Sky? The boy who stayed at this apartment?"

I nodded, not believing it myself. "I just don't get it. Out of all the law schools, he comes to my class to teach."

311

"Teach?" she repeated, setting down her pork fried rice and sitting back in her new couch. "I never pegged him for being into law."

"Yeah, apparently he's in Washington and is interning at NYU. We're supposed to have these cases tomorrow in class-"

"Wow. Are you going to talk to him?" Lavender interrupted.

"I don't plan on it," I said confidently.

"Just talk to him as a friend," she said with a shrug. "Ask him how his life is going, maybe. I don't know."

"He probably doesn't want to talk to me."

She shooed my statement away. "You've had relationships since then, and I'm sure he has too." I picked up my box of Chinese food and took a bite.

~~~~~~~~

"Do you know who's going first?" Paige, my roommate, asked me as we walked into Professor Darby's class.

I shook my head, my long, brown hair falling to the front. "I have no idea. You, probably. You're at the top of the class."

Her cheeks grew pink as we took our seats—in the back this time. "That's not true. If anything, you are."

I snorted, pulling my Mac out of its case and setting it on the ledge in front of me. "No way. My phone call probably ruined that chance."

She shrugged, pulling out her computer. "It wasn't that bad. I mean, you had that hot intern's attention."

I looked up, licking my lips and willing my increasing heartbeat to slow. "What do you mean?"

"What do you mean?"

She laughed. "That guy was staring at you. Even I noticed, and I'm oblivious most the time." I parted my lips to ask her anther question, but heavy silence fell over the room.

312

Nathaniel stood at the front of the room, pacing comfortably. "Okay, good morning everyone."

I breathed in air. His husky, warm voice was the same as I had remembered. "As Professor Darby explained yesterday, we will be having training cases for the next week." I thought I was going to be sick. This was more than torture. He motioned to the middle of the room where a lone chair sat facing the 200-student room. A desk was in front. "I am going to pick randomly from a list Professor Darby has given me, and you will come up and be presented the case you'll be fighting." We nodded, and watched Nathaniel, or Mr. Sky, pick up a clipboard and scan the list.

"Miss Garland?" he called out, scanning the room. I shuddered. This wasn't happening. Paige grabbed my paralyzed arm and swung it in the air.

"Right here!" she yelled gleefully. If only she knew.

He faltered as his eyes met my astounded ones. Mr. Sky held up a hand. "Come on down."

"Told you," Paige hissed to me. I lifted myself from my chair, my legs shaking as 200 heads swiveled toward me. I felt extremely shy as I stepped up to Nathaniel.

He didn't smile, but he didn't frown either. He studied my face and eyes. He grunted, "Take a seat, and study your case for about five minutes."

He turned to everyone. "Miss Garland will have time to study her case, and you all have the same one in your email." There was collected shuffling as everyone in the room went to check their email. "Now keep in mind I will be role-playing as the lawyer. This is all for training under pressure." I took a seat and glanced at my sheet. A father, named Josh, was fighting his ex-wife for custody of his child. She argues that Josh is an unfit parent, and she has illegally denied Josh's legal visits with the child. Easy.

313

I nodded at Nathaniel, who looked surprised I had finished my reasoning. "Who am I defending?"

"The father. I will be defending the mother. Are you ready?" he asked, looking at me. I thought of my defense position and nodded. "Yes." Professor Darby sat in front of me, and nodded to Nathaniel to start.

Nathaniel stood up straighter, pacing back and forth. "Now, I believe my client is absolutely correct with her denial visits. The father is clearly unfit to care for the child, which leads to the correct situation at hand." I kept a straight face.

"Miss Garland, how do you defend your client?" he turned to me, raising an eyebrow.

"I'd wonder over the lack of evidence in the case," I stated. He smirked, and looked at Darby.

Professor motioned. "Go on."

"There is only one eyewitness, which is the neighbor of your client."

"What's your point?"

"My point is that I'd like to see the medical records of the neighbor. Her witnessing an abusing factor may have something to do with her age. Eighty, I suppose? The culture at hand usually allows some rough playing between a son and father that does not rise to the seriousness of abuse. Unfortunately, the son is too young to give testimony. The neighbor, therefore, is a weak eyewitness. If anything, because there is a complaint at hand, the law clearly states a proper eyewitness other than the complainant by himself or herself. Without any proper witness," I paused, "the state has no case against my client." Nathaniel was awestruck with my outburst of knowledge. He looked at Darby, who looked clearly impressed.

"Very valuable observation, Miss. Garland. I believe you have just won your case." Clapping erupted from the students as I smiled and made my way back to my seat without a second glance at Mr. Sky.

~~~~~~~~~

After the end of that period, I decided it was childish to step around Nathaniel. I was past that type of behavior. So, while all students and Darby filed out, I stepped behind Nathaniel. I grunted and stood straighter. His shoulders tensed for a split second before he turned around to face me.

We didn't say anything for a while before I finally broke the ice. "Hi."

He half-smiled. "Hi."

I didn't know what else to say, so I awkwardly looked down, "Okay, well I guess I'll see you tomorrow-"

"Would you like to get some coffee?" He let out a chuckle, "It's been awhile."

I thought. Did I? I had to study for an exam that was a week away...but, after all, when would I have that chance again to tie up loose strings?

So, I smiled and said, "Sure."

315

Forty - Seven

"Small cappuccino, please?" I asked the barista behind the counter, who nodded and wrote my order on a piece of paper.

"It'll just be a few minutes." She nodded to me. I went to hand her a five-dollar bill, when Nathaniel pulled back at the same time. My hand gently touched his when he handed her a ten. He pretended it didn't happen and received his change from the lady.

"How does over there look?" I asked, pointing to the corner of the coffee shop. He nodded and let me lead the way. I sat down near the wall, and watched him take his seat across from me. Awkward silence fell over us, as I scratched at a dent in the table. *Maybe this was a bad idea*, I thought.

"So, what got you into law? I thought you were heading into the direction of veterinary school," he started.

"Yeah, well...Lucy," I paused, "You remember Lucy, right?" He nodded.

I continued, "Lucy said law school would set me up for a better future, and the money would be better."

"Did you even want to do law?" Nathaniel asked, his tone having a bit of edge in it. I parted my lips to respond when a waiter saved the moment and stood at our table with our drinks.

I smiled and took the drink in my cold hands. Autumn was a chilly time in New York. "It's fine. I like it, anyway." Nathaniel just nodded.

"So, what about you, Mr. Sky?" I asked with a smile and light tone. I sat back with my coffee. "How did you get into law? Last time I heard, you didn't want to go to college."

"That was a long time ago," he said, reminiscing then chuckled. The tension eased. "Yeah, well I didn't. But my-" he stopped himself

316

short, swallowing. I just raised a questioning eyebrow, not trying to press him.

"My fiancé urged me to apply late. She had, um, good connections with the deans, so with my LSAT scores and her recommendation, I got in quickly." Fiancé. I didn't know why a twinge of something in my stomach made me feel queasy.

"Fiancé," I repeated, with a forced smile. "How'd you meet her?"

He shifted uncomfortably, gazing into my eyes with a look of something. "She was the daughter of a friend of my mother's."

"When are you getting married?" I found myself asking.

"Next year. It was a fast proposal so..." he trailed off, taking a sip of his black coffee. "How have you been?" Nathaniel asked seriously, changing the subject.

"Fine," I smiled. "I've been fine. You know, everything is really the same. Lavender still has her apartment."

"She does?" He brightened. "I haven't seen her in so long.."

"Two and a half years," I confirmed suddenly, strange irritation growing in the pit of my body as I set my eyes beyond the glass of the window. "It's been two and a half years."

His smile was replaced with a look of sadness, and he leaned forward to murmur lowly, "I'm sorry. For everything."

"I think it's a little too late for that, Nathaniel." I said easily, finally meeting his eyes. Hardness plastered into my expression.

"I know I didn't handle it properly-"

"You didn't."

He put down his coffee, wincing. "I never apologized."

"Or called either."

"I'm sorry." Nathaniel breathed. "I never wanted to-"

"Don't." I shook my head and stood. "This was a bad idea. There's no point in mending our past, because the truth is I don't want to remember." He pressed his lips together.

"I'll see you in class tomorrow," I finished, and walked away from Nathaniel.

~~~~~~~~

The next week was filled with the same cases in class. Some students lost their case miserably, and some, like Paige, won with ease.

"It was fun," my roommate said as we walked out of class. I had avoided Nathaniel's eye contact all week, and it looked like he was doing the same. My phone range, cutting my response to Paige.

"Hold on," I murmured to Paige, who just nodded and looked forward as I answered the call from Lavender.

"Hey."

"Hey! I was thinking we should go on a walk...get some ice cream?" she answered.

I laughed. "How old are we again?"

"Oh, come on." I heard some shuffling in the background. "Ice cream never has an age limit."

I shook my head, smiling. "Fine. I'll meet you at 70th."

After we hung up, I looked to Paige. "Lavender asked me to go get ice cream with her. Want to come?"

"Nah, but thanks. Maybe next time." She smiled and nudged me. "Go have fun."

I kissed her on the cheek, smiling. "See you back in our room." We parted ways at the sidewalk, and I waved for a taxi to drive me to 70th. After climbing into the bright, yellow cab, I called to him the destination. He nodded and made a U-turn. Around fifteen minutes later, we arrived. Lavender stood there, scrolling through her phone. After I paid the driver, I walked up to her.

"Excuse me, ma'am. You're blocking the path," I said in a deep voice.

She looked up, startled, then swatted my arm. "You're obnoxious." We walked to the Ice cream store, ordering our favorite flavors. Lavender got Mint Chip, and I got my favorite: Double Chocolate Chocolate Chip. We walked, licking our ice cream and laughing uncontrollably. Nothing beat these moments.

"Is that who I think it is?" Lavender suddenly asked, licking her cone and looking out over part of Central Park. I didn't even notice we had ended up here, and I hadn't been here since Nathaniel and I had decided to make things work. I had left for Chicago that day.

"Huh?" I questioned, licking my lips.

"Nathaniel Sky," she murmured lowly. My eyes widened. Nathaniel sat comfortably on a large boulder overlooking water. I froze. It must have been a coincidence he was on our boulder.

"Lavender, don't..." I hissed, grabbing her arm to leave quickly.

"Hey, Sky!" Lavender yelled. Nathaniel's head whipped up, catching Lavender's gaze. His grin was inevitable as he jumped down and started to jog over to us.

"Is that who I think it is?" he asked, feet away from Lavender. Lavender handed me her ice cream and grabbed Nathaniel in a hug. He threw his arms around Lavender, spinning her around. Well, hating to interrupt the reunion, I just stood there awkwardly and observed.

He dropped her lightly. "Boy, have I missed you!" Jealousy coursed through me; I didn't feel that way because of Lavender. I felt that way because she had gotten an awkwardness-free perfect reunion. While with myself, on the other hand, Mr. Sky can't even keep eye contact for more than one second.

"Where have you been?" She smiled, taking her ice cream back from my hand.

"Oh, around." He shrugged, smiling.

Finally, he noticed my presence. "Hi, Lindsey."

319

I refrained from rolling my eyes. "Hi." What were we, eighth graders?

"So, tell me everything! Lindsey says you're studying law too," Lavender said, licking. I grumbled inside. Now he knew I was talking about him.

Nathaniel paused half a beat, trying to fathom that I had actually used his name to another human being, then said, "Yeah. I live in Washington right now, interning NYU. This week has been fun with the second year students."

He looked at me. "Right, Lindsey?"

I tightly smiled. "Yep. It's been a blast." Such a blast.

"Well, next time you disappear, you better call." Lavender crossed her arms, half-faking to be angry.

He just laughed, looking at the ground. "Sorry about that. I just got caught up in some stuff." Without thinking, a snort erupted in the back of my throat. They both looked at me; Lavender raised her eyebrows, and Nathaniel pressed his lips into a tight line.

"Sorry," I apologized quickly, and bitterly yet sarcastically added, "just...I find it quite hard to take two seconds out of my day to pick up a phone and call someone." Uncomfortable silence fell over us, and Lavender, as usual, broke the ice.

"Okay! Well, it was nice seeing you, Nate. Promise to stay in touch. Keep me posted on how you're doing." She quickly hugged him with one-arm, and backed up. My ice cream was below the cone now. I nibbled on it, pretending to be lost in thought.

Nathaniel barely attempted to smile, but did so weakly and sadly. "Yeah, I'll see you. Enjoy the ice cream." He paused, glancing at the cone in my hand, and meeting my eyes, "Double Chocolate Chocolate Chip, right?" I parted my lips in shock as I watched him half-smile and disappear back into the park.

Forty - Eight

"I have a proposition," I said quietly at the end of the class, standing in front of Nathaniel.

He raised an eyebrow, a small smile playing at the corner of his lips. "What kind of proposition?"

I swallowed. "I just want to start over. We're adults now, it's time we start acting like it. Okay?"

Nathaniel didn't say anything for a few seconds; he just stared into my eyes. "Fine."

I nodded. "Good."

"So as friends, does this entitle us to a walk in the park today?" I parted my lips in question. What?

"Just as friends, I promise. I have my own girl at home," he reminded me, too sure for the statement. A ringtone from his jacket pocket cut off my response. Nathaniel glanced at the screen, smiling softly.

"Karen," he whispered to me, before answering it. Karen? "Hey, Hon'. How are you?" He turned from me, facing the window. I guessed it was his fiancé, so I motioned to him I was going to leave to give him privacy. He nodded at me without really paying attention. As I left the room, I heard his happy laughter.

~~~~~~~~~

Later that day on campus, an attractive brunet approached me.

"Hi, dear. Would you know where Mr. Sky would be?" She smiled and smoothed down her white dress.

"Natha-?" I stopped myself, realizing it was inappropriate to address a teacher's assistant by his first name. "Yes, he's-"

"Right here," came a surprised, familiar voice behind me. Karen's face brightened, as she stepped around me and threw her arms around Nathaniel.

"Nate!" Her squeal was muffled in his collar. He hugged her lower back, while his eyes were locked to mine. I blinked away.

"I can't believe you're here!" he exclaimed, kissing her cheek. I knew his excited voice, but this most definitely was not it. Nathaniel sounded distracted. I turned to leave, unsure of what to do with myself.

"Oh, Miss Garland?" Nathaniel called to my back. When I turned to face him, his gaze was intense, and the woman's face flashed with quick uncertainty that I wasn't even sure happened.

"Yes?"

"This is Karen, my fiancé." He smiled and tightened his snug grip on her waist. Good to know.

I stepped up to her, holding out my hand. "Nice to meet you."

"And you." Karen smiled warmly, shaking my hand back. "Are you Nathaniel's student?"

I nodded. "Yes, he's a wonderful help to our professor."

"I knew he'd be," she said dreamily, resting her head on his shoulder. He kissed her head and looked back at me. Silence dripped over us.

I checked my phone clock. "Oh - I'm so sorry! I'm late for something, but it was nice meeting you." I waved, and they did as well before returning to Professor Darby's classroom. The only date I was ever late for was Chinese food and myself. Later that night, Professor Darby's blast-email caught me off guard. He informed us all that Mr. Sky would be staying an extra week, due to work that needed to be completed. I groaned in frustration, tossing my Lo Mein in my bedside trash with more force than intended.

~~~~~~~

322

I walked into class a few days later, taking my usual seat next to Paige's empty one. Professor Darby was taking a family emergency day, and Nathaniel was left to teach the class. I noticed Karen, apparently one of NYU's alumni, sitting in the corner with her nose in our curriculum. Paige entered the room moments later, taking her place next to me.

"How'd it go last night?" I asked, smiling. Paige had prepared all week for a date her friend had set up for her.

She made a face, making a thumbs-down sign with her hand. "Terrible."

I puckered out my lower lip. "Sorry, Pai-"

"Miss Garland?" A curt, loud voice boomed suddenly over the room. I glanced upwards, alarmed. The room had somehow become deathly silent.

"Yes?" I asked, blinking at Nathaniel.

He crossed his arms. "Is there something that you should share with the rest of the class?"

I did a double take. "Sorry?"

He sighed impatiently. "I'm sorry, I don't think I made myself clear. I don't enjoy conversations during my lecture time." His tone stung. He stood immobile, taut and swallowing.

I forgot the pairs of eyes on me. I took in our presumably appropriate relationship at the moment and parted my lips, "I wasn't talking during your lecture. You hadn't started talking, and I always respect my teachers when they are speaking." I heard Paige's sharp intake of breath in surprise. I had just talked back to a professor's assistant in front of two hundred peers. I noticed Karen's head rose a fraction in the corner, as she watched the scene taking place.

His gaze softened, then he realized, as I did, that it wasn't just us in the room. "Miss Garland, I'm going to have to ask you to leave." I sat, stunned, but slipped my computer back into its case and retreated down the aisle.

The next day, I walked early into class with confidence. Few students trickled in, only because I was fifteen minutes early. Paige was nowhere to be seen. Nathaniel sat at one of the chairs in the front, scrolling through his phone. His eyes glanced up when I swiftly walked past him up the aisle.

"Oh, Lindsey?" He said my name in a hushed tone. He glanced around at the oblivious students nearby.

I shut my eyes for a second, then turned. "Yes?"

"I wanted to apologize for yesterday." He clicked off his phone and slipped it into his pocket.

I shrugged, strongly refraining myself from falling into the trance of his green eyes. "It's fine."

Guilt flashed in his face, and this time, I was sure of the emotion. "No, it's not. I was out of line when I called you out for something you didn't do. And especially for dismissing you."

My expression softened, accepting his apology. "Okay." I turned to leave, but his hand stopped my shoulder. Chills shot through my body, and I flinched away as I turned back to him again.

He made an inquisitive face as he lowered his hand slowly and stuck it in his pocket. "How about that walk later today?"

"I don't think that's a good idea."

"Please?" he asked, his expression unreadable. I faltered, not thinking it was bright of a teaching assistant to be seen with a third-year student. But his strong gaze that held so many memories made me think twice.

I sighed. "One hour."

Forty - Nine

"I swear! Darby spilled my coffee all over himself!" He laughed, shaking his head and continuing to take small strides as we ambled through Central Park.

"That's funny."

"Yeah, well, I didn't get to drink my coffee," Nathaniel muttered.

I sarcastically puckered my lip. "Poor you." Our familiar banter left an ache in my heart.

He smiled, revealing teeth. "How have things been?"

"With what?" I looked over the vacant park. We were reaching the area we once called "ours."

"With everything. Tell me all about it."

I thoughtfully looked up into the gray sky. "Well, I got into NYU that summer. I was pretty scared to go." I glanced at Nathaniel, whose full attention I knew I held. "The first couple months were awful."

"How so?" We cut over a path onto a grassy area, and ended up of a pathway under low hanging trees. The lighting darkened around us; the shadows and the darkening sky contributed to the eerie atmosphere.

I shrugged. "I don't know. You think the foster system would've prepared me for living alone. I think it did the opposite."

"Really?"

I nodded. "I think I just needed to learn how to do it. Now. I love it."

"Good," was his reply. "I'm glad you're happy."

I half-smiled. "Yeah. I am. Are you happy with Karen?"

It was quiet. I finally looked at him. He was staring at the ground, a thought-consuming expression enveloping his face. "I am. She's amazing."

I smiled. "Good. Are you planning on having children?"

Nathaniel shook his head. "Not now. Maybe in a few years, after college years are finished. But Karen wants them." I laughed quietly to myself.

He looked up, smiling. "What?"

"I never thought of you as a father." I laughed.

He lightly shoved my shoulder. "Trust me, I'm terrified for the day I hold a kid in my arms."

I shooed it away. "You'll be fine."

"Yeah, until I drop it." An easy laugh escaped from my lips. He didn't seem to have changed so much, right? Easy silence fell over us as we walked farther beneath the overhanging trees. A light sprinkling of rain began to trickle off the leaves, but the trees protected us.

"Lindsey." He stopped and clenched his fists, turning to me.

I looked at him. "Yeah?"

"I really am sorry." A tortured look passed his face. "I never intended to hurt you as much as I did."

I swallowed, slight anger rising in my throat as I avoided his strong gaze. "Why did you do it?"

"I told you why."

I shook my head. "No. You didn't."

He took a breath, swallowing and looking as if he were taking advantage of the moments of silence. "I heard Lucy talking to you about your future that day. She said you couldn't possibly continue to travel to New York to keep seeing me, and I started to understand her concern."

"So you broke up with me." I shook my head at the ground.

"Only because I wanted you to have the best possible future."

I bit my tongue to restrain the growing tears. "You were my future." He glanced to the ground with a thoughtful look.

"That still doesn't explain why you didn't answer my calls. You just broke the connection between us. Even Lavender."

"I admit I went about things the wrong way."

"And for that," I said softly, "I will never forgive you."

"Lindsey-" he started.

"You left me!" I yelled, tears rushing down my face and a sob rising in my throat. "You left me."

"I know." Nathaniel nodded, licking his lips. "And I still haven't forgiven myself either."

"I called you for months, Nathaniel. Months. And you never answered. Do you know how often I sat there, going over and over what I must've done? I even went to New York to find you."

He looked up, surprised. "You came after me to New York?"

"Yes. And it was probably the stupidest thing I had ever done." I shook my head, hating him all over again. "You had me thinking it was all my fault." He didn't answer. His eyes sadly bored into mine.

"I think the worst part was realizing that you weren't who I thought you were." Poor, young Lindsey who didn't think her boyfriend could do no wrong.

"I'm sorry, Linds. I know I acted like shit. All I wanted to do was reach out, but I just thought it would make things worse." I shrugged. There was nothing else to say.

"I didn't know you came here." He blinked fast. "Lavender didn't tell me." I ignored the statement and looked up at the sky. It had turned a darker tint.

"I loved you." Again, he couldn't meet my eyes but lowered his gaze to the ground.

The same feeling I had when he had first told me this rolled in my stomach. "I know."

Nathaniel stepped closer, his gaze darting quickly to my lips, then back to me eyes. "I never stopped loving you." I shuddered, more tears threatening to spill. I sensed a certain type of danger. This was bad, Lindsey. Abort. Remember how much he hurt you?

He raised a thumb to my cheek, wiping away a tear. "And I know you loved me too." All it took was just a fleeting moment of consequence-free thinking. I didn't think about the consequences of standing in the open with my professor's assistant. I didn't think of his fiancé. I didn't think at all, and maybe it was the worst thing for me. Maybe it was the best thing for me. The seconds it took for him to reach me was timeless, but the kiss lasted longer. By the time we our lips met with arms clutching each other in a powerful embrace, all I could think about was the familiar feeling of his mouth on mine. His hands wrapped around my cheeks, mine around his neck. The rain's sound seemed powerful in the distance, but all I could hear was my rapid heartbeat. All thoughts, conflicts, and memories faded away as we stood kissing each other passionately in Central Park. It was the moment that tied all loose ends together. I pulled away suddenly, remaining millimeters from his lips as I took a breath.

"I love you," I whispered. A smile found its way onto his face, as he leaned in again, kissing me.

Fifty

I didn't know how to feel about what happened. Had I become that girl? That girl who steals the guy from his fiancé with no thought of how it would affect them? I swallowed hard, consumed in guilt. But at the same time, it faded away once I thought of the feeling of his lips on mine. After three years, our passion had remained. He was everything I remembered; he was perfect, beautiful, funny, romantic. I stopped day dreaming. I stood in mutual horror as I'd, again, forgotten the biggest issue at hand. Nathaniel was getting married. The very thought made me sick to my stomach. What had I done? What had we done? I stared at Karen and Nathaniel. They were clearly in a heated discussion. Karen seemed angry, using her hands for emphasis. They stood privately against one of the brick buildings on campus. I nervously pulled on my side braid, guilt pulsing through my veins. It was official; I was a terrible person. I never should have kissed him. I never should have let him in again. I never should have let myself fall in love with him in the first place. 3:00 am was officially my most hated time of the day. I watched Nathaniel press his lips together and look at the ground. They didn't say anything for a moment until Karen's eyes finally met mine. I started to turn away, humiliated and guilty for overseeing a private conversation. And for kissing her fiancé. Yeah, that was it. I walked away quickly, headed to the only place I could think of. I made it to my car, sitting hunched over, in a daze. In that moment, all I needed was my mom. I pulled out my phone and scrolled to my favorites, choosing her name and letting it ring. By the third ring, her cheery tone answered.

"Hi, honey," she said, "How are you?"

"Fine," I held the phone between my ear and shoulder. I played with my nails.

"You don't sound fine."

329

I paused, wondering what it was going to sound like out loud instead of in my head.

"Lindsey?" her voice was clearer, and the change of volume made me imagine the phone now snug to her ear instead of on speaker. I imagined her in the kitchen and cooking yummy food, or in the barn brushing Red.

"I kissed Nathaniel and he's getting married." I blurted out. Abrupt, much?

She didn't say anything. I cringed, hating myself even more. My guilty conscious continued to skyrocket. One thing was true: it did sound worse out loud than in my head.

"I'm going to ignore the fact that he was in your presence, considering the asshole dropped off the face of the earth," she started, and I smiled at her Momma bear instincts, "but why don't you just start with explaining why you kissed him?" Her tone softened for the second part.

I sighed a sigh I was sure broke her eardrums and paused a beat. "You know why."

"Listen, honey," I heard her start, "You don't need help with this."

"I'm a bad person," I shook my head.

"No," she said, "you just have to talk to him. Remember you're not the only one who messed up." I hadn't even thought of that.

"Also, what do you think it means on his half if he kissed you?" She posed another question.

"You're good at this," I mumbled and gripped my steering wheel.

"I know he made some mistakes, but the Nathaniel you knew is still there. Remember that. You know what to do."

~~~~~

I drove to Central Park, head a bit clearer from Lucy's help. I still felt like I needed to do something, anything, to get my mind off of it all. I needed fresh air . So I drove quickly, out of Queens

330

and into the correct street. Parking my car, I strode thoughtfully through the park. I wanted to get to a quiet place, but without creepy people. I ended up in a new section I had never visited. Large, flat boulders edged their way through a bundle of autumn's trees. While I pondered whether to climb them, my eye caught Nathaniel's shape in the distance. I stared for a moment, not moving. It sometimes felt like my life was right out of a book. He stopped walking once he caught sight of me and pulled his hands out of his pocket. He lightly jogged over to me, stopping within feet.

"Hi."

I shook my head immediately. "We can't do this, Nathaniel. We both know it." Nathaniel made a confused face, but I knew he understood.

I took a breath, making my hands into fists inside my long sweater. "Whether we like it or not, I'm in your past. Karen is your future, and I refuse to risk a future you deserve."

He stared, face blank. I continued, "Listen. You were my first love, and that means something to everyone. First loves are powerful, and they're always special." I was rambling on now, but everything I was saying I felt was true. "You'll always be that person to me, but I'll eventually get over it."

He still didn't say anything. I took his silence as my cue to continue, and I took the chance to say as much as I could get in. "You're just confused about your feelings. Karen is your fiancé, and what we did was wrong."

I took a shuddering breath, avoiding his eyes and looking over the leaves. "It's my turn to let you go." I turned to leave, when his arm pinched my elbow to restrict me.

I met his green eyes, a thin vale of tears developing in my own, and whispered, "Please, let me go."

Nathaniel shook his head. "I've already let you go once. I'm not gonna make the same mistake again."

331

"I need to tell you something." He took his hand away from my arm. I crossed my arms, awaiting his answer.

"Karen isn't my fiancé. She never was." Nathaniel paused, pressing his lips together while he searched my eyes for anything that might signal him to stop. I just stared. Could he get any more confusing?

"I was planning on proposing, and she knew it too, because she found the ring. I returned it months ago. I ended things with her the day she visited me. She was trying to resolve things today, but I stuck firm on my decision." My eyes widened in pure guilt. Was this because of me? It was official; I was the girl who messed up a soon-to-be-married-couple.

"You didn't come between us, I promise," he said quickly, as if reading my mind. "It's just..." He trailed off, looking like he was searching for the right words. "When I was with you, I remembered what it was like to really love someone. Karen was an amazing girl, but I never had that with her. For months now, I'd been thinking of ending it between us—even before I saw you again in class." I tried to concentrate on breathing. What was he saying?

Nathaniel half-smiled, stepping closer and taking me in his arms. "Three years ago, I met an incredible girl in the middle of the night. She sprayed me with mace." He paused and let out a laugh. "I became to know her every day. This girl was stubborn, sarcastic, annoying-" I cracked a smile, "-beautiful. I first kissed her on the side of the road, and she said if I ever did it again she'd call the cops." The memories fluttered in my chest as I managed a laugh.

"I fell in love with this girl, but I later screwed it up. And I promise to make it up to you for the rest of my life." A breath caught in my throat as I covered my mouth with my hands. Nathaniel started to kneel on one leg, pulling a small black box from his pocket.

"Lindsey Garland, will you marry me?"

Fifty - One

"Nathaniel, "I uneasily started, dreading my next words, "I can't." His face dropped.

I swallowed, pushing back the acceptance that was on the tip of my tongue, and lamely said, "I'm-I'm in the middle of a big year for me..."

Nathaniel blinked, closing the small box's lid and standing back up. He took a breath and blinked. "I'll see you in class tomorrow, Miss Garland." Nathaniel left me standing alone in Central Park.

~~~~~~~~

I stormed into Lavender's apartment, letting the door slam into the wall. It was quiet, and I guessed she was out. I'd have to wait until she returned.

"Get out of my house, you bastard!" Lavender's voice screamed. "Or I'll call the cops!"

I sighed. "Lavender, it's me."

She stepped out from behind the wall, sheepishly smiling but still clasping her broom. "Oh. Hi, Linds." I shook my head, stepping into the kitchen and covering my face with my hands as I leaned into the counter.

"What's wrong with me?" I mumbled.

"What?"

I squeezed my eyes before peeking out of my hands. "Nathaniel proposed to me." Her broom fell immediately out of her hand, earning a loud thwack! from the ground.

Her mouth dropped. "WHAT?" I covered my ears, watching her.

"We have to get a dress! Oh, and the invitations! Where's the ring?" She fired off questions, pacing back and forth excitedly.

"Lavender-" I tried to stop her.

"Your mother will die. And Mariella! A pink dress will look adorable on her-"

"Lavender!" I raised my voice, and she stopped. "I said no."

Her face dropped too, hitting me like déjà vu as I had just witnessed Nathaniel doing the same. "What." It was more a monotone statement than a question.

"I said no."

"Why?" she said slowly, not comprehending.

"I said this was a big year for me-"

"You're an idiot."

I frowned. "Thanks, Lav."

She shook her head with irritation, leaving the room.

I sighed, walking after her. "Lavender." She didn't stop, just plopped herself on her bed.

"Lavender." I sat on the edge of the bed.

"I just-" she stopped, shaking her head in annoyance.

"What? Tell me."

Lavender looked at me, pulling herself up and sitting against the bed frame. "I just don't get you."

"What's that supposed to mean?"

"After everything you've been through: the foster stuff, the teenage home, Walter... don't you get it?"

"Get what?"

She shook her head. "He's been through it all with you—for you. For the past three years, I've watched you and seen how hard it's been on you. I know you've been trying to ignore your feelings for him, even though Jack- "

I held up hand at the mention of my ex-boyfriend. "Let's not mention Jack."

"You guys are meant for each other. No one stays in love for that long."

334

I played with the ends of my hair, speechless. "Who says he's in love?"

"Have you seen the way that kid looks at you?"

"Who says I'm in love?" I snorted.

"Have you seen the way you look at him?" She asked in the same tone and blinked calmly. I rolled my eyes, but she continued, "Why can't you just accept that he's everything to you, and to stop running from whatever it is you're running from?"

I was quiet for a moment. "I think I'm scared to commit myself to him again. I don't want him to hurt me like he did."

"Knowing Nate," she smiled, softly smiling, "he won't." I looked down at my hands, until she leaned forward and squeezed them.

"If you're lucky enough to have a guy like Nate, I wouldn't let him go."

~~~~~~~~

Whenever Nathaniel and I would get into small disputes or disagreements, I would always find him in Central Park under our secret rock hangover. That was where I found him at six o'clock. The sun was beginning to set, casting an eerie but pretty glow over the Park. He was sitting under it with his eyes closed and head leaning against the rock.

"Nathaniel." I was breathing hard. I had been running fast.

His eyes immediately opened, and he looked over at me. "Lindsey?" It was like time stopped. But before I knew it, my mind was already made up.

"Yes." I evenly said.

A cloud of confusion ran across his face. "What?"

"Yes. I'll marry you." I didn't want to overthink it. I just wanted to trust my instincts—and jump. For the first time in my life, I was more than sure about that decision. Nathaniel pulled himself up, shocked but smiling. I ran to him, jumping into his arms. We held one another

335

for a little bit without saying anything. The silence was comfortable. I retreated back and let him slide the ring on my fourth finger. It was beautiful; a caret diamond set on a platinum band.

He smiled, wiping a tear off my cheek. "I hope it fits."

I nodded, speechless. "It's perfect."

I turned my finger slightly, frowning curiously at the small symbol engraved on the side. "Is that an-"

"Infinity sign," he finished, looking at it. "On our first date in Central Park, I gave you-"

"A necklace with an infinity sign." I grinned, recalling. I still had it to this day. He smiled, kissing my finger softly.

"But now there's a bigger question." Nathaniel suddenly said, amusement in his tone as he enveloped me in his arms. He nuzzled his head in my neck.

I looked up. "What's that?"

"Where are we going to get married?" he murmured in my ear. I felt chills erupt over my skin. I smiled excitedly, looking around us and then to him with a grin. Like he had to ask.

"I may have an idea."

Epilogue

"Lavender," I whispered, staring into my reflection. Brown hair, the summer sun having given it cutting blonde streaks, curled into loose waves. They fell over my collarbone, spreading over my shoulders and back, ending just below my exposed shoulders. My gaze shifted to my light brown eyes, blinking my mascara-coated eyelashes. My pupils dilated at the thought of him, and familiar nerves swirled in the pit of my tummy. I blinked rapidly, desperately trying to distract myself but failing. My makeup was the best I've ever had, thanks to Lavender. My dress, fitted around my waist, fell like a waterfall and flowed elegantly to the ground. Both our moms, his and mine, went dress shopping with me, because I clearly knew nothing about dresses and makeup and all things involved. It was the most satin and lace and, (was it called chiffon?), I had ever seen. I pressed my lips together, coated with pale pink gloss, and tried to smile in the mirror. My blush dusted cheeks rose with my attempt in smiling, but it came out looking like I was smiling through a painful procedure. My eyes finally darted to her, who stared at me with suspiciously raised eyebrows. "I'm freaking-"

"-shut up. Shuddupshuddupshuddup," she said in her very-Lavender way waving her hands and mimicking a windshield wiper, "I got you this far, there's no way I'm letting you ditch now. I promised him I'd get you down the aisle-" I cut her off with my giggling, turning to her and crossing my arms, "I'm not ditching. I was just saying I was nervous."

I watched her take a breath, her eyes closed in almost what seemed like relief. "Thank, Jesus."

"Wait," I blinked, "What do you mean you promised him?"

"You have a history of running."

I grinned, "I do not!"

337

"Do you not remember the past 6 years of your life?"

It was quiet while we stared at one another; her, with mock-seriousness, and me, with an epic fail in trying not to crack under the pressure. A laugh leaked through, my poker face betraying me. We both fell into hysterical laughter, and I hugged her, holding on tight.

"I love you." I mumbled into her shoulder.

"I know you do," she said over mine, squeezing, "I'm so proud of you."

I pulled back, giving her a half smile. "You know I couldn't have done any of it without you."

"Oh, so now you're admitting to the past 6 years?" I laughed in response, but she knew. I knew she knew. Before him, and even during him, she was my real soulmate. And I hers.

"Aren't you happy I stole those stupid blocks from you?" She grinned.

"No! You were the worst."

"Okay, but you have to admit," she paused for dramatic effect, taking a looonng sip of citrus infused water, "you were so bad at making sand castles."

I laughed. "I was not! I could've been a star."

"You should be grateful I tried to share my killer sand crafting skills with you."

I did a tiny bow to her, to which she carefully flipped her professionally styled hair and graciously accepted the praise. "Thank you, Lavender, for being so obnoxiously intrusive to my playground time."

She stuck her tongue out at me just when the door to her new apartment swung open, my mom stepping in looking as beautiful as ever.

She stopped, a hand flying to her mouth. I swear, I saw a gloss form on her eyes. "I thought I would be prepared for this, but-" a choke cut off her next words, and I rushed to her.

338

"No, no," she waved me off, "I'll be fine." She collected herself, taking another look at me. "He's going to fall over."

I gave her a hug, but pulled back suddenly. "Where's Mariella?" As if on book-worthy cue, the familiar eleven year old came through the door.

"Miss me?" she put a sassy hand to her hip, swishing her hips. Her baby blue dressed swished in response. I squealed, rushing to my sister and throwing my arms around her.

"Careful!" Both Lavender and my mom yelled in unison. I rolled my eyes, pulling back and grinning at my favorite human. "Hey, you."

"I told the whole sixth grade that my sister was getting married in New York. They're all jealous of me."

I pretend-glared. "So, you used me for your own popularity?"

"To be fair, I'm already pretty popular," she said, shrugging. I snorted, but she continued, "but yes, it helped." I threw an arm around her small shoulders, giving her a squeeze.

"Where's Laura?" Mom asked, checking the time on her phone. "We have to leave soon." Nerves swirled in my tummy. Nate's mom had been going crazy for the wedding, wanting to make sure everything was perfect.

"She said she was meeting us there. I think she was doing some last minute stuff for Nate."

"Men." Mariella said, coming forward with a shake of her head. We all fell into laughter.

~~~~

Lavender pulled into a free spot on the busy New York street, rolling to a (read: very) squeaky stop and cutting the engine. My hands gripped the seat, and I stared at her.

"You should really get a new car."

She patted the dashboard, rubbing in small circles. "Never. We've had some good memories in this car."

"Please stop caressing your car," I said, unable to take my eyes off her manicured hands. "But yes. We have." I focused on the first thing that popped into my head, settling my nerves.

"You're a terrible driver!" He screamed as the car lurched forward once more. "Shut up! You're making me nervous!" His eyes were filled with pure terror as he gripped the safety handle above the door. His knuckles were white. The store was on the right, which meant I had to cut in front of three lanes, plus ongoing traffic. That was a problem.

I smiled to myself, taking a breath and looking out the window. A black suburban rolled to a stop behind Lavender in my rearview mirror. Mom, Dad, and Mariella hopping out. Dad snaked an arm around Mom's waist, pulling her in. They gazed adoringly at each other, and Mariella made a disgusted face in the background.

"Your dad looks nervous." Lavender said, and I watched his face - which was, I admit, a tad paler than usual. I watched him fidget with his tie with his free hand.

"Bet you I'm worse," I murmured back, tearing my gaze away. I had only moments now; we had to walk to Bow Bridge, which swooped over the lake where the Loeb Boathouse was. We were having our reception there.

"Linds, look at me." I did, and she gave me a Lavender-look. "This is nothing compared to what you've already done in your life. You could write a book about all the stuff you've been through." She said, pulling me out of it. "Like, a big book. Probably one that exceeds fifty chapters."

I found myself laughing. That sounds like a good book.

"*Very* dramatic," Lavender added, then grew serious with a tilt of her head. She was quiet, and I froze when I thought I saw something. "Lav," I said, leaning closer, "is that a tear?" I couldn't remember the last time Lavender cried. In fact, I could argue she was incapable of it.

"No," she sniffled, turning her head.

"Why are you crying?"

She sniffled again, her glossy eyes meeting mine. "I just feel like the book is ending.

"I'm not dying!"

"know, I know. But, like, I've also just watched you grow up."

I rolled my eyes. "We're the same age."

"Not like that!" My best friend laughed. "You know what I mean. I blinked, knowing exactly what she meant and seeing a visual representation of it. I knocked hard and heard quick footsteps. The door opened and Lavender stood there, her olive skin tone covered by a green face mask. She grinned at the first sight of me, the mask crinkling. Our eyes met, and her grin slipped.

Her eyes widened. "What happened?"

I shoved away tears. "I need help."

"And he's so lucky to have you." I smiled, squeezing her hand. "Seriously, I don't know what he'd do if he didn't."

I made a face. "I don't know either." We fell into giggles, and a light knock sounded against my window. Dad was there, frowning and pointing to his watch.

"We have to be late," Lavender rolled down the window, "it looks cool." I laughed at his face.

"I don't think that applies for weddings. Or if you're the bride. Or if you're twenty five."

"It was cool when I was in high school," Lavender said.

"And college," I added, and she nodded along.

"Okay, you two. Time to go." I swear, I saw a flash of panic in his eyes from that sentence. I took a deep breath, stepping out of the door he pulled open. I took his hand, wobbly on my heels. I hated heels. Lavender joined us, Dad beckoning an arm out to her. She linked arms, and I did the same.

341

"Wait, I need a picture of this," Mom said, taking out her phone and snapping photos. It took longer than it should have, because of her inability to operate technology from this age, but today I felt patient. In fact, I felt so patient I could've stood there all day. Rooted to the ground. For forever. I tipped my head to the sunny sky, enjoying the warmth. Maybe I could stay there and turn invisible. But even as I thought about it, I knew it'd be hard for a bride to blend in. Passerby's smiled wide at me when they passed, and okay, I felt like a princess. I caught Lavender's eye, and she shot me a look, knowing exactly what she meant: take a step. I obliged, filling my belly with air and following my family. They all laughed and chatted, and while I tried to distract myself and do the same, I knew that I was getting closer to him. And the ring. And the people. The bridge loomed in the distance, along with a crowd of people waiting for the ceremony to begin. Suits and dresses swirled together, and I tripped in my heels. Dad caught me though, holding me up. I nervously laughed in response, mumbling an apology.

They all looked to me, probably half-expecting to see me in a white heap on the ground. My gaze fell first on Mom, and she knew.

"Okay, guys," she waved to everyone, "give us a moment." Lavender glanced at me once more, giving me a slight nod and moving to the side with Dad and Mariella. I watched them leave.

"Honey," she said, and I met her calm eyes, "tell me how you're feeling." My lips parted to respond, but nothing came out. How was I feeling?

"It's okay to be nervous."

I swallowed, my throat feeling like sandpaper. "Really?"

"Of course!" She laughed. "I'd be worried if you weren't."

I shook my head, looking to the ground. "I thought it meant that this wasn't the right thing to do-"

"no, that's not what it means. I'm sure he's nervous too." She smiled. Her eyes crinkled.

342

I snorted. "Have you met him?" We laughed together, but I knew she was right. He was probably feeling the same.

"Don't think about all the people. Just him."

I nodded. "Okay. My feet hurt."

Mom laughed. "You and me both."

"Thank you for everything." I said, startling myself. I hadn't even intended to go there. Was I stalling?

"You're stalling," she pretend-glared at me, "and you're welcome. That's what moms are for." I smiled at that, nodding and hugging her. I pulled back, and of course still nervous, a certain calm fell over me. I was ready. But I still had to get there.

"We're ready." She called to everyone, clapping in the air as if herding cats. Lavender joined her, getting ready to assemble in the front of the reception. Mom threw a final smile at me, turning and delicately walking alongside Lavender. The two laughed together about something, diving into an instant chatter. In the distance, it looked like the small group of people were preparing. Multiple heads turned, looking over their shoulders for someone dressed in white. Dad came to me, saving me from walking extra. Pathetic, I know. He held out an arm. I took it.

"Ready?"

I swallowed, nodding and glancing at Mariella. "Take it away." She tossed her mess of blonde curls behind her, marching on with a hand in her pile of pink rose petals.

"She's something else," I said with a laugh. "Good luck with that."

"That she is," he shook his head. He took the first step, knowing I wouldn't. We walked in comfortable silence. My brain needed time to catch up. And if I was being honest, my feet were screaming in pain. Lavender told me to practice so they wouldn't hurt; I obviously didn't take her advice. I watched Mariella drop the petals with flourish. I heard the guests react with a mixture of light laughter

343

and coos, and I refused to look anywhere but the back of her head. Before I knew it, I was walking over the bridge, and my eyes stayed glued to my little sister's head. But in no time, she had dropped all her petals and finished her small moment of fame. She smiled at me before standing with my mom, and when my temporary distraction was gone, it was time for my sidekick to retreat as well. I turned to him, managing a small smile. He hugged me, whispering in my ear, "you can look at him now."

I pulled back, biting my lip to keep from laughing. He winked, grabbing my hand and giving it to another. A familiar hand took mine, and it softly guided me to stand directly opposite him. He squeezed my hands, and my eyes rose to meet his emerald green. He was grinning wide, showing teeth. It took me a second to realize he was trying to keep from laughing at me.

"Shuddup," I hissed under my breath, and he laughed a little harder.

"Nervous?" Nathaniel asked, and even though it was a whisper, I could still tell it was dripping in rhetorical sarcasm. I rolled my eyes.

"Hey," he said, sparkly green eyes glued to mine, "let's get married." A memory swirled into view from the sight of his eyes. The lights turned on shortly after, and by reflex, my arms reached up to cover my eyes. The intruder had clumsily found his way over to the light switch on the wall.

"Who the hell are you?" The boy demanded. His chestnut hair was messy. His green eyes were wide with confusion and red from irritation. My eyes darted to his shirtless chest and red and blue striped boxers. My eyes lingered over the deep indent of abs, and my state of delirium didn't help my wandering eyes.

"If you take a picture, it will last longer," he spit, reaching to the ground and throwing on a gray T-shirt he had taken off moments before.

"Who are you?" I sputtered, ignoring his rude comment.

344

He squinted. "I'd like to think you have the common decency to answer me first. You just sprayed me with mace."

I frowned, not enjoying his attitude, and crossed my arms across my chest. "Lindsey. Lavenders best friend." I explained as if he should've known.

"Oh, I'm sorry that wasn't included in the handbook."

I smirked. "Well, I'm sleeping here."

"So am I."

He tilted his head, able to tell I was thinking about something. I glanced to my parents, Mariella, Lavender, Nate's parents, and some friends I've made along the way. While my gaze swept over the small group of guests, my eye caught someone sitting in the back. Hellen smiled, giving a small wave. She looked aged, maybe a result of the stress from prison, and lines accented the crevices of her face. Her hair was now longer than it had been, which threw me off because I had seen it cut short for so many years. I looked to Nathaniel, who gave me a small smile. He invited her. I looked to the minister next, nodding. It was time. Nate squeezed my hands. Maybe Lavender was right about my story ending. But she didn't realize I was about to start an entirely new one.

Acknowledgements

I never believed that when I was twelve, making up names to characters that my family members threw out and tapping away on my iPad, that my writing would have reached the audience it has. It was crazy to see that readers were starting to connect with characters straight from my imagination; that's when I knew I wanted to be a writer. The Run was my second ever book, following a loosely written book that I like to call an experimentation into the world of words. First off, this book in your hands wouldn't have been remotely possible without the help of Craig Bouchard, whom I met as a sophomore in high school. I am forever grateful for his overbearing kindness, graciousness, and friendship. Besides him, I'd like to thank Jaunique Sealey for her time and tutorage. Our exchange in emails were beyond helpful, and your kindness never went unnoticed! I'd also like to thank my editor, Carole Greene, for having endless patience with me throughout this story. I not only learned so much about the editing process, but about my mistakes and how to fix them. To my mom and sister, who are my biggest cheerleaders. To my dad, who always supported my writing dreams. Overall, I've been truly blessed to have already had this amount of support!

Special Sneak Peak!

into

The Run Vol. 2

I packed hurriedly; shoving toiletries, clothes, and other essentials into my small bag, I swiped the mysterious five hundred dollar check off my hinged bed. I threw a black sweatshirt over my long sleeve, hoping to appear incognito. Checking my phone time, it read 5:51 through the cracked screen.

Exactly nine minutes until my foster mother was back from work.

With trembling fingers and a rapid heartbeat to add to the stress, I raced out of the cramped bedroom and down the steps. It was 5:53; seven minutes. Throwing open the door to the file room, I swiped my prepped file I had noticeably pulled out an inch hours before, and snatched my passport from the inside. Biting my lip, I blinked at my file. Taking an unplanned risk, I shoved the inestimable papers into my bag along with the passport.

"What are you doing?"

I whirled around, my fine brown hair whipping me in the cheek. Breathing hard from adrenaline, I eyed my fellow age-ranged foster brother, who in unbelievably bad timing, stood with arms crossed across his chest.

I bit my lip, screaming inside. "Pretend you didn't just see that."

Ben ran a hand through his red hair, eyebrows raised analytically. "Only if you tell me where you're going." He always had a knack for stalling. Obnoxious, if you were to ask me.

I checked the time—5:57. "Ben. Please."

He squinted, clearly unconvinced of my pleas. Did he not see I was in a hurry?!

The front door suddenly opened within hearing range, followed by clanging of keys and her exhausted breathing.

I looked at Ben with wild eyes.

I watched him, thoughts racing through his eyes as if deciding on what he were to do in the moment. After what seemed like hours, Ben pursed his lips, whispering, "Don't say I never did anything for you."

With that, he strolled out of the doorway and to the front door. His loud warning tone ricocheted as he engaged in pointless conversation to help pass the time.

I thew my backpack on my back, peeking out the door. He had managed to turn her the opposite way so her back was facing me. His glance flickered to me for a split second, as if screaming now! I quickly retaliated and crept down the hallway to the back door. Four steps and I'd be into the outside world of New York City. Two steps and I kept my ears strained for his continues conversation. I reached the door and without a glance back, I took a breath and pushed it open. Stepping out into the semi-darkness, I took off at a cutting run along the house I'd known since I was fourteen.

CPSIA information can be obtained
at www.ICGtesting.com
Printed in the USA
LVHW042102210521
688193LV00015B/1115

9 781087 903309